DEAD OR ALIVE

DEAD OR ALIVE

TEAM SAVAGE™ BOOK TWO

MICHAEL TODD

MICHAEL ANDERLE

LMBPN

DISRUPTIVE IMAGINATION

Copyright © 2021 LMBPN Publishing
Cover copyright © LMBPN Publishing
A Michael Anderle Production

LMBPN Publishing
PMB 196, 2540 South Maryland Pkwy
Las Vegas, NV 89109

First US edition, October 2019
Version 1.01, March 2021
(Previously published as a part of SAVAGE REBORN)

ebook ISBN: 978-1-64202-500-2
Print ISBN: 978-1-64202-501-9

THE DEAD OR ALIVE TEAM

Thanks to our Beta Readers
John Ashmore, Charles Tillman, Crystal Wren, Kelly
O'Donnell, John Ashmore, Nicole Emens, Robert Brooks,
and James Caplan

Thanks to our JIT Readers

Diane L. Smith
Dorothy Lloyd
James Caplan
Jeff Eaton
John Ashmore
Kelly O'Donnell
Micky Cocker
Paul Westman
Peter Manis
Robert Brooks

Editor
The Skyhunter Editing Team

DEDICATION

*To Family, Friends and
Those Who Love
to Read.
May We All Enjoy Grace
to Live the Life We Are
Called.*

CHAPTER ONE

He had been called old-fashioned—hardly surprising, perhaps, since he'd been in this business since the first Bush took his presidential oath. Charles Stafford had been a member of the Pegasus board for over two decades and also many others over the years. He'd headed up various other companies and held leadership positions in all of them, as well as a dozen charitable foundations and even a couple of Minor League baseball teams.

It could be said that this defined who he was. After all, he'd done it for as long as he could remember. His secret was respect. People respected his opinion. They knew he was there to make the business go well and smoothly, a voice of reason to help anchor every generation's free thinkers.

While it wasn't a job everyone wanted to do, it was one he excelled at—and even reveled in, from time to time.

But at the center of his success was the respect he had for the people he worked with and they had for him. Even those who had been forced into conflict with him had always thought of him as a worthy opponent. He didn't like the politics that came with running a business, and he always tried to keep everything he did out in the open. He wanted people to know he had outsmarted them, plain and simple.

Of course, it wasn't always like that, but it was a nice footnote to have on his legacy that he always tried to play the game as respectfully as possible.

Given all that, the reason he was pissed right the fuck off as he marched his way into the Pegasus building was a matter of respect—or, rather, the lack of it in this case. If you called a meeting of the board, it was only respectful to be there in person when they convened. He understood not being in the country when things were happening to genuinely prevent one's presence. Attending an emergency board meeting via a camera and a microphone was acceptable. People couldn't be in two places at once, and those running operations like Pegasus certainly had many other responsibilities across the globe.

And in this situation, having lost two board members— one to death and one to widely publicized arrest and subsequent resignation—in as many months certainly spelled emergency in his book.

But if Dr. Courtney Monroe wanted to assemble the members of the board herself, she could at least extend them the common courtesy to be there.

He wasn't being fair and knew that as he stepped into the elevator with his assistant—a young woman who knew to keep her mouth shut when he was in a mood like this. Monroe had proved surprisingly competent, and now that her little war with Carlson was over, Charles really wanted to see what she could do.

Unfortunately, she wasn't off to the best of starts if this was how she intended to continue.

The elevator pinged to announce their arrival at the appropriate floor. He immediately scuttled off as fast as his limbs could carry him to the conference room where the meeting would be held. He was generally the first to arrive at these events, and the fact that he had arrived late was a deliberate protest against the circumstances.

Most of the members of the board were present, which made Monroe and Anderson notable in their absence. The others sat calmly around the table as Charles dropped onto his seat and tried not to groan. Old golfing injuries had begun to tell on his body, and he didn't much care for it. He needed to see his doctor about upping the dosage of his pills. Being in pain was for people who couldn't afford the best doctors in the country.

"Right, then," Monroe said from the TV screen at the head of the room. "Now that all the members have been assembled—thanks for joining us, Stafford—we can start with the agenda for the meeting. You'll be pleased to hear it's short and to the point."

He chafed at the way Monroe seemed to talk down to him and treat him like he was a freshman in this business, but he let it slide. Instead of a response, he opened the folder that waited in front of his seat, which contained the agenda for the meeting. She wasn't wrong. It was short and to the point.

"Carlson's resignation from his position as CEO of this company has left something of a power vacuum, and especially since the sudden surrender of his shares in the company to…uh…pay for legal fees." Monroe settled her glasses firmly on her nose. "His shareholding was substantial, and as you all undoubtedly know, leaving that large a section of the company without ownership for too long will kill the share prices. I'm sure I don't need to tell you that it's not a good thing. As such, I will make the executive decision to take control of the shares for the time being."

Charles jerked his gaze from the folder when alarm bells shrilled in his head. The board wouldn't ordinarily stand for a power move like that, but the reality was that they had little say. Since the takeover, their power in the company had been reduced to a mere shadow of what they had once wielded. If Monroe wanted to take control of the shares Carlson had left vacant, there was nothing they could do to stop her.

"Of course, I can't keep control of those shares for long," she continued. "We'll hold a selective sale of his position to various trusted members of allied organizations like the Monroe Foundation, among others. Until that point, I will appoint an emergency member to this board, to be announced before the week's end. They will hold the position until it is filled by members more suited to the responsibility."

Stafford wanted to protest. He wanted to tell her that she was a newcomer and needed to respect the opinions of the people who had run this company for years. They had been there since long before she had ever decided to poke her head out from the confines of that jungle she currently visited. But he reminded himself of what was necessary and managed to keep his mouth shut. He didn't like playing the politician, but sometimes, it was critical. It was, he reminded himself, important that Monroe not think of him as opposing any of her plans—not yet. He knew two of the people who had openly butted heads with her, and it hadn't ended well for either of them.

He hadn't known Covington aside from a few meetings, but the impression she'd left was of brash and impulsive arrogance. She had always come across as someone who had so many good ideas that she no longer thought she was capable of any bad ones.

Carlson was a different beast. Charles remembered working with the man's father, and the apple didn't fall far from the tree. He was as sharp as a new suit and equally presentable. The company had thrived under him, too. He was charismatic and knew all the right decisions to make and how to talk people into siding with him.

The man was, quite simply, a force of nature. The fact that he had been arrested was unfortunate. While his methods might have been somewhat unorthodox, he got things done. He'd made the company what it was, and without the interference of that woman and her ex-military sidekick, he would never have been discovered. One could only admire a man who knew what was required and had the balls to do whatever it took. Ruthlessness was something Charles greatly admired.

Monroe and Anderson were, unfortunately, midgets in the shadow of the giant they'd deliberately demeaned. He lacked sufficient words to properly define how abhorrent and inconsequential they were in his eyes. The fact that they so brazenly believed in their moral superiority was sickening.

"I'll announce who will take the position when I return from the Zoo," Monroe continued with a small smile. "Either in person or through our current CEO, James Anderson, who should return to Philadelphia in the next couple of days. And that wraps up my section of the agenda. Are there any questions?"

Charles studied the other members of the board with veiled interest. He knew that each and every one of them had questions they wanted to voice regarding what they had heard. His scrutiny confirmed, however, that none of them would get involved in this. They all simply chose to keep their heads down and hopefully survive this whole debacle without being pushed out themselves. They were all scared of Monroe, not angry at her. That was…pathetic. No, perhaps appalling was preferable.

"Very well, then," she said with another smile as the silence threatened to drag on for too long. "I will be in touch with each of you before the sale to ascertain whether you are interested in acquiring a portion of Carson's shares. Please watch for my emails."

The screen went black and Charles leaned back in his seat, adjusted his four-thousand-dollar suit, and regarded his fellow board members.

"Well," he said to end the sudden silence. "Carlson has been forced out—yes, I know he apparently resigned, but he wouldn't have done so if Monroe hadn't forced him into it somehow—and now, he's locked up. Covington's dead, and you are all hiding in your little turtle shells hoping the big bad doctor doesn't come for you next. What a bunch of cowards." He added a derisive snort to punctuate his statement.

The others simply stared at him in confusion, and some even appeared to be angry. He didn't care. They wouldn't stand up for the man who had all but carried Pegasus into some of its most productive and profitable quarters since its founding. All they saw, now, were the negative repercussions of the bold and ruthless decisions the man had taken. None of that would have been an issue if they'd been able to continue to pretend innocence—or, at the very least, to not be aware of them. These people would merely duck their heads and take whatever the interlopers threw at them. If that was truly their intention, he didn't really give a shit about what they thought.

"It's not cowardice to realize there's a new apex predator in town, Charles," one of the women said. Her expression seemed to suggest that he had single-handedly given all the puppies in the world cancer. "While nothing's been said and there's no way to prove it, we all know she was behind the whole Carlson debacle. Given the timing, you'd be an idiot not to see it. And we've all heard the stories of how she and Anderson use their friends from the Zoo as muscle to force people into making decisions they don't want to make. I don't need to tell you that people who come out of that shit-heap of a jungle are crazier than usual. Keeping our heads down and our mouths shut until all this blows over and Monroe oversteps herself is merely the smart move."

"Smart move?" Charles pushed to his feet and glared around the table. "Is that the term you choose to describe your bending over and taking whatever she wants you to take? No, you need to understand something right now, Madeline. I'm the apex predator around here. Your weak-

7

ness is what allowed Monroe to take over in the first place, and that weakness shows me that it's my time to take over. You're afraid of her when you should be afraid of me."

He shoved his chair away and stormed out of the conference room. The dozen or so board members stared at the door he had slammed shut behind him.

"I have to say," Brian Steward said and closed his folder. "That man seems more off his rocker than usual. I think he's taken Carlson's arrest a little too hard."

"He's taken it personally," Madeline Forbes grumbled and shook her head. "I think he always saw Carlson as the little brother he never had or something like that. He's not happy with how it happened and now, with Monroe taking liberties with the company stock, he thinks it's his time to make a stand. The problem, though, is that he clearly also thinks we'll stand with him because we don't like it either."

Brian chuckled softly. "Well, I only hope the asshole doesn't try to pull us into his stupidity when he realizes we won't join his little revolution."

It took her a moment, but Madeline found herself sharing his laughter. It was infectious, and a few of the other board members joined in before it died down.

"Well, I don't know who he thinks he'll go after," the lean career executive said and brushed her short hair behind her ear as she stood. "But either way, I'll bet you he'll tender his resignation as well within the next couple of weeks."

"Or he'll be dead," Madeline said under her breath as the others stood and prepared to get on with the rest of their mornings. Just like poor Andressa, she thought. The woman had been as tough as nails but had never really understood the kind of woman she had gone up against until it was already too late.

Calls were made to drivers by the group of assistants who waited outside to have their cars ready within in the next five minutes, and most of the men and women on their way out were already making lunch plans. She had paperwork that needed her attention, and she would go to her office on the nineteenth floor.

Jeremiah wasn't sure if he looked forward to the morning with dread or with relief. On the one hand, he knew to expect what would probably be an awkward conversation, but it would also mean a resolution.

If he wanted to apportion blame, he knew he could throw some at Dr. Jessica Coleman. It hadn't been an unpleasant breakup—although he wasn't entirely sure that the concept of breakup was appropriate. They had only shared a couple of nights of passion, after all. The most recent of those had been after a heavy night of drinking and the first had been after a night of mayhem and gunfire and barely escaping with their lives.

They'd had the talk she'd wanted but it hadn't gone well the morning after. Jessica had decided that good pillow talk afterward was to say that Monroe had offered her a job in one of the locations on the west coast and she couldn't exactly tell him where.

He had put up as much of a fight as he could, but they both knew there was an expiration date on the relationship. She was a scientist who would put her work ahead of any relationship she was in, and he was a killer who wouldn't stick around anywhere for too long. It was doomed to fail. All in all, it was best to take control of the implosion and leave before anyone's feelings were hurt.

That had been the idea, anyway. But Jeremiah couldn't come up with a better explanation for his bad decisions over the past couple of weeks.

He knew that it wasn't fair to blame Jessica for his bad choices, but she wasn't around to correct him, and it made him feel better. So long as nobody was hurt, what was the problem?

The shower was steaming hot when he stepped in. He gritted his teeth as the scalding water rushed over his scalp and down his back. It found all the scars across his torso and arms, old and recent, and made them feel like they were new and tender. He drew in a deep breath and vigorously scrubbed himself clean of the previous night's exertions before he stood and allowed the water to wash the suds away. Finally, he turned it off.

Some habits never went away. The old "navy shower" was one of them. He was in and out in under two minutes and dried himself off quickly with the towel the hotel provided. He dressed inside the bathroom because he somehow felt that it would be wrong to do so with someone else in the room.

He had been given the option to take his drunk date back to his place or hers, but his newly acquired paranoid ways told him that neither was ideal. A hotel room seemed the best choice. With the money Pegasus paid to keep him on retainer, it wasn't like he couldn't afford it.

Fully dressed in a gray bowling shirt, jeans, and light

boots, he stepped out of the bathroom. She was already awake.

Pearl, she'd said her name was. He really hoped she had been careful enough to give him a fake name too. She pushed herself up from the bed and the covers dropped away to reveal that she hadn't bothered to put any clothes on since the night before. The long, brown hair, the athletic body, and the obviously enhanced breasts told him that appearance was very important to her. It was a nice ego boost to realize he had made the cut in that way, but as the rest of the night had proven, they were incompatible in more ways than one.

"Morning, handsome," she said, pushed her hair back, and yawned. "Where are you off to in such a hurry?"

"I have a thing I need to get to," Jeremiah replied with a nod and made sure he had all his accoutrements—wallet, keys, phone, and all in the right pockets too. He wasn't sure why that was important to him, but it was. It felt odd to wander the city without a gun, but he didn't have a permit and couldn't afford to be busted with one of his weapons, especially since they were sans their serial numbers.

"Oh, okay," she replied, pulled the covers away, and stepped out of the bed. Nobody woke up looking that good, he noted. Most likely, she had heard him get into the shower and touched herself up. She moved lightly over the carpeted floor and stood on her tiptoes to give him a kiss on the lips. "Well, you have my number. Come again soon. Oh, a pun." She giggled. "I'm punny."

"Right," he said and forced a laugh, suddenly reminded of two things. Why he knew he wouldn't see her again, and why he had come to this hotel room in the first place. He pulled away and moved toward the door in an effort to escape any further morning-after small talk.

"Being dead sucks," he grumbled to himself as he strode down the hallway towards the elevators. "Being without someone sucks harder."

Jeremiah paused as the doors opened and a hotel employee stepped out. He moved inside and waited for the doors to close before he pressed the button for the ground floor.

"Being with an airheaded bimbo sucks hardest yet," he continued, still talking to himself. "Oh, a pun. See, I'm punny too. Maybe we're more compatible than I thought."

He wasn't serious, of course. He doubted that he'd actually saved her number or that he would use it even if he had.

"I need to up my game," he said as the doors opened, stepped out onto the marble floor of the lobby, and moved purposefully toward the front desk. "I suck ass."

They weren't compatible, but he wasn't a monster. He would pay for the room and the raiding of the minibar that had happened the night before, but he wouldn't allow his credit card to be charged after he'd checked out. He wasn't an asshole, but he wasn't stupid either.

CHAPTER TWO

They had focused all their time on bringing Carlson to justice but had never really anticipated the corporate nightmare the man had left. Many shell companies that tied tenuously back to Pegasus now demanded recognition. A fair number of them managed the paperwork themselves as a way to ensure their absorption into the parent companies, but a couple of them proved far more difficult.

Anderson decided these were the ones that been lovingly stroked into solvency by the ex-CEO and felt they should still have the special treatment.

Considering the kind of pressure he assumed Savage had put the man under as well as the damning evidence in the file they'd handed over to the FBI, it was no surprise why the ex-CEO had decided not to fight his charges. There were hints that he might be used as a witness in some other open cases, but from what they could tell thus far, those wouldn't affect Pegasus.

Anja had confessed that she had directed Savage to the

plane Carlson had planned to use to leave the country until the dust settled. The operative himself had been reticent on the subject, but it appeared he'd been convincing enough—no doubt in the way his name implied, but Anderson chose not to ask—and left him for the authorities to find. How the hacker could have believed that their muscle would show any kind of restraint was beyond him. People like him usually made the kind of decisions that would be difficult to live with for ordinary people. That he hadn't gone all-out savage and simply eliminated the target was nothing short of astonishing.

Still, whatever his reasons and his actions, he had ended the battle rather quickly and left Carlson alive on top of that. There was something immensely satisfying about knowing he would live to regret his activities. Scientists were no longer being murdered, and most of the resistance internally had backed down when they heard what had happened. He trusted Savage that none of it could ever be officially linked to Anderson and Monroe. It was doubtful they would survive the shitstorm that would follow if even a hint of their involvement came to light.

But they'd hired the operative because he was a professional and was thorough that way. He had left no evidence and had obviously instilled enough fear into Carlson that he obdurately declared he'd been shot in the knee by an unknown assailant. Anja had supplied the ex-colonel with the medical transcripts of the reconstructive surgeries required. He couldn't resist his smug satisfaction whenever he thought of what their enemy would have to endure. It seemed poetic, somehow.

Anderson scrutinized the paperwork that had been put

on his desk earlier in the day. Courtney had dispatched him all over the country to bring everyone into the fold, but one of the stubborn companies remained troublesome. And from the papers, he could see why.

He wasn't sure if it was because the people were loyal to the problem elements or if they were merely following orders, but materials were being stolen from one of the warehouses. It wasn't overt and the inventory would have seemed satisfactory to anyone who didn't look closer. The stolen stock was replaced with cheaper replicas, which ensured that the numbers tallied and so didn't raise suspicion.

Of course, he couldn't necessarily say it had anything to do with Carlson. It could have been simple greed. People might have realized that those in upper management were in upheaval and decided to pad their pockets in the confusion. It was an entirely human-greed response to opportunity.

Still, one could never be too cautious.

He sent what he found to Anja and asked her in an email to try to investigate whether any of the people involved were living beyond their means or had squirreled a little extra away in their retirement funds. At this point, they had to cover all their bases. He would have called her to let her know what was coming and what he wanted from it, but he never knew when she would be available. Waking her up had proven to be a mistake in the past. She got little enough sleep as it was without his interruptions. It wasn't like this was of vital importance or anything.

Anderson leaned back, rubbed the scar tissue on his arm, and closed eyes in an effort to delay the headache creeping in. He wasn't made for this corporate crap. At the same time, he no longer came anywhere close to what he had originally been shaped into. As much as fighting alongside Savage had made him feel alive again, honesty demanded that he accept that he didn't have another round in him.

He needed to come to terms with the fact that he wouldn't be a soldier, so he might as well be a paper pusher. Unfortunately, it would have been so much easier to adapt to his new course in life if it wasn't so fucking boring.

His phone rang and prompted a groan. He rubbed his eyes again before he lifted it off his desk and pressed the button to accept the call.

"You know, I wouldn't have to call you like this if you would use the earpiece I sent you." Anja's familiar and welcome voice with her soft Russian lilt made her perfect grasp of the English language a little more exotic.

"Forgive me for not wanting to have you in my head twenty-four hours every day," Anderson responded with a chuckle.

"Not all day. Only while you're working. Then I wouldn't have to wait for you to call or, God forbid, have to leave a message."

"It still won't happen. I appreciate the effort, though."

"You'd damn well better," she huffed. "So, what am I looking at here?"

"Well, I emailed you the names and socials of the various people who work at one of Carlson's shell companies." He glanced through the data again. "I want to make sure these people aren't merely selling the missing inventory on the black market or something."

"Why?" she asked and sounded incredulous.

"Because we don't want to chase after Carlson's ghosts without making sure he's the one who actually put all this in motion," he explained. "It means the difference between us sending our lawyers in…"

"Or sending Savage." Anja completed the thought as his voice trailed off. "Understood. I think I can get you rough numbers by tomorrow."

"Don't send them to me," he said. "Send them to Courtney. She's the one who will have the final say on what we do about it, either way. I need to have a chat with our hired gun to see if he's ready to start cleaning shop. I had a couple of ideas I wanted to run by him."

"Where is he now?" the hacker asked. "It's been a while since I've talked with old Jer. I miss his grumpy face."

"Well, he's back in Philadelphia," he said and slid his laptop into the briefcase he now carried everywhere Courtney sent him. "His work for us falls into a highly specific range, and when there's a lull in the need for elimination or physical intimidation, we have to find some way to justify keeping him on the payroll. Running security sweeps, probing the building for possible breaches, and…well, training personnel."

"You're really going to float them in like that?" she asked as he started moving out of the tiny office.

"Float what in like what?" He locked the door behind him.

"Probing? Breach? You can't talk like that and think I won't mock you for it."

"Oh, grow up," Anderson said and punctuated it with a laugh. "This is why I don't want you in my head all the time. Call me when you have something."

"Will do, prude," she replied.

Every time.

He hated how every time he heard the sound of a gunshot, he flinched. It wasn't a new thing either. It was something that had started a long time ago. He'd thought he would get over it, but it seemed to have somehow burrowed into who he was. There would be no getting over it anytime soon and it would likely be a part of him for the rest of his life.

Mistakes were made, yet he was the one who had to live with them. How was that fair?

Anderson shook his head and moved deeper into the warehouse Savage had selected. He gritted his teeth and tried to keep the deeply rooted panic reaction from taking over. A slow breath eased the roiling sensation in his gut, and he pushed himself to approach the source of the noise.

The building looked like it had been abandoned for a while. There were a lot of them around the old Philly docks after they'd moved most of the operations higher up the river once the silt buildup became too much to handle.

Many of the structures were repurposed into a variety of different facilities. There wasn't really much you could do with a massive building that had the sole purpose of storing large containers where they wouldn't get rained on. It wasn't like they could open offices there. As a result, most of them stood empty and had gradually rotted since the companies that owned them had no interest in pouring money into renovations. It was pointless when they wouldn't find any buyers.

The area constantly needed to be cleared of crackheads, which meant that gentrification was still a long way off. That made it the perfect location to train in urban combat.

Anderson managed to circumvent most of the rubble and finally reached a section of the building that still looked to be in one piece. These warehouses always had a couple of offices so at least one corner would be in better shape than the rest. They'd built a small shooting range in this area.

"Keep that right arm up," he heard Savage say. The ex-colonel grinned because the operative sounded like one of the drill sergeants of old, shouting and cursing to make sure that everything he taught was remembered. He knew he would never be able to leave a boot unpolished because of his old sergeant and wasn't sure if he was thankful or resentful.

His abusive nature had imparted skills that had saved Anderson's life on more than one occasion, but the man had to be in retirement by now. By the sounds of things, the operative had endured the same kind of relationship with some army sergeant. He was almost a full decade younger than his boss, though, so the man who had yelled him into shape was probably still in the business of preparing young men to not die in the heat of combat.

Savage looked away from Ivy's stance and took a step back. They both wore anti-flash glasses and earmuffs, which explained why they hadn't heard him coming. It didn't explain how the man seemed to know that he was there before he'd even come into view, however.

"Anderson, nice to see you again," he said with a smile.

The ex-colonel returned the smile and extended his hand for a firm, crisp handshake. "How's the training going?"

Ivy shifted her attention from the pistol she had put on the table. From what he could tell, they had gone through the basics of how to take the weapon apart and put it back together again and now worked through the stances that fit her build best.

It wasn't only about the technicalities of owning a gun, of course. The purpose was to learn about the weapon that you would use and how to treat it and respect it. Anderson remembered that part of his drill instruction very well. Savage was a lot gentler about it, though. While he did want Ivy Anderson to get through all this alive and well, he apparently didn't want her to see him in the way that every grunt saw their drill sergeant.

"Hi, honey!" Ivy waved with a smile.

"Hey, sugar." His smile broadened when she walked up to him, draped her arms over his shoulders, and pulled him in for a kiss. The affection was momentarily interrupted when the big glasses got in the way. They laughed as she raised them and leaned in for a light peck on each other's lips.

"How's the gun training going?" he asked them both. Savage indicated for Ivy to speak first.

"Well, Savage is very patient with me, and he made sure I learned all the minutiae of gun handling before he let me shoot," she said with a laugh. Anderson had been married to the woman long enough to realize her apparent frustration was a good thing. She wanted to improve, and she knew that her husband simply wasn't the person to teach her. Getting along with the operative couldn't be easy, but they didn't seem to be at each other's throats.

Yet.

Savage smiled. "She's a quick study. We've worked through her stances. Isosceles for mid to long ranges and CAR for up close and personal. Using your body is the first step to using a gun."

Ivy rolled her eyes with a laugh and sauntered back toward the table. Her instructor's gaze followed her for a moment before he returned his attention to Anderson.

"She's already familiar with guns and doesn't have too many bad habits I need to break her of," he said with a chuckle and deliberately kept his voice low so she didn't hear him. "I have to say, when you hired me in that hospital, I didn't think training would be a part of the regimen, but it's a welcome break from all the running around I did back there."

"Are you aching to get back into the action then?" Anderson asked. He knew the signs well enough. He'd experienced them himself.

"Like you wouldn't believe." The operative laughed. "Do you have something for me on the Pegasus front? Is Carlson acting up again? Threatening to turn people over to the feds?"

"No, he's still recovering from his latest surgery while in custody," Anderson said. "Did you have to go that hard on him?"

"Well, guys like him won't exactly walk away if you give

them a slap on the wrist and a warning," Savage pointed out dryly. "If I'd let him off easy, he wouldn't learn anything from his mistakes. He would skulk overseas, gather his resources, and prepare for another strike at us. He'd also know all the while that we would be as lenient if we caught him again. Now, though, he knows what to expect next time he tries to pull anything."

"Which only means that the next time he comes for us, he'll look for a killing blow," the older man pointed out as they moved away from where Ivy took her pistol apart again.

"In that case, we have more time to prepare," Savage said with a small smile.

"Fair enough. Anyway, we might have something for you. "Carlson set up a number of shell corporations to run his money and supplies through rather than declare them to the company. They're all being brought into the fold now, but there are a couple that are a little problematic. Predictably, they're the ones that handled all the resource transportation in and out of the Zoo. It might be that they are still working for Carlson, or it could be that someone's greed makes them think they can get away with a little company theft. Anja's looking into it now."

"How is she?" the operative asked as he poured coffee from a thermos into a Styrofoam cup. "Do you want some?"

"No, thanks," Anderson replied quickly. "And...well, she's fine. Jacobs and Kennedy keep her busy on location, which means that any time she has to spare for us is a blessing."

"And that would be awesome if I knew who Jacobs and Kennedy were."

"Right." They'd kept him out of the loop when it came to their whole organization, but sometimes, things slipped. The man seemed to understand that plausible deniability was a factor and that the less he knew about the people he actually worked for, the better.

His instincts in this business were annoyingly and terrifyingly on point. Admittedly, those same instincts were what had saved his life not too long ago, but Anderson still felt he was entitled to feeling a little off about him.

Savage didn't seem to mind. In fact, he appeared to enjoy the way people looked at him—half-awed and half-horrified. An emotional barrier, his way to keep people at arm's length, maybe? Who could tell? It was doubtful that any shrink in the world was qualified to deal with the hot mess of humanity that defined the operative.

"Anyway, there was something I wanted to bring up with you before we started you on another operation," Anderson said as his companion sipped his coffee. "While the mission ended in our favor, there were a lot of luck factors in there we'd like to avoid next time. Most of them involved you working alone instead of as part of a unit. You know, after Coleman—"

"You want me to assemble a fireteam to have on standby if you guys need muscle." Savage nodded and deftly avoided that particular conversational bombshell. "Understood. There's one small problem, though. Most of the people I know who are the right fit for this kind of job are either dead or think I'm dead, which puts a hitch in this plan of yours. The proverbial fly in the ointment. Wrench in the works—"

"I got it." The ex-colonel laughed and wondered how long the man could have continued with the metaphors about how the plan to help him with a competent team was already dead in the water. "Fortunately for everyone involved, there are people—whose names you don't want to know—who know the kind of recruits we have in mind. These would be people recently out of the Zoo or other similarly dangerous places with the skills you might require. We would need you to make sure that they have the right...temperament."

"I thought there weren't any places similar to the Zoo when it came to danger," the other man replied with a grin. "Have you guys been upselling that place to keep prices for the merchandise high?"

"I wish. I could tell you the details, but then I'd have to kill you."

"You'd have to try, Colonel." Savage smirked and looped a thumb in his belt in an arrogant pose. "And then I'd have to beat your ass into the ground to teach you otherwise and haul that ass to the nearest hospital. Neither of us has the time for that."

"Yeah, keep it up with the empty threats, grunt," Anderson replied. He didn't know why, but having someone like Savage around to talk to somehow made him feel whole again despite the fact that a part of him recoiled instinctually from the other man's immersion in his killer persona. While one was a Ranger and the other a Marine, they had both been in the fight together and knew the kind of toll that it took on a man. Even this scant common ground fed a hungry part of him that needed the assurance of something familiar.

"Will you give me the list, or should I turn up at the office to get it?" the operative asked and finished his coffee with a soft sigh.

"You won't need to go into the office for this one." He knew how much Savage hated having to pretend he was simply another employee at Pegasus. "Anja said she'll get the list to you, as well as some last known locations for you to track them from. The people we want for these positions are the kind who know how to live off the grid, so get ready to scratch the dirt."

"Awesome." His grunt spoke real enthusiasm. "Tomorrow, then? So, I have time to finish your wife's lesson?"

"I wouldn't have it any other way. She's shooting for two now."

Savage paused and turned to look at his improvised shooting range. "Wait, what? Is she—"

"Oh, no, nothing like that." Anderson laughed. "I was joking about her having to shoot for me too. Wait, did she say something?"

"Let's not do that, Colonel. Head home and get some rest. You look jetlagged. I don't know how that's possible, but you do."

"Will do. I'll see you at home, Ivy."

"Love you, babe," she called after him before she yanked her glasses and earmuffs on.

CHAPTER THREE

"Run me through the situation again," Jeremiah asked. It was weird to have Anja in his ear again after so much time without her but, like riding a bike, things came back to him remarkably quickly.

Anderson hadn't been wrong when he'd said the potential recruits wouldn't be easy to find. The ex-military types were usually assumed to be people who lived in the middle of nowhere with nothing but themselves, their guns, and plenty of wild game to shoot—and maybe a dog.

It was a hurtful stereotype. Many of the men and women who returned from service initially had difficulty readjusting to regular society, but most of them did it well. They had the help of family, friends, and loved ones as well as a couple of shrinks to get them through the technical shit. When they slipped into their old lives, it was with the assurance that they'd done what they could for their country and walked away with their lives and a group of unlikely friends whom they would never have met otherwise.

The small hitch, of course, was that while the stereotype of the lone ex-military man with guns in the boonies was hurtful, it was based on a grain of truth. And it was that particular grain he now followed. It wasn't like he could ask the well-adjusted veterans to join him on his team to kill anyone who attempted to kill military people on the other side of the world. Most of them would reject the offer, mostly on the premise that they had put that life behind them when they'd left the armed forces and weren't interested in picking it up again.

Or, maybe, they wouldn't be willing to go up against security guards and regular folk for something that wasn't overtly evil. On the surface, the situation they face looked a lot like a regular corporate price war with the volume turned all the fucking way to eleven. Savage wasn't entirely sure how the minds of regular, well-adjusted people worked. While that could be something of a handicap at times, it also meant he was the perfect man to find other rejects and outcasts and evaluate whether they were the right fit for his little team.

"Anja, are you there?" he asked. She had the habit of falling silent, which could mean she had turned her microphone off to talk to somebody else wherever she was. Savage was convinced she was somewhere near the Zoo. If it could be managed, it was actually an ingenious place to set up shop if you never, ever wanted to be found. He knew even he wasn't crazy enough to go there of his own free will, and those who would weren't usually the brainy type.

Then again, there were a bunch of big-assed fucking alien monsters to deal with, so one had to consider that too. Walking the tightrope between crazy and genius was a tiring business.

Jeremiah pulled up to what looked like an old cabin tucked away outside Hector, a small town a little under two hours from Little Rock, Arkansas. He already knew what to expect before he drove in. Small town folks looked out for each other and disliked city folk. He knew he reeked of city folk so anyone who looked at him would do so with a glare or a scowl. Their first instinct wasn't to trust someone like him.

Come on, guys. He'd have to work hard to avoid voicing his frustrations. Still, an inward vent might help him move past it and focus. *It's the twenty-first century. Get with the times and try to understand that not everyone is out to rob and cheat you.*

Although their instincts were probably dead-on in his case. It really was best to not trust him in particular. Almost everyone else who visited, though, likely had good intentions and didn't need to deal with their hostility.

Directions were hard to come by, but he didn't need the directions so much as to get a feel of what the man was like. He was born in the area, everyone told him. His daddy fought in the Vietnam War and was awarded the Medal of Honor. Terry Mixon was a chip off the old block but didn't get half the recognition his daddy did. Whispers were that it was because he was black ops, and all the recognition he received had to be kept under wraps.

There was also considerable suspicion about the government, it seemed. Once again, in that instance, their instincts were dead-on.

The home had been in Mixon's family since the fifties, apparently, and the man had kept up with the times. Water pipes and electricity that didn't require a diesel generator made sure it was a modern house for a modern man. He assumed from his resumé that his target knew how to live with less, but simply because he could didn't mean he enjoyed it.

A minute or two in his SUV outside the front gave him a fair impression of the man. It was a squat, single-story house and well-maintained, which clearly indicated that the man didn't spend all his time with his guns. The wood-work was recently redone, and the varnish couldn't have been more than a couple of weeks old. Preparing for the winter was a serious business around there. It all looked well-done, crisp but not too showy. Nothing was carved into the wood to make it more aesthetically pleasing.

Either this Terry Mixon had hired himself a professional for the work, or he'd done it himself. Either way, it was a good sign. He wouldn't have to talk to someone who hadn't been around people in decades.

Jeremiah made his way to the house with a briefcase in his hand. The front door opened as he reached the front steps, and a tall, gangly-looking man with his blond hair still cut to the military standard one inch on the top and shaved on the side stepped out to meet him. He wore sturdy boots, thick jeans, a checkered shirt, and a heavy sheepskin jacket—heavy enough to keep a weapon concealed, but there was no gun in the man's hands.

"I'm not buying anything," Mixon said in an accent that showed his roots in the area but also his time spent abroad. "If you're selling, that is."

"I wouldn't drive all the fucking way out here if I wanted to sell you something." He smiled as he approached the door. A cool sense of sizing him up glinted in the man's eyes but with no look of hostility. He was taller than his visitor and with a leaner build.

"I'm Jeremiah Savage. A pleasure to meet you." He paused and extended his hand.

The man frowned at his hand for a moment and seemed almost confused by the gesture before he took it. "Terry Mixon," he grunted, his grip firm. "I'd appreciate it if you didn't use that kind of language around me."

"Language?" Jeremiah asked but almost immediately, he realized what he was referring to. "Oh, right. I'll keep it in mind."

Mixon nodded curtly and stepped aside to allow him entry. The inside matched the outside. Everything looked well-made and reliable, but there was a decided lack of decoration. No paintings hung on the wall, for one thing. Everything was clean and ordinary enough not to call attention to itself and lacked sufficient detail to make it memorable.

He had always lived under the impression that a man's home was an accurate representation of his mind. By those standards, Mixon was neat, industrious, and didn't much care for unnecessary bullshit.

"Where'd you serve?" the man asked as he followed him inside. A beagle trotted up the stairs, turned to give the visitor a look, and huffed a soft bark before he continued in the way older dogs did. He still looked fairly healthy, though.

Jeremiah turned back to Mixon and cleared his throat.

"I did my first tour in the Middle East, bouncing around Iraq, Syria—the usual. I'd joined the Rangers for my second and third tours and went all over the world with them. After that, I took time off but rejoined and well... I can't really talk about it."

His host nodded. "I understand. Can I get you something? Well water's all I have. Would you like some?"

"I'm good, thanks," he replied. He wasn't sure how to talk to someone like Mixon. The man seemed reserved, much like most snipers were, which made it difficult to discern what he really thought. "I told you that I'm not here to sell you anything, but what I am here to do is offer you a job. I've seen your resume. It's fu—seriously impressive."

A smile quirked on the man's face at the attempt to keep his vocabulary in check. "Did anything in particular stand out?"

"Well, there was that time you engaged in a heated shootout from fifteen hundred yards out," he replied and folded his arms. "You laid out in the middle of a war-torn town, hid in the rubble for about three days while you waited for the convoy to spring their trap, and you made sure your boys had support of their own. When the time was right, you picked the insurgents apart from a long way out, to the point where they tried to eliminate you with the mortars they brought and almost completely ignored the convoy that cruised through. That was impressive."

Mixon nodded. His expression indicated that he wanted to hear more but was unwilling to participate in the conversation. Jeremiah paused and wondered briefly if it had been a mistake to turn the offer of water down. He pressed on.

"I heard they had a thirty-thousand-dollar bounty on you in Burma at one point when they sent you in to help with the DEA operations in that area," he continued and managed to avoid scratching his jaw lest he look awkward. He needed to appear in control. "You stayed for six months and made sure that none of the drug lords operating in the area got anywhere near any of the windows. From what I saw, you took your longest shot out there—a little over eighteen hundred yards out. Being that close to sea level and with the kind of humidity down there, it was one hell of a shot."

The other man nodded. "You've done your homework, I'll give you that. Not many people were privy to what happened in Myanmar."

"Well, let's say that the SEALs weren't the only ones called in to support that operation." He grinned. "Look, I won't sugar-coat it for you. The work I have will be dirty and off the books. You'll be paid, of course. I approached you because you seemed like the kind of man who didn't mind doing bad things to bad people, and that's the kind of man I want on my team."

His host stared him coldly in the eye for a moment. He had the kind of chilling glare that could easily make drug lords across the world break out into a sweat. Suddenly, he cleared his throat and looked away.

"What kind of bad people?" he asked and wandered over to the kitchen with his visitor following. A small gas stove stood in the corner, but the area boasted no extravagant appliances or furniture—a modern electric heating plate, a fridge, and a table with two seats. All had been cleaned meticulously.

"The kind that gets people killed in the Zoo," Jeremiah replied. He withdrew a file from the briefcase and set it on the kitchen table, leaving it there. "Testing weapons and suits of armor out there in the jungle. Reports from people I trust indicate that they have tested them on marines and grunts as well as the local wildlife."

"The Zoo..." Mixon filled a glass with water before he turned to face him. "I've heard that place is pretty darn deadly without anyone shooting at you as well. Have you ever been there?"

"I have not," he replied and reminded himself that honesty was his best choice in this kind of situation. He talked to a man who deliberately kept his life simple, but that by no means meant that he was a simple man. "Between you, me, and your dog, I don't think I'd survive for very long in there."

"Between you, me, and Buster up there?" The sniper walked over to the file and his fingers skimmed the plain red plastic. "Me neither."

Jeremiah nodded. "The man who foots the bill is a former colonel and Marine recon before that. He's been there, and he's the one who came back with stories about what Pegasus is doing there and with a vision to put a stop to it. The company had numerous ties with military contractors, which is why he and one of the scientists involved, Dr. Courtney Monroe, needed help from someone like me. It turns out that even someone like me needs help from a man like you."

Mixon nodded.

"You won't find anything if you research Jeremiah Savage," he added as his gaze swept the room and noted a couple of hidden cameras. Was that the reason why he'd come in there? "And I'm reasonably sure you won't find anything on my face, but you're welcome to try. You will find something on James Anderson, though, and Dr. Monroe. You don't need to trust me, but you can trust them. You'll find a card with a number in there if you think this is the job for you."

"What kind of deadline are we talking?" he asked as his visitor turned toward the exit.

"We'll have operations to run by Monday next week, or so I've been told." Jeremiah still tried to keep his narrative as honest as possible. "We'll need your answer before then."

The other man merely nodded, already absorbed in the file. The conversation was over, and it seemed clear that there would be no commitment—positive or negative— from him right away. And that, once he made his decision, it would be final.

Jeremiah had been read into Mixon's file, thanks to Anja's efforts to dig it out of the DOD's servers. He remembered his own time in Burma's humid climate and the names they gave the various American teams that had been brought in to help with the country's opioid epidemic. There couldn't be any official interference, of course, but the country's own intelligence services had been read into the operations and approved of them. Nothing overt could be done, but with the Rangers cutting into the supply and the Navy taking out most of their leaders for six months, the cartels were eventually crippled to the point where the local law enforcement could work again.

He'd never known any names outside his own unit except for the tales he'd heard of the man locals called the Saim Nghaat—literally, the falcon, although one of the men he'd talked to said that the less literal translation read "death from above."

For a sniper, he had to imagine it was something of a compliment.

Based on that alone, he was willing to hire him. But the man apparently had principles—the kind that would keep him from operating without a cause to follow. Jeremiah could only hope that destroying an organization responsible for the deaths of fellow soldiers sent into a dangerous jungle would count. He wasn't overly hopeful, but as long shots went, the risk to reward ratio was good enough to merit an attempt to bring him on board.

The no-cursing would be a problem, he mused as he stepped into his car. He grinned when Mixon took a picture of the vehicle with his phone—or the plates, probably. They wouldn't get him anything as it was rental, but it was good to know he was thorough.

"Okay." He started the car and accelerated down the driveway. "Where to next, Anja?"

"Well, the next name on the list is in Chicago," she replied. "Are you sure he'll take the job?"

"Sure? No," Jeremiah replied. "Reasonably hopeful? Also no. But he's one of the best when it comes to long-distance negotiations, and I already know he's a beast in urban environments."

"A beast to help the savage?" the Russian asked. "How fucking poetic."

"Enjoy it while it lasts." He laughed. "The guy will have us saying 'fudge' and 'gosh-darn it' before too long, mark my words."

He continued to laugh when all he could hear was Anja making like she was about to barf.

CHAPTER FOUR

One might think that getting someone away from one of the most dangerous jungles in the world would be an easy task. Or, if not easy, then at least not one that required an inordinate degree of convincing for the parties involved. Charles had never been within a thousand miles of the place himself but considering that a majority of the companies and foundations he was a part of acquired their business out of the Zoo, it was his job to know how bad things were there. The consensus was that things were bad and looking to get worse.

But no, it appeared that Dr. Courtney Monroe had spent so much time there that she didn't want to leave. Still, that might have been because she was a part of a small start-up in the area and, from all appearances, had a personal tie to the people who ran...whatever that company's name was.

"Heavy Metal, right," he grumbled under his breath as his assistant rushed in with new papers for him to scrutinize. Courtney, as it turned out, wouldn't return anytime soon. Despite how many connections he had, he doubted it would be sufficient to persuade someone to fulfill a contract out there. Besides, some poor unfortunate souls had already tried to eliminate her a couple of times and had been beaten into submission—and extinction, for most of them.

The attempts on her life in both countries proved that in or out of her element, Dr. Courtney Monroe was still formidable. Regrettably, her partner was as well—a former Marine with a history and numerous connections to the kinds of men and women who could keep him relatively safe. Carlson had tried to assassinate the man himself with a team of well-armed and well-trained men. All he'd achieved was to embroider Anderson and Monroe's legend and provide even more ammunition they could use in any kind of court battle they might face down the line.

If they were lucky, she would die in the Zoo and he would lack the clout to retain his place on the board.

But he couldn't plan for luck. He needed to be prepared for the probability that she would survive to reach Philadelphia in one piece and still be in control of Pegasus. Carlson had tried to use his formidable power to tackle the problem head on, and he'd failed because he'd underestimated them.

Charles intended to learn from those mistakes. He had made up his mind to be prepared to not only remove them but to have a replacement waiting once they were out of the way. Carlson was, regretfully, a lost cause. The ex-CEO was still recovering from numerous surgeries and was up to his eyeballs in the shit that came when the FBI threw the book at him. Worse, he'd intimated that he did not intend to fight the charges—a sign of weakness that Charles found both disturbing and distasteful. No, he couldn't count on him being there to lead Pegasus out of this quagmire.

"Richard Maven on line one for you," a young man said, standing inside the glass door.

Maven was an old friend, now at the front of one of the largest investment firms in New York, which allowed him to keep his fingers in as many pies as he wanted.

Charles snatched the phone from its hook after the first ring. "Richie, how are you doing?"

"Charlie, it's good to hear your voice again." Maven laughed. "Damn, how long has it been? Last I remember your sorry face was that one time in Monaco—"

"Right after the race. We played poker all night, I remember." It had been a good weekend. He wasn't much of a racing fan, but he was known to spend some of his weekends gambling. Vegas and Atlantic City were his vice capitals, but he didn't mind a trip to Europe with friends when the time could be spared.

Of course, there had been far more vices involved than simple gambling, but he couldn't really talk about that. One never knew when one or another of the country's intelligence agencies might run a tap on one's communications.

"Good times," Maven said. "Anyway, I've had the time to look over your proposal, and while Carlson's shoes will be challenging to fill, I do believe this could be a deal that benefits everyone involved."

He remained silent and waited for his friend's inevitable backtracking.

"However," the man continued after a short pause. "You

know I can't actually take any of these steps to assume control of Pegasus until the current proprietors have moved out of their respective offices—if you take my meaning."

"Of course. I've already worked on the processes required to expedite their extradition," Charles said with a chuckle. "I wondered, though, if you had any—shall we call them suggestions?—for how to deal with the current occupants?"

"Well, you know I can't be involved with any of the internal workings of a company I currently have no place in," he said blandly. "But my assistant will provide you with paperwork on the people who can. They're expensive but top-of-the-line too. They should be perfect for the kind of relocation needs you have in mind."

"I appreciate it, Richie. Are we still on for Thursday?"

"I'm willing to take your money on the golf course any day of the week, Charlie, so Thursday works. Take care." He laughed in parting and the call cut off.

Charles was suddenly reminded why Maven wasn't his first choice for taking up the reins at Pegasus. There were a handful of others, half of whom had turned his proposal down. He didn't blame them since Pegasus stock was almost radioactive at this point. The others had all seemed interested but had shown the same kind of hesitation Maven had. The company was still immensely profitable, but they needed Anderson and Monroe out of the way before they could make any open moves to take over. These contenders also had a couple of ideas regarding who might be up to the task of eliminating them.

There had been a couple of overlaps in the lists

provided, which gave him a good indication of whom to call for a meeting. Charles drew a deep breath and forced himself to regain his single-minded control. Yes, these troubling times made for some strange bedfellows, but he had to believe that any one of the choices he'd contacted was better for the company than Monroe and Anderson.

He had to.

"So why do they call it the Windy City?" Anja asked as Jeremiah put his car in park.

"Well, I assume because it's a city that has a lot of wind," he replied as he stepped out of the car and stretched with a soft groan.

He needed to look into a car he could use on these trips. He'd had discussions with a couple of Anderson's contacts in Philly about acquiring a vehicle that was sturdy, reliable, and unassuming for him to tie to some shell corporation or another. More than anything, he needed to use it without having to worry that his name would pop up on the radar. He liked the name Jeremiah Savage and didn't want to have to change it for a while.

"Yeah, be a smartass to the person you rely on for information," she grumbled.

"I'm a smartass all the time. I can't help it if you or somebody else is on the receiving end."

"Well, the smartass should know that your target regularly frequents the Bailey's Tavern every night, usually comes in at seven, has dinner, and leaves after a fair amount of drinking," she said. "I've never understood people who have a favorite bar. Aside from convenience, why would you have only one bar to go to every night?"

"Well, having a structured schedule for yourself is a part of it," he said as he approached the bar in question. "There's also the feeling of safety. You know the bartender, the owner, and maybe a manager or two, along with the waiters and waitresses. You feel comfortable enough to get completely and absolutely plastered there because you know these people will be around to take care of you so long as you're willing to part with a gratuity or two."

"Well, I can understand that," Anja replied with what he imagined was probably a shrug. "Or half of it, anyway."

"Who the hell calls their place a tavern, though?" Jeremiah asked and studied the parking lot. From the number of cars, he guessed that the place was possibly half full at this point. It was for the best since he didn't want to have to wade through a room full of patrons to reach his target.

"Well, someone who's looking for an old-timey feel, I suppose," Anja said. "But yeah, calling it a tavern is beyond pretentious."

"Well, I'm glad we're agreed on that at least." He stepped inside.

She was right. Calling it a tavern was pretentious, but whoever had named it had obviously put a lot of effort into living up to the vision. Most of the tables were set into booths surrounding the bar that occupied the center of the room—homey while convenient at the same time. He assumed that it used far less space in the center of the room than taking up a full corner of it, and it gave all the patrons a sense of isolation. No, isolation wasn't quite the word.

Privacy? Yes, that was better. Jeremiah surveyed the room in an effort to make out where most of the people sat. They weren't there to go clubbing, that much was obvious. There was a certain aesthetic to it that he liked—a pub feel but without cramming as many tables and chairs into one place that most pub bars tended to do.

"You know, pretentious or no, I think I could get used to drinking at a place like this," he said and edged around the room until he decided he wouldn't locate his target by prowling and making all the patrons anxious.

He dropped onto one of the bar stools and raised his hand to catch the attention of one of the bartenders.

"I'll take a scotch and soda, twist of lime, light on the ice," he said with a small smile. The woman nodded and immediately went to work. In a few seconds, the drink was set in front of him and the money presented pushed quickly into a register before she moved away to another of her customers.

"Should I tell Anderson that his star employee is drinking on the job?" Anja asked as he took the first sip. The scotch wasn't the best quality, but he hadn't really expected it to be around there.

"Well, first of all, I'm an independent contractor so I would be drinking on my time," he retorted. "Secondly, what you would want to tell Anderson and Monroe about is the fact that I'm spending company money on drinking. That would be the infraction. And I wouldn't say I'm any kind of star. Merely...industrious."

"Is that what you call what you're doing right now?" the hacker asked around a burble of laughter. "Being industrious?"

"I'm industriously waiting for the target to show up, yes," he confirmed with a grin.

A couple of the other patrons stared at him, ample evidence that the music playing in the background wasn't enough to cover his conversation with Anja. He pulled his phone out of his pocket to indicate that he was in the middle of a call. Of course, it wasn't routed through his phone, but they got the idea and gestured to tell him that if he wanted to continue the discussion, he would have to keep it down. They were there for the pleasant and quiet environment, after all.

"Right, sorry," he said. "Look, people think I'm crazy talking to myself. I'll have to call you back another time, okay, babe? Love you."

"What are you...oh, I understand." Anja laughed. "Seriously, though, why wouldn't you want people to think you're crazy? It's the best way to get them to leave you alone. I call it the Fight Club method."

"And what's the first rule of Fight Club?" he asked under his breath.

"Don't...oh, I see."

Jeremiah ignored her as he studied his surroundings to make sure he hadn't missed any new arrivals. His gaze settled on a couple that stood and made their way out of the bar. The woman definitely looked drunker than the man. He was tall and lean with a tattoo of a skull wearing a green beret that began at the top of his shoulder. His target located, the operative took a deep breath, downed his drink, and spun on his seat to stand quickly and head after them.

The couple left the bar with him close behind.

"Excuse me?" he called rather than get too close without a warning. The man might not look drunk, but even one drink could stir up the paranoia in an ex-soldier taken by surprise.

His mark turned and Jeremiah realized that he was actually far drunker than he appeared but was simply better at hiding it. Either that or he wore vodka-scented cologne. The man studied him a little blearily and smirked when he obviously realized he had about a foot and a half and possibly a hundred pounds or so on him too.

"What do you want, man?" he asked as he stepped forward and tried to look intimidating. "Can't you see I'm about to get lucky here?"

"Well, I wanted to save you from a night of disappointment." The operative wisely took a step back. "And I'm actually here with a job offer."

"I don't want a fucking job, dumbass," he hissed and glanced hastily at the woman who had already reached his car. "Now fuck off before I have to break your face in."

"I think there's been a misunderstanding," Jeremiah said but clearly, the man didn't want to hear it. He spun into motion, his hand already closed in a fist as he aimed a haymaker with surprising accuracy given his level of drunkenness.

Jeremiah had the advantage of speed that came from a clear head. He took a step back and the swing missed his face by inches. The man lost his balance and stumbled forward into his opponent's elbow. He gave a strangled cry, clutched his broken nose, and flailed at his adversary with his free hand.

The operative responded by gripping the man's fore

and middle fingers and twisted them back until he was forced onto his knees to avoid having his fingers broken.

"Like I said," he reiterated and fixed the hapless man with a hard look, "there's been a misunderstanding. I wasn't offering you a job. I was offering her a job."

They both looked at the woman who now staggered closer to them.

"Come on, boys, you don't have to fight. You can take turns," she grumbled in a decidedly British accent and shook her head. "I doubt either of you is enough to handle me, but maybe if you tag team, we can work it out. We'll talk about the logistics on the way to…was it my place or yours?"

"Not that kind of job," Jeremiah responded and chuckled as he shoved the kneeling man out of his way. "Hi, I'm Jeremiah Savage. And call me crazy, but I don't think your friend here is a Green Beret, despite the tat."

"Well, duh, of course," the woman said.

"And you were going to sleep with him anyway?" he asked and flashed a dubious glance at the man, who now whined over his broken nose.

"Of course. He is—was—hot. You're less hot, but the rating went up now that you beat him up. I'm Samantha Davis, and you can call me Sam. Do you want to get out of here?"

She placed her hand on his shoulder and smiled invitingly.

"Again, not that kind of job."

"Way to kill a lady boner," she huffed. "Fine, what the hell kind of job do you have to cockblock me for, anyway?"

"The kind that requires the skills of one Samantha

Davis, formerly Corporal Samantha Davis of the 22nd Special Air Service Regiment," he said and held her gaze squarely. "Specialist in close-quarters combat and demolitions, and your paperwork reads like a where's where of global terrorist communities and violent insurgencies. You were a very busy woman for about twelve years before you were honorably discharged. The...whys were very carefully hidden by your regiment, which let you retire three years early with full benefits."

"It's none of your business why I was discharged," Sam said and leaned forward, her expression intense. Her reddish hair was fairly short and slid loose from the bun she had tied it in with the sudden movement. "It was a good reason, though. Remind me to tell you about it sometime."

"Maybe over drinks?" Jeremiah gestured at the bar behind him. He couldn't really place her accent. Then again, accents had never really been his forte. She was British, though, he could tell that much.

"Nah, I think I'm done for the day," she replied with a large yawn. "And to be honest, I could really use a job. I've let my skills slide lately, and that won't do. Give me a when and a where, and I'll meet up with you. I expect to be fairly compensated for my work, though."

"I can promise you that the money won't disappoint you," he said with a smile.

"Excellent." Sam patted him on the chest. "Oh, and one more thing. Don't ever tell me that I clean up good."

"Don't you?" he asked and wondered what that was all about.

"Of course I do," she scoffed. "That's not the point. I fucking hate that phrase, is all. It sets me off."

"Well, there you go." He shrugged. "You have the job if you want it. I don't need you to look good. I need you to be able to tap into what sets you off when the time calls for it and make other people a lot less pretty."

"And until then?" she asked, all business now despite her obvious inebriation.

Jeremiah withdrew a card from his pocket. "Don't fuck with the leopard that's looking at you like that."

"What?" she asked, her expression dubious.

"Never mind," he grumbled. "Go home, sleep it off, and be at this address on Monday at around noon." He slipped the card into the front pocket of her shirt. After a second thought, he pulled a twenty out of his wallet and added it to the card. "And take a cab home. You're in no condition to drive."

"All right, Mum." She grinned cheekily. "Will you tell me who you are, then?"

"I told you." He flashed her an amused look as they wandered to the road where, hopefully, it wasn't too early to hail a cab. "Jeremiah Savage."

"Oh, yeah. Well, my name is Fae. Fae K. Namerson. It's Gaelic or something." She punched him in the shoulder. "Come on. It don't take a genius to figure out that it's a made-up name."

"All names are made up," he pointed out, and she rolled her eyes.

"What are you, some kind of wise guy?" she demanded.

"I've been told that the term 'smartass' applies, actually."

"Whatever, smartass." Sam sounded mildly offended.

"So, will you tell me what your actual name is? Maybe a little history? You seem to know so much about me, it's only fair that I learn a little about you. The way you handled the fake back there shows me you're a man of some worldly experience, although your accent pegs you as a local boy. You don't look like the guys the Marines usually churn out. Not Navy or Air Force either. Army, I'd say. You're exactly the right kind of bland they usually produce."

"All that makes sense," Jeremiah replied and raised his hand as a cab neared. "You should go with that."

The vehicle came to a halt beside them as she scowled at him. "You really won't tell me anything?"

"I'll tell you on Monday. Get home safe now, you hear?"

"Yeah, fuck off." She rolled her eyes as she stepped into the cab. He wondered if she'd give the driver directions to another bar. The woman had said she'd had enough, but she'd revealed a very keen insight back there. He suspected she wasn't actually quite as drunk as she had made herself out to be.

"Quite the charmer, this Sam," Anja said into his earpiece as he strolled back to his car. "I can't wait to see how she interacts with our friend Captain America."

"Captain…who?" he asked.

"You know…the 'no foul language' guy. Terry Mixon."

"Oh, right. There's no guarantee he'll join us anyway, so why worry about that now?"

"Well…I guess I should ignore the fact that Mixon just bought himself a train ticket to Philly on his credit card then?" she asked.

"Obviously," he retorted with a good dollop of sarcasm

but couldn't help the smile that crept onto his face. He'd really hoped Mixon would decide to join them. "So, where am I off to next?"

"You're going back to Philly too," Anja said. "Anderson sent me an email. The old-timer says he wants to talk to you. It seems he has a mission."

"I hope it's not training anyone else," he grumbled. "Airport?"

"Airport," the hacker confirmed cheerfully.

CHAPTER FIVE

"So," Jeremiah snarked as he stepped out of the car, "instead of enjoying the last weekend I have before I assemble my team and start to work with them, study up on the people we'll go after—"

"You would have spent it drinking and having a couple more quickly-regretted trysts," Anderson pointed out as he turned the rental car off and opened the door. He ignored his companion's horrified look. "Anja keeps tabs on you, and she fills us in on what you do with your free time. Sue us."

"I have half a mind to do exactly that. You have Anja spying on me?"

"Well, we would," the older man said. He decided against taking his jacket with him and left it on the seat before he closed and locked the vehicle. "But she does it anyway and lets us know what the highlights are. Either way, instead of making stupid decisions and helping drunk women make even stupider decisions—"

"Stupider isn't a word," he interjected. "I think."

"It is too a word, and did I mention 'shut up?' Instead of having the weekend off, you're out here in the outskirts of Los Angeles with me."

The operative narrowed his eyes at his boss. He'd seemed extra snippy all the way there, which possibly had a similar source as his own unhappiness. Although, if he had to venture a guess, he would say that Anderson's reasons carried more weight. Spending time with one's own wife and children trumped going out, getting drunk, and getting laid.

"Which segues excellently into my next question," he said finally to change the subject as they strode toward what looked like a chop shop abandoned for the weekend. "What the hell are we doing out here? You were suspiciously quiet on the flight."

"I wasn't quiet. You napped the whole way," Anderson pointed out curtly.

"I was slee...meditating," Jeremiah corrected. "Meditating. Us bad guys have to meditate before we get our bad going. It's part of my ritual. It's how I tap into my savage nature."

"Right." The ex-colonel's tone carried a hint of sarcasm. "Anyway, now that you're done meditating while snoring, I can fill you on the details of what we're doing here."

"I don't snore," he protested weakly.

"I stand as the tired and grumpy evidence to the contrary. But back to what we're doing here. We're hunting for someone called Edward Smith—which is almost more fake than Jeremiah Savage. Almost."

"And, apparently, we're hurting people's feelings today." He chuckled morosely under his breath.

"Can I fucking finish?" Anderson hissed.

"Right…sorry."

"Edward Smith is the name attached to most of the missing materials from the Pegasus shell corporations," the older man explained. "He's still working for the company, but there isn't anything else tied to that name other than the company contract and this so-called materials workshop."

Jeremiah studied the property as they approached. The business was clearly abandoned for the weekend but that wasn't surprising, all things considered. What was interesting was the mountain of parts from what looked like hundreds of cars stacked on top of each other. All were old and had been dismantled and stripped down to the chassis. Doors, lights, and even trunks had all been removed.

"Say, Anderson, you're the smart guy between the two of us," he said and sneered at the junkyard that was secured by nothing more than a flimsy fence and a chain with a padlock on the gate. "Is 'materials workshop' some fancy fucking lingo for chop shop?"

"Not that I'm aware of," his companion answered.

"Yeah, I didn't think so. Thanks for clearing that up." He scowled and shook his head in real disgust. "So, what were you saying about this…Edward Smith, fellow? He wouldn't happen to have sparkly skin and a craving for B-positive, by any chance?"

"What?"

"Nothing. It was only a weird thought. You know, if this was a movie, all I'd have to do was shoot at the steel padlock and it would break apart."

"And the alternative?" Anderson asked and sounded genuinely curious.

"You wouldn't happen to know how to pick a lock, would you?" Jeremiah grinned as he responded to the question with another one.

The other man merely shook his head.

"Which means we'll have to climb over this damn fence in ninety-degree Californian afternoon heat," Jeremiah complained as he tested the barrier's tolerance to weight. "Of course, it's dry heat, so I suppose it could be worse. Such a fun, adventure-filled life we lead."

He climbed first and made it smoothly to the other side. Anderson took longer and definitely felt more out of shape than his comrade, who even caught him on the way down.

"How are you feeling?" the operative asked and looked concerned.

"I'm...fine," he lied. "Anyway, Edward Smith has nothing to his name other than a contract for a shell corporation parented by Pegasus and ownership of this fucking place. He doesn't even have a social security number or a driver's license."

"A shell corporation paying a ghost," Jeremiah noted. "That adds up."

"He's the one listed as signing off on all the equipment that went missing from the shell corp, which means we need to find whoever is controlling the ghost and politely ask them to give everything back," Anderson returned with a hard smile. "And hope they include the names of the people running them."

"This seems like counter-intuitive legwork when Anja

can usually track them down," the operative observed as they moved cautiously through the veritable car graveyard.

"Well, Edward Smith is the only name actually associated with the missing stuff, and considering that there are some things even I can't do…" Anja sounded off in his ear. "I needed you two to do some of the actual legwork for me to have something to work from. I can trace someone through the baby pictures their mother posts on Facebook, but I can't track people who don't exist. Yet."

"Well, if you keep working on it, you'll get to that eventually," he said in an encouraging tone.

"What?" Anderson asked.

"I'm not playing two parts in this conversation," Savage replied. "If you want to hear what Anja has to say, put your damn earpiece in."

"I still have something against having a still, small voice in my head," the older man retorted. "Call it biblical aversion."

"That's your loss. She's particularly sharp with her wit today," he replied with a grin.

"Why, thank you." The Russian sounded pleased. "I've worked on honing my skills as an entertainer. Actually, I've taken an Internet course in my free time."

"What free time?"

"I have free time," she protested. "If you thought my life merely revolved around getting you lot in and out of trouble, you are sadly mistaken, my friend."

Anderson simply rolled his eyes at the younger man's grin as they approached the only building on the lot. This obviously housed the office and the delivery area and was the only sign of civilization in the otherwise depressing sea of vehicle carcasses.

The operative hesitated and looked around him as something niggled at his awareness. He'd assumed earlier that it was normal for the premises to be closed for the weekend. But didn't chop shops work twenty-four-seven? They'd logically be open when there was a need, whatever the hour, but what were the odds that they would be conveniently shut down at the same time they paid them a visit? Whichever way he looked at it, something seemed off.

"Out of pure curiosity," Jeremiah said as they moved in closer and drew the pistol from the underarm holster he'd brought with him. Thankfully, Anja's weapons acquisition skills had extended to a somewhat scruffy individual who had lurked outside the car rental office and simply handed the weapon over before he melted into the crowd. "Exactly how much did this Smith dude steal? I know it wasn't money, but what value would you put on the property he made off with? Can you make a rough estimate?"

"Well, some of the stuff was actually priceless," Anderson answered. "They were prototypes with hundreds and thousands of man-hours spent on research and development. Courtney gave me approximate numbers on the patent pricing alone and put it at around fourteen million dollars."

"Fuck." Jeremiah scowled and his gaze swept their surroundings once more as he fixed a suppressor on the muzzle of his Glock. "It sounds like Mr. Smith is buying Mrs. Smith a very expensive diamond necklace. And a one-way trip to the Cayman Islands. Do you think it's Carlson? Could he even pull this kind of shit from custody?"

"I can't think of anyone else who would be able to pull this off, can you?" The other man glanced at him, his expression somber. "Besides, this stuff is bleeding edge technology—the kind that even we don't know how to use. It's not like you can simply sell it on the black market. If you steal it, wouldn't it make sense that you'd already have a buyer lined up?"

"Well, just because Carlson is the only person we know who could do this, we shouldn't make the mistake of assuming he's the only one," Jeremiah reasoned. "He might have partners in crime—people he trusted to continue his work if he wasn't around. Or even people who know what he was up to and know that the plans that he had are worth making a quick buck from if placed in the right hands—"

He spun and leveled his weapon as he faced in the direction from which they'd come.

"What?" his companion asked and turned to squint into the stacks of junk around them.

"I could have sworn I heard something clink back there." Savage's voice took on the chilling quality that Anderson was now familiar with. "Like someone used a bolt cutter on that chain instead of bothering to climb the fence."

The ex-colonel paused, but all he could hear at that moment was the loud thump of his heart as it picked up speed.

"How would they know we're here?" he asked. "Fuck, I wish I'd brought a gun of my own. Not that I'd really be much good in a firefight, but I feel naked. Useless."

Savage narrowed his eyes at him. "Well, I can only speak from the experience of having seen you in a firefight once, but I do seem to recall that you were a long, long way away from useless."

"I still needed your help," he reminded him.

"To deal with fifteen trained and heavily armed home invaders. I think it's realistic that you needed help to deal with them."

"I was terrified," he confessed and swallowed as his throat constricted. "Honestly, I had a panic attack. And I only reacted in anger when I realized those guys would kill my family too, not only me. After that…well, protective instincts reigned, I suppose. It was a one-time thing."

"Again—I can only say this from my own experience— wanting to keep your family and the people you love safe isn't a one-time thing." The operative's voice softened as he rested his free hand on Anderson's shoulder. "It'll be a burden on you for the rest of your life and will force you to do and keep on doing stupid things and put the needs of others over your own. Just…draw from that. I know I will.

"You're as close as a guy like me can get to a friend— which is sad now that I say it aloud—and so I'll do my best to protect you. Because…yes, I can hear rusty hinges moving, which means we definitely have company. Take cover and let me deal with these guys. If you really want to be useful, pick the guns up from those I kill and use them. Or use the time to see what you can find in the offices. Take your pick but…stay out of my way, okay?"

Anderson nodded and the uncomfortable pounding in his chest increased, but somehow, instead of panicking, his mind seemed to settle into a calmer place than it had found in a long while. He sucked in a deep breath and made the choice to hurry toward the office building. He appreciated Savage's words, of course, but he assumed he would be a lot more useful if he rummaged through the building and tried to find something worth their efforts rather than try to be a hero.

He could only hope the operative had the situation in hand.

It wasn't a long walk back to the fence where they had climbed over, and he doubted he would encounter any new faces on the way. He wasn't sure who these people were, but there was one thing he could be certain of—if they cut through the chains that secured the gate, they weren't the people who owned the place.

Which meant they weren't there to protect something. They were there to attack.

At the same time, it could be people employed by the chop shop, Savage acknowledged as he checked that he had a round in the chamber and dropped behind what had once been a Chevy SUV. It could simply be that they wanted something and were in too much of a hurry to locate whoever had the keys. That particular scenario sounded highly unlikely, but it was always wiser not to make sweeping assumptions that excluded the simple explanation.

He edged cautiously toward the front and remained in cover with his pistol tucked close to his chest with both hands. His grip tightened on his weapon as he came into view of the gate. A couple of men stood there—on guard, he assumed as he inched closer and found a secure position nearer them for closer scrutiny. The newcomers were dressed in khakis, combat boots, and Kevlar vests. It seemed like someone had come looking for a fight.

Well, damned if they didn't come to the right place.

"Anja, do you have any cameras on our location?" Savage asked, his voice low.

"There are a couple of the cameras that cover the entrance and one on the building in the back," she responded. "They are active but don't feed into any kind of hard drive. I'd say they want security but don't want any trace of what happens there recorded."

He nodded even though he knew she couldn't see him. This close, he couldn't risk making any more noise than was necessary. The two men, armed with submachine guns, watched the entrance but didn't seem overly interested in the spaces between the cars. For now, that was lucky for him, but that luck would change if they saw him coming.

The operative eased in as close as he dared—still a car deep into the stack—before he dropped to one knee and cradled his weapon in both hands. Fifteen yards, he estimated, give or take. Even with the suppressor, it wasn't a difficult shot if he simply chose center mass. Unfortunately, thanks to the vests, he needed to aim for the head.

He squinted to keep the afternoon glare out of his eyes as the man closest to him turned to look at the two black SUVs parked outside.

Savage took another deep breath and squeezed the trigger, and the Glock kicked back into his hand. The target's head snapped forward a fraction of a second after the pop and his brains and blood sprayed across the windshield of the closest vehicle.

The second goon spun to search for the shooter and made the stupid choice out of fight or flight. The operative didn't have time for a headshot. He simply stepped out from between the cars that shielded him and pulled the trigger a couple more times. The armed man fell back a few steps. While the bullets were hollow-points and wouldn't go through the Kevlar, experience said they would still hurt like hell.

The grounded fool stared at him in disbelief as he strode closer to him and squeezed the trigger. A hole appeared on the unfortunate man's forehead and he slumped.

Thankfully, they didn't seem to be professionals—or not to the level that he was, at least. They were good enough for local muscle but probably lacked any real battle experience. It seemed obvious that they'd simply been drawn from the local pool and given weapons and body armor with a lot of hoping for the best involved.

His instincts prickled on the heels of that reasoning. Why would a team meant to protect a chop shop be selected from local muscle? That made no sense at all. Savage holstered his pistol and yanked the submachine gun from the hands of the first man he'd killed. He searched the body and located a couple of extra mags under his vest. It was important to establish where these bozos were brought in from and why. He would search them for a phone or anything else that could tie them to someone who would have to pay for the pleasure of trying to kill him. It would cost them a literal arm and a leg.

He grinned and examined the weapon in his hands. It had no suppressor so his ears would ache by the time he was finished. He would need to remind Anja and Anderson to source protective earplugs—not run of the mill, of course, as his work demanded that they be discreet and not easily visible while still doing the job.

For now, he pushed the thoughts aside, cocked the bolt back, and checked that there was a round in the chamber before he advanced deeper into the car graveyard. His approach was slow and cautious, and he took the time to constantly check his surroundings. He knew the men inside were aware that he was coming for them. They had to have heard the shots, as quiet as they were, and that meant they would be ready for him.

Well, ready for something, he thought with a grim smile. He wasn't sure if anyone on earth could be ready for him specifically, not when he was in that cold-killer place that now directed his actions.

Savage gripped the weapon with both hands and looped the strap over his head, still shielded by the cover provided by the cars. It wasn't much, perhaps. He wasn't sure how much firepower an old aluminum chassis could withstand, but it was better than nothing—and would certainly hurt a lot less than if he only wore Kevlar.

As he moved, his mind ran the scenario. There were two SUVs. Depending on how closely they'd packed them, he would face a maximum of ten men. Two were already dead, and the others would probably advance in a pincer motion. It made sense to try to drive their quarry out to where they expected someone might be standing guard. Of course, they couldn't be sure anyone would be, given the shots they'd no doubt heard, but these dumbasses didn't even have a decent comm system—no radios, no earbuds, nothing. They played off the cuff, which meant the operation was rushed and, most likely, spur of the moment.

Despite that, they had to have a couple of pros in the mix. Someone had to run the operation on the ground. He made some quick decisions as he moved stealthily through the right side of the lot, staying low and listening intently.

"There is a group converging on the building Anderson is in now," Anja announced through his earpiece. "They all look heavily armed, but they... Well, they're all out in the open and don't seem to know what they're doing. Honestly, the quality is disappointing after the last team you and I engaged."

"These are locals, brought in to boost numbers," he grumbled as softly as he could. He froze when he rounded a hulk and the space afforded a clear view of the open area in front of the small building. Six men stood out in the open and peered around like they weren't sure what to do next.

"It's like shooting fish in a barrel," Savage said with an edge of disgust to his tone as he inched closer. "Where the fish literally gave me the gun, the bullets, and pointers on how to shoot them more efficiently."

He raised the weapon and smiled at the comfortable weight of the MP-5 as he stepped forward and pulled the trigger.

As he'd expected, his ears immediately rang painfully as the first three-round burst tore through the open square.

One of the men dropped. Two of the rounds had struck the back of his vest but the third found his neck and drilled through to open a strawberry-sized hole around his Adam's apple. The operative couldn't actually see it, but it was a safe assumption based on experience. The bleeding was fairly minimal, though, since the last round had also severed his spine and killed him instantly.

Dead before he hit the ground. Savage pivoted and selected another target—who seemed to react the quickest to the assault—and squeezed the trigger again. The MP-5 kicked lightly into his hands. Submachine guns were never meant for accuracy, of course, but they did pack as much firepower into as small a container as possible.

That said, the weapon he held was a decent compromise, and the second man fell backward when all three rounds powered squarely into his chest with a force of impact similar to what a mule's kick might deliver.

He wasn't out of the fight completely, but he would take a while to catch his breath and accept the fact that his sternum would probably be a source of pain for the remainder of his life.

The others had enough time to turn and open fire. Thankfully, none of them really had any idea where the original shots had come from and simply released a random barrage of lead all around them in the hope that they might actually hit something.

Savage ducked behind the car, ejected the half-empty mag, and slapped a new one in. It wasn't his gun, and he had no need to conserve bullets. The invaders sprayed ordnance like it was candy and this was Halloween.

"Really?" he asked himself aloud. "That's the metaphor you're going with?"

"Are you talking to yourself?" Anja asked.

"Yep, you know what they say—if you ask your MP-5 a question, you're going crazy." He wouldn't be able to count how many bullets were actually being fired, and honestly, it really didn't matter. It was enough to know that the weapons delivered a constant stream of bullets in all directions, and only a few actually impacted the car he used for cover.

After about fifteen seconds, the shooting stopped and was immediately replaced by the desperate sounds of five men trying to reload.

"My turn," he declared under his breath and stepped out into the open. The men saw him immediately but hadn't managed to reload. Savage knew that every shot would count at this point, so he switched the weapon from three-round bursts to semi-auto. He raised it to align his eyes with the sights and fired.

The first man fell with two slugs between his eyes.

A second a little further away was the closest to actually being able to return fire. Another of the pros, the operative recognized and fired twice. The bullets punched through his neck and lower jaw and he sagged with a strangled moan. It wasn't an instant kill and it would take a while but still make sure that he was out of the fight for the duration.

I could simply pretend I meant to do that. He smirked because none of them would really care much either way.

A third man shoved the mag into the gun and fumbled to pull the bolt back and load a round into the chamber. He targeted him next, pulled the trigger three times, and nodded with satisfaction when, although one of the rounds went high, the other two thumped into his head.

Which left one more, loaded and ready to fire.

He flung himself forward and one of the bullets grazed lightly across his back. With a grimace, he rolled over his shoulder and pushed onto his knees within an arm's length of the gunner who still tried to track him.

Without even a moment's hesitation, he shoved the stock up from his shoulder and drove it between the man's legs. The pain had to have been explosive and the man shrieked as Savage dropped his weapon onto his assailant's shoulder and immediately cupped his hands protectively to his groin. He followed through with a powerful thrust that hammered the stock under the poor fool's jaw. The man sprawled at his feet, unconscious.

At this point, it was a mercy killing. He would wake up with a broken jaw and ruptured testicles, along with a severe concussion.

The operative lowered his weapon to the man's head and fired a single shot. Any more would simply have been superfluous. You could only kill a man once after all.

CHAPTER SIX

The single survivor lay on his back and groaned and writhed in pain as he tried desperately to reach beneath his vest, most likely for the extra mags he kept there.

His struggle looked damn painful, and Savage grimaced as he approached. The thug gritted his teeth and strained until he finally managed to pull one of them free.

"I can't have that." The operative grunted his displeasure and proceeded to kick the MP-5 out of the man's hands. It slid free of his fingers but, still attached to the loop around his neck, it didn't travel far. He dropped to a knee, yanked the loop off, and tossed the submachine gun away.

"Hey, how's it going man?" he asked and searched quickly for any more weapons. He found a revolver shoved into his belt and a knife tucked into an ankle sheath. "That looks painful. You'll want to have a doctor look at it."

The assassin glared at him as his last chance to fight

back was thrown away as casually as one might a candy wrapper.

"The strong and silent type, eh?" Savage asked and smiled as he brought the stock of his MP-5 down on the goon's chest. He screamed in pain and tried instinctively to roll away from the pressure but was dragged back by the collar of his now-ruined vest.

"Well, only the strong type now, eh? Yeah, these babies are effective, which is why they're still in production, and they leave one hell of a mark when they're put to good use. Which is how you can tell whether your bosses actually care much about your well-being. See, if they did, they would have sprung for something a little more expensive but a lot more effective, like ceramic plate weaves. They still hurt, but not the broken-ribs and shattered-sternum hurt."

He twisted the stock into the man's bruised torso again and dragged another cry of agony from him.

"So, I understand that you people are loyal to the man who signs the paychecks, but here's the deal." The operative looked around hastily to make sure Anderson wasn't watching. He really didn't want his boss to have nightmares about this later. "I have...issues I need to get out. Anger, abandonment—a wild concoction of shit that rich kids sit around in therapy for. My parents weren't rich, though, so I learned to take my issues out in more creative ways than screaming into a pillow. I know you don't like me, so if you want me to walk away from this feeling unfulfilled and dissatisfied, make like the world's worst prom date and spill all the goods prematurely. Do you understand me?"

The man stared at him and the defiance bled slowly away to be replaced by a trace of existential horror. As Savage pressed the stock in again, he screamed.

"Okay, okay. I'll tell you everything I know!" he shouted and writhed as he struggled to escape the pressure.

"Awesome," the operative said with an annoyingly bright smile. "Keep your words simple and in English. Who the fuck is Edward Smith?"

"I am," the man gasped. "I'm Edward Smith."

"Well, if my luck isn't simply the best today." He chuckled and for a moment, actually looked amused. "I come to a place looking for Smith, kill guys who come to kill me, and the one man left alive is the guy I'm looking for."

"It's true, I swear to God," Smith gasped. "We're all Edward Smith. We run a small chop operation around here, and we were going out of business after some Colombians moved in across town. Then, these bigwigs appeared out of nowhere a couple of months ago and said they were willing to pay in cash to move stuff out of inventory from a couple of local warehouses. They needed us to move the merch and keep it until some trucks came by to collect. We were supposed to mail them from a PO box in Chinatown to let them know when there was stuff to pick up. They would always leave the cash in there for us. After the first meeting, there wasn't any contact. Okay, there were the truck drivers, but I got the impression they were in the same boat as we were. Especially when one of them showed up with one of our stolen plates. Here, I have the address on my phone."

"Right."

"You have to believe me, man," the wounded man pleaded and hauled his phone out of his pocket to display the address. Savage memorized it quickly.

"I have to do no such thing, amigo," he corrected him. "But I might actually believe what you've told me is the truth because you want me to leave you alive. And, of course, not come after you when you lie in a hospital bed recovering. Because you know that I'll look into your claims, right?"

"Right," Smith quickly agreed.

"Okay, now that we agree on that, I have a couple more questions." He glanced around at the dead men, his expression speculative.

"Come on, I told you everything I know."

"I doubt that," he responded cheerfully. "For instance, I happen to know that small-timers like you don't have access to weapons and equipment like this, so there had to have been some face-to-face contact for that to happen. And I also know that the motherfuckers who sicced you on us didn't only send a group of amateurs to deal with the situation. Which meant they tracked us and then realized they needed to make it a hit and decided to call in local talent."

"Come on, man, we're not...amateurs," Smith grumbled.

"I killed seven people, most of them with their own weapons," Savage pointed out. "And I disarmed you and kept you alive for questioning by shooting you in the chest. You're so far out of your league that you're playing the wrong sport, champ. Now shut the fuck up. And then un-shut the fuck up and tell me which of these dumbasses are the ones who brought you in on the kill? I know it's not the two dumb fucks I killed by the gate."

"It's...that guy," Smith pointed at the first man to die. "And that one. There were only two of them, I swear to Christ."

"I appreciate your help, buddy boy," Savage said. "That concludes the Q and A section of this night's show."

He added a definitive full stop by cracking the stock across the poor man's temple.

"You'll want to talk to a neurologist about that," he mentioned casually to the unconscious man as he stood and approached the men who had been pointed out as the professionals in this operation. He assumed they wouldn't be the actual people who called a hit on the likes of Anderson and Monroe, considering how woefully unprepared they were to handle this situation. No, they were likely tails who were suddenly given a green light for a hit with the promise of a substantial reward delivered to the man who killed them.

He paused while he rummaged through the pockets of the second man. The fact that he'd tackled Carlson on his own and left the executive alive afterward meant that his cover as merely another random man walking around was possibly blown. Anja had made sure that any footage of him was erased, but the chances were good that his picture was out there by now. People knew to look out for him, especially since they saw him with Anderson.

"Hey, Anja?" he said, retrieved a wallet and a burner phone from the first man, and moved on to the second. "I think these guys followed Anderson and I from the airport. They're probably local muscle, but I'm not sure if they have connections. It makes sense that they do to get this amount of weaponry on such a short timeline. Is there any chance you could figure out where these weapons came from and who owns them? It might give us an idea as to who is funding them."

"Send me a picture of the serial numbers," Anja said briskly.

He shook his head. "No luck there. They've been shaved off already."

"Not on the weapons, dummy," she snapped. "From the vests. Kevlar isn't issued randomly. They'd have to have it registered, and you need the pins for that. Just—"

The operative was already working to remove the vest from the man he was examining. Sure enough, on the inside beside the label with instructions on how to wash it, there was a rigid tag with a serial number on it.

"I'll be damned," he grunted and used his phone to take a picture. "Can you track who bought these things?"

"Nope, but I can track who sells them," the hacker said. "While you don't need a permit to own body armor, you do need a permit to buy the vests in bulk and the people who sell them do need to keep a registry of the sales to make sure none were sold to convicted felons."

"Okay, fair enough." He tried not to sound too disappointed. Having been in the army for so long, he'd assumed there were gaps in his knowledge regarding civilian use of combat equipment, and he'd actually hoped that there was more to buying body armor as a civilian than met the eye. He was a sucker for a conspiracy theory.

"This could take me a while," Anja grumbled. "You might want to locate Anderson, and the two of you should probably bug out quickly. That may be an abandoned section of the city, but people heard the gunfire and cops are on the way. I assume that is still a no-no for you, being dead and all?"

"Correct," Savage said. The second man's wallet contained a wad of cash, a driver's license, and no credit cards, along with another burner. He stood and scowled at the burning pain in his back. In the heat and adrenaline rush, he'd totally forgotten that one of the assholes had scored a flesh wound. It didn't seem to be bleeding, but he still wanted to make sure there wasn't any potential for infection.

He stepped inside the building where his boss rummaged noisily through some file cabinets. The operative gave the three rooms a quick sweep before he entered the office where his companion now searched. He had his phone pressed to his ear as he worked.

"That's right," he said as Savage stepped inside. "It looks like some gang war style violence going on in the area. A shit-load of shooting and bodies near a chop shop outside Hyde Park." He glanced at the other man as he stepped in and noted that he still carried the submachine gun he'd taken from one of the men outside.

"Are you finished out there?" he asked.

It took the operative a couple of seconds to realize that the question was addressed to him. "Oh, yeah. I wrapped things up and have a couple of new leads too."

"Great," Anderson replied and returned his attention to the phone. "Oh, yeah, absolutely, it's a fucking warzone around here... I hear you, absolutely. All over the place...

yeah, I appreciate it, Bob. Say hi to Becky for me, would you? Okay, bye."

He hung up and grinned smugly.

"So, Bob sounds like a really stand-up guy," Savage said with a small smile.

"He is." The ex-colonel chuckled. "I did my first tour with him. He got out before I did and took a job in the police force here. He's actually part of the commissioner's office, and they're grooming him for the position come elections next year."

"Hey, that's some really great news." He tried not to sound too sarcastic and failed miserably. "So, did he call to check up or what's the deal?"

"Well, he owes me a favor, so I called it in. We can't be caught here, and apparently, calls poured in about shots fired in the area, which meant we would be swimming in cops in five minutes. This way, they'll mobilize their local SWAT teams, and that gives us about thirty minutes to bug out."

"Well, now I feel like an asshole," Savage admitted and looked more than a little sheepish.

"Only now?" Anderson pocketed a couple of papers he'd found in the mess and gestured toward the door.

"Well, yeah. Anyway, I have a couple of burners I took from the leaders of this attack. I assume Anja's working on them now?" He phrased it as a question to include her.

"You would be correct in that assumption," she said and sounded audibly upbeat about it.

"Fantastic." He smirked, confident that she would turn something worthwhile up in her search. "Anyway, I have a lead on where all the missing merch went. It turns out the guys who ran this shop actually worked for someone and were paid what I would imagine was pennies on the dollar to move all the stuff out of the warehouses in the area and send them…fuck knows where. I have the address for the PO box they were paid from."

"I doubt we'll find anything useful there, but we might as well check it out," Anderson said as they set off toward the exit. They took their time and ignored the fact that there were five bodies and one unconscious man on the ground out there in the baking sun—plus two at the gate who were still out of sight.

"Yeah, we're here for the weekend so we might as well make sure that we follow up on every lead, right?" Savage agreed. "By the way, are you looking into the cars that are parked outside? I'm talking to you again, Anja."

"Oh, right, yeah," she said quickly. "I have the license plates and I'm already running them."

His boss gave him a dirty look.

"Look, you'd be included in the conversation if you'd put the damn earpiece in." He laughed as they reached the exit, skirted the two bodies and the SUVs, and continued to where they'd left their car.

Anderson didn't answer.

———

Charles' eyes snapped open as the phone on his desk rang. He scowled at it for a few seconds. He was tempted to let it go and continue with his nap. Then again, it was the private line—the one even his assistant of the past ten years didn't have access to. It was a secure line, constantly cleaned of taps and wires. He only ever used it for emergencies, and the only people who had access to it were the people who handled his more...delicate concerns. The kind that law enforcement didn't need to know about.

It continued to ring until he straightened in his chair again, yanked the handset out of the cradle, and pressed it to his ear. A click and buzz confirmed that the installed software quickly randomized the connection before a voice could be heard on the other side.

"What?" he snapped.

"Mr. Stafford, this is Addams, your head of security in Los Angeles." the man on the other line said. "Is this line secure?"

"Yeah, it's fucking secure, what is it?"

"This is concerning your orders regarding Mr. Anderson's visit to Los Angeles, sir," Addams continued, seemingly unaffected by his superior's rude tone. "People were brought in to handle the situation personally, as it seemed the man was too close to one of our other operations. It would appear that not all went according to plan. There are police all over the site, so I'm not exactly sure what the situation is, but from all appearances, our assets and the local muscle they brought in are down. There is one survivor on the way to the hospital now. It would seem that Mr. Anderson had help of the professional variety."

Well, that much was obvious, although the who of it was still unclear. He already knew Anderson and Monroe had brought in someone who specialized in this kind of work, and they were good enough to avoid any kind of detection so far.

"There aren't any survivors, do you hear me, Addams?"

Charles said and his voice approached a snarl. Rage had already started to build inside him, and he snatched something up and threw it across the room. It shattered against the wall and he scowled, mainly because it had done little to ease his fury. "And you owe me for a fucking Ming Vase. Twenty-eight grand for the vase. Now, get it fucking done. I don't want to hear from you again until you're ready to give me some good news, do you hear me?"

"Of course, sir," the man said calmly before he hung up.

CHAPTER SEVEN

Anderson looked across the desk to where Jeremiah sprawled in his chair. The operative had decided that the warehouse where he'd trained Ivy was the best place to gather their newly assembled team. They'd added bits and pieces of furniture—all old and definitely the worse for wear but they would serve their purpose adequately.

There was no real reason as to why meeting there wasn't a good idea, but the ex-colonel was a little jumpy. His innate paranoia didn't react well to the prospect of meeting strangers whom he really didn't trust at a fundamental level. The rational, logical side—the hard-assed Marine who knew this was necessary—reminded himself that they were like Savage, or at least enough like him that the man had green-lit them for their operation.

He'd followed his instincts when he'd hired the ex-Ranger, and the man had more than proven himself. For now, he'd trust his operative to get the job done using the best possible people. They'd hired a savage because they needed a savage—and the attack on his home and family proved that he'd done the right thing. He might not like the necessity to bring what amounted to killers on board but damned if he wouldn't play the game by whatever sick rules they threw at him.

On some level, he despised the weakness that compelled him to hire others to do what he wouldn't—or, rather, couldn't—do himself. It still shocked him that he'd been able to defend himself during the attack on his home. But he also knew his scars ran deep. His rage and battle lust had been survival at a purely primal level, the instinctual response of the alpha protecting his family. He wasn't the savage they needed, nor would he ever be. But, while he didn't have that particular hunter-terminator ability, he sure as hell had the instincts.

That was what this recruitment was about—a team honed and hungry to enact the decisions they would be forced to make. Of course, that didn't mean he should dismiss his reservations as only paranoia. His brain was sharp enough to see truths and factor them into the equation. These people would come in with their own reasons and expectations and he was right to be wary. Savage had been so easy because he literally had nothing better to do. His life was over, and he'd been perfectly poised for a role perfectly suited to who and what he was. The newcomers all had lives they would set aside to join their crusade and unlike Savage, they had the luxury of choice.

That, he realized, was what triggered his unease. Anything was possible when people had the power to choose.

"How many did you meet with?" Anderson asked as

Savage leaned back on his office chair and propped his feet up on the desk. He shoved the inner tumult aside and focused on what he knew needed to get done.

"Five. Anja had me hiking out all over the damn place. One of the guys actually got pissed when I wouldn't bring him in and he started a fight. Things got ugly, but I think I handled it well. I told him to cool down, and if he managed to become a little better over the next few months, we'd revisit the issue."

"Will you revisit the issue?" He asked the question despite the obvious answer.

"Of course not," Savage sneered. "The guy was a complete wreck. What he needed was hard-core therapy, not a job. Well, I assume he needs a job too, but not the kind that gets people killed. He needs to dispel all that rage in a healthier way—one that doesn't involve shooting at living target."

"So, about the two you have brought in. Mixon?"

"He was a SEAL sniper with a history of urban warfare." Savage closed his eyes to recall the paperwork he'd read on the man. "I didn't know it at the time, but I actually shared a battlefield with him at one point. His code doesn't always tie in with national and international laws, but he does what's right for the right reasons. It's strict, too—he has a thing against swearing, for fuck's sake. What is up with that in this day and age?"

"Some people use small obsessions to ease the guilt of what they've done in the past." The ex-colonel shrugged. "But if he's the kind of man with a code, why would he join us at all?"

"Well, I made my case as best as I could," Savage admitted. "I liked him for the job, but between you and me, I was surprised when Anja told me he had accepted the invitation."

Anderson smirked. "What about the other one? Samantha Davis?"

"She's British and very against people telling her she looks nice or cleans up well." He grinned at the memory of meeting her. "Our Sam has an interesting history with the SAS and is nuttier than a squirrel turd. All airborne types are."

"Well, that's not a very nice thing to say." The clipped British voice spoke from the doorway. Her tone held a faint edge of humor but not enough to draw a smile from either man. She stepped into the brighter light and Savage noted that she was armed. In all likelihood, she'd taken time to survey the location before she'd approached. The knowledge confirmed his choice. He wouldn't have expected anything less from a professional operative.

"I meant it as a compliment, promise," he drawled and maintained his casual posture with his feet on the desk as she stepped into the small space. Anderson stared at the weapon in her hands and swallowed the swift rush of panic. She was doing what he paid her to do, after all.

"I meant what you said about airborne types." Samantha flashed the ex-colonel a small frown before she focused her attention on the other man and holstered her pistol.

"Oh, yeah, because the people who like jumping out of moving airplanes are the absolute image of sanity and self-control," Savage retorted.

She considered this for a moment, then grinned. "He's got me there."

"You must be Samantha Davis. I'm James Anderson, the...uh, funding party of this little endeavor of ours."

"Charmed, I'm sure." Samantha shook his hand, brisk and no-nonsense. "I did a little research before coming here. You are in the middle of what appears to be a power struggle. I have nothing against that, and I don't even need to know all the details. From my side, I tried and failed at a variety of ways to make a living. It's miserable to survive on a government pension, especially these days. So, if you pay me, I'll stand by you. I haven't turned against anyone before and I don't intend to start, so you don't need to worry that I'll turn mercenary. Oh, and—"

"Don't say that you clean up well. Savage told me." He grinned.

"Well, it's good to know we're all on the same page." She summoned an almost-smile, dropped onto one of the older chairs, and leaned back. "Now, if you wouldn't mind giving me a rundown of the paycheck schedules and what exactly you want me to do, we can get started. I was told the remuneration would be generous."

"You don't need to worry about that," Anderson said. "As Savage here can tell you, we have a generous budget for our project. There are limits, of course, but we'd have to work hard to reach them."

"Oh, definitely." Savage sounded distracted. "I can buy my very own island, turn evil, and fight off British secret agents with prosthetic hands."

"Oh, Bond jokes. Very classy," Sam laughed. "So, the rundown?"

"Well, we're waiting for our second new member to arrive, actually." The ex-colonel glanced at his watch and shrugged. "I'd hate to have to do this twice." He glanced toward the door, his expression a little irritated. "By the way, where is our language-averse sniper anyway?"

"I assume he had the same idea as Jaime Bond here and decided on a little recce before he moves in. Of course, he's a sniper so he's doing it from a much longer way out..." Savage nodded as if only half engaged in the conversation. "Give it time, he'll be here. Trust in the tiny Russian in my ear." He smirked at his boss. "And still not in yours, obviously."

Anderson flipped him a middle finger but made no effort to reply verbally to the challenge. Sam pushed to her feet and prowled the area beyond the door. She seemed to prefer motion rather than potentially strained silences. The two men continued to converse in low tones, occasionally interrupted by Anja who updated them on various things while they waited.

Ten minutes later, Mixon confirmed the hacker's report on his status and stepped into the warehouse without any effort to sneak. He also arrived without weapons. Savage assumed he'd stashed them in some nest he'd set up from which to watch the warehouse for the past couple of days. In this area, someone who didn't want to be found wouldn't be if they knew a couple of tricks. Considering the range Mixon might have watched them from, they could have searched for the man over a full mile radius for a week and still had an even chance of finding absolutely nothing.

"Terry Mixon, I presume?" Anderson asked as the man stepped closer to shake his proffered hand.

"That's me. And you must be James Anderson. I've heard good things about you."

"That's...good, I guess." The ex-colonel seemed confused.

"I told him to do his research to convince him to join us," Savage explained. "It was part of making my case. I'm not exactly the most trustworthy of guys at face value, but you might be the kind of person he could get behind."

"So, you admit to manipulating me?" Mixon raised an eyebrow.

"I didn't think it was ever in doubt. I didn't try to be subtle about it."

"You weren't," the sniper agreed. "But it bodes well for our business relationship that you're honest about it. Manipulation isn't dishonest if it's used honestly."

"Well then, I'm glad we cleared that up." Savage shrugged and removed his feet from the table to adopt a more businesslike pose.

"Moving on," Anderson said. "Now that we're all here, how about we get down to the brass tacks of it, yes?"

Mixon took a seat beside Davis and they exchanged names and potted resumes that provided enough to establish credibility without unnecessary details. All that mattered was that they knew what each brought to the table. The rest would follow as they worked together to forge themselves into a unit and learned what they needed to know on the ground.

The ex-colonel pulled a couple of files from the desk and gave one to each of the newcomers. He waited while they opened the folders and scanned the contents in silence, their expressions focused.

"The short version is that Pegasus is responsible for much of the money that goes into the Zoo and most of what comes out," he said. "I'd like that to change, mainly due to the company's complete indifference to the lives of the men and women who risk their lives. There are more details involved, of course, which you'll find in those files. I've taken a calculated risk by sharing this before we have any signatures on paper, but you need to be able to make an informed decision with all the available facts at your disposal."

The two new recruits displayed little reaction but simply waited in silence for him to continue.

"That said, I will need you to sign NDAs and contracts that will enable Pegasus to pay you without raising any eyebrows." He directed their attention to the amount specified at the bottom of the page immediately above the dotted line.

Mixon maintained his deadpan expression, but Davis seemed suddenly thoughtful and a small frown pinched her forehead.

"If you don't sign this document, there won't be any repercussions. However, I expect you to pay me the professional courtesy of keeping what you've heard here today to yourselves," Anderson added, his tone as hard as the look he gave them.

The two exchanged a glance, and Sam was the first one to shrug.

"Hey, this is about three times what I would consider a decent wage for this," she said with a chuckle. "Give me a pen."

Mixon nodded and took the pen Davis had used to sign his name briskly.

"Don't expect me to not speak my mind regarding your methods if I don't approve of them, though," he said. He looked more somber than Savage would have liked, but as things stood, they were good to move onto the next phase. He'd rather work with a man with honest reservations than one who pretended enthusiasm. At least you knew where you stood.

Anderson's part in this was finished, and it was Savage's turn to step up to the plate.

"Well, this makes me feel all warm and fuzzy in my happy place." He stood brusquely and gestured to the others to do the same. "Now, we have a job to do, and there are people out there who want to make sure we don't get it done. It won't be a Sunday picnic, so get your head in the game up front."

He retrieved the two files and handed them back to his boss. "Mixon, you're overwatch on Anderson. Make sure he and his family stay alive and well. Davis, you and I will track down some stolen merchandise. We don't particularly want it back, but the bastards need to pay for it. And, of course, we'll ask them why they bothered to steal it in the first place. I'll run through the details with each of you individually. Welcome to Team Savage. You start your new life tomorrow."

CHAPTER EIGHT

"So, when you said we'll start tomorrow—"

"Yes, I meant exactly that. It's tomorrow, and we've started." Jeremiah fixed Sam with an expression that spoke exaggerated patience. "What's the problem?"

"Don't you think taking a gal to Mexico on the first date is moving rather quickly?" she asked and peered through the scope of her rifle at the villa they'd had under surveillance for the last hour. "Don't get me wrong, I like your style, but I'd also like to know where this whole thing will go from here."

"Well, the simple explanation is that we traced the money paid to some lowlifes who stole from us to this address. Usually, you would expect criminals to avoid a money trail directly to their residences, but I imagine the tax officials in Mexico are a little laxer regarding the drug money tied to a cartel boss' home."

"Either that or they know they'll be fed to the guard dogs if they show up to collect," Sam replied, still focused into the scope. "Although I'm sure the man who owns this place is a stand-up guy who made his fortune selling porcelain dolls or something."

"No, from the electronic security, I'd say he made his fortune in IT," he quipped.

"Yeah, because the amount of physical security around the place screams innocence." She shifted a little to find a more comfortable position. "Seriously, I count at least fifteen patrollers with body armor and assault rifles. Wait—how the hell do you know about the electronic security in the place?"

"Let's just say that I have a tiny—and, I assume, hot—Russian whispering all the details in my ear." Savage grinned.

"Damn hot," Anja said through the earpieces they were both connected to.

"Well, shoot, Savage, why didn't you tell me you liked hot Russians?" Sam glanced at him with a smirk.

He had the oddest feeling Anja smirked as well.

"What's more important, they like me too." He shrugged carelessly. "I clean up good. What can I say?"

Sam chuckled and turned back to her scrutiny of the target location. "Ass," she grumbled under her breath.

She had selected the weapon herself from the fairly military-esque arsenal on offer from Anja's "friend." Given the wide range available, Savage thought she'd made the right choice. They had debated over the points of the operation on the drive over and ultimately decided that her grasp of the intricacies of long-distance shooting was firmer than his. As a result, she got to play overwatch while he actually operated as the ground force.

That was how these things worked. They played to

their individual skills for the most effective and efficient result. She was also a new member of this operation and he didn't mind giving her the simpler task of providing him with cover as he raided the home of a heavily guarded cartel boss.

He'd heard the stories of how the organization was fairly sadistic when it came to punishing people who crossed them. That truth left him unmoved. They had crossed him first, which meant he had to prove to them that he was even more sadistic and more than willing to engage that part of himself. If they responded with their usual cruel aggression, he'd happily reciprocate.

It wasn't a flawless plan, but it did have simple brute-force appeal. The straightforward approach also suited the timeline they worked to, and he didn't mind having to improvise along the way.

Besides, most of the cartels didn't bother to hire from a widening pool of members with former military back-grounds to protect themselves, considering how expensive it was. They usually recruited one former special forces—usually FARC—and expected them to train others in the business of keeping them safe.

The remainder of the teams were generally low-level enforcers—former police and friends and family of the boss in question. As it turned out, nepotism flourished among the drug cartels.

"Okay, do you have your facts straight?" Savage asked. The killer side of him had been silent, but it now stirred and jostled for supremacy. "I'd hate to barrel in there and end up dead because you forgot to convert imperial to metric."

"Oh, please." Sam laughed and shook her head dismissively. "Stop stalling. I'm well aware that our little nest is seven hundred meters from the location. I have a laser distance locator on the scope of this little beauty"—she patted the weapon in her hands—"and am more than confident that I can punch through any of the body armor our little friends down there are wearing. Which, incidentally, is why I asked for armor-piercing rounds instead of the hollow points you wanted to go with."

"Fair enough. Okay, so I'm officially out of things to stall with. Time to put myself in the crosshairs of a bunch of angry coke addicts with military-grade weapons. Yay me."

Savage eased reluctantly away from the sniper nest she had set up and approached the road where they'd left their car.

The heat would kill him. He grimaced and stepped into the vehicle that had baked under the one-hundred-degree sunlight for the better part of an hour while they made their preparations.

It occurred to him that Thanksgiving was still a couple of months away. Not that the holiday had any relevance for a man who technically didn't exist. He only really thought of it because there was a very real possibility that he'd end up like one of those dry and chewy turkeys nobody really wanted to eat until everyone was drunk and no longer cared.

He put the car in drive—no, first gear since they had rented a car with a stick shift. It had been a while, but he had spent a few years driving in countries where automatic gear shifts were considered a luxury not everyone could afford. Even with this, though, he'd had to readjust to the delicate dance to use the clutch, change gears, and accelerate.

They'd enjoyed a few laughs on the drive there. He'd ground a couple of gears and even stalled once before he settled into the new routine. Despite the humor in it, he knew familiarity with the vehicle might well save his life. Who wanted to stall if you needed to make a hasty getaway?

The winding road made the drive a little longer than a simple hike would have been. It had also allowed them to park and set their nest up out of view in the thick shrubbery that surrounded the Alvarez home.

"I stand by my earlier statement that this is a bad idea," Savage said as he pulled the old VW to a stop in front of the heavy steel gates of the mansion. No one had paid particular attention to the mild protest, of course, and this did give him a few moments of possible surprise he could use. Casually, he stepped out of the vehicle. It was too hot for a coat, unfortunately. The first thing the guards would see when they peered through the cameras was a man with a shotgun, an assault rifle, and a pistol walking up to the gate.

"We need to time this perfectly, okay?" he reminded Anja as he stepped in front of the barrier and focused on the men who approached on the other side. They looked more confused than alarmed. He could imagine that one man walking up to a house surrounded by heavily armed men, despite being well-armed himself, could easily be considered insane.

Which was exactly what he wanted them to think. He

couldn't merely storm the fortress. Guile and cunning were needed, or things would go badly.

"I know, okay?" Anja replied. "I have it working perfectly from my side."

"Well, if I get started and you don't come through on your end, I'll look stupid." He scowled when the dozen guards who had broken away from the patrol gestured at him and laughed. "And I hate looking stupid."

"Don't worry, I have your back, sexy American." She chuckled.

"Yeah, yeah, keep it in your pants, sister," he retorted in as sexy a growl as he could manage.

"*Qué estás haciendo aquí?*" one of the men shouted, coming in closer. "*Vete o dispararemos!*"

"Do you need a running translation?" she asked.

"I think I have the gist of it." He raised his free hand and projected the most intense, arrogant attitude he could. In this heat, it was difficult to keep up the act, but his teammate responded immediately, as planned.

Sure enough, when his hand raised, the heavy metal gates began to swing back and opened wide enough for him to enter. The surprise and confusion on the men's faces were palpable as Savage stepped calmly through the gates and waved his hand again. He smirked when they closed obediently.

"Come on, boys," he said to stunned onlookers. "You have to admit that looked as cool as fuck."

Their immobility and apparent inability to shoot the man who had strolled into their domain like an otherworldly apparition confirmed their agreement with his less than eloquent summation.

"If you thought that was cool, though..." He pointed finger guns at two men selected at random. "Wait until you see this."

He mimicked a hammer cocking with his right thumb. Sam took her cue and delivered a neat, red-blossomed hole to the target's head. He teetered a couple of steps to the side and fell and his brains erupted across the perfectly manicured grass.

Savage cocked his left thumb and another man dropped. It seemed to confuse them further that it wasn't the one he had pointed at. Still, it made sense for his teammate to eliminate the one who was actually drawing his weapon.

"That's right, bitches." Savage raised the assault rifle hanging from a strap and aimed it at the men who stood in shock and bewilderment. "I have a big fucking gun too."

"Demonio!" one of the younger guards screamed as he abandoned his weapon and backpedaled. The others were distracted by one of their own quickly breaking ranks, and while not all of them were as superstitious as the first, Savage could tell they had real doubts about engaging.

This was his time to capitalize and he selected his targets. His weapon carried armor-piercing rounds, too, that would penetrate even the better-quality body armor these men wore. Of course, the slugs wouldn't do as much damage once they actually reached flesh, but he could live with that. He pulled the trigger and nodded with satisfaction when a third man slumped heavily against one of the others.

He rapidly identified a second target as Sam acquired her third. Simple teamwork between him and his sniper partner enabled them to sweep through the dozen men before they even had time to try to return fire.

The young man who had tried to flee, thinking their attacker had demon powers, was the last to die. Savage didn't have much sympathy, even though the kid seemed barely a year over twenty.

Still, the youngster hadn't stood much of a chance. He could hardly be expected to hold firm, especially when he had been dutifully raised in an environment that called for holy water first and asking questions later.

Savage ejected the empty magazine from his M16A7, retrieved a spare from his pocket, and slapped it home before he chambered a round.

"That was good shooting back there, Sam." He smiled and strode toward the mansion ahead at a calm but brisk pace. His gaze searched the location to identify where the other guards were stationed.

"Do you have eyes on the others? Either of you?" he asked finally when his search revealed nothing of value.

"It looks like most of the outside is undefended," Samantha said. "You have a clear approach to the house."

"And the doors are already unlocked," Anja said. "It feels like cheating when they use these smart houses—like they don't mind when someone like me slips inside and controls their lives. There were three men who rushed into the basement when the shooting started. They have an armory there, so I locked them inside."

"How secure is that locking mechanism?" Savage asked and paused to peer into the house he found unlocked, as promised.

"They built a nuclear bunker around it, all tied with a

pretty bow with some of the best electronic security that money can buy," the hacker replied.

"Let me guess—a system a friend of yours designed?" He trusted her, but he also didn't want to be shot in the back by someone who had slipped through under her radar.

"Hell no, I designed that shit." She laughed.

"So, if it's that secure, you're talking about three very untrained, very angry men in a room full of what I can assume is a significant stash of military-grade weaponry."

As if on cue, the entire building shook and a loud roar exploded from the basement. "Well, I guess that proves the point I wanted to make—that they might actually do something for our long-term benefit."

"I hear you loud and clear." Her laugh sounded almost evil. "Anyway, I locked our target in his bedroom on the second floor. He was in the middle of his siesta, so the only weapon he has access to is what appears to be a very expensive Colt Army with naked women carved in ivory on the handle. Obviously, it still fires, so keep your guard up. Oh, be warned. Our friend's siesta did include a couple of younger women in bikinis."

"I doubt they'll be in bikinis by the time I get there." Savage sidled up the marble staircase without incident and reached the heavily gilded doors that hid Alvarez' personal quarters. Their background was old oak but the structure itself was cast iron, which made it impossible for anyone to force their way through.

Thankfully, he utilized something subtler than muscle. He gestured dramatically with his hand as Anja opened the doors to provide entry.

"When it's only you around, it looks lame," she said as she closed the doors behind him.

"It felt cool, and that's all that matters." He grinned and paused a few steps in to peer at the cameras above him before he swept his gaze over the large, very lavish apartment. The concept behind it appeared to be a statement of authority. Like the entire mansion, it boasted of wealth, power, and influence, a less than subtle statement declaring superiority and projecting invincibility.

He wondered vaguely if his target's inner sanctum would reveal the real human essence of the man or was simply another extension of his façade, like his home.

Savage negotiated the living room, alert for possible dangers, and admired the art decorations. They screamed money, of course, but even he could appreciate the classier pieces even though he'd never be tempted to own them himself.

Soft cries and whimpers issued from a couple of women inside what he assumed was the bedroom. A moment later, harsh curses clearly indicated that the man within knew his life was in danger.

The operative stepped into the room and made a rapid sweep of the corners before he focused on the people. No security men had rushed to defend their employer, but their absence didn't necessarily mean he could relax.

A somewhat confusing scene unfolded. The two women were, as he'd assumed, naked. Both were young and perky and definitely not his type, but he could see the attraction. Alvarez would definitely be a man who went through a mid-life crisis in style.

One of the women huddled in the corner of the room.

She sobbed and covered her ears and tried to make herself as small as possible.

The second was held around the neck by the third person in the room, a tall, corpulent man with a greying mustache and a pot belly. He bellowed in Spanish for the girl in the corner to shut the fuck up and brandished the classic Colt revolver in his hand.

The room fell silent when the trio caught sight of the intruder, who took another step into the room.

"Look… Al—can I call you Al?" Savage said and trained his weapon casually on the man in front of him. "I'm not here to kill you, and while I really don't care if you shoot either of these girls, I'd rather you didn't kill them. They seem innocent, for starters. Besides that, having to conduct these negotiations is stressful enough without the prospect of being distracted by two dead nubile girls."

Alvarez peeked out from behind his human shield. "What the fuck are you talking about?" he asked in almost perfect English.

"Which part? It was something of a monologue back there and covered a few points."

"You're not here to kill me?" the man asked. "Then why did you kill all my guards?"

"In my defense, three of them killed themselves while trying to break out of your armory." He shrugged and fought a grin because honestly, he didn't think his opponent would appreciate the humor. "And…well, while I don't want to kill you, I doubt you would have taken my suggestion that you give me the money you owe very well if you had fifteen or so armed goons around you, right?"

Alvarez nodded. "Good point."

"Now, let the girls go and we can have a chat, hombre to hombre." Savage butchered the pronunciation deliberately and the other man actually winced.

"And if I don't?"

"I'll be forced to shoot the girl in front of you through her right leg," he explained calmly and took another step forward. "It's armor-piercing ammo so it'll hit you in the leg—or maybe the kidney. I can't really guess accurately with you behind her, but it'll be one or the other. And it would make this conversation far more difficult."

The cartel boss took a moment to think before he finally let the hammer drop gently forward on his weapon and released the girl in front of him.

"Get out of here," the operative said. "Both of you."

He wasn't sure if they could understand him, but they had most likely intended to do that anyway. In fact, they didn't bother to even attempt to gather their clothes before they scuttled away without a glance at either of the two men.

"Now we talk, yes?" Alvarez asked. "Hombre to hombre, and you don't kill me?"

"That's right." Savage smiled when the man set his pistol aside and lowered his own weapon in turn. Of course, the Mexican could have a weapon hidden somewhere, but the fact that he wore a bright red speedo and nothing else made the prospect unlikely.

"What do you want to talk about?" the cartel boss asked. "Although I would like to know which of my friends gave me up. Professional courtesy, as I'm sure you'll understand. I give you what you want, and you let me take my revenge on someone who isn't you."

"I would, but honestly, I'm simply tracking the money." He fixed the other man with a hard look. "The money you're taking from Pegasus."

"Who?" Alvarez narrowed his eyes in thought. After a second, they widened as the name suddenly clicked into place. "That stupid asshole Charles? If I give you what you want, you won't kill me?"

"No, I won't kill you, dumbass." Impatience colored his tone and he wondered how many damn times he'd have to repeat himself before the dickwad believed him. "You owe over fourteen million dollars, American. Plus, another ten grand I spent on incidentals—no, you know what?" He stepped closer to the abandoned Colt and inspected the ivory handle which was, as a matter of fact, engraved with naked women. "I'll take this, and we'll call it an easy five grand."

"That sounds fair." Alvarez looked a little regretful but nodded toward a painting on the wall. "My personal safe is behind that. The code is eight-seven-five-three-six-six-nine."

Savage tucked the weapon into his pocket once he'd checked it to be sure it wouldn't fire before he approached the artwork. Sure enough, there was a safe behind it. He smirked at the unsurprising cliché as he punched in the numbers. It clicked and opened to reveal what looked like far more than fourteen million.

"Do you have a bag somewhere?" he asked Alvarez and turned to face him. "I forgot to bring one of my own and —oh, never mind, I found one." He retrieved and opened an expensive burlap, which had obviously been left there for this precise purpose. Silence settled around the two men as he started counting the money he slid into the bag.

"Will you go after Charles?" the cartel boss asked finally as Savage worked quickly and quietly. "Because if you don't, I'm afraid I'll have to go after you. I need to make this look good, or my people will think I'm weak. So, you are either someone I've hired to target the man and I wanted you to prove your skills to me personally, or I hunt you for revenge."

"Don't threaten me." He smirked but his tone was cold. "It's not a nice thing to threaten your friends."

"You are breaking into my home," Alvarez shouted.

"I didn't say close friends," he grumbled under his breath.

"My men are all dead," the man countered.

"Fine, acquaintances, then. Out of simple curiosity, how much money do you have in here?"

"A couple of months' worth," he answered with a shrug. "Your money is all in there. You don't need to worry."

"I'm not worried, pal," Savage said with a smile. "That's fourteen million and...did we say five thousand?" He dropped another stack of bills inside before closing the safe again.

"An honest mercenary." Alvarez looked genuinely confused. "What a delightful surprise."

"I'll tell you what, big guy. If I don't take care of this Charles guy, I'll return half this money. Not the five grand, though. I need that to cover my personal expenses. You know how these things go. So, are we agreed?"

He stepped closer and proffered one hand while the

other held the assault rifle. The cartel boss looked more confused than before but shook briskly.

"Agreed, Mr… What do I call you?" he asked.

"I'm Savage," he replied with a small grin and shook the drug boss' hand once again to seal it.

"Well, obviously."

He opened his mouth, a little startled by the comment, and blinked before he realized that the truth of his name had slipped right over the man's head. Well, there was no need to correct him on it, so he smiled and released the hand he now realized was clammy with sweat.

"Consider me another sadistic, savage merc. But not one for hire. Not by you, anyway."

The bag was a little heavier than he'd anticipated, and he grunted as he shouldered it before he made his way back toward the exit. Once he was out of eye and earshot of Alvarez, he pushed into a jog. While the conversation was civil enough, he knew the cartel lord would not easily forgive this little incident. They needed to get out of the range of his wrath—and out of the country—before a veritable army of crooked cops and angry goons initiated a manhunt.

"Are we clear for departure?" Sam asked once she saw him leave the building.

"Yep, and we should probably make it a rapid exit," Savage replied, not quite out of breath by the time he reached the car. He bundled both weapons and cash into the back seat and slid behind the wheel to start the engine. "Pack up the nest and meet me where we were parked."

"Copy that." Five minutes later, Savage eased to a stop from where Samantha was visible lugging all the equipment. She added her pile to his and fell into the passenger seat, and he floored the accelerator to take the out of there before she'd even fully closed the door. A cloud of dust puffed indignantly behind them.

"I've cleared a route for the two of you to leave the country," Anja said. "You might want to move the weapons and cash from the back seat and put it all somewhere less visible before you reach the border—or anywhere near civilization for that matter. Your safe window won't last for long, so I suggest you avoid scenic roads."

"Roger that." Savage chuckled.

His companion covered her earpiece as she leaned over to whisper, "She's…uh, scary."

"I can still hear you," Anja pointed out with a trace of amusement.

Sam pulled back and mouthed the word scary at him in a way that demanded a hearty laugh in response.

CHAPTER NINE

It wasn't like he'd lived a life of excitement and danger before Savage had knocked on his door. Not literally knocked, of course. The figurative challenge or call or whatever he might call it was far more demanding.

The man had seemed...familiar. Like an old face from the past, peeking in uninvited. He hadn't longed for action again, and perhaps action was something of a misnomer anyway. He'd always remained far back and stared at the world through the lenses of a scope—that small, perfect window—before he killed them.

And he'd gotten rather good at it too. People told him that what he did was complicated. They produced numerous numbers and papers to show him how complicated it would have been for everyone else, but for him, it simply wasn't. He hated the fact that they all thought he was doing something spectacular when the real truth was that he did the coward's thing. His particular brand of false heroism was to hang back and allow other people to die while he helped a lucky few to survive.

He drew in a deep, steadying breath. Of all the places in the world to work again, he'd never thought it would be Philadelphia. He'd visited the city before, of course, but never thought he would do his work this close to home. There were rules about not working on US soil, but he didn't really think those rules applied in certain situations. People were out there killing soldiers, men and women who put their lives on the line to defend their country, and nothing was done about it. Well, until now.

At first, he'd simply read the files. They'd stirred enough interest for him to call friends who had served with various units. Most of them remembered Anderson and agreed that he'd been a man of strong determination in the field with even harder resolve to save his men when he'd been taken off. The circumstances that resulted in him being pulled from active duty were tragic, and he'd evidently made it his duty to keep anything like that from happening again.

Then he'd been forced into an operation. Mixon hadn't been able to find any real details except that any military personnel tied to it had died and been shipped back from various locations. The process followed the predictable Pentagon response when they tried to cover something up. The paperwork on the operation was light and most of what was there had been redacted. The message was clear. It had been written, handed to the corporation in charge, and edited before they sent it back.

The sole sponsor of the operation had been a company called Pegasus which was, interestingly enough, the company Anderson had immediately quit the military to join.

He wasn't stupid and could connect the dots. Someone with the ex-colonel's history wouldn't make a change like that so suddenly without a reason. Savage had told him the reason was to make sure the killing stopped. He didn't trust the operative, but he trusted his superior to make the right call. Not only that, Mixon was there to help him save the lives of the men and women in the field. He felt this was an honorable enough cause to break him out of his retirement.

That sentiment still applied, even if the job so far had been merely overwatch for Anderson. He'd make sure the man survived long enough to fulfill his intentions, while Savage and Davis were sent off to find something or... someone. They hadn't really filled him in on the details.

His mission was boring, obviously, but a pleasant kind of boring. He was able to let his mind drift freely while it effortlessly did what everyone thought was so amazing and difficult. He studied the world around him—without a scope this time—but with the single-minded purpose to locate and identify possible danger.

Anderson had told him that any threats he saw should be handled with extreme prejudice. In retrospect, that was a good thing since extreme prejudice was really the only way he knew how to deal with this particular kind of problem.

Mixon tilted his seat back a couple of degrees in response to his body's need for occasional movement. Undistracted, his mind continued to work like a sponge and absorbed anything and everything as his eyes sifted and studied every inch of his surroundings. No threats had made themselves apparent as he watched Anderson take his wife and kid out to a nice dinner. He wasn't sure what kind of restaurant it was, but whoever called their place Interlude deserved the prize for most pretentious restaurant name ever. With a plaque, he decided, like when someone became a Guinness world record holder.

"Who takes their kid out for a date night, anyway?" Mixon asked while he chewed on the beef jerky he'd brought along for the trip.

"Well, I suppose it makes sense," he mused aloud when he felt the need to answer himself. "The man thinks his family is in danger—with good reason—and he wants to make sure they're safe. He's hired someone to keep him safe so it would make sense to let that person protect the rest of his family too. It's like someone sharing their Netflix account, except I'm the account in this situation."

Yes, he was talking to himself. He'd learned the habit in the various dull moments of watching over a city while he waited for his second of an opening. It was important to be able to enjoy his own company since SpecOps rarely teamed him up with a spotter on those missions. He'd needed to learn to enjoy his own company and did so mostly in silence. Sometimes, though, this included being able to hold a debate, argument, or conversation with himself to help pass the time.

He took the last bite of the spicy jerky and tucked the packaging into the plastic bag he'd brought for precisely that reason. It was a company car, not his own, and it was good manners to return a vehicle in as good a condition as you got it, if not better.

Mixon's gaze drifted to the inside of the restaurant as Anderson leaned in to kiss his wife. The young son made a face and his parents laughed and continued the kiss despite his exaggerated protest.

They seemed a nice family. He had thought of having one himself and even met a few girls who fit the criteria. There weren't many out there who could tolerate a man of his particular eccentricities for too long, however, and they ended up leaving.

It was for the best, really. He'd had a hard time enduring their eccentricities as well. But he'd been willing to try, at least.

Anderson seemed similarly eccentric, and he'd found someone. Of course, whether he'd found her before he'd turned eccentric was up for debate, really.

Mixon took a sip of water. He'd put himself on a timer to stay hydrated but avoid overindulging. There were aspects of keeping someone under surveillance that he really felt were a last resort. Once they had finished their day out and headed back to the apartment building, he would be able to relax and get some sleep.

He could tell why Anderson didn't always have his family locked up in the place they called home. Honestly, gold depositories were less secure. The ex-colonel might have used himself as bait, but he didn't seem the type to use his family as bait too.

Then again, his wife had a career of her own to pursue. His superior hadn't enlightened the sniper as to what that was exactly, but she had a job that kept her busy. And the young one needed school, which meant that lives needed to continue despite the threats.

Which, of course, was why he was there.

He'd followed the tyke to school, returned, and tailed

Anderson to fetch the kid again and the mom from the firm where she worked, and directly to dinner from there.

Ah, that was why they'd brought the boy along for date night.

He shifted in his seat and squinted sharply at an SUV that pulled up outside the restaurant. That particular parking space had to be paid for, but nobody left the vehicle to do so. The windows were tinted so it would be impossible to see inside at this hour. There were always ways around that if one made the effort. He looked around to confirm that only one car had arrived.

If the police would show up, that would be fantastic. He could see if the new arrivals would move to avoid a ticket. Unfortunately, another hasty sweep of the area confirmed that he'd have no such luck.

He stepped out of his car, a nondescript blue sedan, and retrieved his phone from his pocket as he strolled casually toward the car. His one-sided heated debate would hopefully allay any suspicions the occupants might have.

"No, Amber, you said I could have him this weekend," Mixon said to nobody in particular. "I have the whole weekend planned. Come on. You can't change the schedule like that."

People avoided conversations like the one he faked like the damned plague. Anyone who heard him would immediately pretend they hadn't. Those who noticed him would instantly forget him—including the group of men inside the car, hopefully.

While the tint provided little more than shadows, he could discern five people inside, bulky and pressed together. Weapons too, he acknowledged if the barrel aimed at the roof of the SUV was any indication. This was another group of people keeping an eye on the family but for very different purposes. His role was as a protective detail, and you didn't need five people with guns for that.

Black SUVs were the kind of vehicle usually chosen because they were big and, while obtrusive, common enough that people wouldn't give them a second glance while on a busy street. They were large enough to disguise a large motor and armor and the tinted windows could be used to conceal bullet-proof glass.

All these benefits added to a significant advantage when you sent a hit squad to eliminate a troublesome former colonel.

He maintained what he felt was an Oscar-worthy conversation while he swung away and returned to his car. It included threats of lawyers, a little making up, and more anger to embarrass people into not looking while he armed himself with the weapon given to him by Pegasus. Well, Savage, technically. There wasn't much he could carry across state lines without drawing the police and all the other alphabeticals onto his tail.

The operative had, it seemed, something of an armory, all with the serial numbers filed off. It seemed pointless to worry about the problems that would arise from that if the police got involved.

All these disconcerting truths meant it was best not to use a gun unless absolutely necessary. Not only would it attract all the wrong kinds of attention, but he also didn't want to have to jettison the only weapon he had.

"No, I can't tag along with you," he shouted into the phone and strode in the direction of the vehicle once more.

A plan began to take shape in his head. "I have my parents coming over for Thanksgiving, that's why. It's the last weekend before the holidays—which you've made all about you, I don't need to remind you—and I deserve to spend some time with my son. Ow! Fudge."

He stumbled against the SUV, banged his shin painfully into the protruding bumper, and finished the maneuver with a trip and roll alongside until he reached the door.

"There's a darn fudging car in the way, parked all the way up on the fudging sidewalk," Mixon yelled belligerently. He swung a hard kick at the bumper, followed by another at the tire. With the phone still held close to his head, he released a string of his almost-curses and vented his frustrations on the vehicle in a way that would both annoy occupants inside and make the passersby look elsewhere.

"Hey," a man shouted as he finally slid out of the SUV and fixed him with a hard glare. He was dressed in what looked like an expensive suit with a holster hidden under the jacket. That little nugget confirmed Mixon's instincts as to their weaponry and purpose. "What the fuck do you think you're doing?"

"Watch your language," he snapped in response.

"What?" Confusion was immediately followed by alarm and shock as he staggered and clutched his throat. Blood squeezed between his fingers from the cut Mixon had inflicted with the knife he'd hidden with his phone. He shoved him back into the passenger seat of the vehicle and thrust in behind him.

"I said watch your language," he muttered as he scrambled over his sagging victim and drove his knife toward his next target.

Cars were tricky places to stage a fight, but it was always easier when surprise was on your side. It was the one place where no one wanted to take advantage of superior numbers to use firearms.

The driver jerked his head up from his phone and surprise registered briefly on his face.

"Sorry about this." The operative stabbed his blade into the broad chest before the man even registered the extent of the danger. It sliced smoothly through the Kevlar lining in the suit and plunged easily into his heart. One twist brought instant death. Mixon grunted his satisfaction. At least, with the driver eliminated, he had a reasonably captive audience.

He yanked the passenger door shut to keep the curious at bay. The sound seemed to snap the three gunmen in the back from their shock but before they could fully react, he plunged his torso through the gap between the seats.

The SUV shook as two of his adversaries punched wildly at him and the third tried to club him with the stock of the submachine gun that was obviously his weapon of choice. One of the fists landed a sliding blow on the operative's cheek, but the heavy weapon missed and connected with a dull thunk against the cheek of the lucky assailant. His luck immediately ran out, of course, when Mixon shoved his blade with the full force of his scramble behind it. There was no resistance as it plunged into his stomach, then yanked it out and thrust it into the man's groin and twisted to sever the femoral artery.

The man in the passenger seat hadn't yet succumbed to

his wound although his groans suggested he wouldn't last long. Still, he flailed wildly with one hand as if to help his teammates despite the blood that seeped and gurgled around his labored breathing. All he managed to do was turn the radio on as his fingers fumbled on the dashboard. The loud, heavy beat provided an intense but almost incongruous counterpoint to the life-and-death struggle.

Mixon grimaced and wiped the sticky handle of his knife on his victim's thigh and hefted it more firmly. The man's hands clawed at his wounds, but a quick glance confirmed that he'd be dead in a few minutes based on his rapid blood loss.

Two men remained, but the one on the right seemed momentarily distracted by his teammate's imminent demise. Their partner jostled the wounded man in an effort to free up a little elbow room as he started to draw a combat knife from a sheath on his belt. The operative moved quickly but awkwardly. With his legs half in the front of the car and the difficult angle, he wouldn't risk a strike that would either miss or do little damage. For now, he struggled to keep the knife in its sheath while he tried to wrestle his body through and into a better position.

He grunted softly when the man to his right punched him hard in the ribs and forced the breath out of his lungs in a rush. His body contracted and his weapon slid from his hand, but he used the impetus to drag his legs through into the back seat area and drive his knee into the man's nose. It was made so much easier by the fact that he had ended up all but on his adversary's lap

"Fuck!" The thug recoiled and shielded his broken nose.

The assassin on his left had used the distraction to draw

the blade completely. Weaponless, Mixon lunged across the now very dead man in the middle to grasp the wrist holding the knife.

He groaned and struggled to breathe while he grappled in his clumsy position to gain some kind leverage over the man who still held a dangerous measure of control over the weapon.

Strong hands snaked around his legs when the thug with the broken nose tried to drag him off his teammate. The operative grunted and kicked out and his assailant yelped when a boot connected hard—hopefully with the swollen and painful nose, he thought belligerently.

"Yeah, you get her good!" someone yelled from outside. Three younger men stood there, and one laughed and pumped his hips suggestively.

Under any other circumstances, Mixon might have laughed. Typical of that age, they'd immediately thought someone was having sex inside the vehicle. Thankfully, the tinted windows would preserve the fallacy of an amorous encounter long enough for him to get the job done before anyone thought to ask questions.

He released his grasp on the man's wrist and his surprised adversary cursed when the blade nicked his own cheek with the unexpected jerk free. The operative lashed out with his boot again to deliver another blind strike into the assassin at his rear.

The blade swung toward him and he rolled instinctively off the dead man's knees scant seconds before the weapon punched into the beefy thigh. For a moment, Mixon almost panicked at the thought that he might be trapped in the tiny gap between the man's legs and the back of the seats.

His hand clawed the carpeting and closed around the sticky comfort of his blade. Adrenaline surged and with a yell, he pounded his other fist into the exposed groin of the man who raised his weapon to strike. The assassin keened and doubled over, and the operative grasped a handful of his assailant's hair to haul himself free. As he pushed out of the narrow space, he swung his knife underhand and into the thug's chest. For a desperate, wild strike powered mainly by desperation, it might actually count as a miracle. The metal sank deeply and without resistance, directly above the fifth rib, to bring almost instant death.

He dragged the knife out to free a splash of warm blood as the last heartbeats pumped a few times before they ceased entirely. The silence was absolute, a breath-holding moment that rushed in as the adrenaline-charged impetus faded.

When his pulse had calmed, he turned to the last man, who seemed to have lost all will to fight.

"No." His final target twisted, scrabbled at the door, and managed to pop the lever without tearing his gaze from the operative.

Mixon clutched his collar before he could throw the door open and leaned forward to make sure it was closed.

"I really am sorry." He honestly tried to be as empathetic as he could, but the effect was no doubt hindered by the somewhat macabre sight of him sprawled over the two dead men. His adversary fumbled to draw a knife to defend himself, but his movements were slow and jerky—the kind made by a man in shock who looked his own end in the eye. He wasn't quick enough, and Mixon's deft swing severed his carotid artery with a precise, practiced motion.

The man uttered a garbled sound of protest and slumped against the door. His fingers clawed frantically in an effort to staunch the blood flow, but a few seconds later, his eyes lost their focus and the body sagged.

Mixon dragged in a deep breath. He crawled over the dead men to the door on the street side and cracked it tentatively. Hopefully, he'd attract less attention if he exited there. One of the men had hung a coat over the back of the seat and he yanked it off and fumbled a few times, half unbalanced on his awkward perch, until he managed to get it on. It was a little large but would suffice, and the dark color would probably hide any blood he and it had collected.

As he patted his victim's pockets to retrieve what he could—only a single cell phone, in this case—he acknowledged that the apparent argument had been a very effective ploy. No one, including the would-be assassins, had noticed his gloves, something that might have been a dead giveaway. They'd all been too busy avoiding looking at him to see what was right under their noses.

Which meant fingerprints were something he wouldn't have to worry about. He didn't think he'd left blood behind, and of course, no one could predict the odd hair falling out. Still, with the amount of blood and gore around, his paltry offering would hopefully slide into the comfortable space of contaminated fluids and be unusable.

Mixon shrugged, slid out of the car as casually as he could, and adjusted the coat as he strolled toward his car.

He grinned when he felt the weight of the knife he'd also taken where it nestled in the back of his waistband. It was a good blade, a little longer and straighter than the one he'd taken from Savage's armory and with a keen edge and good balance. His grin broadened. They would call him two-knife Terry from this point forward.

No, that was stupid, but it was also amusing.

Once safely in his car and away from curious eyes, he took the phone from his pocket, pressed the button for an emergency call, and dialed nine-one-one.

"Hello, operator?" he asked, disguising his voice. "I saw a couple of folks fighting in a car. Or screwing, maybe. Or both. I couldn't really tell. Either way, it was very disturbing, and if you could send someone over that would be great. Oh, yeah, the license is AMP 299, and it's parked in front of the Interlude restaurant on 42nd. Thanks."

He hung up and lobbed the phone out of the window into the oncoming traffic. Anderson, with his wife and kid, stepped out of the restaurant, blissfully unaware of the sinister relevance of the SUV they walked past on the way to their car.

"Why did I do it with a British accent?" he asked himself and shook his head as he started the engine to pull onto the road behind his charges.

CHAPTER TEN

Anderson stepped out of the apartment and onto the terrace overlooking the city of Philadelphia. It was a clear night—something common during the fall, he was told—and the nightlife was booming.

Thankfully, the accommodation provided by Pegasus was well elevated so all he could really hear was the occasional honk of a horn above the veritable white noise machine a city became at night.

Even though it wasn't their apartment, he knew Ivy would have an issue with him smoking inside the house. It apparently had something to do with their son learning bad habits despite the fact that he didn't smoke that often, and when he did, it was only cigars. They'd discussed it a few times and disagreed each time, but he didn't feel like having the conversation with her again. It had been a nice night, they'd both had a good time, and he didn't want to shadow things with a pointless debate.

For tonight, she won, and he had his cigar out on the terrace where he blew lazy smoke rings into the quickly chilling evening air. Once winter arrived, he wouldn't smoke outside anymore, he knew that. One way or another, he'd find a way around the restriction.

He sighed and took in the sights and the sounds of the city below him. Despite the metropolis ambiance, it was peaceful. He was almost a quarter of the way through the cigar when the door to the terrace opened.

"Come on. I'm smoking outside—what else do you want?" he demanded. He glanced toward the door, ready to have the argument again, but it wasn't Ivy.

Mixon carried himself well, a tall man and lean and lanky, with his blond hair cut to the pristine one inch demanded by anyone in a military march. He was at least dressed in civilian clothes, which was a plus, except they weren't the same ones he'd seen the man wearing when he kept an eye on Damon in school. That observation was faintly alarming.

"I keep myself free from most vices these days, but I don't expect the same level of restraint in everyone else," the operative said with a small, bemused smile. "By all means, smoke away. Although maybe avoid it in front of your son?"

"He's eight. He'll understand that it comes with special occasions." Anderson shook his head. "No, you're right. I'm merely imagining having this debate with my wife. It's complicated."

"It usually is."

"In the interests of wildly changing the subject..." The colonel moved closer to his visitor but puffed a lungful of scented smoke away from him. "Did anything happen at the restaurant that you think warrants my attention?"

"At the restaurant proper?" Mixon asked with a shrug. "Nothing at all. But outside the place though... I really thought I'd kept it as subtle as possible. I didn't want to disturb what looked like a happy moment with the people you love."

Anderson nodded. "I appreciate that. And it was— unless you know what you're looking for. To me, an SUV arriving at the same moment we order the check is a little suspicious. I saw you walk around it twice, kick it, and jump in with one of the occupants."

"Right." He chuckled ruefully. "Well, they were armed and ready for a fight—one they didn't expect from me. I disposed of them and alerted the authorities afterward. The police scanner app I have on my phone said five bodies were found in the car, stabbed to death using a knife or some other sharp instrument. The officers on the scene said that it looked like a savage gangland hit."

The ex-colonel smirked, took another hit from his cigar, and exhaled the smoke away carefully. "Honestly, that does sound like something Savage would do. I do appreciate you taking care of me and my family like that."

"I'm simply looking after you, boss," Mixon said with a chuckle. "If you don't mind, I think I'll turn in now."

"You do that." He patted the operative gently on the shoulder. "Get some rest, and I'll see you in the morning."

"Will do, Colonel."

"Don't call me that," he said as the other man turned away.

The sniper swung to look at him. "I thought you Marines had this thing—once a Marine, always a Marine, right?"

"I'll always be a Marine, no doubts about that. But I was never cut out to be a colonel."

"Whatever you say, boss." It was better than Colonel, Anderson mused, but not by much. Either way, he let the man go about his business. They would see a lot more of each other, at least until Savage returned from his little vacation to Mexico. From that point forward, things would be far more interesting.

He'd assumed that Anja would have been in touch by now, and the fact that Courtney hadn't called him once all day told him that she had. For some reason, he'd been kept out of the loop. That would change, though, once Savage arrived.

By virtue of his previous rank, all the military people assumed he was the one in charge of this operation. He was a ranking member, of course, but that didn't mean that he was in charge. Thank God, he was a little lower down the pole than that.

He took a deep drag of his cigar, closed his eyes until he could feel his lungs burning, and released it into the air.

Now that he thought about it, maybe Ivy was right. Besides, smoking outside gave him a sense of freedom that didn't come when he did it inside.

A lot of complaints had come from closing the street off, mostly from the owners of the local businesses that were interestingly high-end. You didn't get stuff like this in the more gentrified neighborhoods these days, which made it all the more satisfying when he told the pompous asses who talked about how many calls the commissioner would receive about this in the morning that they could shove it.

Sure, it would probably be his ass and his badge the next day. No longer would they call him Officer Angelo Cruz a week from now. It would be worth it, though. More than worth it.

Seeing their faces when he told them there was no way he would open the street to let a bunch of pompous rich folk trample all over his crime scene was all he needed to justify his decision.

Of course, the commissioner wouldn't see if that way, especially when the news came that no evidence could be found at the scene of the crime.

Make that a terrifying lack of it. They would need a DNA swab to determine that, but there were many guns in the car, although no shots fired. There was also a lot of blood, but the knives he found on the scene were all left clean. The men were all killed wearing body-armor-infused suits that had to be a lot more expensive than anything a cop would ever see, and yet they all drove in a cut-rate SUV with stolen plates and no serial number attached.

"So, what do you think?" Detective Soza, one of his oldest friends, asked as he walked over to where Cruz had a sip of his neglected coffee.

"Would you believe me if I said it was gang-on-gang violence?" he asked, finished the lukewarm liquid, and winced as it went down.

"No, I don't think anyone has bought that particular pile of bullshit," the other man said with a chuckle. He pulled a pack of cigarettes from his coat pocket and tapped one out. After a moment of thought, he offered one to Cruz, who shook his head.

"Six months without touching one of those cancer cylinders," Cruz said with a chuckle. "But thanks."

"Six months, huh?" Soza looked impressed. "I'm proud of you, man. I know how long you've tried to kick the habit."

"Thanks. So, if it's not gang-on-gang violence, what the hell are we looking at? I sure as fuck can't tell."

"Well, unless we're looking at a gang war between Calvin Klein and Armani, I think we can rule a gang hit out," Soza said and shook his head vehemently. "Beyond that, though, I draw a blank. Maybe the forensics team will have better luck finding something."

The warehouse sprawled in the early morning light, apparently as deserted as ever. Of course, he knew better. Anderson stepped out of his car and studied the structure with a scowl. On that particular morning, he questioned why he'd bothered to get up this early. For some reason, people were keeping him out of the loop and the irritation that caused wasn't only precipitated by his constantly lurking paranoia.

When he'd all but made up his mind to confront everyone, Courtney had given him a call after he'd dropped Damon off at school. Apparently, she wouldn't be back in town for a while and she wanted him to pass equipment along to their little team of outcasts.

The soldier in him had immediately responded with a

surge of satisfaction. The conflict they faced and the formidable adversaries ranged against them demanded that they push forward with the group. That would only be achieved by equipping them with superior advantages rather than those provided by the questionable arsenal Savage had managed to pull from only God knew where.

Thus far, the results were promising, and Courtney's supplies would only push them to a higher level. Yet, despite his icy conviction that he would do whatever it took to crush those who'd declared war on them, the tiny tendril of paranoia niggled constantly below the surface. What was there to keep the newcomers from simply absconding with the weapons and the money they already had and dropping off the face of the earth?

Or worse, the insidious little voice suggested, teaming up with someone who might pay them a lot more than they did?

He sighed and engaged his dark, secret enemy to push it back down where he knew it wouldn't stay. His gaze swept the building and he tried to determine if anyone was actually there. Their team had been hired partly because they were good at keeping themselves hidden. Would he really be able to tell if they were around if they didn't want him to know?

Which, of course, reminded him of his real source of irritation. He hated not being in the know. About more things than this, obviously, but it was easier to focus on what was in front of him. He sighed and circled his car to drag a couple of heavy bags from the trunk. It seemed petty to complain that he'd have to lug both of them to the warehouse, but the damn things were heavy, and he really wasn't in the mood.

He leaned down to grasp one of them when it slid a few feet away. His startled gaze settled on Savage who stopped him, grinning like an idiot.

"Hey," the man said. "How was the family dinner? Did Mixon do his work?"

"Well, yes, obviously." Anderson chuckled. "How's Mexico this time of year? They don't exactly have fall or winter there, so I assume the sun was shining? Birds chirping?"

"Oh, it was all right." Savage rumbled a laugh. "There was a lot of gang violence there, though. It really got in the way of me enjoying my time there. Actually, it made us cut the visit short."

"No shit?" The two men stepped inside the warehouse. "There's been a rise in gang violence around here too. People dying and getting knifed and shot all over the damn place."

"That's the condition of the world these days." Savage tried for wise and regretful, but it fell short at sarcastic.

Davis was already there, waiting for them with a box of doughnuts and a thermos of coffee.

"You look like shit," he observed as he filled a plastic cup with coffee and took one of the pastries. This was breakfast for them, mostly because neither had the time or the supplies to make the toast, egg, and bacon breakfast Anderson had enjoyed.

He was lucky to have Ivy, he realized as he sat on the table between the two of them.

"We're waiting for Mixon to show his face before we

get started." He felt sorely tempted to try one of the dough-nuts. They looked freshly baked, coated in glaze, chocolate, or sprinkles—or some ungodly mixtures of the above, which still looked delicious in the way only junk food could.

The sniper arrived before his temptation proved irre-sistible.

"How's it going?" Savage asked after a sip of coffee.

"Well, I dropped a kiddo off at school this morning," he responded. "Then followed the mother to make sure no one tried to make an attempt on her life before I came here."

"Did anyone notice how he didn't answer the question there?" Sam asked and raised an eyebrow at the others.

"No. No, he did," Savage said with a grin. "He simply wants us to infer what he meant by it. I'll go with grumpy about having to do a school run when you don't have any kids. Oh! I think he wants to drive Ivy and Damon to school instead of following them."

Mixon scowled as Davis laughed. Anderson shook his head with a chuckle.

"I don't think Ivy would like having a driver like we're suddenly rich people who can't stand to do any physical labor on our own," the ex-colonel commented wryly.

"Wait, who's Ivy?" Davis asked.

"My wife." Anderson raised his hand. "And Damon's my son."

"Oh, nice." The woman immediately lost interest in the topic of conversation and focused on the doughnut in her hand

"Anyway," their boss said and brought their attention

back to him. "I was sent some equipment I think will give you an edge on the people you've gone up against."

"All three of us?" Savage straightened. "Was there any action around here? Monroe didn't fill me in. Neither did Anja, for that matter?"

"Who's Anja?" Mixon asked.

"That's…complicated." He wondered how he would explain a Russian woman feeding him all the vital intel for his missions. "What happened while I was gone?"

"Oh, five guys tried to jump Anderson and his family while they were out to dinner," the sniper said. "I handled them."

"Right, good work." Savage nodded, his expression a little smug like he'd been proved right and liked it. "Anderson, carry on."

"Thank you. Anyway, Pegasus has run considerable weapons and armor testing for the open market in the Zoo, and while their methods were brutal, we can't argue with the results. I've brought some of those for you to try."

He hauled one of the bags onto the table, unzipped it, and removed a few weapons, which the team studied with real interest. They seemed roughly based on existing weapons, but also…not. Savage focused on a pistol that lay on the table and opened the case it was stored in. It looked like a revolver but with a long, heavy barrel.

"That prototype was developed in that North Carolina testing site, actually," Anderson said as the operative examined one of the magazines, rounded and shaped like a cylinder but with no place for the new rounds.

"They called it the beast in the files I saw," their superior went on to explain. "The rounds are very thin, magnetically-charged nickel alloy needles. The long barrel is made from a magnetic charging station that activates when you pull the trigger. It's virtually silent when fired because of the suppression built into the long barrel that mutes the usual crack when the needles break the sound barrier. And these little strips here"—he displayed a long strip of tiny little needles all strung together—"have about a hundred rounds in them before you need to reload. That simply requires fitting another strip of these inside. We only have five reloads made thus far, but I assume none of you will need to fire a gun five hundred times?"

Savage picked the weapon up, loaded, and flicked the safety off before he fired it down the range. True to form, the rounds rocketed ahead with little more than a whoosh and punched hard into the chest of the dummy. On impact, they left holes in the Nirvana shirt Savage had put on the mannequin but didn't seem to faze the plastic minion.

"It doesn't look like it has much stopping power," Savage noted with an expression of disappointment.

"Oh...right, there was something about that," Anderson said. He dug in the bag to retrieve what looked suspiciously like a manual. "Here it is. The brittle texture of the round will drive it through armor and clothes—and even walls—better than armor-piercing rounds, but when it encounters soft materials like human flesh, there is a power...uh, absorption. It says here the needle splinters and transfers all the power into the body."

"And turns Gussie's insides into Swiss cheese," Jeremiah said and studied the weapon with renewed approbation. "Or would if he had any insides. Anyways, dibs."

"Why do you get dibs?" Davis protested.

"I called dibs, that's why." He grinned, replaced the weapon in the case, closed it, and drew it closer. "What else do you have, Anderson?"

A few long hours of show and tell came and went during which they tested a variety of weapons and pieces of armor. Nirvana Gussie was put through his paces and eventually had to be replaced by his friend Nessie when he was too damaged for continued use.

Each of the three operatives selected the weapons they preferred and fitted themselves with the new body armor Pegasus had developed. Although lighter and more agile, the display on Gussie and Nessie proved capable of keeping damage from most of the weapons to a minimum. Of course, the sniper rifles the two newer team members wielded proved to be more than a match.

In the end, Mixon had to leave to pick Damon and Ivy up and bring them to the warehouse as it was time for her shooting lesson.

The new weapons and armor were packed away quickly, and Savage was there to help her take her pistol apart.

"Let me help you with that, ma'am," the sniper said and stepped in from behind to take the weapon from Savage's hands to make his own inspection. "Consider it part of your package deal—to teach you how to defend yourself. As you know, I've been tasked with keeping you, your husband, and your kid safe from harm for the duration of this... Well, for the duration."

"Right," Ivy said and narrowed her eyes at him. "What do you think?"

"Well, you might want to improve your time." Terry

smiled to take the sting out of the words and handed the pistol to her. "But the form is impeccable. Practice to improve your time should do the trick."

"Yeah, you're teaching how you lot have been taught to fire," Davis said with a chuckle and strolled toward the group. "Which isn't too bad, but as a girl, you need someone closer to your particular measurements to give you finer tuning. Come on, lads, git. We need girl time here."

Savage looked at the two men and two women around him and shrugged. He wasn't paid enough to have to deal with this many people all at the same time. Sometimes, it was best to simply leave others to get on with it. He walked away from the range and to his so-called office where he poured himself another cup of coffee.

The other two men conceded defeat and left the women to get acquainted. They joined Savage at the desk.

"Davis is telling her how the isosceles isn't a good stance for a woman who lacks upper body strength to absorb the kick of the pistol," the ex-colonel said and frowned as he watched the two women working.

"She has a point," Mixon ventured as he poured himself a cup of the coffee. "Weaver helps you keep your balance better, and if you fit her with the new armor you have over there, you won't need to worry about leaving your side open to gunfire."

"I never liked Weaver, myself," Savage grumbled.

"You look like one of those guys who's CAR or bust, eh?" The sniper laughed.

"When it comes to my style of shooting, balance and precision aren't really something to worry about." His grin said it all. "It's about how many bullets you can get into the air as quickly as possible. Hell yeah, CAR or bust."

Anderson chuckled softly and winced as the firing started on the range. "I think I'll head home now. I have nothing to do at work and nothing to do here."

"Just a heads up, but I think I'll let Davis give your wife shooting lessons from now on." Jeremiah pushed out of his seat and stretched.

"They do seem to be getting along like the proverbial house on fire. I'll call you tomorrow. Courtney said she'll have work for us by then."

"Looking forward to it, Colonel."

Anderson shook his head and walked away. There wasn't any point in correcting them. And, if the truth be told, he rather liked the title—or the genuine respect that it embodied amongst those who really didn't have to use it. He'd tried to convince himself that he was someone else now that the military was behind him, but...well, once a Marine, always a Marine. No matter where he was, he'd been shaped to command, no matter what they called him, and damned if that wasn't exactly what he'd do.

Once he worked out what the fuck everyone was keeping from him.

CHAPTER ELEVEN

He would never understand how people chose to do this—or claimed to enjoy it—but would certainly never admit it.

On one hand, to walk around and get a little sunshine on a bright day was always pleasant, but he could do that without having to trek all through creation with bugs taking a slice of him every step of the way. Worse, he had to try to whack a tiny white ball across the grass, only to walk or drive another fair distance to whack it again. And, horror of horrors, he had to wear his delighted executive smile and pretend to love every minute of it.

People called this a sport, but he never really understood why. The real game was the play that took place behind its civilized veneer. Like everything else, Charles had learned it from his father. He'd also learned the far more gratifying power it unleashed for those who were willing to pay the price. While he often cursed the nagging injuries that manifested with greater discomfort and regularity, he had to admit that it had, when played by his rules, brought many more benefits than irritations.

Of course, he had always been of the opinion that the game-related conversation was always better achieved over brandy and cigars and that exercise and sunshine could be acquired in other ways. He liked swimming, for one thing. It remained a sore point that he'd always been strong at that and even reached varsity on his school's team until his father pulled him out to start his career in business. He'd never forgiven the old man for that, but the old bastard was dead, and Charles had forced his three siblings out of the will in retribution for their lack of sacrifice. He'd learned that from his father, too.

Forgiveness was overrated, anyway, and thoughts of his revenge helped to make what was still an onerous pretense a little more bearable. It reminded him how much he had in the game, as it were.

"Everett," he said with a smile as today's golfing buddy walked over to him. His caddie jogged to keep up with the man and Charles suppressed a surge of annoyance. Despite being a full ten years older than he was, Everett Pedersen had managed to stay in shape. It wasn't unthinkable that men twenty years his younger might even be jealous.

A game with Maven was still tucked in the wings, scheduled for a later date that week, and he was pleased that he'd arranged this particular outing first. Despite the age disparity between the two of them, he liked the man, and the feeling had always been mutual. They shared representation on various foundations and charities and were well aware of each other's accomplishments. A sense of mutual respect had always existed between them, enough that Charles usually suppressed his dislike for the game to join him for a few hours out in the Florida sun to whack at a little white ball with clubs and a ridiculous smile on his face.

"Charles, my friend," Everett said with a chuckle as the two men hugged for a second.

"You look like a fifty-dollar bill," he said briskly.

"And you look like a hundred, old sport." It was an old joke between the two since it had been established early on that with his thick, bushy beard and scowling features, Everett was the very image of Ulysses S. Grant. Charles, with his balding head and calmer appearance, looked a lot like Benjamin Franklin.

The game began without prelude and Everett took an early lead. Charles' dislike didn't mean that he wasn't skilled—he had played since he was sixteen—but against someone who genuinely enjoyed it, he didn't offer much of a challenge. That said, he didn't much mind if the right person won. His satisfaction came from elsewhere, after all.

"So," he said once they were far away enough from the club that they could speak privately without any concern that they would be overheard, "did you have time to look over my proposal?"

The other man looked up from the little white ball on which he'd focused with a small smile on his face. "I did. It was thorough and made for some very interesting reading."

"Does that interest in the reading translate into any other kind of interest?" he probed.

"Absolutely," Everett replied with a chuckle. "For one thing, Carlson and I had a number of conversations, and I actually helped direct a fair number of military contracts his way. Having a majority stake in a company whose shares are rocket-high and climbing is always interesting. Of course, that is assuming your confidence that you can turn the current abysmal state of the company around."

Charles had hoped he wouldn't bring that particular thorny caveat up. Of all the potential candidates to take over the company, Everett remained his first choice—the one who would sweep Pegasus into the kind of future Anderson and Monroe simply would never grasp. As such, he needed to tread carefully. While he couldn't avoid the blatant truth, he also didn't want to make any admissions that might scare the man away.

"There is something I wanted to bring up with you, about that," Everett continued and refocused on his ball on the fairway before he took a heavy swing at it. He smiled and shielded his eyes against the glare to watch as the white spot rocketed against the blue sky. When it dropped on the smoothly clipped grass on the other side of a pond, he turned his attention back to his companion.

"And what might that be?" Charles fell in beside him as they strolled over to the golf carts where their caddies waited.

"Well, first and foremost, the fact that you've offered me something that isn't even yours," Everett said bluntly. He slid his club in his golf bag and turned to face him.

"Well, yes, we do have a current CEO, but that will change—" He began what had been rehearsed many times with many other acquaintances he'd contacted.

"Will it, though?" Everett interrupted. "No offense, old friend, but your attempts thus far haven't gone quite as well as promised. Don't give me that face," he snapped as Charles suddenly looked annoyed. "Yes, I've kept tabs on this ever since you sent the paperwork to me. Too many power changes in a company are bound to make stock prices plummet, and I've already prepared myself to take a lion's share of the stocks put on the market in a couple of weeks. If you can't get your affairs in order before then, I won't need you to put me in a position of power in Pegasus. I'll do it myself."

He fought to keep the angry red from suffusing his face. In front of the caddies, he'd been spoken to like he was a child. Everett didn't bother to wait for him either and simply drove off to the other side of the pond. Charles remained where he was and heaved in a couple of deep breaths to calm himself before he yanked his phone from his pocket and tossed his club at his caddie. The young man ducked to allow the steel rod to career over his head before he raced to retrieve it.

Part of him wished he'd had better aim. The kid didn't deserve it, but he might have felt better with a little violence under his belt. He dialed quickly and connected to the secure line in his office before he dialed again.

"Good morning, sir," came the chocolatey voice on the other side.

"Shut up," he snapped. "I need our current contract to be finished and I need it done now."

"I'm afraid that with your limit on spending, our interested parties are still disappointingly few and of...lesser quality."

"Then up the price." He glowered at his golfing partner in the distance, who calmly studied his ball with no indication that he was even slightly ruffled by their confrontation. "This contract needs to be done before next week."

"What kind of limit are we prepared to reach, sir?" the contact asked.

"Push it to half a million for now, excluding the applicable local fees." His private expenses could bear that easily. They could absorb far more, but he wanted to give himself room to increase should the resources obtained by his addition of funds prove ineffective.

"I'll update the contract sir," the mellow voice said. "Have a nice d—"

Charles cut the connection quickly and shoved his phone back into his pocket. He scowled at the caddie, who looked like he might be tempted to run away rather than have things thrown at him. He shook his head, took his seat in the cart, and motioned for the lad to drive after Everett.

Damn it, he would probably have to arrange for the club to give the kid a raise after this.

There was too much light.

Taking a nap proved to be impossible under these conditions. Amanda worked outside and kept the door open, and he could hear her arguing with Connie over the AI's lack of manners. Connie had probably joked about how she hated to see her go and loved to watch her leave or something like that. It seemed the electronic irritation was going through a phase.

Did AIs go through phases?

The question was something that would keep him up all afternoon. Sal opened his eyes regretfully and pushed off the couch in the living area. He wasn't sure why he didn't simply go to bed given how exhausted he felt, but he didn't want to go to his room. Despite everything, he didn't really mind being around to hear the hubbub of his little base. Being around the people he'd grown to care about was comforting, oddly enough.

He breathed deeply and stretched. Maybe all he needed was coffee. That would do better than a nap these days.

Ever hopeful, he wandered into the kitchen to see if there was anything left in Amanda's pot. He would ask Madigan the niggling question once she returned. She might not know much about AIs and their emotional phases, but she would definitely have a few choice opinions on the subject that would be entertaining.

"Salinger Jacobs." A voice spoke from behind him and he turned quickly. Courtney stepped down from the stairs. She'd obviously just woken up and wore one of his shirts. Jet lag was killing her as it always did, and it would take a day or so for her to bounce back from her latest return from the States. She liked jumping back and forth between her responsibilities in Philadelphia and those in the Zoo, but the price was the fact that her body could never fully settle into a solid sleep schedule.

Oh, right, he recalled blearily. That was why he hadn't gone to his room for a nap. He hadn't wanted to wake her up.

"What are you doing up?" Sal asked. She draped her arms over his shoulders and pulled him down for a kiss.

"I missed you, is all," she said with a smile, her head

tilted teasingly and perhaps even invitingly. "And the fact that I've already slept for six hours which, to be honest, is about the longest I've slept over the past year or so."

"It doesn't mean you can't sleep in, right?" he asked and rubbed her back absently. "You could always take a day off and try to fit in some of that resting and relaxing people talk about. I hear it's all the rage in California."

"Oh, please. The people in Cali haven't heard of relaxing for at least a decade." Courtney laughed. "And I was resting and relaxing until Anja sent me an alert on my phone and woke me up. I checked what it was, and I couldn't sleep after that."

"I'm sure I could help you with that." He grinned lasciviously before he leaned in and kissed the tip of her nose. "I seem to remember you being very tired after our morning calisthenics."

"People have said I need to get more exercise in." She grinned cheekily.

"Hey, Anja," Sal shouted.

"Yeah, that's what a girl likes, hearing her guy shouting another girl's name," Courtney grumbled.

"What?" the hacker yelled from the server room.

"Why are you sending Courtney messages? You know she's supposed to be resting right now. She gets enough stress without you adding to it."

"I didn't send her anything." Anja stepped cautiously out of the dark room with all the computers and looked like she hadn't slept in days. "She has her phone set to receive automatic updates on the Pegasus situation."

"It wasn't really about Pegasus, per se," Courtney said. "It only said that one of our board members added personal funds to a foundation he opened. A cool quarter million. It's weird that it doesn't seem like a lot of money anymore—that is weird, right?"

"Wait, what?" The Russian frowned as she stretched and swung to ease her back. "What foundation?"

"Something called the Ferros Deduction."

"Oh…oh, crap," Anja said softly. "Ferros Deduction is an online messaging board for…well, all kinds of crimes. I use it myself, but I always lay low and never buy, only sell. If he's added money there, it means he's put funds up for a contract. Which member of the board was that?"

"Charles Stafford." Courtney checked her phone for the name again, her expression one of distaste. She hadn't much liked the man or his attempt to challenge her, and maybe her aversion had been well-founded.

"Oh, right, I remember that name." The hacker snatched the phone from the other woman's hand and tapped the alert before she pressed a couple of buttons—digging deeper, Sal assumed. "Well, the foundation he put the money under is called James Anderson, so that can't be good. I guess the positive side is that it's not under your name too, although I'll dig into that as well. What this means is that he put an open contract on Anderson. Well, technically, he put a lot more money into a contract on the colonel's life, which means a much higher echelon of killer will be enlisted. I need to warn him."

Sal narrowed his eyes. Anja talked like she no longer even realized they were there. He knew he did that sometimes too, but he'd never realized how annoying it was from the other side of the conversation.

Well, monologue, technically, but why split hairs?

"Drop him the info, plus everything else," Courtney said with a smile. "And see if we need to hire a counter-hit to keep him safe."

Anja had tossed the phone onto a counter and started to make another pot of coffee. She continued to talk to herself in a mixture of Russian and English, which Sal suddenly realized meant she wasn't talking to herself but rather to someone over the headset she wore. How had he missed that?

Courtney burrowed closer to him and press a light kiss to his cheek.

"You have grown a little bloodthirsty," he said with a grin and returned the kiss with far more demand on her lips.

"Come on," she whined and dragged the last word out over three or four syllables. "I've read R and D papers for the past forty-eight hours, give or take a couple of hours of sleep here and there. I'm not bloodthirsty, I'm horny!"

"It's weird how your brain associates research and development with sex. I like it."

"Of course, you do. You might even consider what we do some very interesting research of our own, all things considered."

"Right." Sal nodded with mock seriousness. "Biological research is my forte, now that I think about it."

"Well, I think I'm the one who will run tests." She bit her bottom lip with evil speculation. "You're merely a test subject. My very…proactive test subject."

He chuckled. "Well, I'm always down for a little more physical testing. Let's get to work."

The two of them started walking back to his bedroom and Anja stopped her work to watch them.

"Like fucking rabbits," she grumbled in Russian and shook her head. It wasn't like they had anything more important to be concerned about or anything.

Well, they didn't really. That was why they paid people like her and Savage to take care of the situation. Which meant they had done all they could and worrying about it would only stress Anja to the point of distracting her from her work.

Maybe it was best that they stuck to fucking like bunnies and left the work to the professionals.

The hacker grinned and filled a mug with coffee, horrid as it was, and shuffled back to the server room. She had work to do.

CHAPTER TWELVE

Mistakes were made, many of them by herself. She'd simply wanted to be nice. The place had seemed like such a sausage fest since she'd joined the team, and with the only other woman looking like a fish out of water, she'd made the decision to try to make the woman feel more comfortable.

That had been the first of many mistakes. And like most errors in judgment, it had seemed like a good idea at the time. Teaching Ivy to hold a gun in a way that suited her body type better had been relaxing. Girl time was at a premium in her line of work, and time when she didn't have to hide the fact that she could name every single bone in the human body while she broke them was even more at a premium.

It had been a kind of give and take, really. Ivy seemed like she had been starved for a social life—something that sometimes happened with people in her situation, when all the people whom she could interact with had very little in common with her. The conversation had deviated from talking about guns and turned to life stories and ended up with her heading out to coffee with Ivy while the two of them had gotten to know one another. Anderson had taken Damon back to the apartment to give his wife the freedom to actually do something a little normal for once.

After their coffee session, Sam had returned to the apartment she'd tried to settle into ever since she'd arrived in Philly. She'd enjoyed the excursion but believed that would be the end of it unless Ivy wanted another girl's time out, which she would have been glad to acquiesce to.

The magnitude of the mistake hadn't become apparent until Anderson called later that night as she'd prepared for bed. He'd told her that Ivy had taken a liking to her, much more than she'd liked the stoic Mixon. It seemed that while the man had all the makings of the perfect bodyguard, the fact that Ivy trusted her made her more suited to protecting the woman and her child.

She'd listened to the long explanation with unusual patience—and yes, that had been mistake number two. He'd detailed his concerns that the people who had targeted him weren't averse to snatching or murdering his wife and child to accomplish their ends. She couldn't fault either the logic or the emotion that precipitated mistake number three.

Sam had actually held her breath when he asked her if she'd take over bodyguarding duties as he had to head off to inspect some of the research sites that had been moved to the city. Mixon, of course, would be his ever-present shadow once he was freed of his role on the home front. As part of the changes, the two newer team members had been briefed on who Courtney was and how she fitted into the bigger picture.

The visits were usually Monroe's job, he explained, but with her stuck in the Zoo, he needed to take over and relay everything back to her. She wasn't sure how he would accomplish that. Maybe with Anja's help. She smiled when she recalled the other welcome feminine presence in the operation. Despite her being a disembodied voice, she somehow still checked the like box.

His request had been politely phrased and really made her feel all warm inside. She had honestly felt it was a worthy thing to do to be a bodyguard for Ivy and Damon.

The pleasurable fuzziness had dissipated quickly, though, when her alarm had gone off at the ungodly hour of seven in the morning. It didn't matter that she had been used to getting up early in the military. Just because she was used to it didn't mean she liked it.

Fuck those guys.

She'd rolled out of bed amidst a stream of all the curses she'd held in during her time around Mixon. The ongoing vent brought a sense of relaxation she as drove to the apartment building where Ivy and Damon lived and walked them to her car.

Anderson had also asked her to look like a driver—something about keeping up pretenses. It seemed Mixon had trouble with the school drop-off since rich parents didn't much care to have a strange man hanging around their children. A couple of calls to the cops had forced the team to rethink their strategy. Her mistakes had provided the perfect solution to this particular dilemma. She gritted her teeth at the double whammy. Not only was she babysitting this early in the morning, but she had to act like a chauffeur while doing so.

Well, a chauffeuse, technically.

Damon had talked non-stop during the whole drive, which made Sam's headache worse than it already was. From the bleary-eyed look on Ivy's face and the massive cup of coffee in her hand, she assumed her new friend felt similarly drained of energy.

The child didn't seem to notice. He talked about a video game stream that he'd watched the night before with his father, going over the latest updates of recently released DLC for a looter shooter that now involved a man based in the Zoo. It apparently included beasts resembling those seen in footage released from the jungle. It was interesting, she had to admit. She had a couple of friends who had gone into that place with the troops at the British base on location as well as a few others who were retired, like her, and had been paid handsomely to head out into the most dangerous place on earth.

Not all of them had come back. Those who had didn't like to talk about what they'd seen. They told her a little, mostly about the money to be made and how it wasn't enough when you had to face lizards with acid saliva that could melt through steel bars and hardened titanium-weave armor suits.

No, she thought, and let her mind wander as she followed the map on the HUD of the windshield to the school. She considered herself a woman of the world, willing to take any job if the money was good enough. And from all that she'd seen and heard, there would have to be a lot of money involved if she was ever to set foot in there.

There was something about that place that simply wasn't right. Especially in the way it affected usually rational people. They either loved it or hated it. Either way, the place stuck with them for the rest of their lives, and Sam wasn't willing to make that kind of commitment to something.

She turned into the lane that led to the drop-off point for the kid and scowled at the long line of limos and armored cars. This was a private school, she realized, one Anderson would never have been able to afford on his government salary. Being the CEO of a controversial company and having a price on his head had at least brought one advantage. She only hoped it was worth it down the line.

It was little wonder, though, that the rich parents so obviously in evidence had recoiled at the idea of Mixon lurking around their little darlings. They obviously felt their wealth entitled them to dictate their own terms of comfort and safety. And Anderson and Savage had been right to be concerned. Rich parents meant connected parents and before you knew it, the alphabet soup would show up because someone's dad played squash with a director and decided he wasn't wouldn't let Weave, Straina or Ellisandrex worry about a strange man.

Rich people were weird. Somehow, the down-to-earth Anderson family were automatically excluded from that sweeping judgment.

She eased in beside the school and leaned back in her seat while Damon gathered his belongings.

"Sam?" Ivy said and leaned forward. "I...uh, to keep up with appearances, would you mind opening the door for

Damon? All the other chauffeurs are doing it, and we don't want to stand out."

"I'm a chauffeuse, technically." She suppressed a growl of irritation as she undid her seatbelt and stepped outside.

And immediately realized she was underdressed.

It didn't help to know that she was probably the most qualified of all these buffoons in slick uniforms and fancy hats. She wore the new hi-tech body armor Anderson had acquired for them, along with a sawed-off prototype shotgun that fired explosive pellets and one of the nifty ceramic knives.

Over that, she wore a trench coat, a black Metallica shirt, jeans, and combat boots. If standing out was bad, she easily rated God awful.

Not that she cared. She felt like she was doing people a favor anyway, and damned if she would dress up for the occasion. Let everyone dress down to her level. At least then, they'd be able to do something if anything happened that required them to take action. She'd tried running and fighting in a fancy suit before. It hadn't been a pleasant experience.

She moved to the passenger side and opened the door as Damon bounded out.

"Thanks, Aunt Sammy," he yelled as he sprinted at full tilt toward the school doors.

"You got it kiddo," Sam said with a grin that she amazingly didn't have to fake. While she didn't like being called Sammy since it was a boy's name, she could endure it when it came from freckles and a silly grin that was missing a couple of teeth.

Her gaze followed his retreating figure as she closed the

door and leaned on the car. Didn't kids hate school? This one seemed delirious with excitement and continued his headlong sprint until he vanished around a corner.

"Hey." The voice broke into her thoughts and she turned as one of the local bodyguards-slash-chauffeurs wandered over to greet her. He was tall and handsome in that quarterback kind of way, which spelled not her type unless she was five tequila shots in.

"Cheers, mate," she said and tried to remember the classes about body language she'd taken back in high school as an elective. She really wanted him to go away without having to tell him that.

"You're new around here. I haven't seen you at the morning drop-off before." His chuckle sounded a little smooth and overly confident. "I'm Jason, nice to meet you. Are you British? You have a British accent. I actually have an aunt who lives in London."

It had only been the one class, she recalled regretfully. And she'd napped through most of it.

"Sam," she replied and despite her irritation, took his proffered hand and shook it. "I'm a Yorkshire gal myself."

"Look, I don't want to tell you how to do your job or anything, but the people around here expect a certain standard when it comes to those who drop their kids off." Jason's smile was polite but had a slightly supercilious edge. "Honestly, I dig the nineties rocker outfit as much as the next guy, but if parents see you hanging around their kids, they'll throw a fit. Rich people do that, am I right?"

She really should have paid attention in that class. Was it something about...posture? Stand up straight and fold your arms to say you don't want to be talked to? Something about putting up a metaphorical shield?

"You look good, but I'm sure you can do better." The idiot rambled on, unwittingly digging himself deeper and deeper into a hole he had no idea existed. "I bet you clean up great if you put some effort into it."

Sam's eyes refocused from her search to confirm that Damon had safely vanished into the school and turned to face the man. Her features were calm and collected as her trench coat swung open to reveal the body armor and, more importantly, the shotgun she had tucked under her arm.

"Look here, Jason," she said and made every effort to keep her voice low. "I've tried to be nice and social-like to keep from antagonizing the locals, but you done pissed me right the fuck off. I've killed twelve...ish men in the past week or so, and don't think I won't mind turning you into lucky number thirteen-ish. Don't ever tell me I clean up well."

He took a hasty step back and she closed her jacket again.

"Now fuck off." Damon was, of course, long since tucked inside the school so she had no reason to remain. She spun on her heel and barely gave the idiot another glance before she yanked the driver's door open and slid inside.

"What happened?" Ivy asked as they eased back into the traffic.

"I was teaching the kids out there what being a real bodyguard is like," she said with a grin and glanced at Ivy through the rearview mirror. "That and not to bother me when I'm supposed to do my job."

"The guy out there looked like he was ready to soil himself," the other woman pointed out with a chuckle.

"Then maybe he's in the wrong line of work." She shrugged, pleased to know she hadn't missed anything important in those classes after all.

Courtney should have been there doing this. That was the mantra playing in Anderson's head with every step he took into this new research and development facility Pegasus was opening. They were bringing many people into various different locations. Thanks to the shenanigans underway in Pegasus, most of their reestablishment operations needed to be overseen personally, and Courtney had told him not to trust any of the board members.

Which meant there were fifteen of these locations, and he needed to keep a personal eye on all of them. He would visit and receive reports from all the lead scientists on their research projects. Well, that was the story he fed them, anyway. He'd finally given in and let Anja into his ear since the idea behind this was for her to record and transmit everything to Courtney when she wasn't charging into the Zoo personally and putting this whole plan of theirs in jeopardy.

He'd told her that it wasn't a good idea to keep doing that, but it wasn't like he could tell her not to go. She was his boss, technically, and while he trusted her to make the right decisions and listen to him when he had something of value to say from a company perspective, he didn't actually have a say in how she ran her life.

Which meant he was now forced to listen to one of the lead scientists who explained the various projects they still needed funding for. He had mentioned that the supply still came in from the Zoo despite the upheaval of the ongoing changes. The problem, apparently, was that the Zoo deliveries were behind schedule.

Anderson nodded. "I'll raise that with the various department heads to see if we can't hire more personnel to help shoulder the load. We've intended to initiate expansions to spread the workload a little. This seems like the perfect place to start training them for that, right?"

"Right," the man in the lab coat agreed but looked confused. "Don't take this the wrong way, Colonel, but I thought I would have to sell you on the concept a lot harder."

"I see where you're coming from, Dr. Maschick," Anderson said with a smile. "I really do. And I'm no longer a colonel, by the way, so you can simply call me Anderson. What were we talking about again? Oh, right...well, the current hand at the Pegasus helm actually has her history in research and development, which makes her particularly happy to help you with your work. As it turns out, she's something of a hardass who has most of the board members wrapped around her fingers like..."

"Putty?" Maschick asked.

"I don't know if that's the saying, but sure, let's go with putty." He grinned at the image that created in his head as they resumed the tour. "If the truth be told, expansion has always been a part of the plan. The only thing holding the people on the board back would be the cost to hire and train new people—mostly doctoral candidates and the like —only to have them run off when another company makes a higher offer.

"Thanks to Dr. Monroe's efforts, however, no one will offer them anything remotely better these days, and with the people effectively trained in all these new facilities, we will turn work around much faster. Once that's done and we're all back on schedule, we can open other facilities and expand, all with new and trained people working with the highest salaries in the business and on the cutting edges in their respective fields."

"Don't take this the wrong way, Co—Anderson," Maschick said as they continued the tour. "But you're nothing like most of the other military people we've encountered before. They seemed to think this was something that needed to be rushed or scrapped. We had one of them running a facility once and ended up losing more money than we saved. Which was why he was sacked, of course, but still, that seemed to be more of a cultural issue than only with the one man."

"Oh, no, don't get me wrong, I'm one hundred percent like the other military people you've met." He chuckled dryly. "You have to remember that Dr Monroe is the specialist here. While I cannot pretend to have her indepth knowledge of the work undertaken by this and other facilities, I still have sufficient understanding to relay the relevant details to her. She will make the call about which projects are still worth running, understood?"

Maschick nodded and made a face that Anderson couldn't quite read.

"I don't suppose you do any of the research that goes into the weapons production, do you?" he asked and looked around as if in an attempt to answer his question at a glance. He'd worked hard to establish a brisk, no-nonsense, but also approachable persona and hopefully lower the man's reservations. While he definitely didn't all the scientific knowledge and understanding at his fingertips—and couldn't be expected to—this natural ignorance could be readily extrapolated to include a broader vagueness that his companion would hopefully not question.

Courtney and Anderson still had far too many unanswered questions, many of which related to the military projects. With his history, it was entirely natural that he would evidence an interest in that side of Pegasus' activities. Hopefully, with a few questions thrown into the mix in an almost casual way, he could ferret out a few tidbits of information that might open up a new line of inquiry.

"No, all the projects we run here are for civilian purposes," Maschick said. "We're developing goop pulled from the Pita flowers—you know, the one most of our competitors sell as anti-aging cream. We've developed it into fuel and found ways to make it recyclable, among other things. These are useful developments with patents either to be sold or maintained for Pegasus, whichever profits the most."

"Right." He paused for a moment before he grinned disarmingly. "And where are the facilities that handle the weapons development? The ones that work for the government."

"Well, I actually have a friend running one of those," Maschick said with a chuckle. "They moved those to Vegas.

Well, Nevada, anyway, since those are the most isolated places, which allows them to actually run proper weapons tests."

"Interesting," he said, careful to school his features into mild interest rather than suspicion while he made a mental note of the information. None of the networked facilities had been moved to Nevada, which meant there were still locations working outside the Pegasus umbrella. That was...worrying. It also confirmed the vague, nebulous suspicions that had nagged at them all. Too many potentially lethal unknowns had yet to be unearthed and accounted for.

His phone vibrated, startling him out of his thoughts, and he yanked it a little irritably from his coat pocket. He scowled at Courtney's name on the caller ID.

The unexpected call was even more worrying. He was still connected to Anja through his earpiece—her occasional snide comments an ongoing cheerful reminder of her presence. She'd gone quiet for a while, thank goodness, but if Courtney wanted to talk to him, she could have simply used Anja's connection.

The unexpected communication was an anomaly, and he hated anomalies.

"Sorry," he said and turned to wave his phone at Maschick in apology. "I need to take this. It's the boss."

"Of course," the doctor said with a chuckle. "I'll be here to resume the tour when you're finished."

"I appreciate it." He tapped the accept call button and moved somewhere that didn't have any prying ears.

CHAPTER THIRTEEN

"You're talking too fast," he said pointedly. "You...okay, slow down and tell me what it is that you know. Use your words the way they're meant to be used—you know, with spaces between."

"Ugh, fine," Courtney mumbled irritably on the other side of the call. "It's not that simple, though. We have a renegade on the board—Charles Stafford—and it would appear that he put a hit out on your life. And an expensive one at that."

"Oh, wow, that makes me feel all warm and cuddly inside." Anderson let his sarcasm drip from his words although he didn't really mean it. Perversely, it was oddly flattering to know that the people who wanted you dead were willing to pay top-dollar for it. Then again, the fact that they tried to kill him at all was something he needed to get used to. Had he allowed himself to slide into complacency with his own fireteam now in place? They'd sent assassins before. The fact that they'd failed meant the worst was yet to come.

"Look, if you need me to head back to help you to deal with this shit, I'm sure I can put my business here aside," Courtney said. Anderson could hear a rumble of protest on the other side, but he couldn't tell who it was. Probably Jacobs, he mused.

"I don't think that's a good idea." He shook his head firmly. "The fact that they have a hit out on me and not you is suspicious on its own, considering you're the figurehead for all the changes we've made here. The only reason I can think of why they don't have a hit out on you too is that you are still near the Zoo. They have vivid memories of what happened the last time they tried to kill you there. Hell, I still have vivid memories from that time."

"Would you believe me if I said that I do too?" she asked with a dark chuckle.

"I'm torn between my own memories and the fact that you've actually been in the Zoo the longest. Technically, you should be the one it affects the least."

"And the fact that the nightmare we saw that day still haunts me should be enough said, I think." Her voice took on a somber note.

"Hell." Anderson forced a laugh. "Now, I actually think we could lead all these people who want us dead out there with you and the Zoo will take care of the evidence."

"Yeah, take care of, digest, and shit out before too long. If they're lucky, of course."

He laughed despite the fact that none of it was funny at all. These days, a dark sense of humor was all he could really manage. When he thought about it, the fact that he still had a sense of humor at all was a miracle on its own.

"Ah, no matter, we'll deal with it on this end." He

nodded decisively. "Haven't you heard? We appear to have had an uptick of gangland violence in this part of town. Horrible business, really. I hear five men with guns were killed outside the restaurant where I had dinner with Ivy and Damon."

"Oh, golly me, that is terrifying," Courtney said and ran with the joke. "Why, that makes me wonder if I should even return to Philly at all. It's probably a good deal safer around here."

"Yeah, that joke will never get old. While we have Davis and Mixon working with us to keep things running smoothly around Philly, I thought I might make it a little more difficult for people to find and kill me by taking a road trip."

"Will you and Savage have a bonding experience on the road?" Courtney sounded amused. "Become bros. Have an adventure, start talking like surfers while you smoke weed and try out all kinds of new ideas. And all that before the two of you meet a couple of happy go lucky ladies who make you realize how much you've missed living life to the fullest?"

"That was...oddly specific." He wasn't sure he wanted to delve into either the fantasy or its possible sources.

"It was a movie I watched," she admitted. "Or maybe a book, I don't remember. Bro-bonding fiction is usually my go-to. That and sci-fi action. All kinds of fun shenanigans, actually."

"Well, the reason for the proposed road trip was something very interesting that the lead scientist here in the Wolven facility said," Anderson explained. He spoke quietly and paced around the small research lab that still hadn't been unpacked and seemed rather low on the list of priorities of the people there. "He told me the people running most of the military weapons testing were all moved to facilities in Nevada."

"But we don't have any testing facilities in Nevada," Courtney pointed out.

"That was exactly what I thought," Anderson concurred quickly. "It would seem that most of the military testing equipment was moved by Carlson before we actually arrived, which is what I plan to take Savage to investigate. If I had to guess, I'd say most of the scientists and researchers were kept out of the loop, which would explain why Dr. Maschick provided me with that little nugget so flippantly. If we can bring them back into the fold, we can find out who was in charge of moving them and if they're still with Pegasus."

"Fantastic," Courtney said enthusiastically, then drew in a quick breath. "Wait a second. You and Savage won't rush off to Nevada to gamble away all the company funds I left at your disposal, will you?"

"I have company funds at my disposal?" he asked.

"Forget I said that," she snapped.

"Nope, too late," he replied. "In all seriousness, though, with this new hit and the higher stakes, staying on the move does seem to be the best option right now. We still haven't managed to establish how the bastards knew we'd be at the chop shop, although Anja is adamant there is no evidence that our systems were compromised. That leaves the option of more conventional or old-school surveillance techniques as a viable possibility. It wouldn't have been difficult to track us on public airlines. If they are watching, a moving target with no clear or obvious purpose could confuse them a little—or draw them out if they think I'm vulnerable."

He paused and frowned before he decided to simply go ahead and say it. "And if you'd rather return to the States, I'd suggest you adopt a similar policy. I'll make sure to use most if not all the company funds at my disposal."

"Ugh, fine." Courtney sounded aggravated and Anderson thought he could hear her roll her eyes if he actually tried. "But don't do it all on red or something like that. Let Savage play a little. He has the potential to simply scare everything so shitless it coughs up, so maybe we can actually pull a profit from this."

"I'll get right on that. Okay, I'll talk to you soon."

"Damn right you will. Stay alive, Anderson."

"Will do, ma'am," Anderson said and smirked at the indignant gasp.

"Did you just 'ma'am' me?" She almost sounded angry.

"Sorry...going through a tunnel... Losing you... I... you..." He continued the stutter for a few seconds before he hung up. She wouldn't believe the charade, but she wouldn't bother to call him back for that kind of awkward conversation.

He hoped, anyway.

Maschick still waited patiently for him when he stepped out of the room.

"I'm sorry, doctor, but I'm afraid I'll have to cut this visit short." He shook the man's hand. "Trouble at the office and it can't wait. But I'll be sure to pass your notes on to Dr. Monroe, and if there's anything I've missed, feel free to email me."

"Of course," Maschick smiled but looked a little disappointed. "You have a nice day now."

Anderson nodded and headed back the way they'd come, his phone in his hand. When he was out of earshot, he opened his contacts list and brought up Savage's number.

Meet me at Pegasus building. Urgent! He sent the text as he hurried to his car. Savage wasn't the type who liked conversations for their own sake and would appreciate that the message was concise and to the point. If he was in any kind of trouble and couldn't make it, he would call or text a response. He'd do the same if he needed more details. Otherwise, he would arrive at the Pegasus offices and assume he had been called in for an emergency.

"He'll know what that means," Anderson said to himself with a grin. He turned the car on and grinned when the engine revved delightfully in the underground parking of the testing facility.

Behind him, Mixon eased onto the road a short distance back. The ex-colonel grimaced when he remembered how close he'd come that morning to telling his shadow not to follow. It had been a momentary foolishness, but he'd learned his lesson. For better or for worse, their foresight in bringing in the new team members had been wise, and he was grateful for the fact that the quiet sniper took his responsibilities seriously.

CHAPTER FOURTEEN

The elevator dinged softly to grab her attention and that of the other five women in the conference room with her. A man stepped out as the doors parted and looked around. He appeared decidedly uncomfortable in the building, stiff and hard to define. Rather than a suit, he wore a leather jacket over a gray bowling shirt, a pair of worn jeans, and boots. His brown hair was cut short and a hint of scruff traced along on his jawline. Greenish-brown eyes seemed to change color with the light.

The receptionist jumped out from behind her desk and circled it to talk to him. He looked a little surprised and took a step back when she smiled and talked over him before she handed him a folder. He smiled that thin-lipped smile of his as she directed him to the other conference room on the floor. Anderson was waiting for him there.

As the man entered the room, the receptionist broke away and headed into the secretaries-office-slash-confer-ence-room. Marie was a younger girl, barely over twenty, but her likable nature and quick mind for the gossip around the building had made her something of a hit among the newcomers in the room.

"Oh, my God," she said with a grin as she prowled the table and kept her gaze discreetly on the two men in the opposite conference room. "How hot is he?"

Alexandra glanced at the receptionist, then tilted her head to examine the two men.

Apparently, it was a popular move.

"Don't all look at once," Marie shrieked and looked utterly abashed. "Are you girls completely unable to control yourselves? Jesus."

Alexandra waited a moment before she looked once again. She could see it, although it wasn't the obvious kind of hotness. She'd seen him around before, of course, but she'd never caught a name. He had the look of the quintessential tough guy, and there was some attraction to that, but there was something else there too. She couldn't really place it—perhaps the mysterious look of a man with secrets?

Marie pushed her shoulder with a finger. "Come on, Alex, could you be more obvious?"

She looked away quickly. "What do you know about him?"

The girl grinned. "Anderson introduced him as Savage. Does that sound like a fake name to you or what?"

"Why would he have a fake name?" one of the other secretaries asked and leaned in closer, the better to hear the gossip that was sure to come.

"Here's my theory, okay?" Marie dropped on one of the seats and waited until she was sure she had the attention of all the women present before she continued. "Well, he doesn't look like he belongs in a place like this, right? Where even the interns need to wear suits and ties? He looks tough, right, like those fake tough guys? But then I saw a scar on his arm when he took his jacket off, and my dad was in the Marines and he has a scar like that. Bullet scars. So he's not simply some tough guy, he's ex-military."

"Anderson is ex-military too," Alexandra mentioned and still tried to catch the odd glimpse of the men out of the corner of her eye.

"Right?" Marie agreed, "So 'Savage,'" she said with air quotes, "is here doing business for people who just got into a position for a company with government contracts. So I've heard, anyway. I'm not actually supposed to know that, but I get memos and stuff. And again, it's in the family, so I can put two and two together and get four, you know what I'm saying?"

"Stay on topic," Alexandra said.

"Oh, right. Anyway. What I was thinking was that... well, he's probably tied up in Delta force or something like that. He's retired but he's brought in by his friend, Anderson, and they'll work together on this and be all covert with their operations around here. For the good of the company."

"I would let him run his covert operations all over me if you know what I'm saying," Miranda, another secretary said with a soft giggle.

One of the other secretaries, Gina, raised an eyebrow. "You know, I've been writing a kind of...novel of my own that he would work perfectly for. Nothing professional, of course. But I've struggled to come up with the male character for the book, and damned if he doesn't fit that bill to a T. Or a B, in this case."

"Do tell?" Alexandra asked and moved closer without even thinking about it. Gina always said her writing wasn't professional or anything like that, but from what she'd managed to share over their time together, Alexandra had realized that she was actually pretty damn good. She mostly wrote short stories and romantic stuff that Alexandra usually avoided, but it was still interesting enough to grab her attention. Most of the other secretaries poised themselves to hear more.

"Well, the story was about a guy—the hard ex-military type with a dark past—being brought in out of the cold," Gina said, knowing she had a captive audience. "He's kind of gruff but with a heart of gold. You know the type. Anyway, he's sent in to retrieve vital information from a company. Enter our female protagonist, Valerie, who has a dark secret in her past as well. She's a secretary at this company, working to pay her way through med school, and she ends up with her hands on the drive that has the data our military man needs."

Alexandra let her mind churn over the idea, replacing Valerie with herself. She was the one who had the information without even knowing she had it, and Savage came to retrieve it.

"Anyway, our guy finds out that she has it, but he also discovers that the people involved in the company she works for know she has it too, and are coming to kill her," Gina continued. "He pauses. He knows that bringing her along for the ride would complicate his mission, but he can't simply leave her behind. Not if her life is at risk. So he drags her along to enter into a world of spies, and back-stabbing, and death, and she's right there beside him."

Yes, she was. Alexandra didn't have any translatable skills into that sort of situation, but she was a quick study. She could learn how to do it on the go, letting him protect her while protecting him right back. He would come to see her as less of a damsel in need of help and more like a partner, a friend, and maybe even…

"I can totally see it," the other woman continued. "He needs to protect her. At first, he thinks it's only about the data, but he starts getting feelings. He's not a fan of them, but he can't help them. They have to go on the run. They end up alone in a hotel room, giving them a quiet moment together after they risked their lives and she struggles to cope. He sees it and relies on instinct. He's not the kind of guy who usually comforts people, but he does. He strokes her cheek. She smiles, and there's a connection. She leans in and they kiss…"

Gina's voice trailed off, but the silence she left behind was enough evidence to tell that she had incited the imagination of all the women present.

Marie was the first to react. She shoved up from her seat and looked a little flushed as she straightened her dress. "Well… I think I need to get back to the front desk. Some—ahem—filing needs to get done over there."

"Right," Gina said with a nod as the other secretaries pretended to get back to work.

Their minds were all on something else entirely. Alexandra could only speak for herself, of course, but she felt like it was time to take that lunch break she'd put off today.

"Hey, Gina?" she said as she stood and headed over to the door. "If you ever get around to writing something like that, I wouldn't mind…you know, proof-reading it."

"Oh, yeah me too," one of the other secretaries said with a smile.

"I'll let you girls know," Gina replied and chuckled as Alexandra made her way out.

CHAPTER FIFTEEN

Savage narrowed his eyes and peered at the conference room across from the one where Anderson had situated himself. A group of women of all ages had gathered there, dressed in pantsuits and suit skirts, all with some variation of the office-approved haircut. The receptionist he'd thought was a little too loud had joined them too, he realized.

"Who are they?" he asked as the other man initiated the connection with their team in the Zoo.

"Them?" He looked up from his work. "Oh, they're personal assistants for various members of the board. I've learned to ignore them the more time I've spent here."

"Shouldn't they have their own offices?" The operative leaned back in his seat and released his gaze from the somewhat daunting gaggle of womanhood. "I would think so. They need somewhere permanent to work."

"They're personal secretaries," Anderson explained. "That means they travel around with their bosses, so there's no need to maintain offices for them in our various locations. I don't think so, anyway. I was dozing off when Courtney explained the process to me."

"I'll be sure to forget you ever said that, boss," he said with a grin. "Right up until I need something from you, and then it works damn well as blackmail material."

"Fuck you." The other man grumbled under his breath but loudly enough for him to hear it and smirk cheekily in return.

"So, what am I doing here?" He moved to sit in one of the padded and definitely more comfortable office chairs surrounding the conference table, then spun it a little before he stopped the swing. "Your message said it was urgent but didn't really say why. I was in the middle of..."

"Insert preppy sorority girl's name here?" Anderson asked, raising an eyebrow at him.

"I have some standards," Savage grumbled. "But basically, yeah. So you'd better have a good reason for dragging me away from Candi with an I."

"Does my getting an official hit put out on me qualify as a good enough reason? Besides, the ones with an I at the end of their names are always the crazier ones."

"Yeah, I do attract the crazy kind of woman, I've found." He propped his feet on the conference table and folded his arms across his chest. "An actual hit on you? Do people actually do that? I thought it was something they only did in movies. Like...open? To anyone with a gun and a death wish?"

"It's more complicated than that," Anderson said and shrugged as if the explanation required too much effort. "But basically, yeah. If you're rich enough and have the right connections out there, you can contact all kinds of people willing to kill for the right price."

"Did Anja have something to do with finding out?" Savage asked.

"Well, we can ask her if this connection ever actually works." The ex-colonel tapped the piece of tech that was apparently the problem with sharp irritation.

"You can tell him that hitting it won't solve anything," Anja said in Savage's earpiece.

"Anja says that you should keep hitting it. That'll do the trick."

"What?" the Russian snapped indignantly.

"Really?" Anderson looked like a kid whose parents had let him raid a candy store. Or an Apple store, depending on their preferences.

Jeremiah was about to continue the charade when the link went online and opened a video channel between them and the Zoo team. At first, all they could see was a startlingly close-up shot of someone's nostril.

"I really didn't need to see that today," he groaned and covered his eyes. "I just had Chinese."

"Sal!" a voice hissed from the other side of the connection. "You're standing too close to the camera."

"Oh, right, sorry," A younger man stepped away hastily to give them a view of a darker room with computer equipment in the background. The kid didn't look old enough to be in a place like that, but if the cut under the tank top he wore was any indication, he certainly had the build for it. He looked tanned, too, although Savage couldn't tell whether it was genetic or courtesy of the sunlight in the Sahara.

His gaze traveled over a few more people in the room. He recognized Dr. Monroe from their previous meetings, although she looked different with her blonde hair loose and wearing comfortable clothes instead of the suit he always saw her wear. A tall woman with short, dark hair and dog tags around her neck stood near a smaller, paler woman seated on an office chair.

"Savage, let me introduce you to our Zoo-based team," Anderson said with a smile. "You already know Dr. Courtney Monroe, of course. This is Madigan Kennedy"—he pointed at the dog-tag woman—"and that's Salinger Jacobs. They and Dr. Monroe are the founding members of our little group here. They have a company in the Zoo called Heavy Metal."

Considering the suits they wore there, Savage could see the connection to the names. He nodded agreeably in response to each introduction.

"Oh, don't forget about me," the smaller woman said with a voice that was very familiar to him by this point.

"It's nice to finally see the face behind the voice, Anja," he said with a wide smile.

She grinned and spun in her chair in the background.

"Good to see you again, Mr. Savage," Monroe said with a smile. "You're looking well."

"Right back at you, Doc. So, what's this I hear about a hit put out on my boy Anderson?" He paused when the former colonel cleared his throat loudly. "I'm sorry—my man Anderson."

"That's not why I cleared my throat."

"Well, how the hell am I supposed to know what you

identify as?" Savage twisted in his seat to look at the man. "I'm not a mind reader."

"Asshole." Anderson chuckled and shook his head.

"Anyway," Monroe said before either man could resume the banter. "How about we get down to the problem at hand? Anja's sources were able to track a payment made into an account in Anderson's name."

"I assume these people aren't paying into his 401(k), right?" He looked at his boss. "Do you get a 401(k)? Or do you guys get a share of the company situation."

"I like this guy," Jacobs said with a chuckle and nudged the woman introduced as Kennedy.

"No." Anja cut into the conversation and pulled a couple of windows up on the screen. "They paid it into an international fund used by people looking for… Well, there isn't a nice way to say it, I suppose. People willing to commit illegal acts for them. This way, the money can't be traced in either direction and allows the payees to stay anonymous. The target name is usually the name put on the foundation segment—"

"Can't we skip to the relevant part, please?" Monroe asked and turning to face Anja.

"No, wait, I think this is all very informative and relevant to the mission at hand," Savage said. "Plus, I think we should all know more about how she has access to all this very illegal information. You should know, Anja, that Pegasus has a very strict no-felon hiring policy."

"Is that why they never officially hired you?" the hacker asked with a sassy grin at the camera.

"I never did anything…overtly illegal. It's simply that there's a flurry of gang violence around these parts, and I happen to be involved in many of the situations. It's not my fault, right?"

Anderson smirked.

"Technically, neither did I," Anja said with a grin. "I was merely surfing the net and happened to stumble upon the various members of unknown origin engaging in various illicit practices and immediately reported them to the proper authorities."

"You're my inspiration, Anja, I hope you know that." He pretended to get choked up. "A true blue…Russian hero."

"Focus, people," Monroe snapped. She sounded like she wasn't at all amused by the bantering. "Thank you. Anja, if you could continue?"

"Right. Anyway, the payment that was put into Anderson's account is already in excess of half a million dollars. It's effectively doubled over the past week or so. Considering the number of people who have applied for the work, it seems a lot of heat will come down on him over the next few weeks."

"How much is a lot?" Savage's voice took on a more serious note.

"Well, I can't really say about the talent involved." Anja turned back to her computer and tapped her keyboard quickly. "But there are many local cartels involved that delegate their work to hitters to keep them busy and make money when there isn't anything for them to do in house. Honestly, I think we can calculate the numbers to be in the metric shit-ton region."

"Huh." The operative scowled. "Do you guys want me to run interference on these people?"

"No," Monroe replied. "We have already identified the

source of the hit—Charles Stafford. He's a board member I butted heads with recently and appears to have been something of a Carlson loyalist. Anja will continue to track his movements and collect data we can use against him. In the meantime, the safe option—especially for Anderson—is for him to stay on the move with security with him, and to have another team with the family."

"Okay." He narrowed his eyes as he considered the possibilities. "What kind of staying on the move did you guys have in mind?"

"Thanks to a conversation we had with one of the facility leaders in the area, I was told about a couple of locations out in Nevada that work with Pegasus materials," Anderson said.

"But—and this is my best guess—we don't have any facilities out in Nevada."

"Give the man a pot brownie," his boss said with a chuckle. "I thought about sending our little team to investigate and try to get our stuff back if needed. But since I have to be on the move, and considering that Davis and Mixon have actually begun to establish a little chemistry with my family, I think they should probably stay to keep an eye on them and make that their full-time job."

"Oh, they'll love you for that," Savage said with a grin.

"Wait, so the two of you will head out to investigate new facilities in Nevada?" Jacobs asked. He looked inordinately suspicious.

"Yeah, how do we know you two won't head out there to investigate the slot machines?" Kennedy asked, her lips pursed disapprovingly.

"Everyone knows craps is my game," Anderson said with a shrug.

"I like blackjack, although you can't really call it a game, or even gambling really," Anja said. "It's all about the cards. Get them all right and you'll make money hand over fist."

"You know they throw card counters out, right?" Savage asked. "They don't even break their knuckles anymore. Instead, they put them on a blacklist that keeps them out of any of the casinos in the state. I've heard they even share their lists with the casinos in Atlantic City."

"Sure, that's an issue if you're stupid enough to go in there yourself." The hacker snorted derisively. "For me, I hire someone and supply ocular transmission lenses for them to wear, get them in, make them about ten thousand dollars, and pay out on half of it."

"Wait, how do you get them to pay your half if they're the ones with the money?" Savage asked.

"I actually had a problem with that a little while ago," she confessed. "I reminded the guy that cheating at cards is actually a felony in Nevada and I had a whole lot of evidence of him doing it hanging around unused in my hard drive that I could turn in to the nearest member of the Nevada State Police."

"But it's not illegal," Savage replied. He remembered reading that somewhere. "If he was only card counting, he'd simply be banned."

"Well, he didn't know that." She laughed a little smugly. "I had all his school records and could see that he had never interacted with any kind of law in any capacity, so it was a calculated risk on my part. As it turns out, I'm great at math."

"Anyway," Jacobs interjected. "Will you guys use this to hide out until the heat dies down, or will you actually investigate?"

"Well, they'll be there anyway," Kennedy replied. "Two competent former special forces should be able to handle it. You only have one Marine on your team, though."

"Oh…shots fired." Jacobs chuckled. "You got anything for that, Army?"

Savage shrugged, not sure what wordplay he could offer. He felt comfortable taking jabs from Anja and even Anderson and giving them back too, but Monroe, Kennedy, and Jacobs were all a step above. In simple terms, he wasn't sure what kind of jabs he was allowed to throw their way.

"Well, I'm thankful I only have to carry one Marine around," he replied by way of compromise.

"Well played," Jacobs said. "Honestly, I don't get to make any of the jokes myself."

Savage narrowed his eyes and studied the other group quickly. From the way Kennedy chuckled and shook her head, he could tell there was at least some sort of mutual respect. Beyond that, though, something in the body language indicated something more intimate, which wasn't as surprising as the way Monroe interacted with him. It wasn't an in-your-face thing, more a light touch on the shoulder or a smile when he was talking that suggested… again, intimacy.

Was he…no. He couldn't be. Well, the world was more progressive these days, and people were far less judgmental about the intricacies of modern relationships.

He was not one of those people. The truth was, he

judged all he liked, especially since he was in a position to do so as much as he wanted since he made the same mistakes. He couldn't comment, but he could judge all he liked.

"I do get to make fun of geologists, sociologists, and art majors," Jacobs said, and Savage realized that the kid was still talking. "But I can't really get into the inside jokes for the armed forces guys. I leave that to Madigan here."

He punched her in the shoulder, and she smirked as she nudged him in return. The operative frowned but again, refrained from comment.

"Well, I think that settles the business on this end," Monroe said. She seemed to have similar thoughts to Savage. "Do you think you can handle spreading the work with your team, Savage?"

He nodded in response. "I joke, but like Anderson here said, they do seem to have developed a working relationship with his family. I think they can protect them while Anderson and I check out the slot machines and make sure they're all working."

"You joke, but I don't want to cite all the laws that prohibit that kind of behavior, Savage." The woman only vaguely sounded like she was joking.

"Understood, ma'am." He nodded briskly and pushed up from his seat. "We'll make sure the fraud is covered up as neatly as possible and give you all the plausible deniability that you need."

He grinned and she rolled her eyes as Anja killed the connection. Anderson looked at him with a trace of respect in his gaze.

"Even I don't feel safe taunting her like that," the ex-colonel said with a chuckle as he gathered the papers he had on the table. "You do know she was able to put a full team of assassins in the ground on her own, right?"

"On her own turf, sure." Savage cackled. "Give a five-year-old time to prepare and they'll Home Alone that shit like there's no tomorrow. What do you think a full-on veteran of the Zoo can do?"

"So you're saying she doesn't intimidate you?" Anderson asked. He frowned into the other room, where the secretaries remained and seemed to be working. It was still business hours, so it wasn't actually surprising, but he really wished they might go and take a late lunch and give them the floor to themselves.

"I'm not saying I wouldn't watch my back around her," Jeremiah said as he followed him out into the common hallway. "And I'd definitely put serious planning into trying to get a hit on her. But it's my job to make sure to know how to kill anyone I'm around. That's how my mind works."

"How would you kill me?" his boss asked. "Out of pure curiosity, of course."

The operative looked pensive for a second. "Hypothetically? I'd probably try something from a distance if I were running the operation and had something like, say, Mixon on hand to take care of it. If it were only me and I had to work with anything I could get my hands on, I'd probably choose piano wire and wait for you in the back of your car. Somewhere nice and quiet, where I'd be able to bug out before anyone noticed what happened."

"Respect." Anderson smirked. "You don't think you have a chance against me toe to toe?"

"I wouldn't risk it if I didn't have to," Savage replied. "But that's simply prudent. The idea isn't to prove yourself. It's to get in and out alive. You know this."

"Yeah, but it's been a while," he admitted.

"Don't worry." They approached the reception desk and he noted that the girl behind it stared at him with more intensity than he was comfortable with.

"Hi, Marie." Anderson greeted her with a smile. "Could you email me some requisition forms? I need to run some supervision out of state."

"Will do, Mr. Anderson," she said and ducked quickly to retrieve a sheaf of papers from under the desk. "Will you work with Mr. Savage?"

The operative tilted his head and regarded her with a speculative look while he wondered if he'd ever introduced himself to her. His memory said he hadn't, but he might have forgotten it if he'd done so in the early days when everything had still seemed so new and unsettling. Anderson had also introduced him to a couple of people, he recalled vaguely, so perhaps she'd been one of them.

"He'll help me with some security supervision, yes. Thanks for reminding me, since I'll need to fill some paperwork out for him too. Do you feel like helping me, Savage?"

He shook his head and chuckled. "Hell no. The reason why I insist that I remain your external contractor is precisely so I don't need to fill forms out like that. So, is this a road trip we're planning? Should I stock up on energy drinks and beef jerky?"

"Please." Anderson smirked. "You contract for a Fortune

Five-hundred company, Savage. Around here, we like to travel in style."

"Well, I appreciate the heads up, Richie Rich. Message me about where to meet you."

"Will do." His boss had already begun to sift through the documents he'd been given.

Savage nodded and tipped an imaginary hat at the young receptionist, who still stared at him in an oddly unnerving way. "I'll see you later...Marie, right?"

"That's right, Mr. Savage," she said. A flush touched her pale skin. "You have a nice day now."

"Will do." He turned and wandered over to the elevator. People were weird around there. Corporate America was such an odd place to live in. Give him the social dynamics of an army barracks any day.

CHAPTER SIXTEEN

"So, all that talk about having a nice little bit of work," Sam said as night settled slowly over their little warehouse. "That whole conversation about getting paid and getting some action in—that was all crap?"

"Well, we are getting paid, technically," Terry said. His gaze lingered on Savage who put their new weapons and armor out on the table before he packed them neatly and efficiently. "So not fully crap."

"Whose side are you on again?" She slid down from her seat on the table as Savage shooed her away to lay a blanket on the surface on which to spread the weapons for cleaning before storage.

"I'm on my own side." Mixon sipped his cold coffee and scowled as he looked at the revolver the other man was taking apart. Well, it looked like a revolver, but it had been established in their testing that it was not. He still had a few reservations about these new weapons. "I'm on the side that's getting paid for work he believes in—which in this case, is protecting a family that's been put in the crosshairs by bastards looking to protect their profits by killing my fellow soldiers in the Zoo."

"Well, yeesh, damn son, if you want to bring logic into it," Sam groaned and rolled her eyes dramatically. "But you did promise us more excitement in this job than what we've had. I don't know about Gary Poppins over there, but I'd really like to shoot someone in the damned face. Call it a deep, dark need."

"Don't worry." Savage looked up from taking his new toy apart. "Stick around long enough and I assure you that you'll see a lot of men with guns. You read the data that Anja sent you, yeah?"

Sam nodded. Terry didn't respond.

"A lot of money is going into killing Anderson," he continued. "It won't be long before the people coming after him decide they might have an easier target in his family. I'll keep Anderson moving and safe as well as I can, but that doesn't mean there won't be danger coming your way. Stay sharp and stay on top of the family. If anybody dies, I'll hold you two personally responsible."

"Wait, are you not giving us the green light to kill the assholes who show up to hurt them?" Terry asked, looking up from whetting his combat knife. "Because that would suck some serious balls."

Savage looked up from his work. "Wait, no. What? What did I say?"

"That if anyone died, we'd be held personally responsible," Sam replied. She grinned at his real consternation.

"Ah...no, what I meant was if any member of the family died, or if Dr. Monroe were to die if she returns from the Zoo, then you'd be in the deepest of crappers." Thankful that he'd resolved that, he nodded and returned to his work. "Feel free to waste any idiots who try to keep you from achieving that goal, but at least try to make it look clean. The last guys were found with a bunch of knife wounds, but it was left clean and neat. We need to keep the cops off our trail for as long as possible."

"Right," Sam said. "What last time was this? Did I miss something while on babysitting duty?"

"That was me," Terry replied and raised his hand. "It was when I intercepted the team outside the restaurant, so no, you haven't missed out. But wait, are you saying I didn't do well there?"

"Oh, no, nothing like that. You did a great job. A little too great, in fact."

"You say that like it's a bad thing." Mixon tested the blade and resumed sharpening it.

"What, are your feelings hurt?" she asked.

"That's not the point." Savage sighed as he finished the cleaning and put the weapon back together again. "My point was, it was left clean and elegant, so all kinds of kudos to your skills. I'm not saying you should change anything up. All I'm doing is letting you know that local law enforcement has tracked our movements, and while it's been attributed to gang violence, if it continues, we should prepare for some federal involvement in the situation."

Terry grinned at Sam, who tried to cover her laughter. "I wondered how long you would keep trying to make sure you didn't hurt my feelings. You're a very nice person, Savage."

"A very nice person that's holding a very new and

expensive piece of weaponry he's dying to try out on live targets." He clicked the last pieces of the pistol together and flicked the safety on. "It's best to keep that in mind, eh?"

"I'll keep that in mind, boss," Terry replied.

"Wait, so if I get to kill the guys who try to kill Ivy or Damon, do I get a speech on how I'm doing a great job but I need to be subtler about it?" She leaned in closer. "Is it like your go-to speech, or do you come up with them as you go along?"

"You know, I'll have a very nice one I'll say at your graves," Savage retorted with a nod and took a moment to inspect one of the shotguns. "Very nice. I have individual poems for both of you. I think I might actually cry too. I'll be the one who killed you both, but it'll still be a sad moment."

Sam chuckled and flipped her hair back over her shoulder. "Aw, that's sweet."

"It's okay," Terry replied with a shrug. "I like poetry. Nothing too brainy, of course, or too dark. You start talking about quoting and ravens, and I'll climb out of my grave to smack you over the head. And then...I don't know, start the zombie apocalypse, I guess."

"Don't even joke about that," Savage replied and completed his packing. "We have alien goop making an alien jungle with alien animals sprouting up in the middle of the Sahara fucking desert. How far away from reality do you think the zombie apocalypse really is?"

"Language," Terry protested in a half-hearted way before he nodded. "Fair enough."

"Right, so." He focused on the two members of his team as he zipped his burlap bag. "We need to decide on mission distribution between you two. You'll cover the Anderson family, but there will probably be some missions that the two of you will need to run on the side."

"Oh, I can take care of those," Sam said with a smile. "Terry can take care of the family, and I'll be on call for any of these absolute emergencies that might come up."

"What?" Mixon flashed her an indignant look. "How come I'm the one stuck taking care of the family?"

"Because Terry's a girl's name," she said after a quick pause.

"Wow, scraping the barrel for the world's weakest argument." Savage chuckled.

"Well, Terry ain't a girl," he snapped with a grin.

"And he responds with the world's weakest comeback." He chuckled at the sniper's disgruntled expression and folded his arms across his chest. "Well, I can see I'll leave Ivy and Damon in the absolute best of hands and will in no way reconsider my decision to bring you two on for this job. I trust you can handle the assignments to make sure each of you earns your money individually and fairly, got it?"

"Well, yeah, if this fucking asshole decides to cooperate," Sam grumbled.

"Language," Terry snapped in a warning tone. All Sam had to respond with was to wave the ring she wore on her middle finger. It seemed to be studded with a piece of lapis lazuli, making it almost opaque, yet it still gleamed in the weak light that filled their small, functional section of the warehouse.

"Right." Savage grinned and hauled his bag over his shoulder. "Anderson said he and the family will stay in for the night, so the two of you can take the time off and decide what you want to do with your lives. Come tomorrow morning, though, it'll be full-time security on the both of them, got it?"

"We'll get it done, boss," Terry replied. "You boys have a nice trip down to Vegas. Put some money on black thirteen for me while you're down there, will ya?"

"The guy who can't even stand cursing likes gambling?"

"A man can have his vices, right?"

"Oh, and Savage, you don't give the stripper the hundred-dollar bill until after she's finished the blow job, okay?" Sam reminded him.

"Interesting that you think I need to pay for a blow job," he cracked back. "Very interesting."

She had no response to that, and he chuckled on his way back to the Taurus he'd bought second or third hand from a local who wanted cash and was willing to make a quick name transfer on the vehicle's papers. He heaved the bag into the trunk.

While he hadn't worked with Terry and Sam long, he felt like he could trust them to do what had to be done without too much trouble. They knew what they were doing, and despite the seemingly light-hearted jokes, they would be able to focus on their work. Besides, except for Terry's annoyance with foul language and Sam's propensity to use it, they had begun to work well together. It was good to see them mesh as a team.

He slid into the driver's seat, started the engine, and pressed down on the gas pedal. His night off stretched ahead with no particular purpose. It wasn't like he was the kind of guy to make plans and he needed to scale back on the drinking. He might simply watch a movie, order take-out, relax, and have an early night.

Or he would go to the bar near his apartment. It all depended on the mood he was in when he got home. Considering that the city would be in gridlock thanks to the rush hour, he had a feeling he would need a drink.

***

The message came at around midnight and forced Savage to bring his night of drinking to an early end. Anderson had messaged him on where to meet him and bring the materials they would need for this extended mission. The location was a small, private airstrip just outside the city, with a plane that left at nine in the morning.

The operative generally only needed around five to six hours of sleep to feel rested the next day. A few cups of coffee would be needed for the duration, but he would be able to survive and even thrive on a day like that.

He was up early the next morning and spent about an hour in physical conditioning—cardio, stretching, and yoga that he would never admit to anyone he was adept at, and a quick visit to a nearby gym for a round or two with a punching bag. That done, he hurried home, took a shower, and headed down to where he'd parked his car. The apartment building wasn't high-end but it had its own parking lot for residents, which allowed him to keep his cheap new car parked in a location where it wasn't likely to be robbed or searched. Having someone discover the virtual armory he had stashed in the trunk would be the definition of a bad break.

The traffic around the city had begun to clog when he drove out, but he managed to slip through before things got too rough. Only one or two slow-moving sections slowed him a little, but he was soon out of the city and drove smoothly and carefully into the open areas where private airfields liked to set their operations up.

When he turned through the entrance, no physical guards were present. The only security was a rapid facial scan, likely sent to someone in the tower for analysis. He felt a moment of annoyance as the machine finished the scan and didn't immediately raise the heavy steel barrier, which made him wonder if Anderson had shared his face with the security system. After a few seconds of impatience, the barrier raised and the screen over the scanner directed him to hanger twenty-one with a little map to guide him.

"Appreciated," Savage growled under his breath as he rolled into the field. Sam would love this place, he mused. She had a whole slew of aggressive driving training under her belt, which made her the only one on their team actually qualified to drive a car through a gunfight. From what he'd watched of the training she'd undergone, most of the drivers liked the open spaces left in abandoned airstrips.

He pulled up to the hangar where a small, private jet was being helped out from under a tarp. It seemed an odd thing to do, but perhaps the need for secrecy extended to the owners of the aircraft. He wondered if his boss had specifically requested the plane for that particular reason.

Anderson was already waiting for him. "You're late," were the former colonel's first words as he pulled his sunglasses off. The man looked like he hadn't gotten much sleep. The curse of having a young child, Savage assumed.

"Two minutes late," he replied easily and checked his watch to make sure, even though he already knew what the digital read would tell him. "And that's only because they had some technical difficulties with the machine that was supposed to let me in. You look like shit, by the way."

"Thanks." His companion shook his head ruefully. "Damon was somewhat under the weather last night. Ivy and I took turns helping him get through the night."

"Well, it's Terry and Sam's problem now, I guess." He hauled his bags out of the trunk of the Taurus. "I think you can catch up on those missing Zs on the flight over to Vegas. Which—holy shit, you weren't lying about the style, were you?"

Anderson smirked. "I was not and thank you for noticing. This baby should get us to Vegas in about four hours. I don't really know anything about the details of the plane itself, but I was told that a hot meal and an open bar would be provided, courtesy of Pegasus."

"So, about that whole not using corporate funds for personal enjoyment?" Savage asked and focused on making sure he closed his mouth after the question.

"Well, the plane is a rental, and the whole thing comes with the package we have guaranteed with them." He picked up one of the three bags Savage had removed from his car. "I'm not the one who negotiated this deal with the airway. Since the amenities are already included, it would be a shame to let them go to waste, right?"

"The man makes a good point," Savage replied with a

grin when the former colonel struggled with the one bag. "You got that? It's where most of the hardware is stored."

"I got it." He chuckled ruefully and grasped the burlap bag with both hands to swing it over his shoulder before he jiggled it slightly to settle it more comfortably. "And you know what the best part of taking a private plane is? No baggage checks."

"I can't argue with that." He smirked. "I have to say, I'm excited to try these new toys out in the field."

They stopped talking about weapons when the door of the jet opened and a modest yet professionally dressed stewardess ascended the stairs to wait for them. It seemed unlikely that she would take their talk about weapons aboard an airplane with the same kind of humor. Anderson ascended the narrow stairway first with Savage on his heels and a polite smile in place as the young woman greeted them.

"Welcome aboard and thank you for choosing Apollo Airways for your travels," she said and followed them into the cabin. "Please observe the no-smoking and fasten seat-belts signs when they light up. We have a bar that will be accessible after we reach our cruising altitude and will serve lunch at about mid-flight. Enjoy your journey and let me know if there's anything I can do to make your time aboard more enjoyable."

"Will do, thanks." The operative smiled again as the aircraft eased out of the hangar. He shoved his bags in the overhead bins and helped the other man with the one he'd taken.

CHAPTER SEVENTEEN

Anderson snorted softly when Savage poked him in the shoulder. The operative scowled at the man still sleeping like the dead. His boss had snored at one point during the flight, but thankfully, having spent a disproportionate amount of his nights bunked with his comrades, he'd learned a few tricks to keep them from waking everyone else with their ability to saw wood while dreaming.

Savage nudged the former colonel in the shoulder again, a little rougher this time. His companion woke with a cough and jerked up from the seat, which he'd leaned back as far as it would go. He'd stated firmly that he would get some much-needed sleep in before lunch. The meal came and went, and despite an admittedly half-hearted attempt to rouse him, the exhausted man had slept through the meal to the end of their four-and-a-half-hour flight. They now stood parked a short way down the airstrip of a small airfield just outside the city of Vegas.

"Have we landed?" Anderson asked. He still looked like he could have done with five or six more hours.

"Yeah." Savage raised an eyebrow. "If you'd slept any longer, they'd charge us rent. We'd better get going. There's a car waiting for us outside."

The ex-colonel nodded and pushed from his seat to look around for his bags before he realized they were already gone. He turned to Savage, who patted him on the shoulder.

"Thanks," he growled and rubbed his eyes.

"Anytime." They made their way out and down the steps. The plane circled and headed off into another hangar as they approached the car. Anderson looked around the vehicle.

"Where's the driver?" Anderson frowned and looked around.

"Oh, it was only the car waiting here," Savage said with a nod. "Get in. We'll find somewhere to spend the night in the city and can start on the investigation when you feel a little less exhausted."

"You can't drive," his boss grumbled and narrowed his eyes. "You were drinking all the way here."

"I'll have you know that I didn't touch a single alcoholic drink on the flight over here." He slid into the driver's seat. "I even had a glass of orange juice with that delicious steak and *pommes frites* lunch they served."

"You're an asshole." Anderson sagged into the passenger seat as the engine turned. "Seriously? A steak?"

"A rib eye as thick as my fist. Medium-rare, juicy, right off the pan. Did you know the stewardess on the trip with us is actually a certified chef? Yeah. She is paid six figures a year to cook and be a stewardess for this airline company."

"Six figures?" They rolled out through the gates and followed the single road away from the lonely airfield.

"Totally worth it," Savage said firmly. "Seriously, you must have had a dream about the food, because while she was cooking, the whole cabin smelled of roasting meat. There was more than only that, obviously, like all the herbs and stuff she added to it. Oh, and she basted it in butter sauce. Just…fucking delicious, man. I tried to wake you for it, I really did, but you looked like you needed the rest. There really was nothing I could have done to help."

Anderson chuckled and shook his head as he lowered the window. "Can I tell you something personal? You know, something that doesn't leave this car?"

He glanced at the man and his right eyebrow raised. "Are we that kind of friends? The tell each other secrets kind of friends?"

"That's what I'm asking you."

"Then…yeah, you can tell me something that doesn't leave this car." He returned his attention to the road and negotiated smoothly into the traffic on the highway.

"Okay." The man nodded as if he'd made up his mind. "I had some problems. I won't bore you with the details but after the… You know what happened, right?"

Savage nodded. He wasn't entirely sure, actually, what had happened with Anderson that had the man pulled from fieldwork. There had been a considerable number of deaths and most of the details had been redacted, including the location and the names of the dead. That, of course, meant black ops, but anything other than that was beyond his realm of knowledge.

Still, it didn't mean he couldn't let him get whatever he needed to say off his chest.

"Anyway," Anderson continued, his voice a little cautious. "I was terrified. I would wake with nightmares. I couldn't sleep for fear of the fucking things and I was in trouble. A car backfiring would give me a panic attack— stupid shit like that. Anyway, in the shootout in our house the other day, I had a panic attack before and after. But once it was all over, though, I found that I could sleep better. I was thinking about it earlier. I'm still nervous. Just being out here, knowing I'm on the run with a price on my head... I...get..."

Savage finally looked at him when the car shifted into the auto-drive section of the road. "I think I get what you're saying, yeah."

His companion looked relieved. "Really?"

He nodded. "It's like you...were afraid of getting into a situation where your life would be in danger again, but once you were in that situation, you were terrified but you got through it. You faced your fear and came out the other end intact, and while there's still healthy fear in there, you feel like you can stand up to it again."

"And you don't think being in a situation where my family's life was in danger was a bad thing?" he asked after a moment's hesitation.

"Well, it definitely was a bad thing. But it doesn't mean you can't look for a silver lining here or there. And this doesn't seem like it's something you really need to keep secret."

Anderson turned to stare out the window, his posture a little tense.

"That's not the secret. Right." He kept going, almost without missing a beat. "Anyway, carry on."

"It's weird, you know…" The man finally continued after a pause to gather his strength. "You move away from the whole…uh, fighting for your life, living on the edge, and trying to stay alive thing with the adrenaline and everything that goes with it. Going from that to…looking after Damon, taking him to school, taking him to soccer practice, helping him with his homework…looking out for him when he's sick. I love him. I love Ivy, and I can't get enough of them, but the contrast is…" He shrugged. "You probably think I'm crazy."

Savage drew in a deep breath, his gaze focused rigidly on the road ahead, and gripped the wheel until he could feel his knuckles turning white.

"Oh…" The other man grunted apologetically and shook his head. "I'm sorry, I forgot."

"Don't worry about it." He tried to keep his voice from trembling. "I've put it behind me."

Anderson nodded, clearly sensing that it wasn't a topic he was willing to talk about.

"Well." The operative needed to break the silence that threatened to drag on. "I think a man on the road needs to have a little vacation. With the kind of stress you're under, you could use a couple of days off. How about you get that corporate credit card, check yourself into one of those hotels in the Strip, and lay low for a couple of days? Just get it out there. They have all kinds of stuff a growing boy needs. Massage parlors, nice restaurants… I actually don't know about anything else they might have, but I'm sure they have much more than that. It's not like they can criticize you for taking some time off. You know, with the whole hit out on you situation."

"You do know that I actually believe in what's going on here, right?" Anderson asked with a challenging glance. "And that we have actual work to do while we're here."

"Well, I'm saying I can do the work and keep you updated while you take some James Anderson time, that's all." He grinned at his boss who stared at him with real displeasure.

"You're benching me? And here I thought we had a moment. We were bonding, Jeremiah, and you had to go and kick me off the team. What, do you not like me anymore? Are we breaking up?"

Savage laughed. "Oh, fuck, it's so weird to hear you call me by my first name."

"What, you don't like Jeremiah?" Anderson asked.

"No, I do not," Savage chuckled. "Out of the two names I wear right now, it's the one I didn't actually get to pick. I chose to keep it, yes, because it was my grandfather's name and I'm actually fond of it. But it's a name I was given, to start with, not one I decided to give myself."

"What first name would you choose, if you could? And a follow-up question—why didn't you go with that one instead of keeping Jeremiah? You can go ahead and set the record straight, find a name that fits you better."

"Hmmm... I thought of a name like...Clint. Or maybe Alex or Ian. I like Ian. It has a good ring to it. Ian Savage."

Anderson nodded. "I can see that. Ian Savage. He's a hard as nails investigative reporter with a steely exterior, a heart of gold that he keeps well hidden, and a dark past. His…father was killed in a car accident…or so the official story says."

Savage nodded. "Interesting. The kind of man who would look cool while drinking alone. Usually bourbon, neat. But he possesses the kind of darkness that brings the dames in because they think they can tame it and make it into enough light to make them nicer. But not, of course, enough that the darkness is completely gone."

"Oh, oh. Maybe he's in love with an incorrigible femme fatale," Anderson added quickly. "You know, the kind who's really in love with him but betrayal is simply in her nature. She keeps going to him, and he keeps falling for her, and she keeps on breaking his heart. His steadfast and loyal sidekick…"

"Steve," the operative said as he struggled for a name.

"Right, Steve. He always asks him why he makes the same mistakes over and over again." The man nodded and grinned like he was actually enjoying himself.

"'Well, Steve…'" His voice took on the gravelly quality of someone who smoked a pack a day. "He says as he puts his glass of bourbon down and takes a long drag from his cigarette. 'Some dames are worth making a mistake over.'"

Anderson couldn't help a laugh as his head fell forward to tap lightly against the glove box. "It sounds like we have a screenplay. We should hop over to Los Angeles when we're finished here and try to get some money on this idea while we still can. We could make a fucking mint."

"That sounds like a plan."

"So why didn't you?" the other man persisted. "Ian is a good enough name. Why did you stick to Jeremiah?"

He shrugged. "My mom named me after her father, and that old man was way more than only a name for me. Back at the hospital, it seemed like I had to drop everything in my life to start anew. Keeping the first name my folks gave me seemed like the right thing to do. I couldn't hold onto anything else, but this was something that had heart."

The ex-colonel nodded. "I get it. Still, you should think about it. Maybe keep Jeremiah as a middle name. Though maybe not Ian, not anymore. I won't be able to think about that without my mind going to a black-and-white TV show from the fifties."

"I'll keep that in mind."

"What do you mean, he left the city?" Charles demanded and leaned into his phone. He'd thought that leaving the office for the day would be enough to stem the tide of bad news, but as it turned out, he was wrong. Of course, he'd known it was a bad move to give his professional fixer his personal cell phone number, but sometimes, he needed to be accessible to all members of his staff. He scowled and shook his head in an attempt to clear some of the rising frustration. Getting good help was such a fucking problem these days.

"Anderson and Monroe are both out of the city," replied the soft, civilized voice he never would have associated with the man he'd met. Bruisers like Kelly usually had thick, gruff voices. Even if they didn't start with it, they would work on honing it to make them appear rougher and tougher. It was part of how they played the fear game well enough to make sure nobody doubted how many cans of whoop-ass they could crack open.

And yet the soft voice worked for him. He'd met the man, who simply knew he could beat almost any living being into dust but didn't need to advertise it.

"I know that." He pinched the bridge of his nose and dragged in a slow breath. "Is there any indication of where Anderson went? Can we still make the hit on him in time?"

"That depends, Mr. Stafford," Kelly said. "The information I was able to acquire from our extremely limited access to the Pegasus database indicates that Anderson chartered a private plane with corporate funds to fly to Nevada. If that can be confirmed, we can continue with the hit, but we'll need to be able to make it national with all the fees that might be incurred."

Nevada? Why would Anderson go to Nevada? Oh… right. They had moved many of Carlson's projects to facilities in the Nevada desert, which made it easier to continue testing while they were waiting for clear direction for the future. As yet, the ex-CEO was still recovering from numerous surgeries and every indication was that he would make no effort to actively fight the charges against him. That inevitably meant a long time behind bars.

Yet the man had painstakingly set up an efficient machine that continued to work and flourish, even without word or direction. Had Carlson rolled over, or was this simply part of some long-range plan that required him to allay suspicions while he somehow masterminding his purposes without visibly doing so?

"Shit," Charles growled under his breath. "Make the call and get it done. Double the contract price. I don't care what fees I need to pay. We have to finish this now. And inform our assets in the area to expect trouble, since I assume Anderson chartered the flight for two people?"

"That would be correct, Mr. Stafford," Kelly confirmed crisply. "I'll have it done by the morning."

"Be sure that you do," he snapped and hung up. He didn't need to be that sharp with the single competent member of his team, but there was too much pressure at present to stress about the niceties. Of course, nobody really dared raise their voice against him these days—not even his wife or his kids, estranged though they were—but if he didn't get to let his frustrations out from time to time, things tended to build up and explode like a volcano. And nobody wanted that.

He straightened his shirt and sipped his bourbon before he returned to his lounge where a woman waited for him.

She was tall and statuesque like a model but with a mind that had put her squarely among his top three contenders for the position of the future CEO of Pegasus. Of that list, she was the only one whom some might consider non-American by virtue of her mixed heritage. To him, it made absolutely no difference—he wasn't so patriotic that he refused to think someone who hadn't been born in the country wouldn't be able to take care of Pegasus' legacy. But because Pegasus' growth relied on government contracts, the perception of foreigners could be a sensitive issue for some.

She was certainly different, and for a number of reasons. For one thing, she was already the head of numerous boards that handled government contracts, including a handful from NATO and INTERPOL.

Secondly—and this was his trump card—her father was actually a retired admiral in the US Navy, and her mother being from South Korea was enough to make her seem friendly.

Thirdly... Well, he really, really liked her. Having to deal with her on a daily basis while she worked to bring Pegasus into the modern world would be a pleasure.

"Was that anything important, Mr. Stafford?" she asked, and her long, delicate fingers toyed with the edge of the glass of scotch Charles had poured for her. Her accent was exotic but lacked any of the defining characteristics that would have allowed him to pinpoint anything in particular. For the duration of any particular phrase, she could sound vaguely French, British, Italian, or even American.

"Nothing particularly important," he replied with a smile and dropped into his seat with a grunt. "A little personal business that needed to be decided before the morning. I apologize for the interruption."

"Worry not, Mr. Stafford." She tilted her head graciously. "I think it was an opportune interruption. You told me what you wanted me to hear, and I was given time to digest your words—and numbers, I should add."

"Of course." He chuckled. "And please, call me Charles."

"Charles, certainly," she murmured and let the name roll over her tongue with a hint of an Oxford accent. "I was given time to think on your offer, and I believe I have an answer for you."

"Please, there's no need for pressure," he replied and shook his head cautiously. "We still have issues that need to be resolved—a vacuum to create before any offers can be seriously considered on either side of the conversation."

"Naturally," she replied equably. "Former Colonel James Anderson and Dr. Courtney Monroe still have a firm grip on Pegasus, which makes it difficult to initiate any kind of transition. Of course, we were given time to inspect the histories of the two, and we were surprised to find that Dr. Monroe is actually a founding member of the Zoo company named Heavy Metal, yes?"

Charles nodded and leaned forward expectantly. "Yes… a small startup that specializes in retrieving items of value. They are profitable but small. I don't see how it's relevant to our negotiations here today, though."

"Well, your ignorance would be permitted if various members of Pegasus hadn't thoroughly underestimated this small startup at various times," she replied, and a hint of steel entered her voice. "Those whom I represent have actually done business with them in the past, and from the words of those who interacted with them, I think you can discern our answer—never bet against Heavy Metal."

He opened his mouth to reply but she raised her hand, rose smoothly from her seat, and adjusted her pantsuit more comfortably on her trim frame.

"I apologize for wasting your time, Mr. Stafford, but your own ineptitude in dealing with Anderson and Monroe has only reinforced our lack of faith in your ability to bring us anything of worth from Pegasus. Your own position is in peril. How on earth can you believe that you can help us?"

With her words still ringing in his ears, she smiled and bowed her head gently in deference before she turned and walked toward the door, apparently in the mood to show herself out.

Frustration writhed and clawed into his chest when he realized he could do nothing but watch her leave. A couple of men in suits waited for her and one of them opened the door for her to step out before they followed her to the car.

Charles set his glass on the table with a trembling hand since he felt an overwhelming need to throw it across the room. It was crystal and expensive, and while he knew he could eat the costs, the vivid memory of a shattered Ming vase lurked as a temporary deterrent to his need to vent his rage.

"Fuck." He scowled at the tempting glass and clasped his hands tightly together. He really did need to throw something.

CHAPTER EIGHTEEN

"What makes you think these guys will let us in?" Savage asked. Anderson looked decidedly better than he had the day before. While he'd turned down the suggestion to find one of the hotels on the Strip to rest and let Savage handle the lion's share of the work, they'd still found a nice hotel off the beaten track where they could take separate rooms, clean up, shower, and prepare for the adventures of the next day.

Of course, they couldn't avoid having Anja in their ears any longer either, so that morning definitely marked a resumption of their normal routines. They readied themselves quickly after a hurried breakfast. The operative donned his suit jacket to hide the new and improved pistol he would carry from this point forward.

"Well, they are working for a shell corp that was part of Pegasus until less than a month ago," the ex-colonel said. "Besides, if they still have a man inside Pegasus they answer to, I have to hope they simply assume we're in the same boat and let us in."

"Building this on your hopes and dreams, huh?" he asked with a grin. He'd been designated bodyguard and driver for the duration of the visit, which meant he should be allowed to enter the facility with a weapon. He really was happy about that. Walking into a potentially hostile environment without a weapon would have sucked.

"Yep," Anderson replied with a nod. "You gotta have some faith, man. You have to believe."

"And what happens when you break out into a song and dance about how you have a dream and the performance doesn't convince the security personnel to let us in?" He glided off the highway and down the narrow road that led toward the facility they were inspecting.

"Come on, everyone believes in the magic of hopes and dreams, right?" The other man leaned forward with a mocking look in his eyes. "But yeah, no. If they don't let us in, we'll leave them with a stern reprimand and a reminder of how we'll make their lives hell and careers short. And then, once we've left their ears ringing, we'll break in after hours."

"Ah, foolproof plan B." Personally, he would have preferred to simply break in as the plan A, but he could see why Anderson needed to at least pretend to play things by the book. He needed to clearly show that he'd tried a legitimate option before the more clandestine—and probably more satisfying—alternative

"What, did you have any better ideas?" Anderson didn't particularly like being relegated to the back seat, but nobody would believe a boss who had a chauffeur but still rode shotgun.

"Well, yes, but they mostly involved having a larger

team," Savage said with a nod. "There's one plan that involved poison gas. Oh, I really like the one I need satellites for."

"If you need those, I could get you access," Anja piped up suddenly.

Savage was, thankfully, trained well enough to avoid the frantic swerve that would have careened the car into the light poles that were the only signs of civilization for miles. He scowled when his boss chuckled at the way he'd jerked his head to the left. The hacker had been out of his ear for a while and it wasn't hearing her voice again that was the problem. The way she simply popped up out of nowhere like a Russian, female Jiminy Cricket was enough to make even the most hardened soldier react.

"Have I told you how much I've missed hearing your voice, Anja?" he asked, his scrutiny focused on the gated and fenced-off facility that grew a little clearer in the distance.

"Yes, but you could always tell me a little more often." She sounded way too upbeat for someone across the planet. It had to be nighttime in the Sahara...well, they couldn't call it a desert anymore, right?

"I'll make sure to let you know periodically throughout the day." He shook his head. Anderson watched him through the rearview mirror, his eyes narrowed as if he tried to make something out.

He didn't particularly feel like engaging the man at the moment. He was friendly with Anja, and with the things they'd been through together, he might even say that they were friends. She'd certainly hauled him out of more than a few scrapes and even saved his life. He owed her.

It wasn't the most complicated of relationships and only business-related on his end. For her, it was nothing but a strict business relationship. She knew more about his history than even he remembered, being able to dig through any record that had been digitized over the past five or six decades.

They pulled in closer to the research building and a pair of armed guards who stood outside. The vehicle rolled forward and Savage pulled to a stop just outside the gate. The security officers moved toward the driver's side, but Savage opened the window beside Anderson instead and gestured them away from him. It was best that they didn't get too close a look at him and instead, focused on the official face of Pegasus.

"Good afternoon." The ex-colonel shifted to look out of the window at the two sub-machine gun toting men who looked more than a little confused by their arrival. "I was sent here for an inspection to make sure all the new implementations are going smoothly."

"We weren't told about any such inspection," the apparent leader of the two said and shook of his head firmly. "I don't think I can let you into the facility without some prior warning, sir."

Anderson allowed a mildly disapproving expression to settle over his features and pulled his ID card from his wallet. He handed it to the man. "I am the current CEO of Pegasus. I honestly couldn't give a shit about whether or not you were warned about my arrival. What I do care about is the fact that I've spent five hours on a plane to get my official ass here to run this inspection."

The guard opened his mouth as if to protest, but the

sight of the winged horse on his ID said that the name was familiar and apparently carried a good deal of weight. He backed away quickly, grumbled something to his comrade, and made a gesture that immediately resulted in the gate being opened quickly. Savage took a moment to register that they might be driving into a trap before he eased down on the gas pedal and guided the black car into the facility. They followed the path that brought them under the building and into a small parking garage.

He stepped out first and smoothly pulled a pair of Ray Bans from his coat pocket and put them on. Yes, he knew wearing sunglasses indoors was a douche move, but he also knew he would be judged on his appearances now more than ever. He needed to look the part, and bodyguards always wore sunglasses. Fashion statement or otherwise, he'd read or heard once that it had something to do with not letting anyone see where your eyes were turned. He wasn't sure how that was supposed to trump impaired vision indoors, but hey, who was he to argue with appearances?

He took a moment to scrutinize the garage before he spoke into an imaginary mic on his wrist. "All clear. Let's move."

"Are you having fun?" Anja asked.

"You bet your ass I am," he whispered under his breath as he pulled the door open for Anderson to step out.

"I'd appreciate it if you took this a little more seriously," the former colonel growled. The man drew himself tall in the way most people expected high-level military officers to do. He maintained the attitude and walked with long strides while he held his body unflinchingly rigid. While he had no hat to tuck under his arm, he walked as if he did and headed unhesitatingly toward the elevators in the far left of the garage.

The doors parted as they arrived there to reveal a couple of lean, tired-looking men in lab coats who seemed surprised to see them. Obviously, this was not the greeting party that would be assembling hastily behind scenes. Common sense said that the deeper they got into the facility before that party found them, the better their chances were of actually finding something relevant.

The researchers vacated the elevator quickly, and Savage and Anderson stepped in behind them. The operative made a quick search of the interior before the doors closed to ensure that there were no cameras.

"So, if we do find anything we could identify as belonging to Pegasus," he asked, "firstly, how would we even know what it is? And secondly, how would we actually get it out of the building?"

"Oh, yeah. Anja fitted me with one of those recording contact lenses in addition to working her magic with the other comms piggy-backing or whatever she usually does." Anderson tapped his right temple. "It feeds into the same comm lines as our earpieces and delivers her live video of what we see. She has a…what was it again?"

"I've fed the images of the pieces of tech that were stolen into a recognition matrix on the servers here." The hacker sounded excited like she'd had too much coffee. "When they detect something that is within the Pegasus patent, it'll let me know, and I'll let you know."

"Well, it saves us actually bringing an expert on these missions," the operative commented as the doors opened and released them into the lobby. "That way, you can send as much muscle as you want and leave the weaker links back home, right?"

"Well, you are bringing a specialist with you," she noted.

"What I mean is that on recon missions like these, the people needed for intelligence are usually the weakest link in the security, right?" He faced his boss to make it seem like he was talking to the colonel instead of only to himself. "This way, the weakest link is removed, and all you have is heavy hitters. You know, they really should do that in the Zoo. I saw that they send these 'specialists' on their missions in there when they could have them overseeing it from a comfy chair back on the base instead."

"Yeah, I wonder why they never thought of that before." The Russian now sounded sarcastic. "Oh, maybe it's because the Zoo doesn't allow enough signal through comm lines for a live audio or video feed. Come on, give these guys some credit."

"Noted," he conceded when a couple of men in white coats rushed toward them, followed by a handful of security personnel.

"Hello there, Mr. Anderson," said one of the researchers, a taller, gaunt man with a hawkish look on his face. "We weren't told you were coming, otherwise we would have been more prepared to welcome you."

Anderson assumed the colonel look again and Savage faded quickly into the background, barely noticed by the welcoming party. "I actually prefer it this way. I don't need to see you prepared for a corporate inspection. I need to see this place as it runs on a day to day basis. As such, I don't think we'll need any supervision as we look through your facility."

"All unauthorized personnel on site need to be accompanied at all times," one of the security men said and folded his arms in front of his chest. "No exceptions."

"Fair enough." He stepped forward until he was eye to eye with the man who had spoken and boldly stared a challenge. "How about we run through your weapons testing areas first? First up, we'll check to make sure all the Mark 15 armor suit research branches are on schedule."

"Of course, Mr. Anderson." Hawkish twisted on his heel and guided their small group down the hall.

They turned toward the east wing of the building and proceeded in silence before a couple of men stepped out of another elevator midway down a hall. Savage recognized one of them as one of the security guards who had met them at the gate. The other was a severe-looking corporate type in an expensive suit and tie and a pair of tortoiseshell glasses.

"I'm sorry," the suited man all but shouted and pushed in front of the group to force them to stop. "I'm sorry, but these two gentlemen aren't authorized to see any of the secure wings of this facility, and they have failed to file the inspection forms issued by the great state of Nevada. I'm afraid that I have to ask you to leave immediately, or I will contact the State Police."

Savage suppressed a smirk. Bodyguards had only one resting face—stoic indifference—but whatever stupidity had prompted this idiot to open his mouth had left him with a definite desire to laugh. Did he really think the corporate twaddle and bullshit bluster would work on them?

Anderson turned around to face the man with studied slowness and fixed him with a look that was both measured and dismissive. The bluster faded instantly as the executive took an instinctive step back before he seemed to convince himself that he was in the right and stood his ground.

"You know who I work for, yes?" Anderson asked. He'd evidently decided to give the idiot enough rope to hang himself over the whole state inspection twaddle. "You know, of course, that I'll contact your superiors to advise them that you obstructed this inspection."

"I know that...ahem, I know my superiors would be happy that I demanded to see proper protocol followed by those who claim to be here to inspect the building." His bold response was somewhat quashed by the fact that he looked like he was a loud noise away from flight when Anderson again turned on what his bodyguard decided he would call his authority face.

"Very well." The ex-colonel regarded his opponent coldly for a long moment before he finally drew a deep breath and appeared to calm. The glint in his eye, however, clearly indicated trouble to anyone who knew him. "I had hoped to do this without any of the red tape and establish a real reflection of how this facility worked without any previous warning. However, if you need me to jump through hoops, I'll jump through hoops. I'll need your name, of course."

Savage frowned. He'd really expected his boss to call the man's bluff but decided to run with it for now. The executive faked a smile. "I'll give it to you on your way out. Please, follow me."

Anderson nodded, and the four stepped into the nearest open elevator that would take them down to the garage.

"I preferred not to have to have this conversation where the other drones could see," their adversary said when the four of them were alone. "We hope to maintain good relations with Pegasus in the future, but our arrangement with your company is such that it preserves our autonomy in critical areas of our operations. I would have assumed that, as CEO, you would know this."

He paused for a moment as if awaiting a response but when the other man simply stared at him with an inscrutable expression, he pressed on. "We are under very specific instructions not to let you or any of your associates into any of our facilities. You are welcome to discuss that at a corporate level if you are so inclined. However, if you are seen on or near any of our properties again, we will have to involve the law."

The ex-colonel laughed, his expression colored with a suggestion of derision. "If you intended to call the cops, you would have done so already." He took a small step closer and into the man's personal space. The security guard stepped in to try to separate them, but Savage moved fluidly and shoved him back into the wall. A rough twist directed his hand away from his weapon.

"Thank you, Jeeves," Anderson said with a wink before he returned his attention to his opponent. "Don't make empty threats," he said mildly like he'd suggested the possibility of rain. "I certainly don't, so I'll make myself very clear. I know who you work for and you should definitely look into the kind of trouble he has invited. Examples were made the last time a spring cleaning was required, but we're not seasonal. We deal with the trash no matter what the weather's doing. You'd do well not to get caught in the fallout. Have a nice day."

As if on cue—with help from Anja, Savage assumed—the doors pinged open and allowed the visitors to step out before either man could respond. Not that they would have. The security guard looked confused and a little embarrassed, whereas the executive was pale. He wore the look of a man about to be sick but didn't want any of the puke on his pristinely shined shoes.

The duo strode to the car and Savage held the door open for Anderson to step inside before he took his place in the driver's seat again.

"Well, that was intense," Anja remarked once they were on their way toward the gates. "I wasn't able to see if any of the stuff was Pegasus property, but I was able to find a back door into the cybersecurity. I don't think I'll be able to turn any of the software off since their hard drives are all contained offline, but I should be able to get you guys in if you decided to...oh, I don't know, break in at a later date?"

"We are breaking in, right?" Savage asked, looking up at Anderson. "Plan B."

"Fuck yeah," Anderson replied with a grin. "It would have been easier to do it this way, but once that dickwad showed up, all bets were off. I'd originally thought to simply let him think he'd won—that he'd cowed me into running home to mother—but he pushed my buttons, I'm afraid. I couldn't risk shoving the grenade up his...never mind. Hopefully, he's rattled enough to not consider the possibility of a night raid." It looked like he now actually enjoyed this sordid spy business after all.

Did he really mind that all he'd done was babysit an actual child? No. Terry had never been the kind of man who needed much money. He had been able to survive relatively comfortably on the pension he received from the army, so the payment he now earned from Pegasus hadn't been the incentive that drove him to join the team.

He'd read up on Anderson—the kind of work the man had done while working at the Pentagon, the reasons why he left, and why he'd chosen to do what he now did. What he'd learned was why he'd decided to come out of his retirement and do this job.

When Savage had arrived and left a file and an offer behind, the sniper had never imagined that his job would entail keeping an eye on a surly eight-year-old with authority issues.

He supposed it was a more honorable job than killing people, but there was still the fact that minding little Damon while his mother was out with Sam at the range, getting some training in, was not exactly the best use of his skills.

"Can you help me make a snack?" the boy asked in a whiney voice and drew Terry's reluctant attention.

"I…what kind of snack?" He looked up from his phone and narrowed his eyes, suspicion stirring.

"I don't know," Damon replied with a shrug.

"Why do you want a snack if you don't know what you want?"

"I'm hungry but I don't know what for." He scowled, not a pretty sight.

"Well, what do you think you might be in the mood to eat?" Terry pushed himself bravely from his seat. "Do you want a...pizza? Popcorn? An omelet? Cereal?"

"I'm a vegetarian," the kid declared proudly. "I don't eat meat or eggs. I can eat dairy, though."

"Well, fantastic." The unwilling minder made a face. "I'm happy for you, I really am, but I won't cook anything vegetarian for you."

"Popcorn is vegetarian, and you offered that," Damon pointed out.

"Well, yeah." Terry rolled his eyes. "But the point remains. Humans developed large brains because they started to eat meat. That's a scientific fact."

"Well, it's a theory, but it's been heavily debated in recent studies." He folded his arms.

"Well, da—ndy Joe. Do you want some popcorn?"

"Nah, I want pizza now." The cheeky grin might have been cute if not for the suggestion of smugness behind it.

"I won't make you a vegetarian pizza," Terry stated in a warning tone.

"You're not making me anything, dumbass."

"Language."

Damon chuckled and ignored the reprimand. "Mom gave me money and there's a pizza place down the street. We can order two—a vegetarian for me and a meat-lover for you."

"Well, I don't want a meat-lover. Maybe one with

pepperoni or something." His charge stared at him for a minute before he shook his head with almost adult patience.

"Look, they have an app on my phone. We can look at the menu from there." He handed the man his phone with an exaggerated eye-roll. "Pick out what you want and get the Thai vegan for me."

Terry studied the kid suspiciously as he opened the app. "You're a weird little kid, do you know that?"

"And you're a weird old man," Damon snapped in response with a grin. "Oh, and Terry's a girl's name."

"Keep talking, and you can tell your friends at school that a guy with a girl's name ordered a pizza for himself and didn't give you any." Not his best comeback, he decided. Still, he chose a ham and mushroom pizza for himself and the Thai vegan option for the kid and paid for it with his own credit card. "They should be here in half an hour."

"Thanks, Uncle Terry." The boy flashed him a good-natured smile as he took his phone back.

"Yeah, get out of here. Make sure that your homework's done before the pizza gets here, or you'll have to eat it all cold and soggy."

CHAPTER NINETEEN

"So how does it feel?" Savage asked. "Being back out in the field, I mean?"

Anderson returned his curious glance with a shrug. "I've been out in the field before, you know."

"Yeah, like a decade ago. Besides, you were in the Marines. I bet you had one of your COs holding your hand every step of the way, teaching you how to swim or how to shout like R. Lee Ermey."

"Wait, do they not know how to swim in the Army?" Anderson smirked a challenge. "Do they not teach that there?"

"Well, no, but they usually expect us to know how to swim before we sign up." The operative shrugged expansively. "You know, basic skills like reading, writing, addition, subtraction, that sort of thing."

"Well, they only do the basics with you grunts anyway." The ex-colonel strapped the new body armor to his chest. "They need us to be able to multiply and divide in the Marines. Crazy, right?"

"Nuts. Okay, it looks like everything's ready to go. Anja, do you have an opening for us yet?"

"Well, there's only one way in and out of the facility," she replied and sounded a lot less upbeat than she had earlier in the day. "They have seismic sensors on the fences all around, so digging won't be an option. I think I can get you and Anderson in through the front door, though. Most of the researchers working there have homes in the city, which means that at closing hours, the gate will be hectic, and security won't actually man it. I can hold the gate when it's closing to get you inside, but the two of you need to be able to sneak in close enough to access it while I do it."

"We can do that." Savage nodded briskly. "We don't have any water to swim in, but I think I can walk my friend Anderson here through the intricacies of watching and waiting."

"Hey, I love the fact that you ladies have all these inside jokes to make about your history in the military," the hacker snarked. "But can you focus a little? We're right in the middle of an operation here."

"Are you all right there, Anja? You sound a little stressed. I don't mean to diminish the work you do on your end, because you're all kinds of awesome, but isn't this only run of the mill for us by this point?"

"Yeah, I guess." She sighed heavily. "Sorry. Things are a little stressful on this end."

"Do you want to talk about it? Anderson just started putting his wetsuit on and it'll take him at least a half hour to realize he doesn't need it and another half hour to take it off again."

His companion flipped him off and he grinned.

"It's just…yeah, people around here are fucked up, that's all," Anja replied. "Nothing I need to bother you with. What do you say we get this show on the road?"

"That sounds like a plan to me." Savage accepted her change of focus without question, actually a little relieved that she hadn't taken his invitation to unburden herself. Maybe the moments before a critical mission weren't the best times for help-a-friend. "When can we start?"

He made another slow scan of their surroundings. They'd taken the car off the beaten track and onto a dirt road about a half-mile away from the facility. Under any other circumstances, he would have considered it a literal walk in the park. Unfortunately, they currently stood under the harsh sun that beat down to the tune of over a hundred degrees. That would definitely add extra spice to their little stroll.

"Well, people should start leaving in about an hour, so I guess the two of you should start walking," Anja said. "There aren't any cameras that cover outside the facility and not too many people wander around there except for the two guards out front. But if you do need it, there should be enough brush cover around the site to keep out of sight of any of the people inside the fence. Once you get within fifty meters, though, it might be difficult since they have cleared most of the growth."

"Fair enough." The operative strapped a pack over his shoulder. "Are you ready to do some walking, Marine?"

"You bet, Grunt," Anderson replied briskly. "I hope things cool off before we need to crawl on our bellies to get to the gate, though."

Savage smirked. That hope was unlikely to bring anything but disappointment. He'd been in deserts similar to this one before, and if there was one thing you could count on, it was the fact that the ground that had absorbed heat from the sun all day would remain shockingly hot for at least a couple of hours afterward. Still, he wouldn't be the one to complain about the heat.

Then again, maybe he would. This wasn't a competition over who was the toughest and who could endure the difficulties the best. He checked his pack again. A shotgun was tucked inside, and he carried his pistol in the underarm holster. Other than that, he'd kept it empty in case they needed to haul anything out of the place. Anderson's preparations were similar, except he had stowed a submachine gun in his bag and a Beretta under his arm.

They would be ready if they needed to shoot their way out of the location, Savage mused as they began their slow march toward the facility. The structure sprawled in the distance. They were far enough away from the road that their presence should go unnoticed, but they still remained as low as possible through the unbearable heat and moved as quickly as they could without risking detection.

The area was very similar to some of the places Savage had spent a lot of time in—and Anderson too, from the former colonel's file. Or the parts that weren't redacted, at least. They both looked like they could handle the long haul and had the presence of mind to bring water for their little hike as well. Hydration was something very rarely remembered in combat situations, but dehydration was the kind of thing that could get a man killed. Failing that, it could knock him out of commission for a couple of days for recovery. That simple truth was heavily stressed to the men and women who fought in desert environments.

Although Savage remembered it being something of a factor in jungle situations too. Sometimes, even the professionals forgot how much you ended up sweating in the hot, humid environments.

He shook his head and adjusted their course marginally to the left. The sun was starting to set, and the heat grew a little less intense. It still felt like they were trekking through the devil's ass crack, though.

He indicated for Anderson to cut toward the road when they moved within the right range. It was annoyingly complicated that the gate provided the only point of ingress, but they would manage it one way or another.

The two guards were still in position but lingered in as much shadow as they could manage, even as the temperatures began to drop. They hadn't moved from their location when the duo reached the last of the brush and were forced to come to a halt.

He glanced at Anderson, who shrugged gently and shook his head when Savage moved to draw his pistol from the holster. He didn't understand why his partner would hesitate. They could cover the distance rapidly, and if his shooting skill at the warehouse lately had been any indication, he could kill both guards and hide the bodies before any of the tired researchers headed out.

The other man shook his head again, held his hand in a fist, and pointed at the gate. He intended to wait, then. The operative ground his teeth but didn't argue. After all, he worked for Anderson. The joking moments were a way to keep his boss' attention away from a potentially mission-ending panic attack, but that didn't change their fundamental relationship of employee and employer.

Resigned to the irritation of immobility, he remained crouched behind some dried tumbleweed bushes and grimaced when the sweat trickled down his back. It was too hot for most bugs, but he identified a couple of smaller lizards scuttling from shade to shade. The creatures froze when they saw the two men and darted away a second later.

It was too hot even for the cold-blooded creatures. What did that say about the dumbass humans who decided to build their lives out there?

Anderson keyed his comm unit and brought Savage's attention back to the present. His thoughts had drifted a little since they now waited longer than expected out in the sun. He would definitely acquire a sunburn out there and could only hope it translated into a tan.

A gesture from his companion directed his attention to the gate they needed to access. It pulled open slowly and both armed guards stepped inside. The barrier closed again but opened a few minutes later to allow a silver SUV through. A white sedan followed with an electric car close behind.

"Okay, boys," Anja said. "I hope you enjoyed your time sunbathing, but we now need to see how quickly you can sprint fifty yards, okay? Count it down with me so we have the timing right. Five…four…three…two… one… Go!"

A small hatchback spilled out of the gap and sped away as the two men sprinted toward the gate Anja's efforts now held ready for their entry. It was still a close thing, Savage realized. She wasn't actually preventing the movement, merely slowing it down as they continued to close.

The former Ranger was in better shape than his Marine comrade. It wasn't all that surprising, considering that Anderson had been out of active duty for a while now. He reached the gates first and assumed Anja would be scrubbing the feeds of the cameras he could see turned in his direction. Once he'd slid through the diminishing space, he immediately cut left, his pistol in his hands, and scanned the area around him to ensure that they were clear of any eyes the hacker couldn't hack.

His boss pushed through barely in time, although he had to squeeze in sideways as the gates snapped shut.

"Getting slow there, squiddy?" Savage whispered.

He didn't need any military experience to understand what the gesture Anderson tossed his way meant. The fact that the man was too winded to actually come up with a verbal rebuttal, though, was all he needed to know, and he grinned a cheeky response.

"Okay, the gate is the only way past the fence," Anja said. "But once inside, there are numerous points of entry into the building itself. Follow my lead and I'll find you a place to slip inside unnoticed."

They sauntered away from the road that now had a steady flow of cars heading out of the facility. Although they weren't dressed too differently than the security personnel by design, a close inspection was something they preferred to avoid for the time being.

"Okay, I have a service entrance on the side of the building for you to use," the hacker said decisively. "People working there have already left for the day, and I don't think security will do any sweeps yet, although they should do so in the next couple of hours. I won't have any access to the feeds until you are back in the building."

He nodded, knowing she could see him now from the lens his boss wore. They circled the building warily, with Savage taking point and Anderson keeping an eye on their rear, and reached the door Anja had indicated. It was locked with a physical lock that required a key. He scowled and tried the handle.

"It's locked," he said to her. "And I don't have any equipment to unlock it with. We need another entrance."

"Okay, there's a door leading into the building with an electronic lock I can help you with. About twenty paces from your current location."

"Why do I feel like this is a good-news-bad-news situation?" Savage asked as they hurried away from the door.

"Your instincts are on point, as usual, Jer. You'll enter through a security hub and should probably expect resistance."

"Roger that." Savage flicked the safety off on his pistol and watched as his companion attached a suppressor to his. A few seconds were all that was needed before the two men approached the door she'd indicated. As she'd said, the lock was electronic and tied to a fingerprint reader to its left. After a second or two, the red light over the sensor turned green. He nodded and gestured for Anderson to follow his lead. From experience, the pistol in his hand made a lot less noise than the Beretta, even with a suppressor attached.

His companion nodded understanding as the operative pulled the door open.

Two men stood nearby. Their sub-machine guns hung loosely from their shoulder straps, and they sipped warm cups of coffee. Both immediately looked surprised to see someone use the door. Their instincts were good, though, and they needed less than a second to process the fact that the two newcomers weren't supposed to be there. As one, they reached for their weapons.

Unfortunately for them, a second a all the time Savage needed. While they had yet to draw the weapons, flick the safeties off, and raise them to fire, the operative was bound by no such necessities. He was already poised for the attack and simply squeezed the trigger.

No loud crack or pop resulted, but the whoomph delivered a soft kick against his hand. One of the needles rocketed from the weapon at supersonic speed.

He pulled it again, to be safe, and nodded when the first man dropped. The second had raised his weapon and was almost ready to fire by the time the operative turned his attention to him and pulled the trigger again to apply another double tap. The guard stumbled and squeezed the trigger on his weapon reflexively. When no gunshots resulted, it seemed obvious that the safety was still on.

Both men were down, and blood rapidly stained the floor. He pushed closer to them and shoved aside one of the men's hands as he tried weakly to grab him. As the former Ranger lifted the man's shirt away, he smirked.

"What do you know? The boys in the lab made something very interesting with this gun." Savage glanced at Anderson. "It punched through their body armor and caused all kinds of internal damage from the looks of it."

"I'm so glad you're pleased." His partner scowled.

"It doesn't take a terrible person to enjoy using a new piece of tech." He shrugged and touched the elongated barrel gently. "Then again, I am a terrible person. The worst, really."

"Oh, come on, do you really think I'll believe that?" Anderson asked with a chuckle.

"Hey, you were the one who said you wanted a savage on your side," he answered and grinned. "Come on, we don't have much time. I'd say the moment someone finds these bodies is when the jig is up. We need to work fast."

They took a moment to drag the corpses away from their place on the floor. There wasn't time to clean the blood, but hopefully, it would buy them time to explore the opportunities that had been denied them on their first trip there.

"Okay, the weapons and armor testing will be in the east and north wing," Anja said. "The east wing is closest so you should start there."

"Shouldn't we split up?" Savage asked. "We could cover more ground."

"Well, that would make sense if you wore a fucking transmitter lens," Anja reminded him. "I can access via the comms piggy-back like I always do, but this particular baby has special software to run the searches in real time. We need that."

"Right. Why the hell don't I have one then?"

"I only had time to make the one," the hacker protested. "Come on. You can't expect me to do everything for you. Get a Goddamn move on, would you?"

"Roger that." Anderson pushed forward and took point quickly, leaving his partner to follow. The two had slid into an easy flow like they'd worked together on this type of operation before. They hadn't, of course, but the many overlapping skills between them enabled them to function better as a team. It didn't take long at all to adjust to one another, so responses and actions became more natural the more time they spent as a unit.

They made one hell of a good team, Savage thought with a smile. Even if the man was a Marine.

Alert for any sign of discovery, they made their way through a series of hallways and deeper into the facility. Hopefully, what they found would provide them with a clear view of what the researchers were working on there. Full suits of body armor—power armor, by the looks of it —seemed large enough to probably assume the battlefield duties of a tank. Whole cavalry divisions, Savage mused, could transform from using huge, lumbering vehicles into men traversing the battlefield using suits like these. That was the future of modern warfare.

Some appeared to be too big, though. He knew a thing or two about the physics involved in using gear like those. The bigger you made a suit, the more power needed to be used to power it and the heavier it would be. It could ultimately turn it into a frustrating cycle of diminishing returns.

Some of the prototypes definitely looked too large to be real.

"Okay, after a thought, I wonder if you didn't have the right idea, Savage," Anja said. "I detect considerable Pegasus hardware, but most of it is too big to carry around in a bag. I'll direct Anderson to pick up what he can. While he does that, you head out to find the hard drives of data storage they have in the building. I don't need to see them to know what to look for. They're all physically locked away from my access, so you'll have to pull them yourself."

Savage nodded and included Anderson in the agreement.

"Five minutes, then we bug out," the colonel said firmly.

"Roger that. Okay, Anja, tell me where to go."

She guided him away and deeper into the east wing of the building. He passed a couple of weapons ranges installed to test massive assault rifles—presumably to be used by the suits he'd seen. He broke into a jog as he neared the server room. It was interesting how quickly the facility had simply emptied at the end of the workday. It made him think the people didn't like their jobs that much. Or maybe they were merely understaffed and needed to bolt at day's end to preserve their sanity.

He located his target and scowled when he realized he had a considerable problem.

"Anja," he said tentatively. "There are a lot of hard drives in here."

"Identify those that have a flashing red light," she said quickly, clearly having isolated the comms between her and Savage and her and Anderson to keep them from over-lapping. "They won't be attached to any of the computers, so unplug them from the power supplies and stash them in your bag. We'll have to find another way to get through them."

The operative nodded and checked his watch before he set to work. He had three minutes before he needed to return to his teammate. The man would probably have to leave sooner, even before he did, but that simply meant he could show up and save the ex-colonel's bacon if someone tried to prevent his escape. He grinned as he accepted what seemed to be inevitable.

The burdens of being good at your job, he thought with a smirk.

He had retrieved fifteen hard drives before his watch beeped to signal that his time was up. He'd barely stashed the last one in his bag when klaxons blared across the facility.

"I think we've officially worn our welcome out around here," Savage said. "I don't think we'll be able to leave the same way we came in, though."

"You would be right," Anja replied. "The origin of the alarm indicates that someone has discovered your dead friends."

"Fun times. Anderson, do you copy?"

"I heard. I'm already on my way to you. Anja says she has a way out we can use."

"Look at me, saving your bacon again," the hacker said and sounded like she sported a broad grin. "If you ever come to the Zoo, you'll have to buy me a drink."

"Well, if I buy you one for each time you've saved my life, I think I'll end up buying you drinks all night."

"Don't inflate her ego," Anderson warned a few seconds before the man sprinted around the corner. Thankfully, it didn't seem like there was anyone immediately behind him. He assumed that intruders were to be shot on sight anyway, so no pursuit at this point was likely a good thing.

He still kept his weapon raised and aimed at the corner to ensure that nobody followed until the ex-colonel, winded again, patted him on the shoulder.

"Where are we headed?" Savage asked brusquely.

"One hundred yards down the hallway, you'll find an emergency exit," the hacker directed. "They don't have any way to open them on the outside, though, so once you're out, you won't be able to get back in, understood?"

"Understood!" It emerged louder than he'd intended. "Let's move."

Then again, with the alarms that now blared across the whole building, he had a hard time hearing himself think. Shouting was the only option at that point.

They jogged purposefully through the still deserted corridors. Although it was tempting to proceed in a sprint, they didn't want to careen into another security squad that might have circled from the opposite direction and so restrained themselves. Thankfully, they encountered no efforts to slow their progress.

That changed when they reached the emergency exit door, though. Loud shouts and heavy boots pounded the floors as they reached it.

"Bogeys on our six," Savage snapped and spun to meet them.

It was interesting to bring a new weapon onto the field of battle. He waited with real anticipation until the men spilled into view in pursuit of the two intruders. They saw the operative raise a weapon and the call to take cover went up, but a good third of the men were slow to respond. Two fell without a sound, sporting wounds from needles that had penetrated their body armor with ease.

He even tagged a third in the leg before the remaining guards flung themselves into the nearby labs for cover.

"Anytime you like, Colonel," he shouted. For the first

time since he'd met the man, Anderson didn't object to being called by the title he used to hold and pushed the door open quickly. Savage kept his gaze on the men behind as his partner gripped his shoulder and guided him back through the door. Gunfire erupted from the outside, both suppressed and unsuppressed, and the other man immediately returned fire. The operative slammed the door shut and spun to assess the situation.

Five men to their left struggled to find any cover at all in the open ground between the facility building and fences. Half a dozen huddled on the right, with bodies and blood visible on both sides. For all his time away from the field, the ex-Marine was still a crack shot, even with a suppressor on his Beretta.

Savage raised his weapon, but when bullets whined over his head, he launched himself from his position atop a small flight of stairs and onto the dusty ground below. He landed on his shoulder and winced when a flare of pain surged through his collarbone, but he continued to roll until he was fully prone. Ignoring his injury, he aimed at the men who attacked from the right and pulled the trigger as quickly as he could. It was such a nice change to not have to worry about ammo and mags, he decided. He still had over two-thirds of the strip of needles in his weapon and could realistically shoot all day.

Not literally, of course, but it made a comforting thought.

Anderson stayed on his feet and took advantage of the men who backed away when they realized they now faced weapons that would turn their vests of ceramic armor into swiss cheese. He sprinted towards the fence and heaved his bag to the other side before he clambered quickly to the top. His partner found his feet and paused to watch the man use his body armor to negotiate over the barbed wire on the top. The suit protected him from any significant damage while he remained where he was, sprawled on top of the wire as he fired at the security teams that now seemed a little bolder.

Instinct and training clicked together. Too much time had been spent running this little drill on the training ground—and even on the battlefield—for him to forget how it was done. The maneuver was purely reflex by now and required no thought at all before he spurred himself into action.

He vaulted high and shinnied up the remaining stretch of the fifteen-foot-tall fence. Anderson's arm hung down, waiting for him, and he gripped the man's hand tightly. He was hauled up the rest of the way by the colonel's strength. One of the barbs caught on his right arm and gouged a wound when he couldn't stop himself from being dragged down the other side.

"Fuck!" Savage shouted in the second before he landed hard. The impact knocked the air out of him, and he struggled to regain his feet. He slapped the pistol from his right hand into his left to continue desultory fire at their would-be pursuers as the duo pushed into the desert. They had no idea if they actually headed in the direction where they'd left their car, of course. The priority was to escape the facility with their stolen loot intact. That achieved successfully, they would circle to locate their vehicle.

Besides, night was already falling, and it would be a lot

more pleasant to walk through the desert without the heat of a thousand suns beating down on them.

The two ran on even as the lights from the research facility behind faded. They continued while the shouting tapered off, remained low, and stayed in motion as they zagged and zigged through the thick underbrush. Their steady pace and seemingly erratic maneuvers made sure that following them in this darkness would be impossible.

Finally, after what felt like hours but could only have been about fifteen minutes, they dragged to a halt. Savage actually felt lightheaded and he scowled at the blood that still trickled from his arm.

"Are you...all right there, grunt?" Anderson asked. He could see the bleeding, even if it looked black in the dim moon and starlight.

The operative felt winded himself but he ignored the discomfort and quickly applied pressure to the wound. It hadn't been the best escape he'd ever been a part of but not the worst either.

"Yeah... I think I'll be okay. I need to have this stitched when we get back to the hotel, though."

"We should use the back entrance," Anderson replied as both men dropped to catch their breath. "I have to imagine that a man walking around with a blood-covered arm through a hotel lobby would draw the attention of some of the patrons and employees. It might even warrant a call to the police."

"You have a point there." His voice slurred a little as he pressed a clean rag to the wound. The pressure triggered a stab of pain and he hissed through his teeth but maintained his effort to staunch the blood. "Did we get what we came for? If we only got away with some really expensive paper-weights, I'll be pissed right the fuck off."

"Well, I can't speak for the hard drives you took, Savage, not until I can see what's on them, at least." Anja had sensibly held her silence while the two men made their escape. "But Anderson collected items that should do the trick rather nicely. I only hope nothing broke when you pitched the bag over the fence."

"Break some specimens or get shot," Anderson retorted. "You let me know which you'd prefer."

"You really don't know me that well, do you, Colonel?" Anja asked.

Savage smirked. "Shut up, both of you. Okay, we need to find our car before the people in the facility start scouring the area."

"They don't have jurisdiction over any land outside the facility itself," she said. "They won't pursue you themselves."

"And you know this how?"

"Because they've already called the state police," she replied brightly.

"Fantastic." He muttered an expletive and pushed to his feet. "So we should probably get to our car before the police find it."

"That would be a good idea, yes."

"We need to get all this to Houston," Anderson said as they set off at a brisk walk.

"What's in Houston?" Savage asked and peered at his arm to confirm that the bleeding had stopped.

"Our closest research facility. They'll know what to do with whatever it was we stole. And there are connections there we can plug the hard drives into so that Anja can take a peek."

The operative nodded. "That sounds like a plan. For tomorrow, though."

"Definitely tomorrow."

CHAPTER TWENTY

"This looks like a new building," Savage commented as he scrutinized the area they entered. Although securely fenced off and sealed like the other facility, it had a new-building sheen to it that stood out. These days, when buildings didn't have to look like modern art master-pieces, they could be erected rather quickly and cheaply, while still being resistant to most environmental issues. On the downside, those buildings that did come out that way ended up looking like off-brand Lego blocks a bored child had discarded.

They could always be dressed up to look nicer, but that was like putting make-up on a pig. If you wanted a nicer-looking building, you shouldn't have built it with prefab material.

"It is a new building," Anderson replied and eased out of the passenger side of the car when it finally stopped. There was no need to pretend at this point, so the operative didn't have to look like a menacing, mute bodyguard. His boss had still insisted that he at least dress the part, though. "Pegasus has moved all its research into new locations so we don't have to worry about any of Carlson's influence reflecting back on us. Courtney already filled me in on a couple of locations that have had problems we caught in time—illegalities that had been put in place to screw anyone who took over for him. The guy was a serious big-picture thinker."

"You almost sound like you admire him for it." Savage slid his sunglasses on and didn't mind the look for practical reasons. There honestly was way too much sunlight around there. Too much open space too, he thought caustically. If Mixon were there, he could tell him he was being paranoid—something about a sniper needing a few days to prepare to be in position to take a shot from this distance —and they'd only decided to fly out there the day before.

"Far from it," his boss replied as they strode toward the doors of the building, both boldly emblazoned with the bright blue winged horse that was the company's logo. "The guy was—is—a fucking psychopath, but that doesn't detract from the fact that he knew a thing or two about how to prepare for what I can only think was his inevitable deposing. He was smart. It doesn't mean I liked him or approved of his methods. If that were true, we wouldn't be doing any of this."

"Fair enough." He shrugged and turned his attention to the building ahead. "We won't be thrown out of this one, right?"

"Considering that it's officially tagged to a company I am the acting CEO for, I should think not," the other man replied with a grin as a couple of security guards asked them to stop at the entrance. "Not if they want to keep their jobs, anyway."

"Mr. Anderson," one man said with a quick nod to both visitors. "Mr. Savage. We were informed that you two might make an appearance. Dr. Geoffrey Chance is scheduled to meet you if you'll follow me?"

Anderson stepped in behind the man and Savage brought up the rear of their little convoy. The guard led them deeper into the facility without conversation. The lack of windows and the sheer number of fluorescent lightbulbs gave the whole place a sense of timelessness. No matter the hour of day or night, this place would always have the same lighting. Well, unless one of the bulbs needed replacing.

"I need to point out the potential problems of having a conversation with someone called Dr. Chance," Savage whispered as they were guided through the expansive building.

"What's wrong with that?" the ex-colonel asked and kept his voice pitched low as well.

"Come on. I know a supervillain's name when I hear one." He grinned. "Seriously, if we walk in on him with a cat on his lap and he has an eye disfigurement, I'll call MI6. Just saying."

"Supervillain, huh?" His boss looked like he was actually considering the concept. "What kind of powers would Dr. Chance have? He would have to have picked his own name, right? Kind of like…I don't know, Savage?"

"Asshole. Well, I think Dr. Chance would—and this is

merely my thought—have power over the elements of chance in the universe. Or be able to predict them or something. I don't know, what do you think?"

"Maybe, but that seems less like a supervillain and more someone the superhero would have to get help from." The other man shrugged. "A man who would be able to predict the chances of anything. Someone who makes money betting on sports, perhaps. He made his fortune originally by betting, but he decided there was more money to be had in being a bookie and handling other people's bets instead, becoming a small-time crime lord that's marginally below our hero's radar. Maybe at some point, he becomes a bit of an anti-hero?"

"I like it. How would he get his powers, though?"

"It doesn't need to be powers," Anderson replied and chuckled like a kid. "He could merely have a very keen intellect. Which is why he's below our hero's radar since he deals with actual supervillains."

"You should trademark that shit." They stopped in front of an office with thin walls. He doubted that the man inside would have listened in on their conversation, but it was always better to keep people in the dark when you had a discussion on the hypothetical supervillain uses for their surname. It seemed like a good rule of thumb if you'd never met the person before.

As it turned out, Dr. Chance didn't look anything like a supervillain, Savage thought as they stepped into the man's office. It was one of the few rooms that actually had a window. As the operative peered out into the Houston marshlands a good twenty miles away from any other sign of civilization, he wondered why they would even bother.

They honestly might as well put in one of those new Vision windows that gave you a live view of virtually any famous location on earth. There was a monthly fee, of course, but it had to be better than looking out into mushy nothingness with a couple of small buildings in the distance.

Fuck, everything was so far away in Texas.

"Mr. Anderson, thank you so much for taking the time to inspect our little facility here," Chance said with a broad smile as he moved quickly from behind his desk. At an average height with a lean, trim build and a hint of a tasteful goatee that offset only a trace of baldness, the man didn't look at all like your average researcher.

Savage realized that their host had reached over to shake his hand and took it quickly as he plastered a smile on his face. "Savage. Jeremiah Savage."

"Jeremiah Savage. I like it." Chance nodded brusquely and leaned back against his desk.

"Well, thanks. I made it myself."

"Right." Chance chuckled and glanced briefly from one man to the other. Anderson sat on one of the visitor chairs in front of the desk, but the operative remained on his feet.

"So, how can I help you gentlemen?" the researcher asked. "Your visit was announced, but nothing was said about what or why. We're in the process of initiating all the research again. Some has been set back considerably thanks to the traveling arrangements—not many Petri dishes survive a trip in a plane, you know—but we should be back on track with the previous estimates in about three or four months."

"Well, I know the board will be very happy to hear that." The ex-colonel nodded approvingly. "I'll make sure to give them a note about your performance. But despite appearances, we aren't here to do any scheduled analytics. We'll leave that to the professionals in a couple of weeks."

From the sudden stir in Chance's eyebrows, this was news to the man.

"We do have to maintain appearances, of course, since what we actually wanted to talk to you about are..." He paused and considered the most diplomatic way to describe it. "Well, you don't need to know the details—plausible deniability and all that—but thanks to the efforts of our contractor Mr. Savage here, we were able to locate company property in the hands of very non-company people. Here is an example."

Anderson removed something from his coat pocket and handed it to Chance. It was small—about the size of a modern phone, although a little bulkier—with exposed wiring and no screen. Anja had called it a capacitor, apparently used to store electric power to be distributed as needed.

It was a simple yet integral part of virtually any piece of modern technology, but there was something about it that she had gone on about and even called someone named Amanda to weigh in on it. They'd talked for the duration of the three-hour flight from Vegas to Houston. It was special, apparently, a piece of bleeding-edge tech that was very expensive in the modern market.

Chance retrieved a pair of glasses from his desk and took it from Anderson's hand before he leaned in to inspect it—not the wiring, which was where Savage's eyes usually went, but the back.

"Yeah, you can see here," Chance said and proffered it to

Anderson. "There's the Pegasus watermark hidden in the circuitry. It's hard to find unless you know what to look for. There's a number as well, probably from the patent, so I'll need to check that, but at first glance, it's definitely one of ours. And, if I'm not mistaken, it hasn't reached the open market yet. If you found that in the hands of someone who wasn't authorized by Pegasus, it would be grounds for serious corporate espionage lawsuits."

The ex-colonel nodded. "Well, we'll keep a lid on it for now since we're still gathering information, but that would be the endgame, yes. However, since there's a lot we still need to get going, we'd like to see if anyone in this facility would be willing to continue the work we have going into these and other pieces that were...let's say misappropriated. I understand this might step on the toes of your current research here, but the board would really appreciate you putting this merch at the top of your priority list. They're afraid someone might have reverse-engineered it, and we don't want to be caught on the back foot if anything like it reaches the market before we have the chance to bring it out."

"Right, of course." The researcher nodded quickly. "We have a couple of teams here that are waiting for their equipment to be transferred from the Oregon facility. I can have them work on it until they're ready to go. That way, it will eat as little company time as possible. If I had to place a guess, this would be one of our capacitors for the new suits we've been building, right?"

"I wouldn't know," Anderson replied honestly.

"Give me a sec..." The man circled his desk and typed rapidly into his computer before he turned the screen for his visitors to see. "Yeah, that's a part of the creatively named Mark 17 suits that will roll out in a couple of years. We haven't done much in the way of weapons and armor testing here, but we do have the licensing for it. They don't really mind weapons testing here in Houston, for obvious reasons, so it shouldn't be a problem."

Savage wasn't sure what the obvious reasons were, but he assumed it was because Texas weapons testing laws were considerably laxer than most other states. He didn't even know if that was true, of course, but it was a reasonable assumption. Chance could have meant something else entirely.

"Okay, do you have anything else you'd want us to continue research on?"

"Oh, yeah." Anderson grinned. "There's a bag of it in the trunk of my car. And we also have electronic data we need to transfer to one of our specialists in Philly."

"We have IT personnel here who could probably handle it—" Chance began.

"And I'm sure they're fantastically equipped and prepared to handle it too," the ex-colonel cut in. "Even so, I think it would be best to pass it through Philly first to make sure there isn't anything hiding in the code or something."

"Of course. I'll send Dr. Myers with you to your car to collect what you have, and she can set you up in our server room too. It has the fastest connection in the building and should give you a lag-free connection to Philly."

"We appreciate your help here, Dr. Chance." Anderson pushed out of his seat and shook the man's hand firmly.

"And I will mention your efficiency and work ethic to the board at the next meeting. Keep it up."

Savage followed his boss out of the room as Chance called for someone named Myers to meet them outside where their car was parked.

"Is there anything hiding in the code?" Anja asked through their earpieces. The operative grinned and turned to face Anderson. He clearly had no intention to come to his boss' defense.

"Well, it's not like I know any of the real jargon," the man muttered under his breath. "Only what I've seen in flicks. I only hope Chance doesn't know anything about the lingo either."

"It's safer to assume he does," she pointed out. "His PhD is in electrical engineering, though. That was how he was able to identify the watermark in the piece so quickly."

"I'd say he looked for it almost immediately," Savage said.

"So, what do you think?" Anderson raised a brow in query. "Supervillain or nah?"

"Honestly, he looks more like a gym bro than your average researcher. Then again, my preconceptions and stereotypes of researchers have consistently been blown out of the water over the past few months I've worked for you, so I don't know what to think. He could be a supervillain for all I know."

His boss chuckled. "Well, for what it's worth, I don't think he looks like a supervillain either."

"We should keep our eye on him anyway," Savage said cautiously. "Look into whether he owns any white cats and maybe ask his neighbors if he's prone to cackling evilly in his spare time. Stuff like that."

"I'll allow it." Anderson paused, his train of thought interrupted by a young woman in a lab coat who walked purposefully toward them.

"Mr. Anderson, Mr. Savage?" she asked.

"You must be Dr. Myers." The ex-colonel extended his hand for her to shake.

"Dr. Angela Myers," she confirmed and returned the handshake firmly. "Dr. Chance told me you need to document transferred materials. I'm here to help."

"Fantastic." The three of them headed to where their car was parked. It was in the shade, thankfully, since everything there would be inevitably baked by the sun. They were told that an underground parking garage was in construction, which meant the employees still needed to leave their cars parked in the blazing sun for eight hours a day or more, and that had to suck.

Savage helped to carry most of the equipment still in the duffel bag Anderson had used while at the facility in Vegas. They took it into one of the labs, where Myers brought in a couple of other specialists. Most of what they discussed sailed above both Savage and Anderson's collective heads. Despite their ignorance, they gathered that most of what they'd recovered were components for some of the bleeding-edge suits developed for use on the battlefield, not the Zoo. There were shock-absorbing panels, weapon reloading networks, and dozens more, apparently all from the same suit.

"Well, as much as we would love to keep talking shop with you amazing people..." Anderson spoke finally to divert their attention and kept his tone as light as possible. "Chance said you had a server room we could use to communicate with specialists off-site?"

"Oh, right." Myers laughed as she jogged to the door and held it open for them. "I'm sorry about our distraction. We don't usually have the chance to actually study any of the weapons Pegasus develops. Of course, we'll probably need insights from the people who actually developed the tech we'll look at, but we'll have fun with it all the same."

"You know what they say," the ex-colonel said as they moved out of the lab and into the hallway again. "Someone who loves their job doesn't work a day in their lives."

"Who said that?" Savage asked and narrowed his eyes.

"Hell if I know." The quip drew a smirk from the other man.

"Anyway…" Myers guided them into a room similar to the one Savage had taken the hard drives from. There were considerably more to see and thankfully, he didn't need to steal any of them.

"Do you need me for anything else?" she asked with a quick glance at Savage. "I could show you how to operate the mainframe."

"I think we have it from here, Dr. Myers." Anderson smiled equably. "You can rejoin your comrades in the lab if you'd like."

"Of course." She made her way out slowly and closed the door.

"Was she checking Savage out?" Anja asked once they were alone.

"I think she was," the ex-colonel agreed. "Savage, do you have the hard drives?"

"Wait, what?" Savage asked. "Why would she check me out?"

"Well, I assume it's because of your manly manliness," the hacker responded tartly.

"No, what makes you think she would?" He retrieved the drives from the briefcase he'd lugged about for most of the day.

"Operate the mainframe?" Anja asked. "Are you fucking kidding me? I think she only wanted to spend some time with Mr. Tall, Dark, and Mysterious."

"I'm not...dark," he retorted as he connected the devices into the servers.

"You have dark hair. Does that count?" Anderson asked.

"Yes." The Russian chuckled throatily. "Anyway, plug those babies in and...we have liftoff."

"Are you already connected to the mainframe?" Savage asked.

"Jer, please. I've been plugged in since the two of you walked into the building," she answered snappily. "Nothing interesting came through, so I had to keep myself occupied with your brilliant conversation skills. I do—oh, hello. What's this?"

"Is there something interesting in the drives?" The ex-colonel's expression brightened.

"I'm still downloading that. It should take a couple of minutes, even with the fiber optics you guys have installed. No, I received a notification from that facility's connection to the Internet. Most of the computers are offline and away from external connections, but there are a couple spread around the building with Internet access. Anyway, someone sent a message through a concealed chat room using the same VPN connection as our dearly departed Edward Smith."

"Who?" Savage made a face as he tried to recall why it sounded familiar.

"The name they used to steal our equipment, remember?" his boss reminded him.

"Oh, right. The chop shop." Savage grunted irritably. "Why would someone use that name? I thought it was already burned?"

"Maybe someone didn't get the memo," Anja suggested. "It's definitely coming from one of the computers in the facility. The setup is slick, actually. The brute force encryption tells me the person who put it in place has a brain for this stuff, but whoever is using it doesn't. I intercepted it, though. Should I keep it from going through?"

"What does it say?" Anderson asked.

"Uh...let me see. One sec." The hacker went silent for a few minutes before she spoke again. "It's only 'nine-one-one. Can you meet in an hour?' And it has the address of a bar about thirty miles from where you are now."

The ex-colonel took a moment to think and rapped the table in front of him lightly with his knuckles before he spoke. "Let it through. See if you can't trace where it goes."

"I don't think I can," she warned.

"Either way, we can go to the bar and intercept the meeting." He rubbed the stubble that peppered his chin. "See if we can't find our mole and his handler in one fell swoop."

"Or her handler," Savage said with a firm nod. "Our enemies are probably equal opportunity employers, after all."

"That's downright decent of them," his boss replied. "Hypothetically, of course. Okay, Anja, let the message through. We'll stick around until you've finished downloading all the data and then head over to get our drink on."

"Roger that, boss man," she confirmed brightly.

CHAPTER TWENTY-ONE

"I'll need a beer and a scotch and soda, please," Savage said and moved closer to the bar. He had suggested they stick to non-alcoholic beverages for their time there, considering they were technically working, but since everyone in the bar was drinking, they had to fit in. Anderson waited at their booth, both to hold the fort down and to keep an eye on the door.

"Of course, honey, whatever you need," the tall, leggy, mid-twenties bartender said with a smile and winked as she pulled a beer from the fridge behind her.

He'd spent considerable time in bars like these. They were the only ones that stayed open near the bases where he'd been stationed, stateside or no. While he wasn't proud of what he'd done in those establishments, he wasn't ashamed of his actions either. He'd had a lot of steam that he'd needed to work out during that period of his life.

"Now, is the beer or the scotch for you, honey?" the bartender asked. He looked away from the TV that displayed a college football game.

"Beer's for me, thanks." He chuckled as he put the money down for the drinks. She smiled and winked at him once again before she turned to another patron.

Savage picked the glass and bottle up and pushed through the crowd to the booth where Anderson waited, his gaze on the door.

"Could you be any more obvious?" the operative asked as he set the glass down in front of the man and slipped into the seat across from him. "I think only the truckers playing pool on the other side of the room aren't aware that we're here on a stakeout yet. Don't get me wrong, they're still suspicious, but they don't know the details."

His boss scowled and shook his head. "I'm not used to this part of the job. The waiting, the looking invisible to anyone and everyone who might be watching."

"It's literally the easiest part, dude." He chuckled and took a sip of his beer. It wasn't the best but it was cold, and that was all that mattered in this heat. "You sit back, have a talk, keep one eye on the TV or whoever you're having the conversation with, and another eye on the door."

"And who are we watching for, exactly?" the other man asked as he leaned forward, his voice pitched low.

Savage put his forefinger on Anderson's forehead and pushed the former colonel back into a natural sitting position. "Well, considering that Anja wasn't able to narrow our target down, look for someone who looks out of place. Believe me, from the folks I saw in that facility, any one of them who steps out of a place like that and into a place like this will stand out like the sorest thumb in history."

Anderson nodded and swirled his Scotch. "It's easy for you because you have all these distractions. I'm a man of focus. When I do something, I like to keep my attention on it."

"Hey, I'm a man of focus too," he asserted. "But I know when to turn it off and have some fun, even while on the job. And what do you mean, all these distractions?"

In answer, the other man reached out and turned the beer bottle to reveal a name and number written on the brand label, as well as a time.

"Oh, well... I guess our bartender's name is Cindy with a Y," Savage muttered and frowned at it. "And it looks like she gets off work at about eight. Fun times."

His boss chuckled and shook his head. "Well, I guess this whole...strong, silent, mysterious persona you wear like a fucking jacket is a huge panty dropper."

"Really?"

"How the fuck should I know? I've been out of the game for a while, in case you haven't noticed."

"Well, I assume you and Ivy do something to keep the romance alive. Bondage, food play, something like that to keep things spicy."

"Firstly, how my wife and I keep the romance alive in our marriage is none of your business." Despite the mock-offended tone, he chuckled "Secondly, it's different. She and I know each other. Things are different when the two of you know a thing or two about each other."

"Well, I know that Cindy with a Y gets off work at eight."

"That's not the same thing and you know it."

"Well, I stand to get to know her a lot better if I end up being able to pick her up at eight," Savage pointed out reasonably.

"You might have to fight the other five guys she invited to pick her up at the end of her shift," the other man retorted.

"I have a gun. I won't have to fight anyone."

"We're in Texas, grunt." Anderson laughed. "I'll bet you half the patrons are packing a lot more than you are."

"Fair enough," he replied with a bleak nod but paused when he saw Anderson's expression change. He leaned back in his seat and caught the reflection in the mirror in front of him to see who had walked in.

They were both surprised to see Dr. Chance step into the bar. The man looked about as out of place as Savage had thought. He wasn't as geeky as the other researchers they'd run into, but he was way too clean and way too sober to hang out in a dive like this.

The fact that Anderson and Savage seemed to fit in so well was a statement of character that the operative wasn't a fan of, even if it did work for them at the moment.

"Not a supervillain," his boss noted and took a slow sip before he set his glass down slowly. "But a villain anyway. I'd say we found our mole."

"Now we need to identify the handler," Savage murmured from behind the top of his beer bottle. He continued to watch Chance's movement through the bar with the mirror, adjusting his position slightly to keep him in sight.

The researcher seemed oblivious to the fact that he now had an audience and pushed through the crowded room toward the bar. Cindy with a Y was there to greet him. The operative couldn't make out what she said, but he assumed she had asked if he wanted a drink. Chance indicated in the negative. After another few words were exchanged, the woman directed him to another corner of the room near the back exit.

He moved out of the range of vision with the mirror and Anderson kept an eye on their target while Savage took another sip of his beer. Keeping his movements natural was of the utmost importance.

"He's moved to the corner," his boss said to keep the conversation going since it was important that it didn't look like they'd suddenly stopped talking when the man arrived. "He's...shaking hands with a big guy. Like...linebacker big."

"Okay, look away for a sec so I can get a view," he instructed with his eyes fixed on his drink until a few seconds after Anderson complied. He shifted back in the booth and put his foot up. The new position gave him a more natural view of what was happening. Anderson hadn't lied when he said the man was big. He was seated, but if his shoulders were any indication, he was a mountain of muscle.

"What are they meeting for, though?" the other man asked after a moment of silence. "And are we sure they're not meeting up for anonymous sex or something?"

"Well, far be it from me to keep a potential relationship off the list of possibilities," Savage replied. "But if I had to guess, the linebacker looks like he's top and Chance seems a little too tense for that to be a comfortable situation."

"Oh, God," Anderson snapped and shook his head vigorously. "Why...what makes you think that I wanted that image in my head?"

He merely shrugged and tilted his head with a speculative gleam in his eye. "Okay, right. We can't let this meeting end. I need you to circle to the back exit, and I'll make sure Chance comes around to meet you there. You can take him, right?"

"Who, Doctor I Dig Rocks? Are you kidding? The question, of course, is if you can handle the mountain over there."

"Of course I can handle him."

"Without using weapons? If you intend to do this, we need people to be alive afterward, and it needs to look like a bar brawl or something. If the cops come along and see a dude with a bunch of needles in him from your fancy new gun, or see him professionally sliced and diced, they might take it more seriously."

"Right. The cops might get involved anyway, so why don't you take…this." He drew his pistol from the holster and passed it to Anderson, who slipped it quickly under his coat. Not having his weapon was the downside of being the corporate mogul. Who needed to carry when you had a bodyguard like Savage?

"Good luck."

"I…guess I might need a little luck," the operative admitted as Anderson slid out of the booth and eased through the crowd toward the front entrance before he stepped out the door. After a moment to give the man time to get into position, he took another slow sip, shrugged, and stood. He needed to be as obvious as possible. Chance didn't look focused enough to pick up on it, but the man he was talking to seemed professional enough to identify him without delay.

He took another deep, calming breath as he made his

way to the bar and tilted visibly as he sipped his beer to watch the two men as obviously out of the corner of his eye as noticeably as he could without seeming deliberately obvious. It took two or three tries but eventually, the man of granite made him. He tapped Chance on the shoulder and indicated for him to head out of the exit where Anderson hopefully already waited.

As the researcher half-stumbled toward the exit, Savage left his bottle on the counter and moved to intercept. He came to a sudden halt when he was blocked by a veritable human wall.

"Oh…" he grunted and allowed his eyes to climb all the way up the man until he met his gaze. "Shit. Oh, shit, you're a big fella, aren't you?"

He didn't answer and merely regarded him with a hard look. The massive muscles tensed under his shirt in much the same way as his tightened in preparation.

He could see Cindy out of the corner of his eye, but it seemed safe to assume that she'd seen enough bar fights to know when one was winding up. She stepped out from behind the bar and placed a hand on both their shoulders.

"Come on, boys, take it outsi—" she started to say, but he honestly wasn't in the mood to let her finish. He needed every advantage he could get, and she had given him one, small though it was.

He stepped around her touch and drew her in closer and between him and the giant as he pivoted as if to step around the man. As his adversary moved to stop him, the operative checked his momentum abruptly and used it to power a pair of vicious hooks into the massive midsection.

With a muttered curse, he dropped back a step and

cradled his aching fists. It had felt like punching a solid wall, and while he had actually tried that a few times on a dare, he hadn't fought too many brick walls that could hit back.

First, he saw the man's hand raise, and second, stars exploded across his vision and he catapulted back into the bar. People scrambled out the way, anxious to watch but also concerned to escape the melee.

"Okay," Savage said aloud and shook his head to gather his senses again. He needed to adjust his fight plan. Anderson would have to take care of Chance on his own.

Cindy was pushed aside, and she shouted that she would call the police as the man strode toward Savage, who still leaned against the bar. He wondered vaguely if he looked the part of someone who had been caught by a concussion-inducing backhanded slap.

His assailant grasped the collar of his shirt and dragged him clear of the counter. The operative twisted to bring his right arm up and down hard on the man's arm, but the hand remained locked on his shirt. His right foot lashed out at the man's knees and managed to put him off balance for barely a moment.

Savage pivoted in place and thumped his left foot into the bar for leverage as his left elbow snapped up and hammered hard into his opponent's solar plexus. The blow was enough to knock the breath out of the man's lungs and he sagged. Not one to waste a valuable moment, he followed through the elbow with a driving tackle he hoped would actually have impact.

Both men tumbled with a shuddering thud. He knew better than to try to grapple with someone so much bigger than him, so he tagged the man's jaw with a punch before he rolled off him and vaulted back to his feet.

The giant stood hastily as well, although he still struggled to breathe easily.

"Aren't you a bucket full of surprises?" he asked in a surprisingly soft voice as he straightened his annoyingly massive bulk and regarded his opponent warily.

"There's more where that came from, Hagrid." Savage rolled his neck and grimaced at a satisfying click. He raised his hands in the classic boxing stance.

The man wasn't intimidated, however, and barreled forward. The attack forced the smaller man to back into a wall and he raised his hands to block a huge haymaker aimed for his head. He knew what would come next and honestly, at that point, all he could really do was admire the fact that he'd been pinned down so easily.

Even with both his hands positioned to block, the overhead blow launched him powerfully into the wall behind him. There was no way to halt the uppercut that followed immediately and hammered painfully into the right side of his ribs. Those that hadn't fully healed yet cracked ominously and he gasped reflexively for air.

Thankfully, he didn't need to focus on the next series of motions that came naturally for him. Muscle memory, taught over long, rough hours of close-quarters combat conditioning, kicked in. He knew that while it wasn't advisable to grapple with someone who was easily twice his size, that didn't mean there was nothing he could do.

He brought his elbow down hard on the man's wrist and felt more than heard the crunch that followed as it dug deep into the exposed soft tissue between the bones. As the giant struggled to pull himself away, Savage grasped the collar of his shirt and used it as leverage while he pounded his head forward. His forehead collided painfully with the man's nose. Another crunch accompanied a growl of pain and he rapidly thrust his right foot on the wall behind him to propel himself forward. A superman elbow strike connected with the man's exposed jaw and he stumbled back to sprawl on a nearby table.

The operative dropped once again and sucked in a deep breath. He couldn't bring himself to press his advantage. As much as he was tempted to do so, he didn't want to think he was in any way winning this fight. There was a reason why there were separate classes in professional fighting rings, and that was because someone as comparatively small as he was could land as many blows as he wanted on the bigger, slower target, and the man could take it. The giant, on the other hand, merely needed one good strike and he would be out like the proverbial light.

Hell, he'd landed a soft blow to his body, and that alone had left him almost ready to tap out.

"I have to thank you," his opponent said in that annoyingly soft voice as he shuffled off the table and wiped glass shards from his clothes. "It has been a while since I've had a proper fight, and it's good for the heart to get the blood rushing. You have to know that you can't win, though, don't you?"

Savage shrugged. "It never stopped me from staying in a fight before," he responded belligerently.

It was false bravado, and they both knew it. He was almost tapped out of tricks and seriously regretted his decision to give Anderson his gun. Of course, it would be cheating, but at this point, he was involved in a fight with a man who was easily six inches taller and about a hundred pounds of muscle heavier. It wasn't a fair fight, to begin with.

Then again, he'd already won the real fight he was there for. Anja would have let him know if Anderson needed help, which meant his partner had acquired Chance by this point and was hopefully extracting some useful and actionable intel from the man at that very moment. He merely needed to wait it out until the cops showed up.

And sure enough, a few seconds later, the welcome sound of sirens wailed. The bulkier man looked around before he relaxed and drew in a deep breath.

"I'll beat you again sometime," he said with a smile.

Every instinct in Savage's body told him to take advantage of the larger man's distraction, but he also knew that distracted didn't mean unprepared. And honestly, he didn't need to be knocked out and wake up in a holding cell. He lowered his hands as well and grimaced when his jaw and ribs suddenly ached as the adrenaline bled from his system.

"Another time, and another place, Fezzik," he said and tried not to show any weakness while he raised his hands above his head. He couldn't help a flirtatious wink at Cindy the bartender, but her interest in him had cooled, it seemed, and she merely rolled her eyes. A couple of cops burst through the front door with their guns in hand and yelled at the two men—who were already surrendering—to put their hands above their heads and get down on their knees.

He was a little slow to comply with the last instruction

and his legs were kicked out from under him. The cold steel of the electric handcuffs snaked around his wrists.

The operative couldn't help a bad feeling that he would run into this amicable mountain of muscle again when the police wouldn't be around to bail him out.

But that was a problem for later, he decided as he was dragged out of the bar and shoved into a police cruiser. He had to hope that Anderson had better luck with Dr. Chance.

CHAPTER TWENTY-TWO

He'd had most of the night to deal with Chance. Thanks to Anja's ability to dig into the man's past—and find all kinds of nastiness there—and feed all the relevant information into Anderson's ear, he was able to intimidate his captive without having to resort to violence. He wasn't sure who, but someone out there had to admire his restraint. Leaving Savage behind to deal with what had to be the harder of the two challenges hadn't been flattering for his ego, but sometimes, you had to take a hit for the team.

In all honesty, from what Anja told him about what was registered for Savage when he was locked up, his operative had taken a hit for the team too.

The ex-colonel parked the company car in front of the police station and exited hurriedly. Bail had already been posted and he was simply there to pick the man up. Spending the night in a holding cell couldn't be a comfortable situation, he thought, and he had to be aching to get out, right?

He entered the station and displayed the barcodes to indicated that the bail had already been posted. The officer allowed him into the back where the cells were.

Surprisingly, the prisoner certainly wasn't chewing through the bars to get out. In fact, it looked like he was still sleeping it off. The officer tapped the bars noisily to wake him and he scrambled off the narrow bed almost before his eyes had opened.

"Oh...fuck me," Savage growled as he shook his head and clutched his side. He appeared to regret his precipitous action.

"I'm sure there's a line starting outside." Anderson chuckled as the cell door was opened to allow Savage out. "You look like shit."

And that, unfortunately, was an impressive truth. The whole right side of the man's face was swollen and splashed with bright red and dull purples. Ice would bring the swelling down, but Anderson had the feeling that his face was the least of the man's worries. Anja had shared the medical report that revealed a couple of bruised ribs, another possibly cracked, and a concussion as well as bruises and lesions across his knuckles and elbows.

"You should see the other guy," Savage retorted. He still held his left side tenderly as he stepped out of the cell and scowled at the attending officer.

"I did." He patted the man on the shoulder and ignored the involuntary wince the gesture caused. "Concussion, broken cheekbone, broken nose, and a twisted wrist. A couple of lesions and bruises on his face."

"That's... not very inspiring although it sounds about right. Between you and me, it was a fairly one-sided fight. I was lucky the cops showed up when they did. Did you see the size of that motherfucker?"

"I did," Anderson said. "And you should know that… well, it won't stay between you and me." He tapped his right ear.

"Fuck," Savage snapped. "The cops took my earpiece."

"I turned it off," Anja said in Anderson's ear. "For all they know, it's only a Bluetooth earpiece. You'll get it back on the way out."

The ex-colonel relayed the message to Savage, who still looked like he could use more medical attention. The hacker had told him on the ride over that some first aid had been applied to his injuries after he'd been written up, but it was very unlikely that it would be enough.

"I need to have a chat with the sheriff," Anderson said. "Courtney said she had the corporate lawyers give him a call earlier today to let him know that you would be released and no charges would be pressed, either by the bar or the giant you fought with. Not that it really matters, but the bartender said that the colossus started it anyway."

Savage nodded and looked genuinely relieved. "I appreciate it."

"So do I." He patted the other man on the shoulder and dragged another groan of annoyance and pain from him. "I'll fill you in on the details later when we're not in a police station."

"Fair enough."

The two men stepped into the local sheriff's office. The man in question obviously had nothing against playing to every stereotype possible, having a Colt Army in a frame above his desk, a Stetson hanging from the hat rack, and every kind of cowboy paraphernalia Anderson could think of. These included but weren't limited to a selection of horseshoes hung over the door, a bullwhip, and pictures of the man himself atop various horses and bulls.

It was a cultural thing, he thought. It had to be. He didn't judge, of course, but it still felt more than a little cheesy to him.

In Sheriff Francis' defense, despite the greying hair, the man had the leathery skin and lean build of a man who spent his days off working hard on his ranch when he could. He looked like he genuinely enjoyed the lifestyle and there was nothing bad about that.

"Mr. Anderson, I presume?" Francis asked as he pushed from his seat and shook hands, dutifully ignoring Savage. "I'm sorry for making you come out here like this, but we like to make sure all our bases are covered. We can't simply release the brawlers without some kind of assurance that they won't do the same thing again, you understand."

"Of course. Although I'm sure you understood from that interview you told me about that my man Jeremiah here wasn't the one who started the brawl."

"Oh, no doubts about that, with other witness accounts coming in with a couple of Internet videos making the rounds," Francis replied and chuckled. "I actually had a look at one of the better ones. Your boy here knows his way around his fists.

"He's had some training," he agreed noncommittally.

"I don't doubt that, but at the same time, we need to keep the peace. And it's like our mothers told us, it takes two to fight." The man nodded emphatically like he'd imparted an untarnished pearl of wisdom.

"I appreciate you letting him out this soon," Anderson said, anxious to move the process forward. "Even with all things considered. I think you'll be notified by the people at the bar that they were monetized for all the damages, including the possible revenue from yesterday and today to be sure. They said they won't press charges. Everything was done on paper, too—very open and official. Pegasus doesn't take well to having employees look bad, even if they are outside contractors."

The sheriff leaned back against the front of his desk before he moved a little to speak in a conspiratorial tone. "You know, between the two—three—of us, I'm not a fan of holding bar brawlers. Of course, they have to pay up, but most of the guys I lock up for throwing fists merely need to let off some steam. In all honesty, with all the gang violence seeping out from the city into our little county here, I'd prefer to leave the holding cells open. Things are getting worse around here, I'll have you know."

Anderson nodded and looked appropriately concerned. "Well, I'll make sure not to take up any more of your time with this business. I can assure you that you won't hear another peep from Jeremiah."

"Appreciated."

"How long do you think you'll plan to hold the bigger man since he's the one who's actually open to criminal charges?" he asked and tried to frame it as simple curiosity.

"Oh, him?" Francis asked. "His bail was posted before he was even admitted into one of our cells. It looks like he has friends in high places around here too, and someone was in a hurry to get him out. He can't leave town, though, since there will be charges pressed against him by the local state attorney. It'll only be a misdemeanor, of course. A small fine and maybe a couple of weeks in the slammer."

"Right." The ex-colonel straightened and assumed a more businesslike demeanor. "Look, we'll get out of your hair, Sheriff. Again, I appreciate your understanding in this matter."

"Any time, Mr. Anderson." The men shook hands quickly. "But make sure this one stays out of his cups and in a peaceful state of mind, you hear?"

"Loud and clear, Sheriff, loud and clear." He nudged Savage to exit the room first and they moved quickly to the counter to finalize his release.

"What'd you guys pay him?" the operative asked after they'd stopped to collect his personal effects. "There's no way a straight-shooter like that lets a couple of brawlers out of jail without some serious palm-greasing."

"I have no idea what you mean, Mr. Savage," Anderson said and managed a suitable degree of indignant outrage. "In other, completely unrelated news, Sheriff Francis is running for State Senate next month. While he lacked a little in campaign funds, the shortfall has since been rectified by a handful of very generous anonymous donations."

"God bless democracy and the legal forms of bribery that come with it." Savage chuckled and shook his head, a slightly disbelieving gesture he maintained until they were out of the building and headed to where Anderson had parked the company car. "Anyway, now that the only listening ears are halfway across the world..." He paused to put his earpiece in. "Hi, Anja. Now that we're alone, how about you share what Dr. Chance told you last night?"

"How are you feeling, Jer?" she asked. "You look like shit, by the by."

"Yeah, Anderson filled me in." He turned to his boss as the former colonel slipped into the driver's seat. The man paused and waited for him to groan and moan as he eased himself gingerly into the passenger seat.

"Well, with some help from Anja, I was able to have a nice chat with Dr. Chance during your night in the slammer," the ex-colonel said and handed Savage's weapon back to him before starting the car. "He doesn't appear to be very deep in this. She uncovered a couple of instances of very...interesting spending on his part over the past few years, way beyond his means. It stands to reason that the most terrifying thing in this country is pissing the IRS off."

The operative chuckled. "People underestimate the relentless pressure tax collectors have in them."

"Right. Anyway, he was very happy to share the details once I'd uncovered his dark secrets. Well, Anja uncovered them, of course. I merely displayed them. He went through the common lines of 'I don't know anything' and 'I'm not the one you want.'"

"More cliché than 'it's not you, it's me' and 'I think we should see other people,'" Anja snarked. "It's like, come on, we know you are bad guys. They could at least put some effort and creativity into their excuses."

"I hear you, Anja." Savage grunted softly when the car hit a bump on the road.

"Do you need to have that checked?" the ex-colonel asked. He could make all the Army jokes he wanted, but that didn't take away from the fact that his companion was a tough guy, to a fault. He would absorb as much pain as he thought he could and treat himself afterward. He wouldn't complain, but if he winced and doubled over thanks to his ribs hurting at the wrong time, they were both dead men.

"That depends on what we learned from our friend Chance, doesn't it?" he asked and glared at him like he had a bead on what his boss thought and didn't approve.

"He said he wasn't told anything directly and has always dealt with your big friend each time he needed face-time with his handlers. He called him Mr. Kelly, although I'm sure that's a fake name. Anyway, he said he managed to do some digging into what happened to the items he'd managed to sneak out of the building, and all he could track down was a name—Charles."

"Which makes it the second time we've heard about someone called Charles being behind this whole thing," Savage replied. "I think I need to find this Charles Stafford and have a talk to him."

"You'll have the opportunity when we're ready," his boss assured him. "Chance also mentioned that most of his deliveries were done personally and he was consistently directed to a little bar in New Orleans. He always dealt with the same person, although no names were exchanged. Our man would take days off to visit the city every few months, drop a couple of the items off, and get paid."

"Let me guess, most of Chance's spending happened in New Orleans?"

Anderson nodded in response. "Chocolate for the smart kid. So, since there's no real schedule on looking at the bar, how do you feel about getting medical attention?"

The man shook his head. "I should probably have it checked out, I agree, but we can do it in New Orleans. That way, even if I need to be out of action for a couple of days, I can still make myself useful by scanning the place or something. Does that sound all right to you, or will you hover over me like a mama hawk?"

"Sue me for wanting to make sure the grunt covering my back isn't whining and groaning instead of actually doing what he's paid to do," Anderson snapped but with a grin that took the sting from the words.

Savage opened his mouth but seemed to lack an appropriate response and quickly shut it again. The minutes slid by in silence while the two men drove through the barren wilderness outside the metro area of Houston. A couple of businesses thrived here and there in the open spaces. He finally leaned back and laughed.

"Of the three destinations we'll visit, two are Vegas and New Orleans." He shook his head with a rueful chuckle. "I'm not saying Courtney will think you're taking a vacation since she knows better, but the rest of the board will probably want to look at your receipts."

"You don't need to worry about that," Anderson replied. "Most of the hinky financial stuff I've done has been pulled out of untraceable petty cash."

"That's adorable." Anja laughed. "But seriously, I've been careful to make sure you two are covered financially from the board's perspective on Courtney's orders. It's more work than I think you two are really worth financially, but what can I say? You tickle me in a nice place."

"Well, that's an image I won't get out of my head," he complained.

CHAPTER TWENTY-THREE

Savage scowled as he looked around with real distaste. The street was way too crowded for comfort. He didn't like being out in the open with so many people around him. It made him feel exposed and vulnerable with the overwhelming barrage of bodies, sounds, shapes, and colors that flashed incessantly in his vision. If there were ever a time where he and Anderson were more vulnerable, he didn't recall it. If anyone intended to hit them, it would be there.

There had been no news on any changes in the contract on Anderson yet, he reminded himself. Not from Anja, at least. He doubted that Courtney would want them to be left out of the loop on something so important as a hit on her partner in Pegasus, but she was deep in corporate cover, and honestly, he didn't know her very well. He had no clue what kind of greater good she would consider to be worth it to leave Anderson dangling.

It occurred to him that what they were doing was basically dangling the man and keeping him on the move to keep him safe. Maybe something done to allow for a larger picture wouldn't be the worst thing in the world.

It would still be a dick move to keep them out of the loop, but that could simply be his overanxious caution at work. They were compiling data on Stafford like they had done with Carlson, and to move too soon would be plain stupid. Also, he had no doubt that Anja would notify him the moment she picked up on any direct threat.

"How are your ribs feeling?" Anderson asked and stepped a little closer.

He looked at his boss and retained his scowl as he tried to convey his irritation. The man had hung around like he wanted to make sure he was okay, and while he appreciated the sentiment, he also had to know that hovering while he was getting better was detrimental to his progress.

"It's fine," he assured him finally and took a step to put a little distance between them. "I'm a little sore and still recovering. These wraps don't do much for my mobility and— Look, man, I appreciate it, but you don't need to be around me all the damn time. I think my body knows how to recover on its own by now."

"Have I been too clingy?" Anderson made a face. "Come on, man, you should have told me. I've been like this ever since Damon got sick and they told me to stay with him. Sorry."

"Don't worry about it, and again, I appreciate the sentiment." He nodded brusquely. "But honestly, I think I simply need some help from a nurse. And not one who's found in a hospital, if you know what I mean."

His boss narrowed his eyes. "Wait, you want one of the nurses they send to nursing homes?"

"They send strippers to nursing homes?" They adjusted their route to walk toward the building across the street from them. There were still too many people around—an uncomfortable number of people, actually—and he hoped the new destination might ease that.

"Wait…come on. That was a joke," Anderson said and shook his head vehemently.

"Yeah, I know, but you suck at it since you gave up so easily." He grinned and nudged the man in the shoulder.

"Wait, how many strippers have you slept with?"

"Do you want an actual number?" Savage frowned as he considered it. "I…well, I don't remember any from when I was married, so that's easy. And it wasn't too many overall, I don't think. Maybe one or two at bachelor parties. No—no, damn it, not my own." He snarled the protest when he saw Anderson's grin and knew exactly where his mind was going. "Not at my own. I would never have done that. Anyway, after the divorce, I spent most of my time overseas so didn't actually get much time here. Not that many in total, after all. More than most folks, though, I suppose."

His boss shrugged. "First of all, I wasn't going to say you cheated on your ex-wife with a stripper at your bachelor party. I thought I'd put that out there. Secondly, well… You know what, never mind."

"Oh my, have I stumbled on something of a fetish of yours?"

"What? What the hell are you talking about?"

"I don't know." Savage shrugged. "You seemed focused on the strippers so I thought it might be something you wanted but were afraid to bring up with Ivy. Do you think that, once we're finished with this, we could go to a strip club and maybe work out what you want? That way, you will have built up the courage to encourage Ivy to do it."

Anderson narrowed his eyes at him but paused when they reached the entrance. "But you're the one who brought strippers up. Why... I...I don't feel comfortable talking about my wife like that to you. Sorry."

Savage shook his head apologetically. "Sorry, I don't mean to pry. You seem a little uptight and in need of relaxation. I've met Ivy, and she seems like an encouraging woman who wouldn't mind trying out new things with you."

The ex-colonel dragged in a deep breath as he looked around as if afraid someone might overhear them. "I mean...sure, whatever. Ivy is the best, and yeah, I have hang-ups of my own that I'm not comfortable addressing with anyone, including you."

"Again, I don't want to pry." He placed a hand on the man's shoulder. "And it's not like I'm a relationship expert or anything like that. Far from it. You and Ivy seem as strong as ever. I'm sorry, I don't want to intrude. It started out as a joke and got a little closer to reality than I intended."

Anderson chuckled. "Don't worry about it, man, and I appreciate the concern. It's not like you don't have some good points."

"I'd go easy on suggesting that your wife strip for you, though," he added as they stepped inside the club. "Pro advice. Build up to it, you know? Ivy probably won't slap you, but I've been slapped for the suggestion. Keep that in mind."

His companion laughed. "Thanks, Savage. I think I needed this."

"I have no idea what you're talking about." He felt better for having his weapon tucked into his under-shoulder holster, although he doubted that he would have time to use it in these kinds of close quarters. Precious milliseconds would be lost in simply bringing it to bear effectively. Still, its solid presence made him feel a little less vulnerable. His left hand hovered around the knife secreted under his belt for quick access. He sincerely hoped he wouldn't need it.

Stepping inside revealed very little that he couldn't already guess from the outside. New Orleans was one of those cities that was usually in a state of celebration. Of course, the time for Mardi Gras was long past, but that didn't mean people couldn't celebrate around it. Tourism was a huge money-maker for this city, and when the weekend rolled around, people liked to have a good time without needing a calendar-based excuse for it.

Shots were distributed while lively pop music covers were played by a live band. A section had been partitioned off, which indicated that a DJ would take over when the band needed a break. This wasn't the kind of place Savage usually frequented since the loud noise tended to give him a headache over time. Still, he could understand the appeal for people who were about a decade younger than he was.

"Fuck, I'm old," he grumbled as they made their way through the busy interior.

"Come on, thirty-two isn't that old," Anderson retorted.

"You're right at the peak of experience and physical viability. I really don't know what you're complaining about."

"I'm simply shaking my cane at the youngsters and shouting at them to get off my lawn, is all." His mood improved a little when one of the dancing women sidled up against him. "Then again…"

His enjoyment vanished, however, when he realized a couple of security people now waded through the crowded dance floor to reach them.

"I'm sorry, sirs, but I'll have to ask the two of you to come with me, please," the female bouncer said calmly. The girl who tried to get his attention made a move to tell the woman to shove off, but the sight of a gun in her holster was enough to make her back down. It also immediately got the duo interested in seeing what it was that they wanted.

If worse came to worst, Savage still had his knife. The woman's holster had a buckle that still held the gun in place, and the safety was on too. It wasn't the safest situation to be in, but it wasn't untenable, at least for now. If things started to go south, he would make sure Anderson was out of the way before he stepped in. He wore some of that new light and useful body armor, but his idiot boss didn't.

He had given him all the nasty looks and nagging he could before they left the hotel. At one point, he'd even told him directly to go back to his room and get some body armor, hoping the words and attitude might trigger the dad in him and remind him that he'd likely said much the same thing to Damon more than once. But damn, the man was stubborn. Not only that, he was the boss. Aside from physically manhandling him into a suit, there really had been nothing more he could do. He had to assume there was a reason, even though it made no sense and his job a lot harder. If they ended up in a firefight, Anderson would have to stay back and let Savage handle it.

They were led from inside the dance floor to a flight of stairs that ascended to what looked like a VIP section of the club. The area was closed off with its own personal DJ and a group of mostly women danced in an open section.

There were three booths, each stood in a corner of the square room, where some of the other patrons were drinking, eating, or indulged in a card game. He wondered vaguely how they could hear each other over the dance music. Maybe they had some sort of sound isolator in there that kept the music out? He wasn't sure if that even existed, but with all the technical advances, you couldn't really be sure. So much new tech was coming out and even more these days with the Zoo out there to provide more and more surprises.

Savage glanced at the fourth corner to the back and left of the room and immediately realized why they were there. The booth there was larger and more expansive and appeared to be a more private and exclusive VIP room with its own security. Five people sat in comfortable chairs, four of them women and dressed as skimpily as they could possibly be while still vaguely described as dressed. One man lounged in the back, his arms around two of the ladies.

"Alvarez," he said cheerfully. "Is that you?"

The man looked up from his companions and grinned

broadly when he saw the two men who had been brought in. "If it isn't the savage. How the hell are you?"

He gestured at the two armed bouncers beside him and another in front. "Right now, I'll go with confused."

"Oh, come on, man." The Mexican chuckled. "You did me a favor at home. Setting the record straight put me in good standing with my superiors. You know how I hired you to get rid of this Charles man who's given us so much trouble? You've made your way through the world and I have to say, my organization really approves of your initiative."

"No…hard feelings then?"

"The way I see it, you're saving us money." Alvarez indicated for the two men to step inside. "I'm sorry, but my people won't let you enter without searching you first. I assume you came in armed?"

Savage nodded. "Of course."

Anderson's glance suggested caution. He obviously wondered if he knew what he was doing, and he nodded assurance. If it ended poorly, it wasn't like the man would be able to say I told you so.

The bouncers moved in brusquely and, in Anderson's case anyway, professionally to frisk them for weapons. The female bouncer looked like she was taking her sweet time as she ran her fingers down the operative's chest and his shoulders and drew his pistol out of his pocket suggestively.

His eyes widened when her hands wandered into areas that were unlikely to contain any weapons. "Will you buy me a drink after this?"

She didn't respond but backed away from him quickly.

Without meeting his eyes, she gestured that he was clear to go. She hadn't seen the knife hidden in his belt buckle, which was encouraging. It was a two-inch blade that he could pull out in a pinch. It obviously wouldn't do much damage, but if the aim was to kill Alvarez before he was murdered himself, it would do nicely. Revenge was always sweetest when it couldn't be returned.

Savage dropped easily into a seat beside the Mexican. Anderson, for his part, looked rather uncomfortable about the situation, and he really couldn't blame him. They were in an isolated place with a cartel boss who had reason to want them dead.

"So, I've tracked your actions through the US," their host said with a furtive glance around him. He also kept his voice low, which was encouraging. "To be honest, you have a very particular...style. We have all that talk about gang violence in our country, but the savage makes us look like girl scouts, am I right... What was your name again?"

"James," Anderson said softly like he wanted as little to do with the conversation as possible. "And yes, you are, in fact, right."

Alvarez grinned and sipped lazily before continuing. "I'd like to know how close you gentlemen are to catching this Charles. I need something to report back since I have it on record that you are working for us toward that goal."

"Here's the situation, Al." The operative leaned in closer and spoke in a confidential tone. "We intercepted one of his inside men and he told us he was supposed to make a drop here. I honestly didn't know that you would be here to receive it."

Undeterred, the cartel boss chuckled. "I see. So, it was

in the stars for us to cross paths again, my friend. We were told to wait here for some geek scientist who comes periodically with information and...well, tidbits we're not supposed to ask questions about and merely pass along. We're also not supposed to ask questions about where we send them. We merely call a number, and someone comes in and takes it away."

"Okay, here's what you'll do. We'll get a drink, stick around for a couple of songs, and then we'll leave. Once we're done, you'll call that number. They'll ask you what data you have, and you say you have information instead. Tell them you know they're looking for a man named James Anderson and that he's staying at the Palm Hotel on the intersection between Wood and 49th. We'll be there, and we'll be waiting for them."

Anderson glared at him, clearly alarmed at the amount of information he had shared. It was the reaction he had been waiting for, of course. It would get Alvarez's attention and make him realize that James was actually this James Anderson. The ploy was something of a gamble, but based on his past interaction with the man, he thought the chances of it paying off were good. They seemed to be under the heel of this Charles character, and he guessed that Alvarez wanted to get him and his organization out from under that heel more than they wanted a single payout, however tempting it might be.

He also counted on the cartel boss having a very clear recollection of what had happened on his visit to Mexico. He would hopefully assume that turning on Savage now would end with a lot of bodies, including his own. Self-preservation was one hell of a motivational tool.

The man sent him a measured look and smiled. "You would do this for me?"

"Hey, I figured I owe you one for my shenanigans in getting you to hire me. Besides, I really don't want to repay half the down you shot my way and I won't give you the other half. We already discussed this, but that's gone on expenses. You know how it is, right?"

"Of course, my friend. Now that we are done with business, how about we have that drink, eh?"

"Do you mind if we get our weapons back?" Anderson asked, his eyebrow raised.

"Sure, why not? We are all professionals here, yes?"

"Yes." Savage smiled as the bouncer handed his pistol back, and he tucked it quickly into its holster. "You really need to talk about professionalism in your own crew, though. They missed something the first time around."

The man narrowed his eyes when Savage tugged out the small knife that was secreted into his belt buckle. "Well, I thank you for pointing it out, and it will be brought up later when we're alone."

He eyed the woman, who looked abashed and backed away slowly.

"So…" The ex-colonel shoved his pistol back in his holster. "How about that drink? I've been dying for a Manhattan."

"Make that two. You know what, Manhattans all around."

CHAPTER TWENTY-FOUR

Anderson glanced irritably to where Savage sat with no apparent care in the world. The man had a habit of looking like the universe didn't affect him. Admittedly, his ribs had healed somewhat and the strap with a topical anesthetic would make sure they wouldn't cause him too much pain. Treatment had reduced the swelling in his face, making him look less like someone dying from anaphylaxis and closer to his original, rugged self.

It was difficult to tell if he was actually fine or was merely pretending. He honestly didn't like it when people were that difficult to read. While he'd had a couple of hard cases in his unit back in the day, he'd also never figured out how to handle them. It made him feel out of control and antsy.

The duo sat in the fading afternoon sunlight and watched one of the local parades. The pleasant ambiance made him feel the man was actually all right with his situation. He was a hard case, there was no denying that, but he wasn't a liar. Savage didn't hide his pain. He used it when necessary, but he also wasn't stupid enough to charge around in a very dangerous occupation without making sure he was all right.

Well, except for that time when he'd burst into Anderson's country home and helped him fight his attackers off while being injured himself.

Maybe a little stupid, then.

"I don't get it," the operative said, his gaze focused absently on the people walking on the street below. "It's not Mardi Gras. This celebration should be months away. Do you know what it is these people are actually celebrating?"

Anderson shrugged. "Being alive? I don't know, but the hotel obviously knew about it—otherwise, they wouldn't have provided us with these." He indicated the basket full of colorful plastic beads that had been out on the small balcony they now sat on when they'd checked in. This was Anderson's room. Savage had taken one down the hall but considering that the man with the price on his head was Anderson, they'd thought laying the trap in his room was the best way to go about this.

Savage smirked and focused on one of the floats moving down the street with a handful of young women dancing on top. When they saw the men watching them from the third floor, they uttered a cacophony of loud whoops, pulled their shirts up, and called for them to throw beads down. He obliged with a chuckle.

"I have to say, I don't hate this," he said and sipped his beer with a scowl.

Anderson narrowed his eyes. "With the painkillers you're on, do you really think it's a good idea to drink? It's one thing to have a couple of drinks at the club, but you might want to avoid drinking too much."

"Don't worry about it." He grinned as a couple more women on the street flashed him in exchange for beads. "I talked with the doc, and he prescribed me painkillers that go well with alcohol, actually. I remember that because I thought I was high when he told me about it. It's this new thing from the Zoo, apparently. Expensive, but hey, if Pegasus is footing the bill, what the hell, right?"

The other man smirked. "Honestly, I think Pegasus were the ones who developed it."

"Wait, Pegasus has a pharmaceutical division?"

"I'm reasonably sure they're the ones that first started making money from the stuff taken out of the Zoo, so maybe?" He shrugged a little impatiently. "I may officially be the CEO, but we both know my role is focused more on the current threat and the…uh, military aspects of it all. The truth is that I know only enough to get by, and I bullshit through the rest. Courtney and that sidekick of hers handle everything else, so I'm seldom put in a situation where I have to know all the details. It's a big company and they have fingers in every kind of pie imaginable. Whether that includes straight pharmaceutical as opposed to beauty treatments or whatever is not need to know."

"We have fingers in all kinds of pies, Anderson," Savage grinned and threw another pair of beads to a couple more flashers. "Pegasus is a we now."

"Fuck you."

The operative squinted in surprise as a handful of women—who looked like they were barely old enough to start college—thought they would give the flash for beads the old college try. He obliged their courage.

"I'm easily bribed," he explained when his companion flashed him a disapproving look.

"Clearly." He passed the beads in his hand to Savage. "I need to go inside and get another drink. I'm obviously too old and too taken to do any of this."

"Believe me, man, you're lucky." He scattered their beads over the railing.

"Yeah, if this story ever comes up in the future, be sure to tell Ivy I took the high road and didn't see anything," he yelled from inside as he tugged a couple of tiny bottles of bourbon from the minibar and poured them into a glass. He wasn't taking any painkillers so could afford to be liberal.

"I'd joke about that," Savage responded. "But I don't want you to shoot me in the back in case you feel you need to cover your tracks and make sure the story of how you peeked at younger women exposing themselves to us never leaves this room."

"I didn't peek." He shook his head vehemently.

"I hate to interrupt what I'm sure is a very vital and important conversation," Anja broke in through their earpieces. "But I'm getting interference near your rooms that tells me someone else is using an encrypted channel in the same area. The cameras in the hotel indicate that you are about to have some company."

The operative pushed to his feet and entered the room to close the door firmly behind him. Anderson assumed there was impending violence and he didn't want anyone on the street to have their festivities interrupted by the sound of gunfire and screaming.

That was what a good neighbor did, after all.

Savage drew his pistol, clicked the safety off, and yanked a combat knife out to hold in his free hand as he indicated for Anderson to move away from the door.

"How close are they?" he asked as he stepped in behind the door and assumed a defensive position.

"The hotel only has one camera covering the elevator, so they should be seconds away," the hacker replied.

He nodded and eased in opposite where the door would open, giving himself cover as he heard it unlock. Someone had found something that could override the keycard lock. He sucked in a deep breath and adjusted his grips on his weapons. The light was on so any attackers would know there was someone in the room.

Anderson ducked behind the minibar with a SIG in his hand, the barrel elongated with a suppressor. He promised himself to track down one of those needle-shooting guns Savage had. While they weren't readily available, it wasn't impossible that other prototypes couldn't be sourced—or that someone would be willing to replicate it for sufficient incentive. It was a little bulkier than the average pistol, but it only needed to reload after firing a hundred or so times, for one thing. The silence aspect also made it even better than a suppressed weapon, so all in all, the pros far outweighed the cons.

The door opened slowly and an MP5 slid around the corner. Anderson pulled back instinctively. He tried not to make a sound and was wildly aware that his heart raced at a hundred miles an hour. There seemed no doubt that they would hear it and open fire. The minibar fridge would cover him for the most part, especially if all they had were 9mm rounds. But small fridges and the concrete walls they were propped up on weren't made to absorb gunfire. To rely on them to be all the cover he needed was the kind of gamble people made for money, not their lives.

The first masked man pushed through the entry and predictably, he immediately swept the room. Savage came in from behind him and squeezed the trigger on his specialized weapon. It still seemed unnatural that a weapon like that would produce no sound. Anderson couldn't help flinching as the weapon fired with the barest hint of a whoosh and the intruder who had taken point dropped without a word.

While he didn't see the exact moment when the needle punched into the man, he did see him succumb almost immediately with blood leaking out the back of his head. Another whoosh and thud felled a second man. Anderson eased around the corner and paused. One of the men was tangled with Savage, having gotten in too close to shoot. A fourth member of the attack team stood near the door and tried to place a shot around his—no, her, he realized as her mask came down—comrade in arms.

He worked his way cautiously from behind his cover. She was too focused on the other fight to notice him until the suppressor pressed into her temple. Her eyes widened in surprise as Savage hauled the man down in an expertly executed judo flip that felled him with a solid thud. The operative flipped his gun quickly and used the grip as a club to deliver three hefty blows—one to the assassin's head, once on the jaw, and the last on the cheekbone to draw a splatter of blood. The man curled and another strike hammered home on the back of his head before his body went limp. It wasn't possible to tell if he was dead.

"It's not worth it," the woman said and dropped her weapon hastily. "Not for my share of a million bucks."

The sub-machine gun swayed, caught in the strap that hung from her neck. Anderson reached over to undo it quickly and kicked the weapon away.

Savage straightened slowly, his face and clothes splattered with blood.

The ex-colonel looked at the blood that now began to seep onto the room's carpet. If he wasn't dead from the strike to the back of his head, he definitely was now.

He looked at the operative, who calmly adjusted his pistol into to the proper grip, a little out of breath.

"Are you good?" Anderson asked.

"Better now. Are you going to kill her or what?"

The woman stared at him, fear in her eyes. "You don't need to kill me. I promise."

"Did you even search her for another weapon?" he demanded and aimed his gun at her too.

"Come on, man, we don't have to kill her." He hadn't actually searched her for any other weapons, which was probably a good idea now that he thought about it. He ran his hand hastily around her waist until he found her sidearm as well as a combat knife she had attached to her belt.

"Careful there, buddy." Savage grinned. "I might have to tell the wife that your hands wandered as well as your eyes."

"Seriously, you just killed three guys. Can you at least

show some professionalism?" The ex-colonel snorted and flung the weapons aside.

"Not cool, dude," the woman said and shook her head.

"You don't have a say in this." The operative took a step closer. "And I have already killed three people, so unless you want to make it an even four, you'll to need to share some juicy gossip, okay?"

"How is four even?" the other man asked.

"It's an even number. Come on, Anderson."

"I'm not being paid enough for this," the woman muttered.

"To be fair, we're not paying you either," he replied. "On the other hand, if you fill us in on who you were supposed to report to, we can... Well, let you get out of this alive."

"Look, we got our contract from the people at the Research Triangle," the gunwoman said. "There was a monetary prize involved, of course, but they were simply going to pay us out of the contracts."

"The...the Research Triangle?" Savage asked and looked confused.

"Is that...*the* Research Triangle?" Anderson asked. He, at least, seemed to have a better idea of what she meant.

Irritated, the operative pressed the barrel of his weapon firmly against her temple.

"You'll have to be a little more explicit, sweetheart. The Research Triangle is an academic region or something. I don't have the time or the patience for this kind of bullshit story."

"No, you don't get it. Wait—let me explain, Goddamnit."

He glanced at the other man who nodded. "Okay, but I

want the truth. It's up to you whether you walk out of here or not."

"Yes, yes, God…" she whispered. Her eyes closed as she sank against the wall and anticipated the trigger-pull that would end her life. "I swear, I'm not lying. There's the Research Triangle everyone knows about—with the universities and all. That's in North Carolina. But there's a building in DC where all the government research grants and contracts pertaining to the military go that they call the Research Triangle. It's a fucking joke—you know, because of the research stuff and because this stupid-ass building is actually built in a triangle."

"You guys are associated with the Pentagon?" He looked startled for a moment.

"Not directly," she replied but her eyes remained tightly closed. "We're associated with one of the Pentagon's domestic contractors as independent agents, brought on for strictly blacked-out stuff. Look, this is the comm unit they gave us to let them know that the job was done."

Savage took the device and glanced at Anderson, who seemed to have as much difficulty processing this as he did. They were being attacked through official channels. Exactly what kind of pull did this Charles Stafford have?

"Are you going to kill me?" she asked after an uncomfortable silence. She did at least feel safe enough to open her eyes again.

"Fuck me," Savage said bitterly.

"I'm not… I'm flattered, but no thanks," she replied.

"What?" He snapped his gaze back to look at her. "No. Shut up and let us think of a way to get us all out of here alive and in one piece."

"I'm part of the 'us all' I take it?" she asked and gave them each a hopeful look.

Anderson shrugged. "What kind of options do we have?"

The operative shook his head. "We have three bodies to deal with and I don't feel like explaining this situation to the police, do you?"

The other man shook his head definitively.

Savage nodded and tapped at his ear lightly. "Hey, Control, do you read me?"

"Wait, why am I Control all of a sudden?" Anja asked.

"Because I don't feel like saying your actual name in front of the hostile."

"Oh, good point," she replied and sounded like she was grinning. "I like it. Can we call me Control for every mission?"

"Will you stop calling me J—by your affectionate nick-name for me?"

"Yeah, that won't happen," she grumbled.

"And you have your answer, nice and gift-wrapped. Now, are there any police alerts for our location?"

"None at the moment," she said.

"It's not like we made much noise," Anderson pointed out.

"Right. What are our chances of cleaning this situation up here before anyone notices the bodies and calls the police?" Savage queried and lowered his weapon. Anderson kept his pistol pointed at the attacker, just in case.

"You can't walk a couple of bodies out of that room," Anja said and definitely sounded less than optimistic.

"Three bodies," Anderson clarified.

"That's still covered by the expression a couple—look it up," Anja interjected quickly. "What are you thinking, Savage?"

It was interesting how she called him Jer as a rule unless they were in dire situations like she understood the fact that there was a time and a place for their inside jokes. Anderson couldn't help a small smile.

"Well, if this were any other time and any other place, I could change the names on your registration, erase any footage of your having been there, and let the police put this down to another incident of gang violence," the hacker explained.

"And why can't we do this now?" Savage asked.

"If the Pentagon are interested in finding their people again, they would find ways around that," she snapped.

"They're already coming after me anyway," Anderson reminded them. "We merely need to make sure that law enforcement doesn't come after us too."

"Okay." Anja paused for a moment while she worked. "I can erase any footage of you being in the hotel and change the names and everything on the system, but thanks to your little stunt out on the balcony, you two have popped up on all kinds of social media. I can corrupt and change it, but I'm not God. Something will get through if anyone looks hard enough."

Savage nodded. "We don't need to be invisible, merely hard to find. Do what you can. We'll leave the bodies in here, and…you—" He turned back to the woman, who still had Anderson's gun aimed at her head. "I assume there's someone waiting for you downstairs in the getaway car? The fact that you came in with that much firepower and without any suppressors tells me you don't mind making a mess, but you would need to get out quickly. Can you lead us to them?"

She nodded.

"Good, then we only need to do a quick wardrobe change and we'll be right down." He immediately began to strip down the assassin closest to his size.

The men changed quickly and took turns to keep an eye on their hostage before they were both dressed as their attackers. Both looped the sub-machine guns around their shoulders, but Savage kept his pistol ready behind the woman. They gave her weapon back to her since it would appear odd that one of the party wasn't armed when they exited, but they removed the magazine and ejected the round in the chamber before they returned it.

"Let's go. Service elevator to the basement parking lot, right?" Savage asked, and she nodded.

"I'll clear a path for you," Anja said. "Oh, and I've already altered your reservations to different names and will add another week to your stay. Put the do not disturb sign on the door and you should have time to get the hell out of Dodge before anyone discovers the bodies."

"You're the best, Control," Anderson said and pulled his mask up as they left the room. They moved quickly as their hostage seemed to understand that they wouldn't mind leaving her behind if she made a scene. They found an empty service elevator waiting and stepped inside. It was all electronic and tied to the hotel's Wi-Fi, which meant Anja could operate it and deliver them directly to the garage.

"Keep scrubbing, Control," Savage instructed as they

stepped out and swept the area to ensure it was abandoned before moving out. The gunwoman guided them through the garage to a large black SUV.

"Why is it always an SUV?" The operative wondered aloud as they approached. When they were a few paces away, the passenger side door opened to reveal a fifth man who leaned across from the driver's seat and stared expectantly at them.

"Did they put up a fight?" he asked. "Is that why you guys took so fucking long?"

He had no time to react when Savage yanked the gun away from the woman's back and pulled the trigger. The unsettling whoosh of the needle dragged magnetically through the elongated barrel fast enough to punch into the man's forehead. He dropped wordlessly in the driver's seat.

The operative turned the woman to face him. "Look, as of right now, you are as fucked as we are. If you head back and try to report what happened here to your employers, they will eliminate you. Nod if you understand."

She did.

"Your best chance at surviving from this point forward is to take this SUV, drive out to a swamp, dump the body, and disappear." His voice had taken on the cold, commanding quality of a man in a hurry and on a mission. "If I see you again, I will kill you. Do you understand?"

She nodded again.

"Do you think anything that I've said up until this point is a lie?"

She shook her head.

"Good." He appeared to believe her. "Now get in that SUV and get the fuck out of here."

She broke away from him quickly, scrambled into the vehicle, and shoved the body into the back seat. As deadly as the needle gun was, it didn't make much of a mess, which was another plus in Anderson's book. The door slammed behind her and she started the engine and peeled out of the garage.

"Do you really think she'll disappear?" Anderson asked as they removed the masks.

"If nothing else, it will keep her thinking long enough for us to disappear ourselves." He shook his head as he turned his pistol's safety on and tucked it into its holster. "It was either that or kill her, and I thought the two of you had a nice connection."

"Fuck off," his boss snapped.

"I've wiped you guys from the system and I turned the cameras off on the garage, so if you ladies are done hugging it out, I think it's time to get out now." Anja sounded more professional than usual.

"Will do, Control," Savage said with a grin as they jogged to the company car, fell inside, and he eased out of the parking space.

"What will police think when they don't find bullets in the bodies?" he asked. The automated garage system opened for them before they even reached it. "There can't be many people dead from splinters propelled at super-sonic speeds, right?"

"That is actually a fantastic question." Anderson looked intrigued.

The agent leaned back in his seat and checked to make sure they weren't joining the parade route before he pulled onto the road. "They've seemed content to blame all this shooting on gang violence, but at some point, they have to figure out that gangs aren't this well armed."

"I guess we'll have to have to cross that bridge when we get there." Anderson sighed. "I honestly don't look forward to that. Anyway, where to now?"

"Well, you heard her," Savage said. "The Research Triangle—this secret building, I mean—is only a couple of miles out of DC. Anja, can you run a trace on this little device she gave us?"

"Will do, once I'm finished wiping your faces off of every camera I can find." The hacker sounded unhappy. "I have software that's scoured the social media sites using face recognition, but I need to inspect each one manually before I tamper with it. It'll take me a while. Thanks for that, by the way. Couldn't you have kept your asses inside for the parade?"

"We'll make sure not to get involved in local festivities in the future."

His boss agreed, although his reasons probably differed from the other man's.

"I'm no good at this," Ivy complained. She yanked her ear muffs off and looked over to where her companion inspected the weapon she'd handed back.

Sam narrowed her eyes at the woman. She was doing reasonably well, all in all. You couldn't expect everyone to have the same proficiency as a trained professional, but the fact that she was surrounded by those and even had a husband who was Special Forces created lofty and frankly unrealistic expectations about where she should set her standard. She was more than comfortable telling her pupil that not getting her pistol shots into the ten-ring from thirty yards—or even the seven-ring—was perfectly acceptable. Frankly, she wasn't even sure she could pull that particular rabbit out of the hat every time.

She could get it right most times, but she'd been brought in as one of the best, after all. If she had to train a civilian, she couldn't have the woman thinking she needed to be a crack shot after only two or three weeks. Hell, Sam had been at it for most of her adult life.

Maybe she should have left the training to Terry. He was better at long-distance shooting than she was anyway. From what she'd heard from him and read in his file— provided to her by Anja—the man was something of a freak. He would hold Ivy to the kind of standards she held herself to and get her there in a shorter amount of time. Assuming the woman didn't simply quit out of frustration first.

"You simply need practice, girl," she said patiently and made sure the SIG's barrel had cooled before she disassembled the weapon quickly and placed the pieces on the small red felt blanket. "Look, you've been frustrated with shooting practice a lot lately. Why don't we move on to hand-to-hand? You're getting better at that part of it."

"I used to do PE." Ivy shook her head, clearly still irritated. "I guess I'm frustrated with other stuff and I feel it more when I'm on the range. I'm sorry."

"What has you frustrated?" Sam set the last piece in place and gave the other woman her full attention.

Ivy started to put the pistol back together, working

almost reflexively. They'd done this enough times for her to be able to do it without needing to pay attention, even if a couple of seconds could be shaved off if she did.

"I'm worried about Jim," she said softly. "It's not like him to not try to contact us, right?"

She nodded. "Savage has kept them busy and on the move too, remember. They need to stay one step ahead, and since keeping you and Damon safe is up to me and Terry, he shouldn't worry about you guys."

"You're not used to being in this position," the woman commented. "Having to comfort people in a bad situation?"

"I'm doing my best here."

"I know, I know. I'm sorry." The woman slid the last piece home and placed the weapon into her instructor's hands. "I haven't been the easiest person to babysit."

"Hey, I like a challenge." Sam handed her the magazine. The compact weapon held fifteen Parabellum rounds, which Ivy now loaded smoothly and precisely.

"If you really looked for a challenge, you wouldn't have worked as a babysitter," she retorted and finished with the loading before her companion handed the weapon back to her. Weapon safety had been drilled into Ivy for days before her instructor had let her shoot the damn thing. She checked that the manual safety was on before she slipped the loaded mag into it and nodded when the slider slipped forward to automatically chamber the top round. Satisfied, she aimed the pistol into the range, effectively pausing the conversation as earmuffs came on, and focused on the dummy down-range, still thirty paces away.

Fifteen rounds later, she'd gotten a little closer to the center but it was still a wide spread. Again, it wasn't at all bad for a beginner to hit a human-sized target in center mass from that range with a smaller pistol.

She still looked annoyed as the range was cleared and the other woman walked over to collect the paper target that had been taped onto the dummy, replacing it with a new one.

"Look…" Sam shook her head firmly as her pupil glared at the target like it owed her money. "Why don't we take a break from this for the rest of the day. Girls like shopping, right? We can go shopping or do something girls normally do."

"I'm not a big fan of shopping, actually."

"Thank God. Neither am I." She breathed a sigh of relief. "What do you like to do?"

"You'll laugh," Ivy grinned despite her residual irritation.

"I…can't promise that I won't, I suppose."

"Well, I happen to be a big football fan," she explained. "And there just so happens to be a football game happening tomorrow. Vikings and Eagles, right here in Philadelphia."

"Wait, you're talking about Handegg, aren't you?" Sam asked. "Because I grew up playing real football. You know, where you kick an actual ball around with your feet?"

"Well, Jim isn't that big a fan, but he got me some season tickets. I'm going to the game. You can come along, if you like, and see how a real sport is played—or to babysit."

Sam rolled her eyes. "Ugh, fine, if you insist. But I can't promise I'll enjoy it."

"Hey, if you're only doing your job, who says you have to enjoy it, right?" Ivy flashed her a challenging look.

"So long as you're paying for the food, I think I can find some way to enjoy myself. Handegg is the one where the blokes wear big padded armor and really tight trousers, yeah?"

"I...think so," Ivy said and narrowed her eyes.

"Like I said, I'm sure I'll find some way to enjoy myself." Sam grinned. "Now, try the target one more time and we'll give you some knife practice."

CHAPTER TWENTY-FIVE

Savage looked around the plane with a sense of real bemusement. He still couldn't wrap his head around people flying on planes they had rented for themselves. It was such an odd, weird strata above his usual station. He could see the appeal of it, of course. He'd flown coach more times than he could count, and it wasn't a picnic. You got to your seat—that was only wide enough to hold someone his size while severely lacking in leg space—and were stuck with one and sometimes two people. It was like the weirdest kind of lottery since that person or those people were randomly selected and would be who he would share that ridiculous space smaller than most beds for the duration of the flight.

Not here, though. Here, he shared a space larger than most New York Apartments with only one other person. Well, technically, it was with four other people if he counted the pilot, co-pilot, and stewardess, but was he really supposed to count staff in the number?

Staff? He felt a little disgusted at the thought. It was

such a bourgeois way to think about people. How sickening was that?

Anderson stepped out of the cockpit and strolled to the passenger seats. He settled comfortably on the one across from him.

"Well, we should land in a couple of hours," the former colonel said as he shifted a little and stretched his legs. "I explained that we had to take a couple of detours. The pilot said he didn't need to know why, winked at me, and added that 'bitches be crazy.'"

"He thinks you're cheating on your wife and you're flicking around the country to throw her off your trail," Savage said with a nod. "I assume these pilots have to deal with more than a few promiscuous husbands."

"Fuck, that's what I thought," his companion agreed.

"Come on. It's not like he'll go over to Ivy's place to have a little chat about what you've done or anything," he pointed out.

"It still pisses me off that people take one look at me and assume I'm some sort of high-baller businessman." The man shook his head with real disgust. "Especially not the kind that flies around the country to tag with his various mistresses."

"Not to play devil's advocate or anything," Savage said but sounded like that was exactly what he would do. "But you are the CEO of a Fortune Five-hundred company with government connections and all, and you fly around on a private jet. So you are, technically, the kind of high-baller businessman kind of man they think you are. Just saying."

Anderson shook his head and leaned forward. "What do

you know about the Research Triangle?" he asked and changed the subject.

"Absolutely nothing." He made a face. "Army Rangers don't actually have much connection with the scientific side of the military spectrum. Even the ones working with special forces. The only one I ever heard of was the area in North Carolina—which is what I imagine most people will think of when they hear the name."

"That's the beauty of it." Anderson nodded but his expression was unusually grim. "Aside from the obvious play on the research theme and the actual shape of the building, the name itself is what guarantees its continued secrecy. No one who isn't actually in the know would even suspect that it was either a building or located in DC."

Savage smirked. "I can buy that. It has all the makings of governmental conspiracy. So okay, Mr. Former Colonel, sir, what do you know about this damned Research Triangle?"

"Well, considering I had a much higher security clearance than yours, I'll say a fucking lot more than you."

"Yeah, yeah, yuck it up," Savage rumbled. "What do you know about the place?"

"It's the research building that's officially tied to the Pentagon," Anderson explained. "It has a really long name officially, but it's known as the Research Triangle as we've already explained."

"Sure," Savage agreed. People who nicknamed government buildings weren't exactly known for their creativity, after all, even if they had certain nefarious purposes that their pretense actually served very well.

"Right. Anyway, that's where they send all their internalized research," Anderson continued. "They keep most of their staff there too, which means that if anyone reports to someone there, they report to someone who works directly for the Department of Defense."

"Okay, so let me get this straight." The operative raised his hand, his frown evidence of his deep thought. "Our target—the person who is working for this Charles guy or who could give us what we need to eliminate him—will be working inside a government facility, yeah?"

"Correct."

"And we assume he knows who we are—or who you are, anyway, by probably me as well by now—and has been tasked with killing us. Given that, walking in with Anja'd-up papers is probably out of the picture, right?" His frown slid into a deeper scowl. "Oh, and let's not forget that the building houses top-level clearance research. I assume—since they're downsizing and leaving some of the secret research to the companies that have lobbyists in all the right places—they'll have the dual security threat of both top-level corporations and the worst of the most paranoid government officials?"

"I..." Anderson looked a little startled but tried to follow Savage's logic. "Sure...yeah, that sounds about right."

"Awesome." Savage laughed. "And we'll still break into this top-of-the-top-of-the-line secure building without any open means of ingress and with our target waiting for us and knowing at least one of our faces. That's no biggie, I guess."

"I can see you don't have much confidence in this plan

of ours," his boss challenged. It was fairly obvious that he had a few doubts of his own as well.

"So, what are we thinking in terms of solutions for our problems? The whole situation is just begging for an underdog story."

"We are the underdogs in this story, right?" Anderson asked.

"Obviously."

"Well, not to toot my own horn here, but you under-dogs have one hell of a secret weapon," Anja piped up.

"She's talking about her, isn't she?" the ex-colonel asked.

"Yeah."

"Shut it," the hacker said crisply. "Unless the two of you think you can charge into the Triangle by yourselves?"

"No, we obviously don't think that, Control." Savage shifted in his seat and smiled. She liked the nickname and considering that she had been there for him more consistently than anyone else in the world, he liked to reward her now and then. If they were in a face-to-face kind of relationship, he would have suggested they go out for a drink and maybe catch a football game. But with their parameters being what they were, he had to get the small things in when he could.

And from her tone of voice, he could tell his nickname had the effect he'd intended.

"Well, considering you two couldn't get in there without my help anyway, I think it's smart of you to admit it."

"So, do you have a way for us to get in?" Anderson asked. He really needed to move on to something concrete

—and doable, hopefully. "Can you get us through all the hardware they have around the building?"

"Yes," she replied with far more confidence than Savage thought she should have. "Although it'll be a little unorthodox and less pleasant as ways of entry generally go."

"Is it worse than trekking through hours of blinding sunlight out in the middle of the Nevada desert?" Savage asked. "Because been there and done that. I don't want to do it again, but I'm perfectly willing."

"Considering they don't have deserts in the Washington DC area, I think having the two of you trekking through the desert, as you say, is off the table. Unfortunately, that's the good news in the good-news, bad-news tandem."

"What's the bad news?" He was almost afraid to ask.

"Well, a host of old sewer tunnels run beneath the building," the hacker said cheerfully. "I'll send you the precise maps, but given the size of that building and the fact that they haven't built anything beyond chemical vats to contain the hazardous waste coming from that place, you can assume the sewers will be in use. While they should be large enough for you to walk through, you will be walking through...well, you know, sewage."

"Fan-fucking-tastic." Savage rolled his eyes. It wouldn't be his first time to infiltrate a building via the sewer system—and in some of the countries where he'd done it, the sewer systems didn't have any of the guidelines they had in the US. That had inevitably meant he'd spent hours crawling through duct-size tunnels of gross. He'd needed scuba gear to get through it, but he'd done it. Never let it be said that Jeremiah Savage couldn't handle getting his hands dirty.

"It can't be worse than the Nevada desert, right?" Anderson asked stoically.

"That's a seriously weird choice of last words, but okay." The operative grinned and pressed the button that lowered his seat into a prone position. He intended to get a nap in. The new painkillers were hell on his body clock.

There was an old saying—it never rains, but it pours. Charles couldn't help but feel it applied in this particular situation. He didn't usually like to base his business practices on anecdotes but, as with most things, they seemed to have their place and their time.

Anderson was a slippery bastard. He was only now coming to realize how slippery. Word about the man breaking into one of the Nevada facilities had been cast aside, initially, until other information about recovered property finding its way into a Pegasus location had reached his ears through various sources. The attempts to retrieve it—or at least slow its acquisition down—had failed miserably. Ultimately, it had ended with the man whom he'd sent to take care of it in jail after a brawl and his asset in the wind.

News about how the attempt on Anderson's life in New Orleans had also ended badly had left Charles wondering if the entire proposition wasn't merely cursed from the beginning. He was a dyed-in-the-wool skeptic who didn't believe in ridiculous things like curses. But when things went this bad so often, it was difficult to resist the impulse to think that some kind of higher power had interfered in his business.

Of course, resist it he would. And well, too. Covington had been arrogant when she'd tried to handle Courtney on her own. Carlson had been too engaged in saving his legacy in the company to be able to enforce his will properly. Charles lacked the encumbrances and distractions of his predecessors. He had underestimated Anderson too, but he wouldn't make that mistake again. Tying the attack back to Haynes had been a mistake, but it wasn't a complete loss. The man at least knew well enough to hire from the outside.

But as of right now, he needed someone on the inside. He needed a professional.

Charles took another sip of his bourbon and scowled when he noticed the ice inside had already begun to melt. He hated that because it diluted the burn as it rushed down his throat. With an exaggerated sigh of irritation, he picked up his encrypted phone and quickly punched in a number that he'd dialed a lot over the past couple of weeks.

The tone twisted and whirred as it settled into the encrypted channels he always used to handle this kind of sordid business, and after a few seconds, it dialed the number.

He actually startled when he heard a phone ring directly outside his office. A man stood over his secretary but spun aside and now walked toward the semi-transparent glass doors of his office.

His secretary complained and protested vociferously, but the visitor simply ignored her.

Finally, she decided to get a jump on the situation, stormed toward the office herself, and opened the door.

She looked flushed and frustrated—not her best look, he realized—as she stepped inside and barely moved out of the way as the behemoth maintained his direct path into the office.

"I'm sorry Mr. Stafford—he insisted," she said, her frustration rampant. "Do you want me to call security?"

Charles honestly pitied the men who would try to throw the man out of a building.

"That's quite all right, Alicia," he said. He shrugged and replaced his phone in its cradle. "I was actually calling Mr. Kelly for a conversation. Why don't you take an early day? Get a jump start on the long weekend?"

"Are you sure, Mr. Stafford?" She glanced hesitantly from her boss to the giant who regarded her with a faintly amused expression.

"Of course. Have a nice weekend, dear." He smiled as she made her exit.

"You called?" Kelly asked once the door had shut behind her.

"I'm sorry about that." Charles gestured for his visitor to take a seat. "She's a good girl and a good worker, and has an ass that won't quit, but she's a little difficult to handle sometimes."

The other man smiled, looked around, and decided against taking a seat. It was probably a wise decision as it was actually doubtful that the small chairs in the office could support his weight. As he moved in closer, though, the evidence that he'd taken something of a beating became very clear. Bruising had barely begun to recede in his cheek, and a bandage covered what looked like a broken nose.

"You don't need to apologize to me, Mr. Stafford," Kelly said in response with that unnervingly calm and quiet voice. "Shall we get to business? I assume you called me for a reason, so I'll let you speak first."

Charles smiled and set the very natural questions about the man's face aside for the moment. "Anderson has proved to be a bigger and more annoying problem than I thought he would, and that's a conservative deduction. I think we need to update the contract on him. Expand it and put more money on it. I want as many bodies on this as possible."

"Of course, Mr. Stafford," Kelly said. "I agree that an update would have been necessary—as well raising the price—regardless of what problems Anderson might cause you."

"What do you mean?"

"Well, I think you know by now, but I've had a run in with the muscle Anderson has brought into his fold." He touched his bruised face lightly. "Knowing what I know now, I think I understand why Carlson had such trouble handling your man."

"The muscle?" Charles asked and frowned as he considered this. "He did that to you?"

"I can assure you that I gave better than I got, Mr. Stafford, but that's not the point." He still sounded like nothing would ever force him to raise his voice. "The point is that the man Anderson brought in to keep him safe is smart. He's reliable and well-trained—former military, obviously—and might be one of his friends from the

Marine Corps, although I have some doubts considering his particular fighting style. Army, I'd say. Upper-tier, though. Green Berets, at least, but most likely a Ranger."

"You could tell where he's trained from his fighting style?" He quirked an eyebrow, not quite sure whether to believe this.

"It's a very distinctive style," Kelly replied with a small smile. "With that in mind and considering that the two appear to work in tandem, I'd say you would have to pay better to get the kind of personnel with the necessary skills interested in the mission. Either that or simply have the sheer number of people that might enable you to get lucky."

Charles nodded. He took another sip of his drink before he sighed softly. "Fine. Double the price on Anderson's head—and maybe add a little extra if they manage to eliminate the muscle as well. I want to know more about this guy, but Anderson is still the priority. I don't care about the fees. Get this shit done today. I'm tired of it."

Kelly nodded and tweaked his suit nonchalantly to straighten its perfect lines. "Consider it done, Mr. Stafford."

CHAPTER TWENTY-SIX

It was quiet—too quiet, almost. He studied the very confined space and made a face. The sewer tunnels weren't as cramped as he'd thought they would be, but the decision to bring masks was a good one. It had been Anderson's idea, of course. Savage had thought he could cope without too much trouble.

He'd been proven wrong and damned if he didn't know when to admit it. Even with the masks on, the place was a terrifyingly inhuman place to be. They both wore plastic suits that were supposed to keep the sewage and the smell away from them. They helped a little, obviously, but he still felt like he would never be clean again.

Behind him, Anderson muttered a curse when he slipped but managed to regain his balance. A fall was the only thing worse than having to walk through the nightmare.

"I bet you didn't think you would do any climbing through sewers when you were offered that CEO job, huh?" Savage grinned.

"I knew from the start it wouldn't be a cushy desk job," his boss admitted and shook his hand to remove some of the grime that had gathered on his rubber glove when he'd caught himself from falling. "But to answer your question, no, I did not think I would trudge through sludge, much less break into a government facility through their sewers. You'd think they would have some sort of security system in place down here to keep exactly what's happening from happening."

"There is," Anja interjected, and Savage had to literally flail to prevent himself from faceplanting in sewage.

"I will never get used to that," he complained.

She continued to talk like she hadn't heard him. "Those wires you can see running along both sides of the tunnels there work as antennae for the drones they send down there for maintenance, but they also work as hyper-sensitive motion sensors. However, instead of setting the sensors to automatically activate an alarm, they put them to register on a marker in their system and they send a drone to automatically investigate. All I really had to do was follow the line until I found a weakness in their system. I've intercepted all the alert messages since you got down there."

"While I do appreciate the lucky break involved," Anderson said stiffly, "that kind of alert system isn't used very often in government buildings. It's definitely not used in the buildings that have as much classified shit as the Triangle, so why are they down to this now?"

The hacker paused for a moment, apparently searching through any kind of database to find the answer to his question. Savage shook his head. He hadn't even thought of that. He had started to get a little too used to having Anja cover his ass and might have grown a little sloppy after all this time. He needed to shape up or he would be caught with his metaphorical pants down and with nobody to help him.

She wouldn't cover for him for the rest of his life. He couldn't get used to having her in his ear.

"Okay, it looks like they only activated this new system a couple of months ago," Anja advised them. "They constantly received false alarms they couldn't track, so they made the whole system double back into the security network."

"Is there anything in there about what actually triggers the alarms?" Anderson looked thoughtful.

"I don't know—a software glitch or something? I could look around for it, but that would expose it to them too, and as of right now, we need this to be as broken as hell. Why are you looking a gift horse in the mouth?"

"So the horse doesn't bite me in the ass later on," Savage grumbled under his breath.

"I heard that," she snapped.

"I said it aloud, didn't I?" he replied with a grin.

"If you two could keep your lovers' quarrels to a minimum?" It seemed like the former colonel was a little on edge although there was no indication what annoyed him to the point of lashing out. It could have been his and Anja's bickering, of course, but he wondered if there wasn't some kind underlying cause to his annoyance. He had been far away from his wife and kid for a while now and having a kill order hanging over your head was never a pleasant experience. The man needed to lighten up a little. Maybe they could go out and get a drink together after the mission was done. Chatting over beers would help him get over his homesickness.

Savage suddenly froze in place. His body told him something, but it took him a couple of seconds to realize what it was. The first hint that something was off was the change in the color palette around him. He wasn't quite sure why that was what he'd chosen to focus on. Their flashlights were powerful enough to give them a good view of where they were going, but everything that wasn't the dull grey concrete of the sewer tunnels had been black until the odd hints of blue and green that now spread across the walls.

"Anderson?" Savage gestured around them. "Do you see this or am I going crazy? A stroke, maybe?"

"Are you talking about the change in colors of the moss on the tunnels?" The other man swept his flashlight across the walls. "No, you're not having a stroke. The jury's still out on the crazy, though."

"Hilarious." He refocused on his surroundings and a sense of dread slowly filled him. He couldn't explain it, but with every step he took, the voice in his head grew louder and louder. And no, it wasn't the usual voice in his head. That one had a Russian accent.

An inner prompting overrode his logic and told him to turn and walk away.

A hesitation in Anderson's body language told him the man had a similar feeling.

When they reached a corner in the tunnels, a soft, repetitive clicking emanated from the way ahead. The operative held his fist up and signaled for his companion to stop.

"Hey, so...Anja," he said, his voice pitched as low as he could. "About those alarms being tripped..."

"What about them?" she asked seriously. She'd obviously sensed the dread in his voice. "If there is some sort of invasive plant species growing down there, it could have compromised the wiring in the tunnel walls."

"I'm starting to think it was something a little more mobile than your average mushroom colony," Savage grumbled and fumbled in his suit to draw his pistol. He wasn't sure what it was, but he knew he didn't want to meet something that clicked like that. From the sound of it, the whatever it was didn't want to meet him either. It sounded suspiciously like a rattlesnake's warning to stay away.

Unfortunately, there was no way for them to get into the Triangle but through...whatever it was, regardless of whether they intruded on its territory or not.

Something cold swept over him as he started to move forward against every warning in his gut telling him not to. Anderson followed close behind, having drawn his own weapon and tucked it over his flashlight. There was no way to know if guns would be necessary, and they would both feel foolish if it turned out to be rats. But feeling foolish was fine if they were alive to do so.

And...well, what they found could be described as some kind of rat. Maybe.

"What the fuck?" he asked.

Anderson didn't say anything as their flashlight illuminated a creature about the size of a Great Dane. The protruding jaw and elongated incisors along with the grey fur mottled across its back were rat-like, but that was where the similarities ended. The legs were long and attached higher on the body like an insect's, although there were only four of them. The tail hung over its body with a rattle at the end, which quivered as the clicking grew louder.

"Seriously, what the actual fuck?" Savage said again. The creature looked as surprised to see them as they were to see it, and after a moment during which all three stared at one another, it voiced a screeching roar. The bottom half of its jaw split down the middle to reveal a pair of fangs that seemed to actually elongate as the monster attacked.

"Shit!" Anderson yelled, and Savage raised his weapon and pulled the trigger. The first needle drilled through the creature's forehead but showed no sign of stopping it. Without even slowing, it barreled across the ten paces or so between them in the tight, claustrophobic tunnels. He squeezed the trigger a few more times and the needles rocketed into the monster's head over and over with no apparent effect. Anderson's weapon fired consistently from a few paces behind him, but his bullets proved as ineffectual.

The creature maintained its furious assault and he flung himself to the right to avoid it. The other man dodged left and they cleared enough space for the creature to upend them as it careened past.

Something slashed across his cheek and he recoiled

instinctively. The lethal tail whipped past him as he pushed himself around the spindly legs while he maintained his fire. The rounds finally seemed to have an effect and blood had started to flow from its various wounds. Its legs struggled to find purchase on the sludgy ground. The two men maintained their barrage and it finally dropped to screech and roar in distress.

Savage scrambled to his feet and stood over the monster that now writhed in pain. He raised his weapon and pulled the trigger a couple more times, aimed at where he assumed the brain would be, and it fell still.

Chittering from behind him dragged his attention from the dead creature and he spun as a group of smaller versions of the monster hurtled off in the opposite direction. Its young, he supposed in a kind of shocked stupor, and while the mother defended her brood, the offspring themselves would flee the attackers.

Anderson looked oddly at him and narrowed his eyes as he moved to offer a hand to help him up.

"What did you do that for?" he asked as he took his hand and found his feet.

"It was a mercy killing," he pointed out. He removed the chamber on his pistol to check how many needles he still had in the strip he currently used. It was enough—a good five or six magazines' worth. "Whatever the fuck that was, it was an animal defending its territory. We needed to go through it to complete our mission, so we did. It doesn't mean we have to leave it bleeding and dying out here, much less deal with the young."

Anderson nodded. "I understand that. But...Anja, did you see that?"

"There are no cameras down there, so no," she replied. "What was it?"

"It looked like a giant crossbreed between a rat and some kind of insect."

"Don't forget the tail," Savage reminded him. "The tail had a rattler like a rattlesnake, and it..." He touched the cut on his cheek.

"Right, the tail. Do you know if any of the Research Triangle projects are dealing with anything from the Zoo? Anything at all?"

"What does this have to do..." Savage started to ask, but he paused. He'd seen the videos. The monsters had always seemed to be a nightmarish form of the animals that lived on earth. If anything could explain what the hell they'd just seen, it was that. "Wait, you're telling me it was a Zoo monster?"

"Well, technically, it was a sewer monster," his boss said. "But the same principle applies, I guess. By that I mean it comes from the same source."

"Oh, shit." He shook his head and dropped to his haunches beside the creature. The blood seeping out from the dozen or so wounds across its body was a dark blue—or maybe purple. The flashlight didn't do a great job of showing it well.

"Oh shit is right," Anderson hissed. "How the fuck are there goop animals in the sewers? In the States?"

"If they were running tests on Zoo stuff, I guess that would explain how," Anja said. "But these places have some secure ways to dispose of waste. You wouldn't simply wash your hands. They went through some rigorous processes to make sure nothing got out."

"Courtney tells me that all it takes is a couple of cells," Anderson grumbled and patted his companion on the back. "One mistake, one guy cutting corners because he had a hot date and a timeline... Considering she's studied this stuff for a while, I'd say she knows her stuff."

"Dr. Monroe knows all the ways this goop can kill us. Got it." Savage pushed up from his examination of the creature. "The fact that we have this stuff out in the wild—and here—has me worried. I thought we were putting all kinds of work into isolating the problem in the Sahara. Knowing that it's all the way out here and simply waiting for a mistake..."

He let his words trail off. He'd seen the kind of monsters people faced in the Zoo. Only videos, of course. From what he'd read on Anderson, the man had a closer look. Dr. Monroe and her Heavy Metal team had far more than that. Even based on the little he knew, having critters like that rushing into heavily populated areas would end badly. Very badly.

"We need to alert these people about what they have growing in their basement," he said as they started to move again. "You know, once we're finished with all this crap. Just make sure their drones come down here with flamethrowers or something and tear this whole place apart. We don't need a Zoo Two: The Zoo goes to Washington situation on our hands."

"Agreed," Anderson said almost under his breath. "For now, though, we need to get through this damned sewer, into the Triangle, get our intel, and get out. So, Anja, do you have any changes on our vector?"

"Nope," she replied. "Keep moving forward and you should reach your destination in about half a mile."

"Let's keep moving. And keep our weapons out in case we run into a daddy rat-insect that doesn't like the fact that we killed mother dearest."

His companion nodded grimly. Not that he needed the reminder. He would have kept his gun out anyway.

CHAPTER TWENTY-SEVEN

"I'll never get the smell of sewer off me," Savage complained in a low tone as he peered around the lab Anja's entrance had led them into. They'd removed the rubber hazmat suits they'd worn, but something unpleasant still lingered. He wondered if it would always linger for the rest of his days.

Anderson wore the scrunched-up look that said he had a similar problem. They were dressed in combat gear with the body armor given to them by Pegasus, and both carried weapons. Just because they were inside didn't mean they wouldn't run into any resistance. They were there after hours, but there would still be security prowling around the place.

He didn't want to have to kill anyone, though. That was why Anja had them enter to retrieve the intel during the off hours.

There seemed to be no way to actually ignore the stink that clung to every fiber of their being. He managed to stop himself dragging in a deep breath and instead, rolled his shoulders and sighed heavily.

"We need to keep moving," Anderson said softly. There hadn't been much conversation between them the rest of the way through the tunnels. Neither of them wanted to talk about what they'd seen down there. The fact that this stuff was shipped out to every corner of the globe and that it could actually do the same thing it did in the Zoo was something they both needed time to digest.

"I'm wondering, though," Savage finally said as they hurried on through the triangular building. "That seems like an odd combination, right? Insects, rats...sure, okay, but a rattlesnake? Where did that come from?"

His companion shrugged. "I won't pretend to know anything about anything but given that they test the stuff for human use, it's possible that the combination of insect, rat, and reptile might have something to do with that. This goop...learns. It adapts and soaks in any DNA that it has been subjected to and extrapolates from it and builds on it. From what I've seen in the Zoo, it tests and tries things out. I don't know how it works, but it's effective."

"Obviously." His chuckle was dark and humorless. "However much of it that came down was enough to start a whole mushroom farm and bring that monstrosity to life, and then it had babies. So—"

"We're pretty damn fucked," his boss interrupted.

"Well, I was going for something more elegant than that, but that works, yeah," he agreed. "Back on topic, though. Anja, do you have any idea where we're going?"

"Well, we're working off the tracker you picked up from that merc you so mercifully released," she replied and sounded a little more subdued than usual. "I have it down to an IP address, but it's basically shared with the whole wing of the building. You'll need to do some physical investigation when you get there."

"Well, is there any way to narrow it down?" he asked and scanned the hallway they were in. "I don't know if you've noticed, but this place is kind of huge."

"Don't get sassy with me now, Jer." She chuckled. "You boys are in the right wing, but you need to look for a room with the name Brian Haynes on the door. It's from his office."

The operative nodded and glanced at a camera he didn't doubt she already had access to.

"You're looking as hot as ever, Jer. You might want to rethink the haircut, though."

"I cut my own hair," he protested.

"Yep, that's what I mean. Okay, I have access to the building details. It looks like Mr. Haynes is on the second floor. Room 207. Chop chop, boys."

"Who is this Haynes guy?" Anderson asked when they found the stairs.

"A low-level bureaucrat—a glorified accountant from the looks of things," the hacker replied. "Exactly the kind of man who would fly low enough on the radar to allow him to get away with this kind of shit."

"It sounds like our kind of guy." Savage guided them onto the second floor and located the room in question. He was the first through the door and secured the darkened office before he called Anderson in and turned the lights on.

"Okay, Anja, what are we looking for?"

"The office computer is where everything will be stored," Anja explained. "I can't access it from here, so you two will have to run through everything yourselves. Just make it all easily accessible, and I'll take it from there."

"I don't think she trusts us." He grinned.

"Well, I leave all the shooting and breaking bones to you guys, don't I?" she reminded him as Anderson turned the computer on. "Leave all the IT stuff to someone who knows what they're doing, okay?"

"On that topic, can you crack the computer pass—oh, never mind." The ex-colonel let his words trail off when he saw she had already broken in.

"Like I said, leave it to the professionals." She sounded smug. "Savage, keep an eye outside and make sure nobody walks in on you guys. The second floor is in a camera blind spot. Budget cuts, I'm afraid. You'll have to be my eyes and ears."

He didn't say anything as he moved toward the door. They'd left it cracked, which made it easy to monitor the corridor. To be safe, Savage turned the light in the office off. There was no sense in giving their position away.

"Is Savage sulking?" the hacker asked, presumably of Anderson, who tapped the keyboard.

"I think he doesn't want to tell you how awesome you are," the man replied without looking away from the screen. "He doesn't want to inflate your ego or something. And yes...maybe a little sulking."

Savage flipped the man off to avoid saying anything aloud. He was sulking—only a little—but a hint of worry nagged at the back of his mind.

"What's up, Savage?" she asked. "Don't worry, I've given

Anderson a list of things to do and we're on a private connection. Tell him you're going to secure the hall."

He nodded. "Hey, I'll make sure that none of our security pals are coming this way."

The other man remained focused on the screen as the operative stepped out of the room and closed the door before he moved down the hall. He positioned himself closer to the stairs and elevators so he could keep an ear out for anybody approaching.

"Are you alone?" she asked.

"Yeah."

"I know we didn't have the kind of relationship where we can talk about things before," she said tentatively. "But...well, I think we've grown closer over the past few weeks, and if you feel like the whole situation needs to be talked about... Well then, maybe...you know."

"I appreciate it, Anja," he said softly and leaned against the wall. "It's just a thing, I guess."

"Wow, that's a little too specific for me." She chuckled but sounded oddly nervous.

He smiled in response. "Yeah... It's...uh, the whole Zoo animal thing. Not that I have a phobia of Zoo animals or anything. You know what I mean, right?"

"Right, a monster straight out of the Zoo is a little hard to handle," she agreed.

"It's not only that," Savage said. "I don't want to say something and come off as a coward. I stayed clear of the Zoo for a reason. I can handle humans and the atrocities that come with them. Shooting people isn't difficult once you realize how terrible they are. But the animals...that's a whole other ballgame. Not only is it terrifying, but if I wanted to shoot animals all day, I wouldn't have gone into the military."

"I think I get that." He recognized the background noise that he had come to associate with her leaning back and the seat groaning loudly in protest. "It's a whole different ballgame."

"It's probably stupid," he grumbled and folded his arms. "But combat is a mental game more than anything else, and I would be out of my depth. It's…different. There's something in me that makes me feel like there would be a block. Kind of like a writer's block, but for shooting things."

"Oh, well, that makes sense." She didn't sound even a little sarcastic, which worried him more than he would have cared to admit. "Anderson's calling you back into the office."

"Right." He straightened quickly. "Thanks for the talk. And thanks in advance for keeping it between you and me."

"That depends. Will you buy me something pretty for my silence?" she asked as he moved toward the door.

"Well, I won't buy a bullet with your name on it," he offered.

"Ah, the gift that keeps on giving." The hacker sighed. "Deal."

He nodded and stepped into the office where Anderson was still working on the computer.

"Were you talking to yourself?" the former colonel asked and looking at Savage, who merely pointed at his ear in response. "Oh, right. Anyway, I finished transferring all the files to Anja and thought you might want a quick look at this."

The operative circled behind the desk to see what the

other man stared at. A picture of a man displayed on the screen, older and dressed in a golfing outfit. He was talking to someone they recognized very easily.

"The big guy from the bar—what was his name?" Savage asked.

"Mr. Kelly. And do you recognize this guy he's talking to?"

Savage leaned in and narrowed his eyes. "He does look familiar. I think he was at one of the board meetings. Older guy, sticks to himself for the most part."

"Charles Stafford, one of the oldest members of the board. He's been around forever, almost since the founding."

"So that's our elusive Charles, huh? I don't know why, but I thought he would be taller."

"Kelly over there is tall enough for the both of them," Anderson pointed out. "My question is, why does some low-level government accountant who plays middle-man to shady deals for extra cash have this picture on his computer?"

"Blackmail material?" Savage asked with a shrug. "Kelly has to have some shady connections. Putting those two together can't be the best situation for Charles, not with how the guy is attached to his squeaky-clean image."

"We already know that Charles is the man behind this. We now also know his connection to Kelly—which links him to our friend Chance. We should be able to handle him."

"Well, handling him is one thing," Anderson pointed out. "Lifting the price he has on my head is quite another.

We need to have a game plan that might kill two birds with one stone."

"That we do. But for now, we have what we need, right?"

"I have it all here," Anja confirmed. "You boys are good to go, and the security guys don't do their rounds for another half hour at least. Get out of there."

"Back into the sewers we go." Anderson forced a chipper tone as he shut the computer down.

Charles looked up as Kelly stepped back into his office for the second time in as many days—which was annoying enough on its own, but it was also necessary. There wouldn't be time for anyone to deliver these kinds of messages, and Kelly's voice was so unnerving on the phone.

The man tilted his head in query when his host moved to the mini fridge in the corner of his office, retrieved a bottle of water, and poured some into a glass. He pulled a small tablet from inside his coat pocket and dropped it inside.

"The damn motherfuckers are giving me ulcers," he hissed by way of an explanation as he sipped the medicine-infused water before he returned his stare to the giant of a man standing across from him.

"You called me," he said and folded his massive arms across his equally huge chest. "What can I do for you, Mr. Stafford?"

"They got to that dumbass Haynes somehow," Charles said with a significant glare. "He was both stupid and paranoid, a very dangerous combination. Apparently, he thought he might cover his ass by collecting incriminating evidence of our work together."

"How do you know about it?"

"You have your contacts and I have mine," he said dismissively. "But in the interests of collaboration, let's say I have an IT person who owes me a favor or two. I collect by making sure he keeps an eye on Haynes and other persons of interest. He has installed spyware on the man's system—I don't understand the ins and outs of it but it's apparently cutting-edge, undetectable, and monitors his usage and communication. That was how we discovered the evidence he has compiled. More importantly, however, he received an alert of unscheduled usage. It appears that someone—and we have to assume our particular someones —raided his office after hours and copied files from his computer."

"Is security aware of this?" Kelly asked.

"I do have a pet security guard—low on the food chain but eager to please—whom I approached. Security is blissfully unaware of any intrusion, but it would appear that their footage is conveniently missing." He took another sip from his glass and grimaced before he returned to his desk. "It's them. No doubts about it. The only question is what the fuck are you doing to fix this problem?"

"My options are limited by your budget," the other man pointed out.

"Double the money," Charles snapped. "No, triple it. I want every person with a gun and a need for money to hunt these fuckers now." What was a paltry three million in the bigger scheme of things?

His visitor nodded. "I'll handle it personally, Mr. Stafford."

He watched the man leave and glared at the glass in his hand. He would give anything for it to be bourbon, but his doctor had told him that alcohol would only make the ulcers worse. He needed to reduce his intake of fat, alcohol, and stress.

Well, so far, it was two out of three.

CHAPTER TWENTY-EIGHT

The smell would never wash off.

Savage scowled at the clothes he'd placed in the bags the hotel provided for guests who requested dry cleaning. He wished the people involved all the luck in the world, but he wondered if they wouldn't simply throw the garments into an incinerator and eat the charges that came with him trying to get his clothes back.

He wouldn't blame them. The fact that he'd worn a rubber suit throughout the trip somehow hadn't helped with the smell. The only problem, of course, was that he'd worn his body armor underneath, and that couldn't be dry cleaned or scrubbed. While the fewer fibers would make the smell less pungent, it was still there.

From his fairly limited experience with the gear—and the hasty glance he'd had at the manual back at the warehouse—the armor was strictly wash by hand, which he had started to do in the shower. It smelled of cheap yet strong motel soap now, but time would tell if their adventures down under would have a lasting effect on it.

Thankfully, he'd brought spare clothes that didn't smell of toilet, which he quickly pulled on. Anderson needed time off, a fair amount of venting, and a little alcohol, and damned if he wouldn't get it to him.

He stepped out of his room and moved to the one across from his, where he knocked three times on the door.

His boss opened it and narrowed his eyes when he saw him standing there. "What's up? Is everything okay?"

"Oh, yeah. I thought you might appreciate going out for the night, getting your drink on, and lightening up."

"I think I'd rather get some sleep."

"Come on, man." He fixed the man with a firm look. "It's been a stressful few days. I say we get the fuck out of this depressing hotel and find someplace to have a quiet drink and something to eat. Nothing fancy but enough to kick back and relax a little. It'll do us both good to do something halfway normal for once, and if we keep a low profile, it'll be safe enough."

Anderson considered it for a moment, then shrugged. "Okay, I'm sold. I'm just...I need to get some clothes on."

"What were you—no, you know what, I don't want to know." He closed his eyes and shook his head vehemently.

"I was taking a shower, asshole," the man snapped. "Meet me downstairs in the car."

"Yeah, right. I'm your babysitter, remember? That means I sit until the baby's ready."

Anderson slid into their booth and set two beers on the table. "So you're telling me that you wouldn't be fit for combat in the Zoo? Is that it? How does that add up?"

"It's doubt, man," Savage replied and drew his beer over. "I'm not sure that if I stood up against one of those monsters, I'd be any good. And that doubt is enough for me to realize I might not have what it takes to be good enough in the Zoo."

"You took on that critter in the sewer well enough," he pointed out.

"It was reflex. I simply didn't have time to think about it and had the gun out. When I have time to think about it, the doubt kills me. The point is, I like animals better than I like humans. That's why I'm so much better at killing people."

"You like me well enough, right?"

"There are always exceptions that prove the rule. I like Anja well enough too."

The ex-colonel chuckled softly. "So, is that the reason why you wanted to come out for a drink? To talk about your feelings?"

"Hey, you were the one who asked why she wanted me outside for a minute," he replied. "No, the drink is because...well, you seem like you've had a rough time lately, and I thought you might want to take some time to unwind."

He smirked and shifted into a comfortable slouch. "Don't think I don't appreciate it. And yeah, I do miss Ivy and Damon. I was getting used to being around them a lot more lately, but it's not like I don't enjoy what we're doing here."

"Well, the point is we both need to relax. Here's to unwinding." He raised his glass and clinked it softly against his companion's. "That means no talking about the job, no reminiscing about any old days, or dreaming about times gone by. We drink and let the night play out. One night with nothing on the agenda, what do you say? People think you're having a vacation anyway, so you might as well enjoy it a little. As long as we don't lose sight of why we're out here ducking from all those idiots who want you dead, we should be golden."

"Yeah, whatever you say. Let's finish this beer and we'll see how it goes from here, what do you say? I didn't feel like getting all heavy with the emotions tonight anyway."

"That sounds suspiciously like a plan."

They sat in silence for a while, simply enjoying the drink and the quiet ambiance. Halfway through the mug, Anderson jumped a little before he pulled a vibrating phone out that displayed a blocked number.

"Should I answer it?" he asked. Savage had already finished his beer and his fingers tapped on the empty glass as he considered the question.

"Anja said she encrypted our lines, so it should be safe. Either way, keep the call short, eh?"

He nodded and pressed the accept call button. "Hello? Oh…hi, baby. It's so good to hear your voice again."

"Baby?" Savage mouthed.

"Ivy," Anderson spelled out silently.

"Speak of the devil," the operative said a little louder than he should have.

"Oh, yeah, that's Savage…what? No, we were talking about you and then you called, that's all," the man said quickly and defensively as he flipped his companion a middle finger and earned a broad grin

"Should I leave you two lovebirds alone?"

Anderson didn't answer verbally. He was clearly already deep in conversation with his wife, a clear enough indication for the other man to get lost. Savage grinned, picked his mug up, and bowed his head in playful surrender. He teased but he was happy that Anderson was talking to his family again. It made him feel all warm and gooey inside although he honestly didn't know why.

Sure, joke about it. That'll make all your own problems disappear.

He drifted to the bar to allow his boss to have his conversation without any more distractions. He needed another drink anyway. It had been a while since he'd got his drink on properly, but with his responsibility and the ever-present threat hanging over Anderson, he'd have to shelve his desire to simply break loose for another time.

In some respects, he was a bit of an alcoholic and was willing to admit it. He could function without it—and had if the past couple of weeks had been any indication—but that didn't mean he would turn the vice down when it came his way. He was sure it was a healthy attitude to have. As long as he didn't let it interfere with what was really important, that was okay.

Savage reached the bar and placed the empty mug on the counter while he waited for the bartender. The man was talking to another patron—a woman in her late twenties by the look of it. He didn't want to stare, but the expensive jewelry around her neck and wrists didn't seem to match the jean skirt, flannel shirt, and Stetson she wore, although the richly tanned boots did.

His habitual scan of his surroundings soon revealed, based on the outfit, that she was a part of the bachelorette party that occupied most of the far side of the room. They weren't being too loud, but the night was still young and they weren't that deep in their cups yet. Besides, this seemed like it was only the starting point for the party. Strip clubs had to be on the agenda.

The tender finally realized he had other patrons waiting for him at the bar and tore himself away from the woman with a nod at Savage.

"A lager, thanks," he replied with a smile. The man nodded and pulled one of the mugs from the shelf behind him. He frowned a little as he watched the woman he'd been hitting on move down the bar toward Savage with interest in her eyes.

"Look, honey," she said, and her voice milked the Alabama accent. He honestly couldn't tell whether it was real or not. "I'll be honest with you. I'm thinking about breaking my one rule in a bar and buying you a drink, but it'll have to be a hell of a lot stronger than a lager."

He turned to look fully at her. She didn't look quite drunk enough to make him consider calling her a cab rather than accepting her offer. And he'd gotten involved with far less classy women over the past month or so. The least he could do was let her buy him that drink. It would be rude to refuse.

"Here's what I'm going to do," he replied as the bartender placed his drink on the counter and he paid the man for it. "I'm starting off light with a lager, to warm myself up. But if you're buying, you pick the juice, and we'll see if it makes us both happy."

She tilted her head and smirked before she turned to the bartender. "I'll have another Pina Colada, and if you could get this gentleman a..." She paused and made a show of studying him. "He'll have an Old Fashioned."

Old Fashioned was always a safe bet, he mused. It was good enough that nobody disliked it, and it wasn't fruity enough to make people turn their noses up.

She couldn't be the only one playing the game, though, he thought. "Oh...you're good," Savage said with a chuckle. She winked and leaned in close enough to whisper in his ear.

"You have no idea how good I am, sugar," she murmured softly, and he chuckled as her hand drifted across his chest to find the firm planes under his shirt.

"Savage," he whispered. "You can call me Savage."

"I'll bet I can. And you can call me Caroline."

"A pleasure to meet you, Caroline." He caught her hand as it trailed suspiciously low on his torso.

"Hey, Bea, come over. We need to toast," one of the women at the party called, and "Caroline" turned to scowl at her friends.

"I'll be waiting right here...Caroline." Savage winked and took a sip of his beer.

"Ma'am?" the bartender asked as she moved away from the bar.

"Put them on the tab," she called over her shoulder and jogged to where a toast actually meant a line of shots.

On the tab, he thought. She was buying him drinks and

putting them on her party's tab. He had to admire that kind of thriftiness.

The tender eyed him, almost as if to make sure that he didn't actually drink until she returned. There was an odd kind of loyalty between bartenders and their patrons, and he had to respect that. He raised his beer to the man before he took a nice long draught.

"Hey there, honey!" a woman said a moment before she slapped him on the shoulder. He almost dropped his beer and coughed discreetly when a little went down the wrong pipe.

"Honey?" he asked. A short, perky redhead sporting all the right kinds of curves grinned cheerfully. "Isn't that a little familiar?"

"I plan on getting all kinds of familiar with you, big guy." She tilted her head to study him with avid interest. "Do you feel like buying me a drink?"

Honestly, he wasn't quite sure what the situation called for. Caroline had bought him a drink, and it seemed like he needed to be loyal to that. Then again, he'd always been partial to redheads.

"Stick around, dear," he replied and smiled at her. "And I might."

"If that isn't all kinds of mysterious." She inched forward to swing up on a barstool, but her eyes flickered, and her gaze settled somewhere over his shoulder.

"Find your own man, you little skank," Caroline screamed as she shoved him out of the way and dragged the redhead off the barstool to toss her to the ground. She used her boots to hammer a kick into the other woman's stomach and dropped to deliver a punch but Savage interceded.

It irritated him that he had to intervene. Caroline looked like she was about to beat the redhead senseless, and he couldn't have that happen, not over him. He grabbed her by the wrists and hauled her off the prostrate woman.

"Let me go, asshole," she yelled and tried to shake him off. She was unsuccessful and he managed to step between the two.

"Throw another punch, and you will regret it," he snapped and pushed her back into the bar when she tried to swing at him after he released her. He turned to glance at the other woman. Except for a low groan, she looked like she would be fine.

"Are you all right?" he asked, and she nodded.

"Just keep that crazy psycho bitch away from me," the redhead replied and took his hand to help her up.

"That's probably a good idea." He smiled apologetically before he returned his attention to Caroline, who had recovered and now tried to attack the redhead again.

"You get the fuck back," Savage snapped and pointed a finger at the woman. It was usually an effective trick. People respected the finger-pointing. It was a show of dominance without actually showing any dominance.

"Or what, big guy?" she snarled in response as she backed away from his finger. She regained her courage quickly. "Men like you are all so full of shit. You posture and get all manly, but when it comes time to actually do something, you wuss out. I wish that once—just once—a man would treat me like he would any other man."

And that taunt marked his all-out-of-patience level. He stepped in and saw the shock on her face a second before his fist collided with it. The mostly harmless punch to the jaw wouldn't leave that much of a bruise, but she fell back with a soft grunt and crumpled.

"Wish granted," he stated softly. Most of the patrons had fallen silent and the entire crowd seemed to have witnessed what had happened. There didn't seem to be too many disapproving glances since most people present knew she was a bitch, even those in her party. They were simply surprised that he had actually acted on it.

Savage didn't feel like confronting them about it. He was all for equality, and if a man had challenged him like that, he would have done precisely the same thing.

That said, he didn't much want a drink anymore. He wanted to punch something and keep on punching until it couldn't punch back. It nagged like an itch in the back of his mind that had started when he'd punched Caroline and wouldn't stop until he let it out.

Maybe time at the gym would resolve it. Their motel didn't have one, but there had to be someplace open in the area where he could punch something. He rolled his shoulders in an effort to ease the rising tension and resisted the urge to wait for her to come to.

Anderson was still on the phone and didn't seem to have noticed anything, too engaged with talking with Ivy. He didn't want to interrupt and made his way quietly outside for some fresh air.

CHAPTER TWENTY-NINE

Anderson missed most of what could only loosely be described as a fight as he finished the call with Ivy. She told him that while both sides of the line were encrypted, it was still best to keep the call short. He couldn't deny that it was nice to hear her voice again. The worst part, of course, was how much it hurt when she had to hang up.

He did catch the part where Savage clocked a blonde woman dressed as a cowgirl across the jaw and walked out of the bar like he didn't give a crap. That was fun, he had to admit.

He drained his beer to the dregs and pushed out of the booth to move quickly to join his comrade. He jogged to catch up since Savage walked at a brisk pace.

"Hey, hey, slow down there, buddy," he called and gripped the man by the shoulder to stop him in his tracks. "Are you okay?"

The operative paused and looked tense and unsettled.

"Yeah. It's just…you condition yourself to finish the job when it comes to violence. I'm not built to walk away from a fight anymore. When I do, it's like an itch that won't go away. I'm used to it, though. I simply need some fresh air."

Anderson nodded. He'd known that about the man when they'd hired him. There had been a frank discussion with Courtney about what they would do if he went off the rails. Bringing Heavy Metal in to deal with him had not been taken off the table. The more he saw of him, however, the more he realized the man had an odd yet rigid kind of control over himself. He was a beast, absolutely, but a beast that knew what he was doing and how to handle himself in more ways than one.

Besides that, he wasn't fully sure that even the Heavy Metal team in all its armored glory wouldn't have a hard time dealing with Savage when he was in one of his moods. The kind of mood he suppressed right now.

"In all honesty, I think someone upstairs did me a huge favor," Savage continued. "I was about to get down and nasty with the crazy blonde. I've made bad decisions in my love life and that was one mistake I don't think I would have walked away from."

"What about you and Dr. Coleman?"

"Jessica said she needed time to think," he grumbled. "Then she took Monroe's offer to head up one of the facilities in… I don't even know where. She made her choice and it wasn't me. Hell, I can't even blame her. It was a good choice."

"Don't be like that." Anderson patted his comrade on the shoulder. "Although I do agree. You dodged a major bullet with the blonde cowgirl."

The other man chuckled and shook his head, but his face went dead a few seconds later and eyes narrowed as he stared at the parking lot—and more specifically at the trio of black SUVs that had pulled in and parked at the far edge of the area. A group of men stepped out, toting more than a few weapons.

"Oh...shit," Anderson whispered softly as both men dropped behind the nearest car. "How did they know where to find us?"

"Well, there are a number of possibilities." Savage drew his weapon and checked the strip inside. He had enough for a firefight, but probably only one, although he hadn't had to reload once. "It might have been the call. Or it could be someone saw us and turned us in to the people hunting us. It could even be that they're not looking for us."

"How likely is that last one?" he asked. He had a feeling he wouldn't like the answer.

"Not very." The operative slapped the chamber into place, his expression grim. The ex-colonel drew his own weapon, checked the mag, and flicked the safety off.

"We can't fight that many of them out there," his companion pointed out. "They'll flank us in no time. We need to get out of the open."

"Back to the bar?" Anderson glanced around them. The man was right. They would get picked apart out there in the open.

But Savage shook his head. "Too many witnesses and too many innocent people caught in the crossfire. We need an exit strategy. Until then, we can stall them. Anja, do you hear that? We need an exit strategy now."

"I'm working on it," she responded, having apparently listened in on everything they'd said thus far.

"Anderson," he said softly. "Stay behind the car and give me cover fire. I'll take them on a merry little chase until Anja figures out a way for us to get out. Understood?"

The ex-colonel nodded. It was a tactical choice, he knew that. They were there to keep him alive. That was the operative's sole purpose on this trip and that was exactly what he would do.

So why did it suddenly feel so shitty?

Savage didn't wait for him to agree with the plan but immediately pushed out from behind the car. Anderson needed a moment to realize what he was doing before he got with the program.

The chances were their attackers didn't actually know what his bodyguard looked like, and they definitely wouldn't expect him to walk toward them in the parking lot. He kept his weapon tucked out of sight and moved with the stumble-shuffle drunk people tended to use. At face value, he was simply a man leaving a bar after a few drinks and would probably make the wrong choice and try to drive home.

The ex-colonel peeked out from behind the vehicle, his pistol trained on the group of men who started to break into search parties. They had a general location but didn't seem to know where he was precisely, which was a comforting thought. A group of five walked toward Savage, seemingly unaware of who he was. They paid him no attention as he fumbled in his pockets in search of his keys or perhaps his phone.

Damned if the guy didn't know his craft.

At almost the same moment that the group seemed to notice someone approaching them, one dropped back after the distinctive metallic whoosh that Savage's pistol made when it fired. The sound repeated as the target crumpled. His four comrades looked confused before a second man succumbed to a pair of needles delivered with precision into his skull.

It wasn't until the third man died that they realized they were being shot at.

They swung their sub-machine guns up to return the favor. A fourth assassin was eliminated before the weapons clattered to life and Savage circled quickly to hammer the butt of his pistol into the last man's skull in two blunt strikes. He shot him calmly a couple of times to finish him off.

The death spasm triggered a single, three-round burst. The bullets fanned harmlessly into empty air but still alerted the other two search parties to where their quarry was.

"Shit," Anderson hissed. He twisted to watch the ten men converge on where the other man had ducked between two cars when a concerted volley spewed into the night. The ex-colonel raised his weapon cautiously. The assassins ignored him for the most part, obviously assuming Savage was the greater threat. Well, they weren't wrong, but that didn't mean he didn't have a little fight in him as well.

His Beretta kicked back into his hand. The sound of gunshots made his ears ring and mingled with the rapid staccato rhythms of the other weapons. His heart pounded in his chest and adrenaline made everything feel tingly and alive. But the fear was gone, he realized. Something had changed within him, and he had to say he liked it better than he had when everything started.

He couldn't be sure whether that was a good thing or not but damned if he didn't feel alive in that moment. He pulled the trigger and smirked as his two targets tumbled when his bullets drilled into their backs. That was the moment when the others realized they'd been drawn into a trap. It wasn't particularly impressive given that they were still outnumbered about eight to two and no longer had the element of surprise.

Three of the attackers circled and found cover behind the cars. These were pros, Anderson realized. He maintained a steady stream of fire and tried to cover for Savage as well as keep the three breakaways pinned down. It wouldn't last. Their adversaries had more ammo and more patience.

"There's a car coming to your right," Anja said suddenly in his ear. "Get in—now."

He didn't think to question what she'd said. All he could do was move. His pistol clicked empty and he didn't bother to reload but sprinted as quickly as he could toward the electric car that rolled closer. He fell inside and slammed the door behind him.

"I love me some electric cars these days," Anja said, and he pulled back into his seat as the vehicle suddenly accelerated. "Did you know that these cars actually have their engines cued into the car's electronics? And that they have a Wi-Fi connection? How convenient is that?"

The ex-colonel didn't answer as the car veered through the parking lot. He could only imagine that the hacker sat back in her chair and manipulated the vehicle like it was some kind of video game. Honestly, it wasn't a pleasant thought. He clutched the seat to anchor himself as she guided the car on her chosen course. Their attackers seemed confused by this turn of events, and it looked like they had their opening.

They stopped where Savage still held his ground. He saw the car and immediately barreled toward it. Anderson stretched to open the passenger side door and the man scrambled inside. He landed awkwardly but managed to close the door behind him as Anja gunned the engine again.

"I can only get this thing moving at about twenty miles an hour, so not to get all Carrie Underwood on your asses, but someone, please take the wheel," Anja shouted through their earpieces.

The ex-colonel jumped to the task and assumed control of the vehicle as they pulled out of the parking lot and onto the street. Gunfire erupted behind them, but it seemed like the weapons their attackers had brought would have difficulty reaching them over this kind of distance.

"Who the hell is Carrie Underwood?" Savage asked once he'd settled into his seat.

"You don't want to know," Anderson replied and tried to sound calm and collected as they swung onto the access ramp for the nearest highway. "So, Anja, where are we going?"

Sam scowled and looked up from the laptop she used to keep an eye on all the cameras that had been installed around the building.

She didn't really mind that Terry had taken on the job of keeping Damon alive and well while Savage and Anderson were scouring the land. It was a simple fact that she had never been very good with kids, and this one was no exception. He was cool enough, she supposed, but it was draining to be around him all the time.

Enter Mixon.

The man lived for this sort of crap, she thought with a disgusted eye-roll. He helped with homework. They watched sports. As of right now, they played an obnoxiously loud video game, and Terry gave the kid tactical advice on how to flank a couple of campers that tried to control the map that they were playing on.

They were loud about it too. Apparently, they had a bet going that whenever one of them died, they would have to do ten push-ups as they waited for their character to respawn.

If that didn't get rid of childhood obesity, what would?

Sam glanced at Ivy in the kitchen. She'd complained that Terry fed Damon too much pizza and junk food and that damn it, tonight, she would make them a healthy meal. The boy was still a vegetarian, which meant it would be some tofu bullshit or another, but Ivy, to her credit, seemed to enjoy helping her son with his dietary preference.

Honestly, she didn't think she would have that kind of patience. That was maybe why she wasn't great at the whole being around kids thing. And she grew more and more thankful that Terry was there to fill the gap as well as more and more annoyed at the man. He dropped in that moment and worked quickly through his pushups.

She jumped when her phone vibrated insistently and yanked it out of her pocket to see if she recognized the number. She didn't, but she wasn't the kind to simply let it go to voicemail.

"Hello?" She narrowed her eyes and considered which of her I'm-not-buying-anything speeches would be appropriate.

"God damn it, Sam," a familiar voice with an equally familiar Russian accent said belligerently. "Why isn't anyone there wearing their earpieces?"

"We're having some downtime? Is that you, Anja?"

A sigh from the other side of the line seemed to indicate that the hacker wanted to make a joke but didn't have the time. "Just…have someone listening into the comms at all times in the future, okay? But for now, I need you guys to get off your downtime."

"What's up?" Sam asked and gestured for Terry to join her. Damon voiced his annoyance and muttered something about being in the middle of a match, but the man pulled out anyway and looked at her with a questioning expression.

Sam put Anja on speakerphone. "You have both me and Terry here. What's up?"

"Anderson and Savage are in some serious shit," the Russian explained, apparently not knowing or caring that there were children present. "They're heading back to Philly, but once they get there, they'll need your help."

"Tell us what you need," she said softly. The alarm in the

other woman's voice was enough to sober her. Jokes could come later. This was what they had been hired for, after all.

CHAPTER THIRTY

F ucking doctors. What the hell did they know about this sort of shit? Charles knew he shouldn't drink, but damn it, the source of his ulcer problem was stress, and that was better treated by a couple of drinks. And, inevitably, a couple more after that.

In truth, the decanter full of scotch in the corner of his office had been full when he'd started about an hour before, too afraid to head back home without this situation resolved. Kelly had told him that he'd take care of it personally and make sure the word was spread far and wide through his contacts.

It was best to be in the office when the call came in. With Anderson dead, maybe Monroe would take the hint that she wasn't wanted in Pegasus and stay in the Sahara. And from that point forward, all the fucking assholes who had been shooting his solutions down over the past few weeks would come back looking to make amends simply to have an in with all the money that would be made over the next few quarters. He would be able to pick and choose and tell some of the assholes they would have to watch from the outside.

Charles sucked down the last mouthful of scotch from his glass and poured another one. There was only enough for half a glass, which was disappointing. He'd made sure that his secretary didn't stock the stuff anymore after his doctor's orders. Although that wasn't necessarily a problem. He could head on home for a couple of bottles, right?

The red phone rang, and he took a moment to stare at the damn piece of tech. He didn't want to answer it or to hear what might be bad news. It could be good news too, he reminded himself, but was it really worth the risk?

"You're being ridiculous," he told himself firmly and snatched the phone up.

"Mr. Stafford?" Kelly's calm, collected voice did little to soothe him.

"Please tell me that you have some good news for me," he breathed into the mouthpiece. He could smell the alcohol on his own breath, and that annoyed him.

"I'm afraid not. We laid a trap for them in DC, but they managed to give my team the slip. They're still in pursuit, and I have people coming in to try to cut them off. I'll notify you when we have some more news."

Charles didn't care. He hung up, pushed himself out of his seat, and picked his glass up. His eyes unseeing, he stared at the city sprawled below him. He couldn't be sure if he looked in the direction in which Washington DC would be, but he had to imagine that he did.

"Why won't you fucking die?" he screamed suddenly

and hurled the glass at the window. He'd wanted it to make some kind of dent in the window proper, but all he got was the shattered glass that spilled the last of his scotch on the floor.

The last of the scotch.

"God fucking damn it," he whispered and fell into his chair where he sat and simply shook his head. He couldn't help but feel that if Anderson and his muscle died in this mess, it would make it worth it. It would have to be worth it.

God knew he was spending enough money to get it done.

Anderson looked at Savage as the man worked on reloading the needle strip in his gun. They had driven in silence for a while. Anja had told them to start back to Philly and that she was prepping a surprise involving Sam and Terry. All they had to do was get their asses back to the warehouse and they could spring the trap.

That had been the good news, of course. The bad news was that the price on Anderson's head had more than tripled and virtually every hit squad on the eastern seaboard now converged on them. Three million dollars— and who knew how much more by now—was one hell of a payday for these people, and they would come for blood.

He wondered if he should feel flattered that this much time and effort went into removing him from the picture. Courtney would probably have a similar price tag on her head, but considering how spectacularly the efforts to kill her in the Zoo had failed, he guessed Charles would wait for her to return and would focus all his efforts on the former colonel in the interim.

Maybe he should think about heading out to the Zoo for a while. He could persuade Ivy and Damon to fly to the Heavy Metal complex and give them a little education on the place, all while getting them and himself out of the line of fire for a while. They deserved that much at least, right?

The silence was killing him, but it didn't seem right to turn the radio on, not at this juncture.

"How are you boys holding up?" Anja asked over their earpieces.

"All sunshine and roses over here," Savage replied, slapped the magazine back into his pistol, and eased it into the holster under his shoulder. "How are the preparations going?"

"Sam and Terry have their instructions," she replied. "Honestly, they seemed like they were excited to do some actual fighting after babysitting. No offense, Anderson."

"None taken," the man replied with a small smirk. "That said, if they'll be out and about, who'll watch over my family?"

"Well, there's me, for one. There's the security in your building for two. And Ivy has herself a gun and an itch to kill anyone who even tries to harm her or little Damon for three. I think they'll be safe for a short while. You don't need to worry about them right now, Anderson."

"Well, I think I will anyway," the former colonel replied. "It'll help to keep my mind off worrying about our own safety. It feels both noble and a little less selfish."

His companion nodded and looked like he approved.

"There is some bad news, though," the hacker continued. "It looks like our friends at the parking lot had a good look at your plates and they spread the info to the rest of the hordes currently on the hunt. There should be another hundred or so miles still on that car's charge, but you might want to avoid unnecessary pitstops along the way."

"We didn't plan to stop anyway," Anderson replied. "Is there any more bad news? Besides the fact that we had to leave everything we own, of course."

"Not really, although what bad news there is happens to be seriously sucky. On the bright side, I think I might have a way to get the money on Anderson lifted, but I'll need some time on that. Don't worry about it. Focus on staying alive and I'll see to the rest."

"Damn, that ruins my plans" Savage shook his head with mock gloom. "Here I had planned to trust you being awesome and so not stress about getting us out alive at all."

"Don't get sassy with me." She chuckled. "But I appreciate the compliment, as sarcastic as it was."

"You do what you're good at," he replied and patted Anderson lightly on the shoulder. "I'll make sure nobody can collect on that bounty in the meantime."

"Good lad." She added something in what could have been Russian and the connection went silent.

"What do you think about that?" He glanced at his boss. "If anyone can remove the price on your head, it'll be Anja. Once that happens, what do you think you'll do?"

The other man shrugged. "Hell if I know. I simply want to go back home to Ivy and Damon. I want to have dinner with them again and apologize for being away so long. Maybe get Ivy something nice to wear first."

"I think we both know how she'll repay you for getting her something nice to wear." He grinned and nudged the man in the shoulder.

"Don't be gross," Anderson warned. "Although, yeah. Even if it's none of your damn business."

"You might want to remember those tips I gave you back in New Orleans. Just saying." He tried to avoid the half-hearted punch Anderson threw at him with limited success. The electric car was tiny, after all, with very little room to move around in.

"I want you to know, though," the ex-colonel said once the quiet had settled around them again. "I wanted to thank you for watching my back. I know Ivy will have some thanks for you too."

"Well, let's not plot for the finish line before we reach it, eh?" He leaned back in his seat and stretched clumsily. "I'll see what kind of thanks I'll accept from Ivy. Maybe some hot dinners will have to do, right? I mean, Pegasus will cover the financial side of things."

"You can be a real ass sometimes, you know that?"

"I know, but you love me anyway, don't you, Colonel?" Savage quipped and lowered his seat a few notches. "We should be fine while we're on the road but keep an eye open."

"Do you think we should have told Anja about how we had to leave all our clothes and most of our weapons at the motel?" Anderson glanced at the man beside him, who let his eyes drift shut. "I know I mentioned it vaguely in the everything we own comment, but there has to be some cleaning involved in that."

"If all goes well, we'll probably be able to head back there tomorrow or the day after to collect our belongings and check out of the place properly." The operative's eyes remained shut. "If we don't make it, they won't be our problem anyway."

"You're killing me with all this optimism, buddy," he replied wryly.

Savage popped an eye open to glare at him. "My point was that it's a problem for when we get out of this alive. Stop worrying about something we can only take care of once our real problems go away. Stay focused."

The ex-colonel didn't particularly care to be talked to like that, but he didn't want to tell Savage how to do his job. The man had a process that involved a lot of focus, and…a little bit of pre-fight napping, apparently.

He could still feel the effects of the adrenaline that had raced through his body during the firefight. The tingling in his fingers and jittery alertness lingered around the edges of his calm.

And there Savage was, taking a quick nap. The simple truth was that he would never understand the man, but maybe that was a good thing. He couldn't help a small smirk as he relaxed against his seat and watched the miles tick by on the odometer. The car's readout told him they had a little farther to go before the electric car would need recharging.

It might be enough to get them there, but they would possibly have to ditch the vehicle before then. Anja had said that she was blocking the vehicle's GPS from notifying the police that it had been stolen. That was positive, but considering how much she was already doing, he had to assume she couldn't cover that for long. They needed to start doing shit for themselves.

The first step, of course, was to eliminate these teams that had lined them in their sights.

CHAPTER THIRTY-ONE

"What's the news?" Charles demanded brusquely. He'd given up on expecting good news tonight. That way, if any did come in, he would be pleasantly surprised as opposed to the constant disappointment he'd had to endure over these past few weeks.

"The targets are still on the road to Philly," Kelly replied. "I'm en route to intercept them."

He nodded. "Push the bounty to five million before fees but spread it for wide appeal. I want every possible gun in the area pointed at them. I don't care how you do it. Just do it."

"Of course, Mr. Stafford," the man replied, as quietly affable as always.

"I don't want it to be a bullet from a distance," he said suddenly. "I want it to be up close and personal. I want Anderson to know who is killing him. He has to look them in the eye and know that I'm the one. Understood?"

"Understood, Mr. Stafford. I'll handle it personally."

Charles hung up without a final farewell. He didn't care

that he was abrupt. Kelly was a professional and he would understand the kind of pressure he was under. And he would handle it personally. Whether the man meant he would perform the assassination himself—the thought of which made Charles a little giddy—or if he would personally delegate it was irrelevant. All that mattered was that Anderson didn't survive the night.

"It had better be fucking worth it," Charles whispered and scowled at the empty decanter.

Savage studied the open area outside their warehouse. Sunrise was still a couple of hours away, which meant the place was murky and difficult to see. Anderson pulled the car in to park a few hundred feet away from the building proper and the operative stepped out first. His alert gaze scanned the entire area before he indicated that it was clear for his boss to exit.

"So…" The ex-colonel looked around and let his eyes adjust to the darkness. "Just how fucked are we if we didn't get the timing on this perfectly?"

"Right up the ass. With a cactus. The prickly kind."

"That's great. Anja, do you know if our people are in position?"

"Terry's already in position and waiting for you," she confirmed. "Sam, how close are you?"

"I'm still five minutes out," she called. "Why the fuck is there so much traffic at three in the fucking morning?"

"Better make it two," Savage muttered under his breath

as he flicked the safety off his pistol. "Because we are about to have some serious company."

The truth of that statement was immediately evident. A string of cars had already started to pull up on the other side of the damn lot. Most of them hadn't bothered to stop but headed directly toward them. Savage drew a deep breath and stilled his thoughts to take himself into that dark, lonely place in his head.

"Get in the warehouse, Anderson," he said. He raised his weapon and stepped into the cover the small electric car offered.

"I can help out here," the man protested.

"Get in the damn warehouse—now," he snapped and narrowed his eyes. He didn't have time to remind him that he was the one these killers had targeted. They didn't care about Savage as much as they would a bump in the road on their way to some serious cash.

This particular bump, however, would break bumpers and flatten wheels. He liked that analogy. Maybe he'd be able to use it some other time.

The ex-colonel broke away from the car, and Savage breathed a deep breath. The enemy were about a hundred yards away but closing fast. He let the breath out slowly, propped his arm on the car in front of him, and squeezed the trigger gently.

Not having to account for the kick of a firearm was the best, he noted as he fired a pair of needles into the air. At this distance and with the kind of weapon he used, he was surprised that he could even hit the cars. The fact that the needles both seemed to drive through the windshield in the driver's seat area made him smile. The first car that he'd aimed at suddenly veered off course and cut a couple of the others off as the rest continued their hurtled approach.

Anderson had reached the warehouse and ducked behind the heavy steel door. He used it for cover as he started to lay down fire as well. Between the two of them, the six vehicles that had converged on them now were forced to halt barely twenty paces away, and the men inside piled out. Some carried assault rifles, others had shotguns, and there was a myriad of other weapons. One of them even carried a crossbow.

The operative ducked behind the electric car as they immediately opened fire at him.

"Any time you like, Terry," he shouted when a spray of glass rained over him as the windows of the car shattered. The owners would not be happy about the condition of their car after this. He would have to think of a way to repay them.

"Roger that, Savage," Terry confirmed in the distant, distracted voice long-distance shooters used when they had their eyes locked on a scope.

A loud crack echoed above the cacophony of fire-power. A bullet pounding its way past the sound barrier was always an impressive sound, Savage thought. Shouts of alarm vented, and the fusillade paused. The operative peered from behind his scanty cover. The brains of one of the men sprayed across the car. Another loud crack split the air and a second head exploded.

Savage resumed firing, although he lacked the kind of pinpoint accuracy the sniper had. Another assassin fell, most of his chest cavity aerated, then another. This one clutched his leg as one of the needles struck home.

The attackers all came to the decision that they wouldn't be able to attack the warehouse with a sniper breathing down the backs of their collective necks, and that became the priority problem. They had a good idea of where Terry was holed up and, at the risk of leaving Savage and Anderson free to fire on them, they started to lay down fire in the general direction of the sniper.

"Fudge!" Terry shouted through the mic. The sounds of bullets ricocheting around him said that he wouldn't return fire until he'd moved to his new location. The difficulty presented by the warehouse had been to find a secure position that offered a clear line of sight. Rather than entrench himself in a single hide, he'd chosen two or three of the best to enable him to use each, depending on the situation. He'd rejoin the battle once he'd relocated, but for now, they were on their own.

A couple of the invaders remained to lay a steady stream of bullets toward the sniper who had already moved on. The rest conferred, no doubt to plan a strategy to attack the warehouse.

Some looked like they were pros. Even in the darkness, they hugged what little cover there was, mostly provided by the cars they had brought themselves. Of the two and a half dozen, though, about half seemed like they were in a hurry to be somewhere else. Some strafed cover fire while their comrades pushed their way toward the building. Their haste left them open to Savage, who was able to pick them off one by one without even needing to break cover.

More glass shattered and a couple of the bullets aimed

at him punctured the car's tires. At this point, the owners would be better off buying another vehicle. Their insurance would cover stuff like this, right?

Those who had tried to rush the warehouse had either started to fall back or had dropped under the crossfire of Savage and Anderson's positions. The rest, however, were more determined and far more skilled and circled cautiously to use the defender's cover against them. They worked together to overlap their lines of fire while some moved into a position that would force Savage to peek out from behind his cover and expose himself in order to fire on them.

It wasn't an ideal situation, he had to admit, but then again, none of this was. They still had one member of the party who was running unfashionably late.

Worse, the little car he huddled behind wouldn't provide him protection for much longer. The bullets were already blazing through to his side. The only reason why he hadn't taken any of those holes himself was because he was still hidden visually. The enemy simply battered the vehicle with firepower in the hope that someone would get lucky.

That wouldn't last long, he realized. He needed to move.

He made a snap judgment. "I'll need cover here."

"Reloading," Anderson called from behind the door. As soon as the former colonel was ready, Savage sucked in a deep breath, put aside the paralyzing fear of being shot in the back, and sprinted toward the warehouse. His partner pulled out from behind the door and fired as rapidly as he could to spread as much lead in the general direction of their attackers as he could. Terry had obviously secured his new position and added his lethal efficiency to the firefight. For a second, the attackers were caught in a flurry of fire from two sides.

It wasn't much, but it was enough to allow the operative to careen into the warehouse. Unable to stop, he pounded into the wall behind Anderson at full speed. He winced as his shoulder twisted with the impact. The pull had left him tender, but not overly so, although his ribs flared with new pain. Still, he was in fighting shape. He'd been in worse.

"Mixon, you need to get out of there," Savage said and stepped into position where Anderson had been as his comrade reloaded.

"I'm way ahead of you, Savage," the sniper replied. "I have one more position, but that'll be the last." The man would make a final stand and do what he could, but his locations hadn't been great to start with and two were already compromised. If this took any longer, more cars would join the first group, and he would be even more vulnerable. He needed to get back to the warehouse immediately.

He had been in the business long enough to know when his particular skills became his point of weakness.

Savage narrowed his eyes when the sound of screeching tires shrieked over the now sporadic gunfire. For the worst of seconds, he believed it could be their attackers' reinforcements coming in. They wouldn't have the firepower to handle another wave force, not with Mixon relocating.

But as the vehicle hurtled towards the warehouse at breakneck speed, another thought came to mind. He'd watched videos of Sam's driving, both in courses and in the field. Nobody would be able to emulate the kind of controlled crazy she brought into play when she had a car in her hands. He grinned as she brought it in with no apparent attempt to slow and executed a handbrake turn to yank the vehicle around in a cloud of smoke. For a moment, her ploy provided a welcome screen to protect them from the enemy that now scrambled to regroup. Fortunately, no one seemed to have any real idea who she was. For all they knew, she was one of them.

She shoved the door open. "Anderson, get inside," she snapped.

"Just me?" he asked with a glance Savage.

"Yeah, just you," he snarled. "Get inside."

"I won't leave you here to deal with all these attackers alone," he roared in protest.

"What part of 'they're here to kill you, not me' do you still have a hard time understanding?" he asked. "Get in the fucking car, dumbass. Besides, I still have Terry to cover my ass. You need to go."

He nodded. The man clearly didn't like being the first out. He was a soldier, through and through, and if there was fighting to be had, he preferred to be in the middle of it instead of running away from it.

Tough luck. He would get out of there alive. Savage reacted to his boss' hesitation by grabbing him by the collar of his shirt and heaving him into the passenger seat. Anderson voiced little complaint as the operative slammed the car door shut and patted the top of the vehicle to indicate that they were all good to go.

Someone in the ranks gathered beyond the vehicle must have seen something because a single short volley shattered the calm. Sam didn't need to be told twice and she pressed down on the gas. The tires churned another cloud of impressive—and useful—dust as they hightailed it out of the lot, narrowly missing a few of the attackers who tried to bring their weapons to bear and had to fling themselves aside to avoid injury.

Savage ducked behind the door and his eyes scanned the area around him. Some of the attackers had clearly not received the memo that their quarry was currently in flight. These milled around in apparent confusion and a few arguments ensued between some of the groups. The pros knew it, though, and were the first to sprint to their cars to give chase.

He managed to pick a couple of them off before they escaped, then turned his attention to those remaining. They gradually realized what had happened and decided it was time to flee, while Terry's rifle barked with deadly intent from his final position to hurry them along.

CHAPTER THIRTY-TWO

Savage eased back into the warehouse and checked how many needles he still had in his gun. There would be enough and he hadn't even used half of the strip yet. Still, he felt thrifty. They didn't have that many reloads, and he really had no idea where he would find more once those he had were used.

The silence hanging in the air after all the shooting felt ominous, like there was something missing. He didn't like the feeling.

With the slow ebb of his adrenaline, he realized he was tired. He'd been up all day and night with no rest. He'd caught a nap or two here and there but not enough to make him feel rested.

He sucked in a deep breath and made a quick assessment. It was possible that some stragglers had stayed behind to take care of him, seeing him as an easier target.

Footsteps alerted him and he spun, his weapon ready, but immediately relaxed when Terry stepped into the moonlight that slivered into the warehouse, the only source of light around.

"They're all gone," the sniper said and hefted the rifle from his shoulder and into to his hands. "All the cars have gone after Sam and Anderson, which means he's still the sole target. Lucky us, right?"

"Do you think Sam is able to keep these guys off her tail until Anja is done with…whatever the fuck she plans on doing?" he asked.

"I've seen her drive carefully," the other man said, placed his rifle on the table next to their shooting range, and stretched to ease his back. "I've seen vids of her driving like she has a hellhound on her tail. I've talked with her and spent time with her. From the information I've been able to gather, I'd say her pursuers will have to be very talented indeed if they feel they can catch up with her."

He nodded. "I agree."

"Let them have the little fish," a voice boomed from inside the warehouse. "I'd rather have the two of you to myself anyway."

Savage only had the barest glimpse of a massive shadow moving in the darkness. It was closer to Terry, who didn't have time to draw his pistol before something pounded into him and hurled him over the table and into the small brick wall they used as a barrier to the shooting range.

The operative raised his gun and flicked the safety off. He pulled the trigger a couple of times. Whatever it was, the shape moved with alarming speed and was big enough that he knew he had caught it a couple of times before it finished its charge.

He felt his wrist tweak as the massive human grabbed

the gun's barrel roughly and yanked it away. The weapon clattered noisily to the ground, too far away to retrieve easily.

Something hammered into his skull. He literally saw stars as a second painful blow drove into his solar plexus to knock the breath out of him. His body crumpled, but two huge hands grasped him and swung him off his feet like he weighed nothing. His assailant flipped him up and over and he crashed with enough force to collapse the table beneath him. Terry's rifle spun, an odd, distant sight before the pain exploded to suck him into a breathless place of paralysis.

"Fuck me." He groaned when he finally managed to breathe and turned to push slowly to his feet. Everything hurt, but he wouldn't simply lie there. He coughed with the effort and his diaphragm struggled to suck in air, but he was determined stand and to remain standing.

The fact that Mixon hadn't tried to correct him on his foul language was worrying. He peered around in the darkness and his gaze settled on his comrade, who lay still and unmoving. Savage dropped to his knees and quickly checked the man's pulse. It was still ticking, weak but steady. He was unconscious, although he couldn't tell if there was any other damage. But at least he was still alive, he reassured himself.

He located the pistol Terry had tried to draw when he'd been attacked. His hands curled around it and he attempted to identify the model by touch alone. The fucking darkness was a real handicap, and his eyes were still adjusting.

It was a Sig, he realized. Most of those models had a

four-point safety system, which meant it would be good to shoot as soon as he had his finger on the trigger. He didn't like them, generally. They were too bulky and their weight awkward, and the trigger was a little heavier than he liked. They were safe and reliable, though, which explained why Mixon used one.

That said, he didn't really have anything to shoot. The massive bear of a man who had attacked them had faded into the shadows again, annoyingly enough.

"What did you think would happen?" the booming voice asked. Savage could already guess who it was. There couldn't be that many people that size on the planet. The voice held the same nuances as the soft tones Kelly had used before, but they were louder now and carried easily through the warehouse. They echoed in the open space to the point where it was hard to actually pinpoint the origin.

"You'll have to be more specific," Savage called in response. His eyes had started to adjust to the darkness, but even then, all he could really see were shadows on shadows, only slightly illuminated by the moonlight that filtered in through the windows.

"You kicked the hornet's nest," Kelly declared boldly. "You thought you could get away with that?"

"Wait, why are you here after me?" he asked in an effort to buy himself time as he eased toward the office. He'd prefer to have something at his back to avoid an attack from behind. "Isn't your boss' hit on Anderson?"

"There are more than enough guns on Anderson," Kelly pointed out. "I don't really care about him. What I care about...is you."

"I'm...flattered, I guess?" A moment of intuition made

him spin suddenly, but a ham-sized hand gripped him by the wrist and prevented his gun from moving. He pulled the trigger a couple of times and the loud blast did his ringing ears no favors. Kelly twisted his arm viciously until he screamed in frustration and was forced to drop the weapon.

He turned but his assailant stepped in to deliver a powerful backhand across his jaw. The metallic taste of blood seeped into his mouth from where the inside of his cheek had been cut by his teeth with the force of the strike. The giant followed through immediately and hammered his fist into his opponent's lower back.

It wasn't the first time he'd been struck there, although never quite as hard, and he knew what to expect. But even experience couldn't have prepared him for the mind-numbing agony that blossomed directly after. Savage could do nothing but release a low moan of pain as he dropped, clutched at his side, and curled instinctively.

"Oh, kidney shot." Kelly chuckled, stepped over his victim's body, and dropped into a crouch beside him. "That has to hurt. I've punched men in the kidneys before, and those who survived pissed blood for a month."

He couldn't come up with anything to say beyond another groan and tried to roll away, but the man caught his shoulder and yanked him back sharply.

"See, normally, I respect men like you," he explained. He pinched the bottom of Savage's jaw and forced his head up to look at the man who towered over him. "In fact, I do this time too. You're a real fighter. The kind of man with the will and the skills to defeat almost anyone. But I'm not almost anyone, see. Your actions—and those of your boss, Anderson—called my effectiveness into question, so I hope you know that it's nothing personal when I say I'll tear you apart limb from limb. After that, I'll find everyone you ever loved or cared about and act out all the fucked-up shit in my fucked-up brain on them. It's purely business. I need my reputation to remain intact."

Savage looked up from where he writhed on the ground and gritted his teeth. There would be problems tracking his family down, but if the man had his finger-prints, his face, and his DNA? A good tracker with a quarter of Anja's computer skills could piece his original identity together. They could find his family—Jules, Abigail, and even Andy.

It was like something snapped in the back of his mind. He'd spent so much time trying to keep himself under control that he'd started to think it was his natural state, how he was meant to be. Until that moment. He'd run the length of his life in a long, continuous state of half-assed-ness. Until right about now.

Nobody threatens my girls.

Pain seared through his body, but he no longer cared. He shifted and thrust his hand between Kelly's legs, and his fingers found what was between on the first attempt. Driven by the innate need to wound, he squeezed and twisted and the surprise in the big man's face suddenly turned to agony. His adversary screamed and fought to free himself from the vice-like grip until he fell on his back.

Moving was pain, and breathing too, but it no longer mattered. It was like the engine-warning light that people ignored. There would be complications later, he knew that. He simply didn't care.

His screams of rage echoed in his own ears as he climbed over Kelly and allowed his fists to pummel his body as he crawled higher. Kidneys, liver, ribs, solar plexus...he didn't bother to count. The pent-up fury erupted and vocalized itself in the desire to wound and kill. On some vague level, removed from the all-encompassing flood, he supposed a professional might say it was therapeutic.

He continued the violent battering as Kelly curled in the fetal position and tried to protect himself from the ceaseless barrage. Ignoring the futile resistance, he hauled the man back and straddled his chest so his knees locked his shoulders in place to prevent him from even raising his hands to defend himself.

"Here's the thing, asshole," Savage growled through a manic grin lightly splattered with his adversary's blood. "Between your fucked-up brain and my fucked-up brain, mine wins every time. So next time, when you have someone on the ground, kill them. Don't gloat."

Not that there would be a next time, he thought as he pressed his thumbs into Kelly's eye sockets. The larger man screamed and bucked in an effort to dislodge him, but he continued the relentless pressure. Warm blood mingled with the jelly-like vitreous humor and he continued to push until Kelly stopped moving except for the occasional twitch.

Savage pulled away and sucked in oxygen as he fell back. His rage was spent, and the pain flooded back as he clutched his side and stared at the darkness above him.

Terry came to a few seconds later and scuffled in the darkness as he scrambled to his feet and spun awkwardly to find their threat.

"Over here," he called through clenched teeth, and the sniper hurried over to him. He winced when he saw the massive corpse that had once been Kelly.

"Are you all right, boss?" he asked and extended a hand to help him up.

"Never better," he lied. He tried to laugh but it came out as a cough instead. "I think I'll lay here for a minute if you don't mind."

Mixon nodded. "I'll get the medical kit."

He pressed into the ground and held his side, a part of him still stuck on the thought that he wouldn't survive. Aside from anything else, he would need to see a doctor about the damage to his kidneys. And yes, he would piss blood for at least another week.

"God fucking damn it," he groaned and tried to roll onto his side.

"Watch your language," Terry said when he returned.

CHAPTER THIRTY-THREE

Something buzzed and vibrated nearby.

Charles reached out to turn his alarm clock off. He wouldn't go into work today. Honestly, he'd been around long enough that he didn't need to make excuses when he wanted to take a couple of days off. He needed to get himself together, find a way to relax, and let off some steam. Maybe, he thought groggily, he could even get laid. That usually helped him back into the mood.

His hand fumbled for the alarm clock but found nothing but air. The sensation of almost falling was enough to wake him abruptly, barely in time to stop himself from falling over.

Blearily, he studied his surroundings and finally remembered that he hadn't actually gone home the night before. He'd fallen asleep in his chair in his office. It was surprisingly comfortable, although at his age, he knew his back would ache for the rest of the day.

Maybe a visit to his masseuse was in order before anything else. He pushed heavily from his seat and stretched, groaning as he did so. A few annoying and painful clicks in his back left him sore but awake as he relaxed again, although he was also more than a little hungover. He sucked in a deep breath before he straightened his shirt and wandered to the sink in his office. He didn't bother with a glass but sucked water straight from the tap before he shuffled to the toilet to take a piss.

He left the bathroom, feeling a little better, but something nagged at the back of his head. Something had vibrated, something that had woken him up at—holy shit, was it already ten in the morning?

Charles moved through his office and tried to decide what he was looking for. Another buzz from his desk answered the question and he dragged his attention to the phone. He repressed a massive yawn behind his hand as he picked it up and activated it.

He'd received a notification from the Foundation. He felt his blood run cold for a moment as he worked through the password protection to see what it was. Had the account been paid out? Had someone finally killed Anderson?

Excitement made his fingers jittery as he moved through the various encryptions to access the notifications. If the account had been paid out, proof would be offered to show that Anderson had been killed. That was something he wanted to see.

Request to change account name. Confirm? was the first notification.

"What?" He leaned in closer to the screen. There were three other notifications, and he swiped to see the next one.

Request to change account name confirmed. Specify account name change, said the second, and the cold feeling in his stomach turned icy. Any change in account names needed to go through him. The fact that it had already been confirmed without him even having access to it told him that something had gone terribly, terribly wrong.

Account name changed from 'James Anderson' to 'Charles Stafford' confirmed. Account locked until contract completion. Charles stared at the final notification in horror before he let his phone fall from his numb fingers. The account name had been changed to his name. All the criminals with access to the Foundation would see a contract for five million dollars payable on the death of one Charles Stafford.

"Shit," he said and retrieved his device hastily. It hadn't broken, thank God. The new polymer screens were the best at preventing phones from breaking, which meant there was no way for him to think any of this was only his imagination. He checked it again. When nothing had changed, he checked it again to make sure.

The name had been altered. He was now the target.

"Fuck!" he screamed and bolted as quickly as he could to grab his coat and rush toward the door. He needed to get out. The contract had been elevated to a national level. If he could get out of the country, he could get to Bern. He could appeal the contract with the Foundation. They would be able to see that it was tampered with, fix their systems, and put the contract back on Anderson.

It was his only chance. The contract was locked. There

was no way to change it for any reason until it was paid out. They were coming for him now, not Anderson.

"Mr. Stafford?" his secretary asked and looked up from her work. "I didn't see you come in."

"I…spent the night," Charles said, truthfully enough. What was her name again?

"You have that eleven o'clock lunch meeting—" she started to say, but he cut her off quickly.

"Something's come up, I won't be able to make it," he snapped and shook his head. "I'm actually taking some time off, so you can go ahead and cancel everything I have for the rest of the week. And why don't you take that time off yourself? I need some time on my own."

"Oh…of course," she replied but looked concerned at the state he was in. "Are you all right, Mr. Stafford?"

"I'm fine," he lied. Dammit, he didn't have the time for this. The word was probably already out that he was in the building. Attackers would be waiting for him outside, and they would find a way inside if he remained there. His car was in the basement so he would be able to get out of the building without too much trouble.

"Oh…if you could do me a favor?" he asked as he moved to the elevator and pressed the button five or six times. "I'll need you to buy me an airplane ticket. First class, of course, anywhere outside the country. Text me the details, if you could."

"Of course, Mr. Stafford," she said. He knew why she didn't ask any questions. People in her position didn't keep their jobs that way. Their bosses were supposed to be eccentric, and to make decisions like this on the fly was par for the course. It was their job to keep up with the eccentricities and make sure the rich men who employed them were able to do what they wanted with as much comfort and as little hassle as possible.

She would get him that ticket in a few minutes and all he had to do was get to the airport.

When he reached the garage, his driver was already waiting for him. The man was a veteran as well, trained in aggressive driving techniques, and doubled as a bodyguard. And Charles didn't even know his name. He wasn't sure if that was a bad thing. Getting too attached to these people would influence his decision to get rid of them when they inevitably made the mistakes he needed them never to make.

"Mr. Stafford." The man nodded, clearly having been alerted of what to expect by the secretary who had called him. He opened the door for his boss to step into the town car that waited for him.

He circled once Charles was inside, slid into the driver's seat, and eased them out of the parking lot onto the ramp that led up from the underground.

"Where to, sir?" he asked and glanced at him as they waited for the gate to raise and let them out.

"Get me to the airport," he replied and leaned back in his seat. He knew he should have gotten the limo that had a bar. More than anything, he needed a drink.

"Will do, sir." The driver tipped his hat as they emerged into the street. He seemed to know that they were in a hurry and ran lights and stop signs alike as they increased speed on the route to the international airport. A few minutes later, his phone buzzed. He pulled it out of his pocket and smiled to see a link to a one-way, first-class ticket to Tuscany, where he had a couple of properties. It was where he usually went when he needed time off. It was a good call.

Of course, he preferred to have a plane to himself, but a first-class ticket was good enough. With the airline she'd selected, he would have his own room with a bed, a TV, and Internet connection—a little luxury for the people who couldn't afford to have their own plane.

He would buy a plane when all this was over. After all, he had the money for it, and he hated having to sign off to get one through Pegasus. Besides, it didn't seem like he would get any more support from the company.

His eyes narrowed as they pulled off the highway and headed down into an underpass.

"Hey...what the hell are you doing?" Charles demanded. He leaned forward, but all the driver did was roll the partition up.

The cold feeling in his stomach returned. It continued to grow as they emerged beneath the freeway and came to a halt on the abandoned road.

He tried the door a couple of times, although he already knew they had been locked from the driver's controls. The man stepped out of the vehicle, holding a phone to his ear. He spoke in Spanish, from the sound of it, and less than a minute later, a couple more cars arrived and parked around his town car.

"Fuck!" he gasped and fought to open the door again. That didn't work, so he tried hitting the glass. He doubted that he would be able to get through the window and out, but he had to try. There would always be that annoying instinct for self-preservation and damned if he wouldn't listen to it, even if it was one last time.

The men circled. There were nine of them, all toting assault rifles. They handed another one to the driver, who turned to face the vehicle.

This was it.

Holy shit, he'd never thought it would end this way. Charles looked at the floor. He really wished they had gotten him a car with a bar. A last drink—or even a last smoke—sounded perfect. He wouldn't get one, though. The men positioned themselves outside the car and raised their weapons like they were performing an execution. Which they were, he realized, and closed his eyes when the first opened fire.

CHAPTER THIRTY-FOUR

"I still don't believe it," one of the men muttered.

Beason looked up from his phone to see what his colleague was looking at. He peered at the screen where the picture of a rotund, white-haired man headed an article.

"Billionaire and philanthropist Charles Stafford was found dead in his car?" Beason said, reading the headlines. "Shot eighty-seven times in what authorities describe as a gangland-style execution."

"Holy shit, right?" Yuri chuckled. "You saw the contract on him? I mean, five million dollars isn't something to sneeze at, but I'd say these guys were taking something out on the guy, you know?"

"That's not the interesting part," Beason replied. "Of course, you wouldn't find it in the papers, but you can look into where the money that went into the contract came from. Well, it came from a foundation Charles Stafford owned. The guy paid for his own hit. How the hell did that even happen?"

His friend shrugged. "You know he wouldn't do that to himself. And guys like him use their foundations to funnel money, so how would that money reach the account?"

He couldn't help a small chuckle. "With the kinds of connections Stafford had, I'm not surprised he had enemies with those kinds of resources. Seriously, someone is fucking scary smart."

"Let's hope we don't have to go after them," Yuri replied and waved a hand airily. "We don't need enemies like that coming after us instead."

"Is that why we didn't try for that contract ourselves?"

"Well, five million is a lot of money, sure, but the kinds of hitters who would jump on that... No, not worth it. Maybe one day, when we have more muscle on our side and more backing. For now, though, stick to the smaller contracts."

"Your call."

Alvarez leaned back in his pool seat. Life was good, he had to admit. Soaking in the sun and being back in Mexico was a blessing. He didn't really mind New Orleans. The place bustled with all the right kinds of energy. The party atmosphere that had surrounded him while he'd been there had been enough to make him smile. It hadn't been terrible.

But in the words of that ancient American film, there really was no place like home.

While they still ran repairs and maintenance after the savage's attack, most of the damages had been restricted to quarters he really had nothing to do with anyway. Which meant that, as soon as the inspectors cleared the building of structural damage, he was able to live there again.

He smiled and lowered his sunglasses as a couple of women in bikinis pulled themselves out of the pool, smiling and laughing as they moved towards the champagne he'd left open for them. He wasn't in the mood for alcohol yet anyway. At heart, he was an old-fashioned guy. He didn't believe in drinking before two in the afternoon, so he stuck to his coffee and the aphrodisiac presence of the women in his villa with him.

The phone he'd left on the table beside him buzzed, and he scowled at it. He'd specifically told his people he would take the day off. Of course, they could still call him if there were emergencies, but the fact that they couldn't go one day without needing him to fix some problem or another for them was disappointing.

The number was blocked, however. Alvarez quirked an eyebrow before he pressed the accept call button and brought the device to his ear.

"Hello?"

"Al, nice to hear from you," came the familiar voice of the man called Savage. Alvarez couldn't help a smile as he leaned into his seat again.

"Savage, you *hijo de puta*." He chuckled. "How the hell are you?"

"Sun's shining, birds chirping, can't complain," the man replied. Despite his words, he sounded weaker and somehow less vital than the last two times they had spoken to one another. "How are you, Al?"

"Well, I really can't complain." He took a slow sip of his

coffee. "You really came through for us with Charles, my friend."

"I have no idea what you're talking about," he replied. "From what I heard, he paid for the hit on himself. How weird is that?"

"Oh, he did it to himself all right." Alvarez laughed. "It couldn't have happened to a more deserving *culero* if you ask me."

"I'll have to take your word on that. I even sent you half the money you paid me, exactly like I promised. Minus the operational fees of course. You know how it goes, right?"

Savage was lying, of course, but not really. The arrangement had changed somewhat when the man had given him an insight into the money on Charles' head, where he was, and where he was likely to go. It had been a simple matter to call his men in the area to effect the hit. They'd taken their usual commission, not knowing that the five million for the contract had flowed into Alvarez' own account.

So, in a way, the man had paid close to half of the money he'd taken from Alvarez' safe when he'd broken into his home and given him a way to get rid of Charles at the same time.

"In all seriousness, my friend, I think I owe you a great deal," he said softly.

"Considering that we might do business at some time in the future, I'd be willing to call it even if you look on me and my associates kindly when we come to you with opportunities again," Savage said. "I would hate to have to pound my way through your whole security team all over again when I need to get in for a chat."

"Even, then," Alvarez replied with a chuckle. "And I look

forward to doing business with you again soon, Savage man. Take care of yourself. *Hasta.*"

"Nice talking to you Al." He ended the call.

Alvarez pushed himself out of his seat, set his phone on the table again, and stretched.

Fuck it. He would have a drink. It was called for on special occasions like this.

———

Madeline looked over the group that had been assembled. It seemed like emergency board meetings called by someone who wasn't even in the fucking country had become more and more commonplace these days. While she didn't quite approve, unlike the men who had occupied the two seats that were currently empty in the room, she knew her place. She wouldn't rock the boat. Whether or not Courtney and Anderson were competent enough to lead the company was irrelevant. The only important fact was that any person who had tried to take them on had failed to do so.

And hers would not be the next empty seat.

The screen at the front of the room flickered on to display the likeness of a woman Madeline had started to have mixed feelings about. Dr. Courtney Monroe was not dressed like she was about to have a conversation about the Fortune Five-hundred company she spearheaded but rather like she had just gotten in from a morning jog.

People like her could get away with a few eccentricities, she supposed.

"Ladies and gentlemen of the board, thank you for

meeting with me on such short notice," Monroe said with a forced smile and adjusted her glasses. "Allow me to cut right to the meat of the matter. What is this I've heard about Charles Stafford killing himself?"

Madeline looked up from her notes and an odd look settled on her face. "We thought you might know more. Has no one contacted you about it?"

The woman shook her head. "No, I had to read about it in the *Wall Street Journal,* of all places."

The other board members shared glances. Madeline kept her eyes firmly rooted on the screen. She wasn't sure if Monroe was telling the truth—in fact, she was rather certain she wasn't—but of course, it was part of her role to seem like she had nothing to do with the sudden death of a man who had opposed her on the board over the past month or so.

"Well, the details are still under investigation," she said and took control of the meeting herself. "But the financial reports just came in, and it would seem the money that paid for the death of Charles Stafford, may he rest in peace, came from his own personal accounts. We'll let you know if we learn anything more. The IRS is currently scouring his records."

Monroe nodded and looked crestfallen. Either the woman was telling the truth, or she was a fantastic actress. Neither would surprise Madeline.

"In the meantime," she continued with a hasty glance at her notes, "it would appear we now have to fill not one, but two, seats on the board. We have been forced to put off the stock sale for Pegasus until those seats have been filled."

"I have another suggestion," Monroe said. "We push the

stock sale up. We have the power to declare that emergency powers be granted to the rest of the members of the board, constricting the size of the board, to hold the position for a limited time until shareholders can appoint their own members."

Madeline looked at the other members. "Are you suggesting that we have an emergency vote?"

The woman nodded. "I'd be lying if I said that wasn't one of the main reasons why I called this meeting. I will recuse myself from the vote, of course, so hold it and message me when you've come to a consensus and tell me your recommendations. I need to prepare for a trip into the Zoo. You ladies and gentlemen have a nice day."

The line went dead, and the screen blackened as Madeline gathered her notes again. She had spent most of the last few days collecting the names she was willing to submit for the two vacant seats. All for nothing, she supposed.

She looked at her colleagues, who seemed to simply stare at her and wait for her to say something.

"Well, you heard Dr. Monroe," she said crisply. "All those in favor of granting the current members of the board emergency powers to control those sections of the company left vacant, say aye."

Some were more hesitant than most, but all seemed to understand that while Monroe had laid it out as a choice for them, there really wasn't much option.

The vote was unanimous.

"Excellent." Madeline gathered her notes. She would shred them when she returned home.

"Do you believe she really goes into that alien-infested death swamp?" one of the other members asked.

"It's in the desert, William," she explained.

The man opened his mouth to retort but quickly stood down. The tension in the room was all but palpable, she realized.

"You know that she's consolidating," she explained. "She was doubted, and she was contested. She's merely making sure that no one is left who will openly stand against her. It's a power play. She'll select whoever takes the empty seats on the board herself when the time comes. For now, let's allow things to cool down. Once everyone is back and can deal with this rationally, we can revisit it."

William, a tall former model with an MBA from Stanford, shook his head. "Hopefully by then, someone might have some new ideas."

Madeline smiled and stood graciously. "Well, nobody can claim our meetings are boring, anyway. This meeting is adjourned. I'll see you all later."

WOOT! Thank you for reading this second book of the *Team Savage* Series.

I'm a big fan of internet connectivity. So much so that I like to have it everywhere I travel (as I imagine most people do.)

This evening, the cable provider / internet provider up and kicked the bucket. I went from 200 MB download to a big fat zero.

ZERO!

UGGH. I was back to having to use my cell phone data plan, and trust me, I suck up internet like it's cheap and sleazy water with no thought to trying to pay attention to my business videos and what they are doing to my download bill.

When the cable modem stopped working, I had visions of a second mortgage happening in just a few short days.

It was a horrible vision. More a day-mare actually (you know, a nightmare that happens during the day?)

Some boiling of Pepsi and sacrificing of rubber

chickens later, I got the internet modem to connect, and I've been so damned happy ever since. That feeling of euphoria when something goes well in your life hasn't left yet.

I'd rather not go through that again, Mr. Spectrum Cable Provider.

I appreciate you taking the time to read our stories and hope you delve deeper into the ZOO Universe.

There's nothing there to kill you...

Or is there?

Could the nations of the world be doing something in the Sahara we aren't aware of... yet?

Hurry up and go grab *Team Savage* 3 with new words and preeminent ass-kicking, and let *Savages* take you places tonight!

Ad Aeternitatem,

Michael Anderle

www.ingramcontent.com/pod-product-compliance
Lightning Source LLC
Chambersburg PA
CBHW020235110726
47898CB00004B/1269